HOT HEX BOYFRIEND

OTHER BOOKS BY CARLY BLOOM

ONCE UPON A TIME IN TEXAS

Big Bad Cowboy

Cowboy Come Home

Must Love Cowboys

HOT HEX BOYFRIEND

CARLY BLOOM

FOREVER

NEW YORK   BOSTON

Copyright © 2024 by Carol Pavliska

Cover design and illustration by Caitlin Sacks. Cover copyright © 2024 by Hachette Book Group, Inc.

Forever
Hachette Book Group
1290 Avenue of the Americas, New York, NY 10104
read-forever.com
@readforeverpub

First Edition: September 2024

Forever is an imprint of Grand Central Publishing. The Forever name and logo are registered trademarks of Hachette Book Group, Inc.

The publisher is not responsible for websites (or their content) that are not owned by the publisher.

The Hachette Speakers Bureau provides a wide range of authors for speaking events. To find out more, go to hachettespeakersbureau.com or email HachetteSpeakers@hbgusa.com.

Forever books may be purchased in bulk for business, educational, or promotional use. For information, please contact your local bookseller or the Hachette Book Group Special Markets Department at special.markets@hbgusa.com.

Library of Congress Cataloging-in-Publication Data

Names: Bloom, Carly, author.
Title: Hot hex boyfriend / Carly Bloom.
Description: First edition. | New York : Forever, 2024.
Identifiers: LCCN 2024008281 | ISBN 9781538741092 (trade paperback) | ISBN 9781538741108 (ebook)
Subjects: LCGFT: Witch fiction. | Romance fiction. | Novels.
Classification: LCC PS3602.L6575 H68 2024 | DDC 813/.6—dc23/eng/20240222
LC record available at https://lccn.loc.gov/2024008281

ISBNs: 9781538741092 (trade paperback), 9781538741108 (ebook)

Printed in the United States of America

CCR

10 9 8 7 6 5 4 3 2 1

to Amy

CHAPTER ONE

Delia Merriweather did not believe in magic. Not even a little. But as she sat beneath the carefully knotted bundles of aromatic dried herbs hanging from the hundred-year-old rafters in her grandmother's kitchen, she had to admit things *felt* pretty magical.

Steam billowed about the room as Grandma Maddie gazed into the giant pot of boiling water, which fogged the thick lenses of her glasses and made her massive halo of silver curls coil and bounce like a nest of snakes.

Delia took a sip of spiced chai tea to hide her grin, because her grandmother looked like a pint-size, legally blind Medusa. "How's the soup coming?"

Grandma Maddie pointed her face in Delia's general direction. "Did you just say *soup*?"

Unfortunate slip of the tongue. "Sorry. I meant to say spell. Or is it more of a potion?"

Grandma Maddie sighed in disappointment over Delia's question, as if maybe Delia had forgotten that Austin was the capital of Texas, or that the fork went on the left side of the plate and the knife on the right. "We're casting a *spell* that *includes* a potion," she said with a tone of exaggerated patience. "There's a blue moon tonight. Surely, you haven't forgotten the importance of that."

Delia glanced up at the small sign above the archway in the

kitchen that said A FAMILY THAT DWELLS TOGETHER, SPELLS TOGETHER. And it didn't refer to a game of Scrabble.

Most of the folks in the small Texas Hill Country town of Willow Root considered Delia's family a bit quirky or eccentric. The rest thought they were off their collective rockers. Because Delia's grandmother and great-aunts identified as witches. And not New Age witches, either. They were old-school witches of the pointy hat and black cat variety. The fact that none of them could cast an actual spell or concoct an effective potion or utter any valuable curses beyond the occasional f-bomb didn't alter this heartfelt belief.

Their lack of magic, they said, was due to an ancient hex cast upon their ancestors by an evil witch. This was impossible to prove and, therefore, a perfect excuse.

Delia rose from the creaky cypress table and wandered over to the stove. "It's been a long time since the last blue moon. I might be a bit rusty."

The ritual of the Blue Moon Spell was utter nonsense, but it was *delightful* nonsense, and it didn't cause a lick of harm to anyone. Delia loved the loony traditions that filled so many of her childhood memories. Maybe none of the other kids were dragged out of bed to dance in the moonlight or to make fairy circles. But Delia wouldn't trade a single minute of it for all the money in the world.

"A potion is liquid," Grandma Maddie lectured. "We're meant to consume it."

Delia's stomach growled as she eyed the onions and cloves of garlic resting on the counter. It had been a long time since breakfast tacos, and she'd worked through lunch. "It's perfect weather for hot—" She stopped herself from saying *soup*. "Potion."

The first cold front of the season had blown through early that

morning, officially ushering in fluffy sweaters, pumpkin spice anything and everything, and, of course...magic.

"Our spell, if you remember, calls for..."

Delia swallowed uneasily, her appetite waning ever so slightly.
"The boiling of an innocent," she said quickly, as if running the
words together would somehow lessen their comical-yet-horrible
meaning. The sentence lingered in the air—a reminder that it was
all fun and games until somebody mentioned human sacrifice.

"Which is more innocent?" Grandma Maddie asked. "A carrot
or a potato?"

Delia grinned. "I'd say it's a toss-up."

It had been a long time since Delia had first attempted to cast
the Blue Moon Spell that was supposed to break the hex and
restore magic to her family. In fact, it had been on her eighteenth
birthday, which was when she'd officially (insert air quotes) *come
into her power* as the Blue Witch—an auspicious honor bestowed
upon her because she'd been born during a blue moon and also had
a birthmark on her left butt cheek that looked like a pentagram if
you squinted just right.

On that day, they'd returned home from the town's fall festival
to find a mysterious note poking out from beneath their doormat.

With the blue moon, the Blue Witch's power will rise.
133.4 MER
p 32

Excitement had coursed through them, because there was a rare
blue moon that very night. Aunt Thea had recognized the cryptic
numbers and letters as a call number for a library book, so they'd
trotted off to the Willow Root Public Library, where, sure enough,

a book of magic spells and potions entitled *Clavis Hexicus* was sitting right there on the shelf in front of God and everybody.

They'd dutifully carried it to the circulation desk, where Justine Tarte had entered it into the library's system, only to find it didn't exist.

"Well, what do we do?" Grandma Maddie had asked.

Justine had shrugged and handed it back. "It doesn't belong to the library."

Grandma Maddie had discreetly tucked it under her arm, and they'd made a hasty exit.

That night, beneath a blue moon, Delia had opened the dusty, leather-bound book to the Blue Moon Spell, only to discover that she didn't have what it took to break the hex. Because the potion had called for ingredients far more heinous than eye of newt or hair of hound, and things had suddenly become very real and very batshit crazy and very illegal in all fifty states.

Delia had slammed the book shut with a shudder of disgust, and after a moment of stunned silence, her aunt Aurora had finally said what they'd all been wondering: *Are we supposed to boil a fucking baby?* To which the ever-practical Aunt Thea had responded: *Where would we find a pot that big?* Followed by Aunt Andi's proclamation: *But I'm a vegetarian!*

The end result—Blue Moon Non-Baby Vegetable Potion—had since become another beloved Merriweather tradition, albeit not a very often one, since blue moons happened only, well, once in a blue moon.

Somewhere along the way, Delia had come to realize that there was no such thing as magic. The book had been a joke. Everyone in Willow Root knew the Merriweathers believed themselves to be witches, and someone had played a mean, nasty prank.

Grandma Maddie blindly grabbed a handful of herbs from the rafters above her head and dropped them into the pot. Then she nodded at a mound of potatoes on the counter before squinting up at Delia. "Care to do the honors?"

A birthmark on the ass was a birthmark on the ass, so Delia had to be the one to cut the sacrificial potato. Just as she picked up the knife, the back door opened, and then slammed shut, rattling the stained-glass window above the sink. Aunt Thea rushed in, red-faced and panting. "Oh my Goddess, Madora. Did you actually start without us?"

"Six o'clock sharp means six o'clock sharp," Grandma Maddie snapped, looking at her watch. "Timing is important. The magic is in the details."

"So's the devil," Thea said, removing her jacket and hanging it on the back of the chair. Thea was an accountant, so she knew about details. "And speaking of devils, there's a gang of them outside, singing their silly little songs."

Delia groaned. For as long as she could remember, local kids had been gathering outside their home to chant and taunt and occasionally throw eggs at the "witch house."

The house, for its part, cooperated fully by being in a constant state of disrepair, although it had a lovely turret tower, which happened to be Delia's bedroom.

"They're such darlings," Grandma Maddie said. "Did you give them any candy?"

"I cackled at them," Thea said. "And they ran."

"What good fun," Grandma Maddie said.

The back door opened and slammed shut again, followed by stomping and cursing as Delia's other great-aunts, Aurora and Andi, became momentarily lodged in the mudroom doorway before bursting into the kitchen. "Are we too late?" Aurora asked, brushing leaves out of her hair. "I'm starving."

"We're just getting started," Delia said.

Andi stepped in front of her twin sister, holding up a green bag with the image of a black broom on it. "I brought sage from the shop."

Andi and Aurora owned a bookstore called the Crooked Broom, whose inventory was about ten percent books and, in the words of Delia's mom, "ninety percent crapola." Its shelves overflowed with things like crystals, tarot decks, incense, and, of course, Grandma Maddie's teas and herbal remedies.

"We need to smudge," Andi said. "Before Delia breaks the hex."

"Says who?" Grandma Maddie asked.

"Says a bunch of New Age malarky," came a low, sultry voice from the doorway.

Delia clapped her hands. "Mom! You came!"

Fiona Merriweather crossed her arms and cocked an eyebrow. "I heard there would be soup." Tall, lithe, blond, and graceful, she looked very much like the Good Witch Glenda if the Good Witch Glenda was slightly jaded and full of sarcasm. In other words, the exact opposite of the rest of the shorter, rounder, and merrier Merriweathers. Delia had inherited the blond hair, but her eyes were dark brown, and at a whopping five feet and three inches, she lacked her mom's height. Her body had decided to invest square footage in boobs and hips instead.

"There will definitely be *potion*," Delia said, winking at her mom with the gentle reminder.

Fiona considered herself to be in recovery from witchcraft, so she didn't suffer these rituals very often. She'd even moved out of the house in an effort to distance herself from it. But like Delia, she found her family difficult to quit.

"The more Merriweathers, the merrier," Grandma Maddie said. "Oh, and, Fiona, is Hartwell's cat still out there? I saved him some tuna from my lunch."

Fiona gave Grandma Maddie a quick peck on the cheek. "No black cat crossed my path," she said. "And, Mother, you really shouldn't feed strays."

"He's not a stray, Mom," Delia said. "And even if he were, we couldn't let the poor thing starve."

"Yes," Grandma Maddie said. "Especially now that Hartwell is gone…" There was a slight tremor in her voice, and she seemed to lose her train of thought.

Delia reached over and squeezed the older woman's hand.

Hartwell Halifax had been their next-door neighbor for as long as Delia could remember. Two months ago, he'd suffered a massive heart attack and died, alone in his home. Since then, many attempts had been made to get Hartwell's cat to come inside and stay, but he always managed to sneak back to Hartwell's house next door.

Before any serious level of melancholy could set in, Fiona dropped her purse on the counter and said, "This is damned inconvenient. I have an open house tomorrow, and not a single room has been staged."

"Sorry, Mom," Delia said. "I've had a crazy busy week. But everything is on-site. Amy is going to help me first thing in the morning. The place will be fully bedazzled before anyone arrives. Promise."

Her mom crossed her arms. "You haven't bitten off more than you can chew, have you?"

"Are you kidding?" Delia said. "This is how dreams are made. By swallowing whole chunks without chewing."

"That's gross, dear," Grandma Maddie said. She nodded at the knife in Delia's hand. "Get back to chopping."

"Yes, ma'am."

Starting a new business was exciting, but it was also utterly bone-deep exhausting. And Delia should know, because she'd done it about a billion times. There'd been Delia's Dog Grooming, after which she'd tried her hand at personal training, followed by her short stint as a handy-girl (turns out she wasn't very handy), before launching Merriweather Merry Maids, where she'd been the only maid and not a very merry one. Something had gone wrong with each and every one of those ventures, but this one—Southern Charm Interior Decorating and Design—felt different. It felt like an actual calling.

Ever since Delia was a child, she'd been somewhat obsessed with bringing order to chaos, particularly, the chaos of their home, which seemed to be structured around whatever the opposite of feng shui was. She'd eventually given up, retreating to her overly pink and highly decorated round turret bedroom, where she watched hours and hours of HGTV.

Last year she'd taken the bull by the horns and enrolled in an online interior design program. She'd loved it and had graduated with top honors. But unfortunately, she was having a hard time convincing local residents that the same girl who'd recently cleaned their homes was now qualified to decorate them. Living in the witch house probably didn't help, and so far, her mom's real estate business was her only real client.

Fiona straightened. "Speaking of open houses, guess who agreed to have one?"

"Who?"

"Try to guess. He's the last person you'd expect." Fiona winked and nodded in the direction of Halifax Manor next door.

Delia gasped. "No way. You can't be talking about the asshole. And, oh my gosh, you're listing the house?"

The left corner of her mom's mouth curled up, and she nodded.

"That's fantastic," Delia said.

"Who is it?" Aurora asked, fanning away the sage smoke. "And shall we spill his blood? Maybe all we've been missing these many blue moons is the blood of an asshole."

"No, no," Thea said, eyebrows drawn. "The spell calls for the blood of a witch's true love. Not the blood of an asshole. Unless, of course, they're one and the same."

Andi held up a finger and began ticking off the so-called ingredients. "A boiled innocent. The blood of a witch's true love. And an angry spirit."

"An *agitated* spirit," Thea corrected. "There's a difference between angry and agitated."

After the soup, there would be a short but dramatic séance, where they'd try to provoke dead ancestors with insults. It was absolutely the best part of the evening.

"I could have sworn we needed an angry something or other," Andi said.

"What if we literally need an angry asshole?" Aurora asked. "And all that's required is someone with hemorrhoids?"

Delia snorted. "Hemorrhoids might explain Max Halifax's disposition."

Max Halifax was Hartwell's nephew. He'd arrived in Willow Root shortly after Hartwell's death in order to settle the estate. When Delia and her family had marched over with an apple pie (to offer their condolences and also because they were nosy), Max had opened the door like a startled serial killer caught in the middle of dismembering a body. He'd accepted the pie and condolences as if he were accepting a subpoena, and then...he'd shut the door! Without even inviting them in!

Since then, Delia had seen him now and then over the fence, but when she offered a friendly wave, he pretended not to see her. "You'd think that after inheriting a house like that, he'd have something to smile about," she said.

"Not to mention his handsome face," her mom added.

Delia shrugged. "I hadn't noticed his handsome face."

Hazel eyes ringed with black lashes, full lips, dark stubble on a cleft chin, black hair, and cheekbones a girl would die for.

Grandma Maddie grinned. "Whatever you say, dear."

Aunt Andi raised a delicate eyebrow. "So, he's rich and handsome."

"Don't start," Delia said.

"All I'm saying is that his standoffishness might be explained by something a bit of cream could cure," Aunt Andi said.

Aunt Thea grimaced. "Saying that boy was standoffish is like describing a rattlesnake as being a tad antisocial."

"Maybe he's just grieving," Andi persisted.

"Whether he's a grieving asshole with hemorrhoids or a rattlesnake cursed with horridly unforgivable manners, he's asked me to sell the house," Delia's mom said. "And hopefully, he'll let Delia get in there to work some magic with staging."

Yes! Delia's skin literally tingled at the thought. She freaking loved Halifax Manor and had dreamed of living in it ever since she was a little girl. Hartwell had been like a surrogate grandfather, and she'd spent much of her childhood there. Decorating the manor, even if it was just for a staging, would be an amazing opportunity.

"He has a slight accent, doesn't he?" Aurora said. "Where on earth is he from? Someplace exotic, I bet."

In Willow Root, anyone who didn't say *y'all* was considered to have a strange accent.

"Maybe Delia can find out where he's from," Grandma Maddie said.

"I don't care where he's from," Delia said. "I have zero interest in pursuing a cranky rich guy on his way out of town. And anyway, I'm a Merriweather woman. I'm happy being single."

"Just as well," Grandma Maddie said, holding up a knife. "If anyone were to fall in love with Delia, we might have to kill him."

CHAPTER TWO

Max whistled cheerfully as he moved through the large, rambling house known as Halifax Manor. Boxes lined the walls, and the rooms held that particular gloomy echo of impending emptiness.

It was music to his ears. He'd been in Willow Root for six weeks and was ready to get back to his normal life as a venator, traveling the world in search of rare magical antiquities. All he had to do was pack up approximately two tons of stuff first.

Flipping on the light in the library, he gazed at the bookshelves that spanned floor-to-ceiling on every wall. The books couldn't be haphazardly thrown into piles for keeping and giving away. Like many other items crammed into every nook and cranny of the home, some of them might be dangerous.

Uncle Hartwell had also worked as a venator. But unlike Max, he'd been a rascal and hadn't handed over some of the more rare and dangerous things to the Concilium, which was the governing body of the witching world.

Max headed for the bookcases. It was time to get to work, and although any normal person would be overwhelmed by the task, he was—

"Feeling giddy?"

He jumped, even though he should be used to Nikki seemingly popping up out of nowhere. Although at the moment, Nikki was hardly popping. He was sprawled out on the old leather Chesterfield sofa, blackish-blue hair sticking up in every direction and bright green eyes puffy from sleep.

Max sighed. "Another nap? When we have so much to do?"

Nikki stretched luxuriously, yawned, and then sat up and stretched some more. "I did some sleuthing around earlier. And I packed two whole boxes, for your information."

"Wow. Two whole boxes? Only one hundred ninety-eight thousand, or so, left to go. As to me feeling giddy, why yes, actually. I can't wait to get out of here."

Max frowned. What was he going to do about Nikki?

Max had come to Willow Root, a tiny little town with an even tinier witch population, under direct orders from Morgaine Gerard, High Priestess of the Concilium. The high priestess was not an elected position. Whoever had the most power and could attract the most magic ascended to the so-called throne. And for the last couple of centuries, it had nearly always been a Gerard. Max had no choice but to do Morgaine's bidding, which included keeping an eye on the silly Merriweather women next door.

Nobody had told him he'd have to deal with Nikki, too.

"We've got to figure out a way to disentangle ourselves before I leave."

"You make it sound like we're celebrities negotiating a divorce."

Max laughed. "If only it were that easy."

Along with the house and his uncle's antique shop, Max had inherited Nikki, Uncle Hartwell's familiar.

Few witches had familiars in modern times. But Nikki's

attachment to the Halifax family was the result of a centuries-old curse. The key to unlocking it had been lost, and well... Here they were. A man and his imp. Whether they liked it or not.

Like most imps, Nikki typically took the traditional form of a black cat. But Uncle Hartwell had been dreadfully allergic to cats, so he'd cast a spell that would allow Nikki to assume a human form inside the manor and the antique shop. It was technically illegal, but Uncle Hartwell hadn't been known for following rules.

Nikki pouted and gazed around the room with longing. "Why do you have to sell the manor?"

"Why on earth would I want to keep it? The Concilium says I can do whatever I want with it—"

"Unless the Blue Witch uses magic to break the hex before her thirtieth birthday."

Max snorted. "That's in eight days. If she hasn't done it by now, she's not going to. I mean, there's a blue moon tonight. If she's truly a blue witch, Cordelia is at the height of her power. And didn't you tell me she was over there helping her grandmother make soup? Call me reckless, but I'm not worried."

"I'm quite a bit older than you, Max. The fates are nothing if not hilarious. And they love a good twist."

"Screw the fates."

Nikki smirked as if maybe he had, indeed, screwed the fates. "You shouldn't underestimate Delia."

"Lots of people are born during a blue moon. So what?"

"But only one Merriweather. And she has the birthmark."

The Merriweathers were quite properly and soundly hexed. Max had once seen the actual spell, painstakingly preserved and held under lock and key, deep within the historical vault at Shadowlark.

He shivered. There was a rumor that the book—a collection of

Halifax Hexes from the year 1800 to 1899—had been made of human skin. And the spell itself had called for a blood sacrifice.

"And lots of people have birthmarks. Believe me. There is nothing special about Cordelia Merriweather. If she's a blue witch capable of breaking the hex, then I'm Sabrina the Teenage Witch."

"But—"

"She has to break the hex in order to gain any magic, and she has no magic with which to break the hex." He smirked. It was brilliant.

"Except that blue witches under the age of thirty are never entirely magicless—"

"Hush, Nikki."

Nikki crossed his arms over his chest in a huff, and Max remembered (again) that Nikki had no choice but to comply with a direct order from him, and he'd just told him to hush.

"Sorry," he said. "You may speak, of course."

Nikki recovered quickly, although his cheeks were slightly pink. For that matter, Max's felt warm. The situation was awkward.

Nikki cleared his throat. "As I was saying, blue witches are never completely powerless. The hex was meant to stifle *witch* magic, but not—"

"Don't you dare tell me you believe in fairies."

Nikki shut his mouth and raised an eyebrow.

Max sighed in frustration. "Sorry. Feel free to say you believe in fairies. Although surely you can't do it with a straight face."

"Of course I believe in fairies," Nikki quipped. "You do realize that most people don't even believe in imps?"

That was probably true, but—

"Magical beings are in hiding for their own protection, because witches have made sure they're practically powerless—"

"That's not true. Magic is regulated outside of Shadowlark in order to *protect* magical beings. It's necessary. You know that."

Shadowlark was a hidden city run almost entirely on magic. It was considered the Cradle of the Craft, because its libraries and vaults held the oldest and vastest collections of historical documents, genealogical charts, magical antiquities, and, of course, literal tomes of spells, potions, and hexes. Everyone who lived there, including Max and his family, were descendants of the Logos line of witches.

Nikki rolled his eyes as if they were just going to have to agree to disagree over something that was not open to interpretation. "Anyway, just because you can't see them doesn't mean they aren't there."

"But *fairies*, Nikki? Come on."

"Right. There's no such thing as fairies. That's why your uncle was set up here in this house for nearly thirty years, spying on the Merriweathers. Because there's no such thing as fairies and no such thing as blue witches."

"Folklore," Max said.

Fairies were the playful tricksters of the magical world. Max believed they "existed" so people could blame things on them. Missing something? A fairy took it. Spilled something? A fairy did it. That sort of thing. And if a witch child was born during a blue moon and happened to have a blueish birthmark (a fairy's kiss), then they were supposedly gifted with wild and unpredictable fairy magic. This bit of "blue" magic was seen as a gift from the fae, and it only lasted for thirty years.

"It's all based on folklore," Max repeated. "You know how witches are—"

"Oh, I definitely do. You're about to say they're old-fashioned and illusory and egotistical—"

"I was going to say that they cling to their traditional customs, but go on."

In response, Nikki took a gigantic breath, as if he were, indeed, about to go on, because of course, he was. Max had told him to.

Max held up a hand. "Never mind. I didn't mean that."

"Really? Because I could." Nikki's lips curled up just a tad on the left side, while his right eyebrow rose the exact same amount, and *that* was where the term *impish grin* came from.

"Really."

The grin disappeared. "You're no fun. And that's another thing about witches, by the way."

Despite himself, Max stifled a chuckle.

It was his prerogative whether to continue letting Nikki walk around on two legs. But thus far, he hadn't been tempted to undo the spell. It was kind of nice having someone to banter back and forth with.

"So tell me," Nikki said suddenly. "Why did the Concilium order them hexed?"

Max walked to the window and gazed at the Merriweathers' eyesore of a house. Conveniently, they shared a backyard fence. "It was over two hundred years ago." He shrugged, hoping Nikki would take the hint that it wasn't a topic worth pursuing.

"I bet you don't even know why, do you? You witches are so petty, which is another one for the list, by the way."

Hint not taken.

"Illegal love spells," Max said.

"Ah. They're supposedly Cor witches, so that makes sense."

It was a bit unnerving how much Nikki knew about the witching world. But completely understandable, considering how much time he'd spent within it. And he was right. The Merriweathers descended from the Cor line of witches, which made them practitioners of heart magic.

"They once tried to control the witching world by controlling the hearts of men," Max said. "My ancestor, Wilmot Halifax, was bewitched by Lucinda Merriweather, and together, they damn near brought down Shadowlark with their dangerous ideas."

"By dangerous ideas, I assume you mean love," Nikki said with a bit of snark.

Logos witches, like Max's family, were logic-based. And they didn't *do* love. Sex? Yes. Love? Most definitely not. And they'd never have sexual relations with a Cor witch. Way too dangerous.

"Mens omnia cor," Max said, turning back to Nikki with his shoulders squared. He felt a surge of pride, saying those words. "That's our motto."

"Mind over heart," Nikki said. "Saddest thing I've ever heard."

"Love isn't rational," Max said defensively. "Thinking with anything other than the mind leads to bad decisions."

Logos witches didn't date. They didn't fall in love. They absolutely never married. And they were all the happier for it. It gave them the time they needed to devote themselves to their work—protecting and preserving the Craft within the hallowed walls of Shadowlark.

"Wasn't it a Halifax who hexed the Merriweathers?"

Max rubbed his temples. "We really should get to packing."

"That's what I thought. Hexing is your specialty, after all."

"We're rarely called upon to hex anything or anyone anymore. As a venator, I regularly engage in unhexing. But in any case, it seemed appropriate for Wilmot to cast the hex since he was Lucinda's victim."

"Falling in love doesn't make you a victim, Max."

"And to think, Uncle Hartwell could have just taken allergy meds and missed all this wisdom."

Nikki shrugged. "They made him sleepy. And he found me charming."

"Well, I heard he was going a bit bonkers there at the end."

Nikki stiffened, and Max cleared his throat uncomfortably. "Let's get back to work."

Nikki removed four books from a shelf and handed them to Max. "Let me play the devil's advocate for a moment—"

"You quite literally *are* the devil's advocate, Nikki."

Nikki shrugged slightly. "What if you're wrong about Delia?"

"I'm not."

"Humor me."

"Well, if I'm wrong and Cordelia Merriweather breaks the hex on her family, then I guess someone will be required to rehex them."

"I hate to ask this next question, but, ahem, would that someone be you?"

"I haven't spent much time thinking about it, because it's not going to happen. But yes, I suspect the responsibility would fall to me."

"And do you know how to do that?"

Max accidentally dropped a book, and it wailed horribly— lamentatio spell—making him wince and cover his ears. Nikki, who was skittish around loud noises, dissolved into a black ball of fluff and ran out of the room.

It was just as well. Because, no, Max didn't know how to do that.

CHAPTER THREE

Delia wiped sweat off her brow and gave the sofa one last shove with her hip. Whew! She and Amy had pulled it off with twenty minutes to spare. Thank God she hadn't been lying to her mom last night when she'd said she could do it.

She stretched, producing a string of clearly audible popping noises. "Ahh…" she said. "That feels better. My back has been giving me problems again."

Amy, decked out in army-green cargo pants and a cutoff Sex Pistols T-shirt, looked every bit as tired as Delia felt. "You're turning thirty soon, so don't expect that to get better. Today it's moving a couch. Next week you'll throw your back out trying to put on a bra."

"Thanks for the support," Delia said with an eye roll.

Getting the couch onto the trailer late last night—even with all her aunties helping—had definitely given her back a tweak, and it would now be prone to spasms until it settled the hell back down.

"Save that appreciation and gratitude for your bra," Amy said. "Because once you turn thirty, it'll be working overtime, too." Amy held her hands open as if she were weighing cantaloupes…at waist level.

Delia laughed. She'd been a late bloomer, but once things had finally gotten started, she'd gone from a training bra right into a

D cup lickety-split. "Well, my bras might not be pretty, but they can handle my girls just fine. And seriously. Thanks for helping me this morning."

"All joking aside, decorating is hard work," Amy said. "I'm going to stick to catering."

Amy had been Delia's best friend since the second grade, when they'd bonded over their shared status as the social pariahs of Willow Root Elementary. And the last thing Amy was interested in was interior decorating, but here she was, dragging furniture around since dawn, and it made Delia's heart fill to dang near overflowing.

"Why the hell are you looking at me like that?" Amy asked.

"Just wondering what I did to deserve such an awesome best friend."

Amy's cheeks turned a little splotchy, but she waved off Delia's mushiness. "Please. Like you haven't slapped the salami with me at least a thousand times."

Delia laughed. "I really wish you'd stop saying that."

Amy owned a charcuterie catering business called Across the Board. Delia often helped her lay out the food, which yes, usually included slapping down some salami.

"I'm trying to thank you," Delia said. "You've been here since dawn. You helped me unload the truck, move furniture, unroll rugs, hang pictures, and..." She closed her eyes and inhaled. "You even baked cookies so the house would smell amazing."

"Like I said, I'm going to stick with food. This was hard work."

"Just because you make catering look easy doesn't mean it is," Delia said. "It's like magic when you do it."

Amy waved a hand dismissively. "Slice, spread, stuff. No breaking a sweat required. This, however, is heavy lifting. But it looks awesome, and if Fiona doesn't like it, she can—"

Delia's mom cleared her throat loudly from the doorway.

"Oh, hi, Fiona," Amy said.

Fiona raised an eyebrow. "Hello, Amy. What was it you were just about to recommend I do?"

Amy grinned, producing two identical dimples that made it nearly impossible not to imagine a halo over her head, which was funny if you knew Amy. "Let's go with jump in a lake. It's the least offensive."

Delia's mom pretended to bristle, but then her expression changed to one of open-mouthed shock as she took in the room.

Uh-oh. Delia broke out in a light sweat as a spark of panic unfolded in her tummy. *Please don't hate it, please don't hate it, please don't hate it...*

"Oh my God, Delia. What have you done?"

Shit. "We can change—"

"Don't you dare touch a thing!" her mom said, walking to the center of the room. "It's absolutely perfect. Brilliant, even! This house was horrid, and now it's, well, I don't even have the words. Where did you get all this?"

"You'd be surprised what Grandma Maddie has in the attic and the storage shed. And I cut a deal with Ramos Furniture Store. They let me use floor models for staging, and I'm helping with their displays. Also, I've picked up a few things here and there. Garage sales and whatnot."

The house was a plain Jane ranch-style circa 1972. In other words, it was a challenge.

The owner hadn't wanted to spend a dime to upgrade the avocado appliances or replace the gold and orange vinyl flooring or chocolate shag carpet, so Delia had decided to just go with it. Instead of trying to put lipstick on a pig, they went full-on *Brady Bunch*. The shag carpet was in remarkable condition, but it darkened the low-ceilinged room. So, they threw a white fur rug down and placed a knockoff Isamu Noguchi coffee table on it. Next, they'd yanked out the dark velveteen couch and love seat (wagon-wheel print—ack!) and replaced them with a sleek, modern sectional. Accent cushions of gold and sage fit well, especially when paired with the green midcentury hanging swag lamps that Delia had bought at a garage sale and had been dying to use. A heavy macramé wall hanging looked great over the couch, and unbelievably, the earthy floral wallpaper on the dining room wall was actually making a comeback, so they'd accented it with a gigantic sunburst mirror.

"So, you like it, Fiona?" Amy asked, arranging a trio of kitschy retro owls on the dining table.

"I think it's groovy. Hopefully, it won't overwhelm a buyer."

Staging wasn't meant to show personality. It was just meant to make a home feel welcoming and comfortable. But sometimes it was hard to resist. Especially when there was nothing you could do about the personality that was already there. Like in this house. Delia bit her lip as her stomach churned. What if she'd made a huge mistake?

"Delia, are you going to Becca's miscellaneous tea tomorrow?" Amy asked.

Miscellaneous teas were a Southern small-town bridal tradition (a dying one, but the folks in Willow Root loved traditions in general and dying ones in particular). They were huge, extravagant showers with crystal punch bowls and silver coffee service sets and pastel-colored mints, but—here's the funny part—no tea.

In Willow Root, most miscellaneous teas were hosted by Constance Fleming or Violet Wilson, who seemed to be in direct competition with each other over who could host the fanciest event.

"Mrs. Fleming has asked me to decorate," she said, stretching to relieve the kink in her back.

Her mom lit up. "You're going to redo her living room? Oh, Delia, that's great!"

"No," she said, bending to the left and feeling a satisfying pop. "She just wants me to decorate for the shower. Like, you know, party decorations."

In addition to providing gifts for the bride, miscellaneous teas provided opportunities for the hostess to show off her home by displaying gifts in every room.

"Are you kidding?" her mom asked. "Why did you agree to that?"

"I'll give you a hint," Delia said. "And it's green."

Her mom sighed. "Okay. I get it. But you didn't earn your associate's degree in interior decorating so you could blow up balloons."

"I've fashioned a beautiful arch out of willow twigs and definitely plan to do more than blow up balloons. Who knows? Maybe it will get me a few real clients."

"Just don't let her talk you into cleaning," Amy said with a frown. "You're not her maid anymore."

"Don't I know it. And I won't."

"Promise?"

"Swear it."

Delia looked at the dry bar in the corner of the room. "Oh no," she said. "We were going to put a martini set there, remember? It would have been perfect."

"You don't have time to run to your storage unit," Amy said.

Delia gazed at the ceiling fan, thinking. "You know what? Hartwell's antique shop is just a few blocks away. Max Halifax's car was parked out front. He's probably in there packing up, and I bet there's something we can use. And, anyway, I need to talk to him."

Amy physically recoiled. "Why would you need to talk to *him*?"

"So, you've had a run-in with Max, too? He's terribly rude, isn't he?"

Amy pretended to gag, and then she said, "I can't stand him. If I were you, I'd steer clear. He gives bad vibes."

"He's selling Hartwell's house," Fiona said. "I'm listing it."

"Ooh, congrats, Fiona!"

"And I want to stage it for the open house," Delia said. "So, I'm going to run to the shop, pick up something to set on that dry bar, and, you know, flutter my eyelashes, and ask about staging the manor."

"It's too bad you can't buy the manor, Delia," Amy said. "You've always loved that place."

Delia laughed over the absurdity. She absolutely *did* love Halifax Manor. Every nook and cranny of it (and there were so many). But it wasn't reasonable. For one thing, she'd never be able to afford something like that. And for another, it was way too grand. Too huge. And Delia was just one person and intended to stay that way. Merriweathers *always* ended up that way. Delia planned to skip the middle part where hearts were broken and just ride the spinster train all the way to the final stop.

"I hope somebody nice moves in," she said. And then she turned to her mom. "What are the odds that the new folks will honor the My Pool Is Your Pool rule that Hartwell had with us?"

"I'd say the odds are slim," her mom said. "Hartwell was one of a kind."

"Definitely not like his nephew," Amy said with a shudder. "I mean Max Halifax is—"

She hiccuped violently, which was a thing she did whenever she became flustered.

"Oh my God," Delia said. "Do you have a little crush on Max Halifax?"

Amy hiccuped again. "Absolutely not."

"Because he's super cute," Delia added.

"His hotness doesn't overshadow his personality," Amy said, adding a hiccup for emphasis.

Delia's mom handed Amy a bottle of water. "Take a sip, then hold your breath for ten seconds. And neither of you needs to get worked up over Max. He's leaving as soon as he gets Hartwell's shop packed up and the house sold."

Delia thought about the little shop and how every square inch was packed with odd knickknacks and antiques. And how the house was pretty much the same way. It seemed like it would all take some time.

"You know," her mom continued. "That space the antique shop is in would be a perfect location for an interior design business."

Delia's heart skipped a beat. It was almost too much to dream about. Hartwell's shop was right on the town square, across the street from her mom's real estate office, and a block down from the Crooked Broom, where Delia currently "officed" out of the stockroom.

"Maybe. If I can ever afford it. Right now, it's *this* job I need to concentrate on. And that means heading to the antique shop to see if I can find something cool to set on the dry bar. I need a few things like that anyway, and since Max is clearing out the inventory, I bet I can pick up something cheap."

"Good luck," Amy said, hiccuping again. "Just get in and get out."

"I don't have time for anything else," Delia said with a grin.

Max turned the sign on the door to CLOSED. And then, because folks in Willow Root often couldn't take a hint, and he really didn't want to be bothered while he packed up the shop, he pulled a string from his pocket and tied a neat, small knot. Almost mindlessly he muttered:

Cross this threshold at your peril
Unwellness pierces like an arrow
Turn at once or hurry past
With this knot my spell is cast

There. That was done. Now to light the repellant candle, just in case anyone was extra determined. With a simple flick of his pinkie, a thick brown candle on the counter began to flicker, and a string of black smoke snaked its way toward the ceiling.

"Must you?" Nikki asked. He was perched on a stool, elbow on the counter, sipping coffee and flipping through a catalog instead of packing. "That thing stinks. I have a sensitive nose."

"That's the point," Max said. "It's a deterrent."

"Your personality is enough. No need for stinky candles."

"It's hard to know which form of you is worse. The one where you shed massive amounts of hair and dander or the one where you emit a steady stream of irritating-yet-ineffective insults."

Nikki raised an eyebrow. "Are they though?"

Max plopped a box on the counter. "Pack more. Talk less."

Nikki picked up a stack of plates. "Are these ready for a box?"

"Yes, but be careful with them."

"They look like bone china."

Max snorted. "And you don't want to know what kind of bones. But that's not why you should be careful."

Nikki's eyes widened. "Can they kill me?"

"How many lives do you have left?"

Nikki gingerly set the plates down.

"They're mirage plates, dating back to the seventeenth century. With the proper spell, they'll fill up with whatever meal a witch can dream up. But it's only a mirage to cover what's really on the plate. Which would typically be something dreadful and poisonous, of course."

"Of course," Nikki said.

"Use the Bubble Wrap," Max said.

"I have an aversion to Bubble Wrap. And anyway, why can't you just pack up this place with a single knot? Doing it this way is going to take forever."

"Yes, especially if I have to do it by myself. And as I've told you, I must examine every item. Some of this stuff needs special treatment beyond Bubble Wrap, as you well know," Max said. "And some of it is illegal and needs to be turned over to the Concilium. Uncle Hartwell was a bad boy in that regard."

"He was quite the collector. But no harm ever came from it."

"That you know of."

Apparently, Uncle Hartwell had continued to procure magical, charmed, or hexed items after retirement, and not all of them had been nullified or neutralized, a task that often fell to a member of the Halifax family, since they were highly skilled in the art of unhexing.

Reversing spells was like solving a puzzle. And for the times Max couldn't solve it, he resorted to stultifying hexes, which were basically counter-hexes. And since hexes were never permanent, rehexing dangerous items was an irritating reoccurrence.

Thinking about permanent hexes reminded him of the hex on the Merriweathers. It was a perma-tempus hex, which although not technically permanent, was about as close to permanent as a hex could get. Perma-tempus hexes could be reversed, but a "key" was required to do so. And in the case of the hex on the Merriweathers, the key was in a book entitled *Clavis Hexicus* that had been missing for decades. Even if Cordelia *was* a blue witch, she'd never be able to get her hot little hands on the actual spell needed to break the hex.

Max had never been called upon to cast a perma-tempus hex. They required the approval of the Concilium and were typically reserved for people or things deemed dangerous enough to threaten the entire witching world.

The bell above the door jingled.

Max looked at Nikki, who stared back bug-eyed. He'd never been seen in human form by anyone other than Max or Uncle Hartwell.

"Didn't you lock the door?" Nikki whispered.

Holy hell. Had he not locked the fucking door? He'd flipped the sign... He'd cast the spell...

He hadn't locked the fucking door.

"Whoever it is, they won't stay long because of the deterrent spell," Max whispered. "Sit tight. It's too late to dissolve into a fluff ball."

Max waited for the sound of retreating footsteps, because by now whoever it was should be feeling poorly. Possibly wanting to vomit while smothering beneath a blanket of dread and impending doom. Something like that. At the very least, their heart would be palpitating—

"Howdy! Is anyone here?"

How far inside would this intruder venture? They were probably already turning around, ready to bolt for the door...

"Yoo-hoo! Hello?"

It was a woman. And the farther she came into the store, the more likely it was that she'd vomit *inside* instead of *outside*, and how rude was that?

Intensely curious, Max came out from behind the counter. He stepped over a small chest that had once overflowed with a replenishing supply of gold dragoons, stubbed his toe on the leg of a writing desk that housed an ink pen that predicted the future, and ran right smack into Cordelia Merriweather.

Her blond hair was in a ponytail, swept away from a glowing face that exuded optimism and cheerfulness.

Max prickled. Who was she to be impervious to his magic?

She pushed up the sleeves of an oversize yellow hoodie that said LET's RODEO! and rocked back on the heels of a pair of worn brown cowboy boots that should have looked silly but somehow didn't. Big hoop earrings the size of tangerines swung back and forth on delicate earlobes.

Why am I noticing her earlobes?

Slowly, the peeved feeling faded into something a bit…chillier. It crept up his spine, and he had to suppress a shiver.

Delia could only resist his magic if she had a bit of her own. Which she shouldn't have. Unless, of course, she really was a blue witch.

Max swallowed.

An object deemed dangerous enough to threaten the entire witching world had just entered the shop.

CHAPTER FOUR

Max Halifax looked like he'd seen a ghost, and Delia wouldn't be surprised if he had. The shop was packed from floor to ceiling with odds and ends and curiosities of every variety, and most of the stuff was covered by a thick layer of dust. She'd had to fight her way through several cobwebs and their resident spiders while navigating the maze of armoires and chests and tables and chairs. She was mildly relieved to be facing Max instead of a minotaur.

"Hi," she said. "I'm not sure if you remember me. I'm Delia Merriweather. My family and I popped in with a pie? We're next-door neighbors?"

She held out her hand, and Max looked at it like it might bite him. Was he a germophobe? Or maybe he had crippling social anxiety. That would possibly explain his poor manners.

Max narrowed his eyes slightly and then took her hand, giving it a quick, firm shake before letting go. "Yes. Sorry about my behavior that night. I had my hands full at the time."

"We shouldn't have stopped by unannounced. It's just that we were so used to popping in on Hartwell that we didn't give it a second thought. Maybe we should have."

"Second thoughts are always a good idea."

Okay. That was some proper shade, and talking to him was like trying to engage a tree stump. "I believe my mom is your real estate agent?"

"Yes, she is," he said simply. And then he stared deeply into her eyes. "Are you feeling ill?"

She smoothed a few locks of hair that had come loose from her ponytail. "No, I feel fine. Why?"

Max continued staring—the man was not afraid of eye contact—and maybe she was feeling a bit ill after all, because staring into those gorgeous hazel eyes suddenly made her head feel cloudy. Something unfurled slowly in her belly, like a lioness waking up from a nap because it sensed an extremely tasty treat nearby.

"Are you sure you don't have a slight headache? A little nausea, perhaps…"

"God. Do I look that bad?"

Before Max could answer (just as well, since she probably didn't want to hear his response), a shuffling sound drew her attention to the counter, where a man sat perched on a stool in the shadows. "Hello," Delia said. "I didn't see you there."

"That's my cousin Nikki," Max said quickly. "He's a bit shy."

"I'm sorry, but did you say Nikki?"

Max gave her a quizzical look. "I did. Why?"

Nikki had beautiful green eyes. And dark black hair. Between him and Max, Delia was definitely not the prettiest person in the room. Delia gave him a little wave. "I'm just wondering if it's some kind of a family name," she said. "Because that's also the name of Hartwell's cat. Which is kind of funny, if you ask me."

Oops! Nobody *had* asked her, and she suddenly remembered her manners. "Goodness, I hope I didn't offend you," she said, smiling at Nikki. "It's a perfectly good name. It's not like you have a cat name. I didn't mean to insinuate that Nikki is similar to Mittens or Fluffy or Princess…"

She looked at Max, hoping he would save her from herself, because she had more cat names and felt unfortunately prepared to use them, but Max just stared at her as if she were a specimen of something seriously weird in a jar, and well, now she'd lost her train of thought regarding cat names, so yay?

Nikki smiled, and his green eyes lit up in a most pleasant way. "I'm not even slightly offended," he said. "It's just a fun coincidence that Hartwell's cat and I share the same name."

Whew! What a relief. But she couldn't shake the weird sensation that she'd met this guy before. "I'm sorry, do we know each other?"

"No," Max interrupted, shifting from foot to foot like a kernel of corn about to pop. "You two have absolutely never met. Nikki is just visiting."

"Oh? From where—"

"Is there something I can help you with?" Max said, rudely interrupting.

When someone says they're visiting, you're *supposed* to ask from where. It was the polite thing to do. Delia had briefly forgotten that Max Halifax had no freaking manners.

Fine. She would just do her business and get out. She was short on time anyway.

She took a deep breath and glanced around the dim room with its large furnishings casting endless shadows. "I'm looking for something to set on a dry bar. Something kind of groovy. Maybe a martini set?"

Both Nikki and Max looked at her expectantly, as if she were telling a story and hadn't gotten to the plotty part yet.

"Or I guess a pitcher would do. Maybe some highball glasses."

Nikki suddenly snapped his fingers. "Max, she's here to buy something."

"Yes, and also..." Delia dug around in her purse and pulled out a stack of newly minted business cards. "I was wondering if you'd mind setting these out. I know you're not going to be here much longer, but for now, maybe just a few on the counter?"

Max took the cards and looked at them. A slow smile spread across his face, and damn, the man was fine when he smiled. He hadn't shaved, and his face was scruffy in that rugged, sexy way that Delia liked, while also somehow managing to look properly fine and polished. His dark wavy hair was thick and glorious and in need of a good trim, which she hoped he never got, because she liked the way a rogue lock of hair fell over his left eye.

"Southern Charm," he read aloud. "Inferior Decorating and Design."

Did he have a lisp? Or—her mouth went dry—was there a freaking typo? She grabbed the card out of his hand.

Sure enough. It said *inferior* instead of *interior*.

"Oh no! Are they all that way?"

"I'd assume so."

This was horrible! She'd been leaving these things all over town. She was going to be the laughingstock of Willow Root, which was quite an achievement for someone whose family was pretty much already the laughingstock of Willow Root.

Someone didn't like Cordelia Merriweather. Her business cards had been hexed with a simple, elementary-level spell.

"Oh my God," she said. "I've...I've been giving these to everybody."

He literally could not care even one iota less that she was making a fool out of herself via business cards in Willow Root, Texas, but nevertheless, her puppy-dog eyes were doing something weird to his insides. "I'm sure nobody noticed," he said.

"You noticed."

"I'm a stickler for details. Most people aren't." And that was true. "How about this? You run along, and I'll fix your cards. You'll have them by this afternoon."

Anything to get her out of here. His mind felt like it was literally on fire. He had to find somewhere to sit and think and figure out what was going on.

"Really? You can redo my cards? Do you have a printer or something?"

Max nodded. *Or something.*

"You don't mind?"

"Of course not," Max said. "Happy to help."

He wasn't, actually.

Delia smiled, and holy hell. She was pretty when she smiled. And that Texas twang—*you have a printer or somethin'?*—was ridiculously cute instead of annoying.

Well, actually, it was annoying.

And cute.

Max smiled back, which was stupid and unacceptable in light of the circumstances. But here he was. Doing just that.

"Well, thank you. That's so kind—"

Max put a hand on the small of her back. "Let me escort you out."

And lock the door behind you.

A tingling sensation started in his belly and threatened to move lower if he didn't get her out of here. This witch was Cor. Which meant she was naturally gifted in heart magic. Is that why he felt this way?

Hm. Something to ponder.

Delia suddenly stopped short. "Oh!" she said. "The dry bar! I still need a martini set. I swear my mind got a little fuzzy the minute I stepped in here."

Max raised an eyebrow. At least she felt *something*. "We really don't have anything like that. And even if we did, I wouldn't possibly know where to find it. We're right in the middle of packing up."

"Actually," Nikki said. "I think there might be something up front by the window—"

Max shot Nikki a look.

"Never mind. I think we sold it," Nikki said quickly.

Delia squinted in the general direction Nikki had indicated, where there was, in fact, a retro martini set with four multicolored stems in a stainless-steel caddy.

"Oh! Thanks, Nikki. I see it."

She headed straight for it, ponytail swinging.

Max hopped over a wishing well that was the very definition of why you should be careful what you wish for and landed at the martini set just in time to pick it up and thrust it at Delia. "It's yours," he said briskly. "Goodbye, and have a lovely day."

"Careful. It looks fragile," she said, taking it gingerly from his hands. "How much is it?"

"It's on the house," Max said. "Just take it."

"Oh, absolutely not," Delia said. "I insist on paying for this. Go ahead and ring it up."

He had no idea how to do that. He'd never worked in a shop, much less one in the Stray Lands. "You heard the lady, Nikki," he said. "Ring it up."

"Ring it up?"

"Yes. The martini set. Just ring it up."

"I don't even know what that means," Nikki said.

Max sighed. Did the ancient cash register even work? "Ms. Merriweather, that will be fifty dollars." He held out his hand, hoping she'd slap some cash in it and be on her way.

She began digging in her gigantic bag. "Let's see...Does the store still take credit cards?"

That was it. He was dead now. Because even a witch could only take so much.

"No," he said through gritted teeth. "Unfortunately not."

"Can I swing by and pay you later?"

"Yes, yes, of course," he said, ushering her out the door as fast as he could.

"Bye," she said, spinning around. "I guess I'll see—"

He closed the door, locked it, and collapsed onto a dusty, overstuffed chair while Nikki hovered nearby, grinning. "What just happened?" Max asked.

"Cordelia Merriweather came in and stole a martini set while you fumbled about with a tent in your pants."

Max sighed and shut his eyes. He did *not* have a tent in his pants. He wasn't that easy. But other than that minor detail, it was a fairly accurate account.

Chapter Five

Max lay on the Chesterfield sofa in the library, exhausted from going through what seemed like ten million of Uncle Hartwell's books and researching perma-tempus hexes...just in case. Because Delia *had* marched right past two deterrent spells.

Better to be safe than sorry.

The problem was, nobody had used a perma-tempus hex in over a hundred years. And the original hex on the Merriweathers called for a blood sacrifice.

He shivered. He might be an expert on hexing, but murder was not in his wheelhouse.

He forced himself to unclench his jaw. Even if Delia was a blue witch, she wouldn't have any idea how to break the hex. The book of keys was missing. It had disappeared from Shadowlark's vaults, and there was no way Delia or anyone in her family had access to the vaults. And if Uncle Hartwell hadn't been able to find it, nobody could. Uncle Hartwell had literally been famous for finding unfindable objects.

Max yanked his shirttail out of his pants and stretched out, bringing his hands behind his head. He wasn't going to have to rehex the Merriweathers. It was stupid to be even mildly concerned about it.

He breathed in deeply and exhaled. In just a little over a week,

Delia would turn thirty. And then he could put it out of his mind, because even if she was a blue witch, the fairy magic would last for only thirty years. Once they crossed that line—Delia's thirtieth birthday—Delia wouldn't have any magic with which to break the hex.

He tried to imagine what it would feel like to not even *know* you were a witch. Or—a knot formed in his throat—to know it and not be able to practice magic. He thought of Delia's face, all glowing and cheerful. Could you miss something you'd never had?

The knot grew larger, and he had to swallow twice to get rid of it. What was this nagging feeling of discomfort?

"Feeling guilty?" Nikki asked, scaring the absolute shit out of Max, who hadn't even known Nikki was in the room.

Max sat up and twisted his head around to see Nikki leaning against the wall. "I've no reason to feel guilty. I didn't hex the Merriweathers."

"I didn't ask if you had reason to," Nikki said, strolling over and taking a seat in a nearby chair.

"They probably don't even miss their magic. I bet they're like hedge witches in that way."

Nikki snorted. "Have you ever met a hedge witch?"

Hedge witches lived among Strays—non-witch humans—in places like Willow Root, where ley lines that transported magic ran beneath the earth. The magic of hedge witches was minimal and heavily regulated by the Concilium. It was for the safety and protection of everyone, of course. Because Big Magic tended to draw the attention of Strays, and historically, the attention of Strays resulted in unfortunate events. Like witch-hunting, witch-burning, witch-drowning, and other activities that witches would prefer to avoid.

He didn't feel at all guilty about the necessary regulations, and he particularly didn't feel guilty about the hex on the Merriweathers. Forcing someone to fall in love involved stealing their free will. It was the worst offense imaginable. The thought of losing control over not just your emotions but your very *mind*...He shivered.

Whatever this was that he was feeling, it wasn't guilt.

"Cor magic *is* dangerous," he said. "A Merriweather bewitched my ancestor, forcing him to fall under her spell. It wreaked havoc—"

"Are Logos witches built so differently from other witches?"

"What?"

"How do you avoid falling in love?"

"You don't *fall* in love. It's not like tripping over a fucking rock and landing on your face. It's a decision. And Logos witches have decided not to make that decision. It's easy. Love is totally avoidable, unless a Cor witch gets ahold of you."

Nikki shook his head, as if to clear it. "So much deciding."

"You know," Max said, lowering his voice. "There were rumors that Uncle Hartwell was no longer loyal to the Concilium. That he was overly sympathetic to the Merriweathers and the witches in the Stray Lands."

Nikki raised an eyebrow. "And what if those rumors are true?"

"Are they?"

It seemed that Nikki might know the answer, but he just stared impassively, arms folded across his chest. Max could force him to answer, but first, he really wasn't an asshole, and second, he might not want to hear the answer.

"Maybe you're asking the wrong questions," Nikki finally said.

"What's that supposed to mean?"

Nikki sighed and shook his head. "Exactly what it sounds like.

But what do you say we change the subject. Did you take care of that hex on Delia's cards?"

"I told her I would, didn't I?"

He'd kept his word. A quick and easy incantation had reversed the hex.

"Listen, I don't think we should let her out of our sight over the next couple of days, just to make certain she's not up to anything."

He'd decided to let Delia's mother, Fiona, list the house simply because it gave him a reason to keep in contact with the Merriweathers that didn't involve having to socialize with them. With Delia's birthday approaching, it made sense to watch them more closely.

"I was just over there," Nikki said, nodding in the direction of the house next door.

"Oh? And what was our powerful blue witch doing?"

"Sneezing with wet mascara."

"I'm afraid I don't even know what that means."

"It's a horrible thing that results in a string of profanity that would make an ogre blush. But it doesn't involve a cauldron or a human sacrifice. If she broke the hex, I definitely missed it."

Max rolled his eyes, but honestly, it *was* ridiculous to be spying on the clueless Merriweathers. "What's the event?" he asked.

"A shower," Nikki said. "And there's no way you'll receive an invitation. So, you're just going to have to trust that while the nice Southern ladies will be spilling plenty of tea, it's very unlikely that they'll spill any blood."

Max sighed and covered his face with his arm. He wasn't even sure what a shower was. They didn't have anything like that in Shadowlark, but he thought it might have something to do with a wedding or a baby. And Nikki was right, of course. Since the hex had called for a blood sacrifice, the spell to break it would, too. That wasn't something that could be done casually, and certainly not in mixed company.

He was just going to ignore it all with a nice, long nap—Nikki style.

Delia stared at her grimacing image in the antique mirror of her childhood vanity. She'd just redone her makeup, and now all she wanted to do was get these earrings in, but the holes had closed up overnight. Nobody else in her family seemed to have that problem (if you could call healthy and quick healing a problem), and it was a pain in the ass when she made the mistake of sleeping without earrings.

She'd just done a poke-through in the left ear. Now it was time to steel herself for round two with the other ear. She sucked in her breath and prepared to poke—

"Delia!"

Ouch! She hadn't even had to do the countdown from ten. Her mom's bellowing had caused her to stick that sucker right through.

"Up here!" she shouted.

Brisk footsteps echoed determinedly up the stairs, followed by silence as her mother hit the second-floor landing and walked across the rug to get to the final, steep ascent up the turret. There was a small pause, a sigh, and a slight groan as she hit that last step, and Delia used it to get herself in order.

Happy Smile. *Check.*

Squared Shoulders. *Check.*

Facial Expression That Screamed Don't Worry I Know What I'm Doing. *Check.*

The door opened, and there stood her mom, looking perfectly put together with her gorgeous blond hair swept up in a French knot and her makeup subtle and tastefully applied to show off her best features. She wore a camel-colored tunic with a mocha lace cardigan and carried a clutch handbag that matched her shoes, and Delia felt that same momentary spark of pride that she'd felt as a kid when her mom had shown up for school functions.

See? At least one of us is perfectly normal.

It was in sharp contrast to the feelings she'd had when Grandma Maddie or her great-aunts had come to school, eccentrically dressed in every color of the rainbow, loud and exuberant and almost always in pairs or trios when even just one of them would have been too much for the average person to take in.

Her mom removed her sunglasses and scanned the room. "Oh, dear Lord, Delia. This room. Nobody would ever guess you're an interior decorator. You live in a time capsule."

It was worse than that, really.

Her room was in the round turret at the top of the stairs, which was totally awesome, yet also small and cramped and really difficult to decorate because it had no right angles. Nevertheless, fifteen-year-old Delia had made a go of it, and that was why she was basically on the set of *I Dream of Jeannie*, right down to the round purple bed that Grandma Maddie had bought secondhand from a motel that charged by the hour. It even came with a coin-operated mattress vibrator.

"Believe me, I know. But why bother redecorating when I'm not going to be here all that much longer? As soon as Southern Charm Interior Decorating and Design takes off, I'll get my own place."

"I hope you mean that."

"Of course I do. But for now, I can't afford it. And anyway, they're just not quite ready to be left alone yet. Good grief, Aunt Andi left the stove on yesterday. And Grandma Maddie, well, you know how she is. She'll get busy on a project and forget to eat for two days. Oh! And did you know they shut off our electricity last week? Because Aurora couldn't find the light bill and didn't tell anybody—"

"You're not their savior, honey. They're grown women."

"I know, but—"

"You're not their blue witch."

Delia knew that, too. Of course she did! But *they* didn't. And yes, dang it. She felt responsible for them because she loved them to pieces and also because, well, she'd disappointed them by not coming into her power and rising as the great Blue Witch foretold to avenge et cetera, et cetera...

She sighed. In light of that, it just seemed like sticking around to make sure they didn't burn their freaking house down was the least she could do.

"Forget I said anything," her mom said. "I just stopped by to drop off Aunt Aurora's blood pressure pills."

"Oh, thanks. I'll mark the pharmacy off my to-do list then."

"And to tell you I'm proud of you," her mom added.

Delia turned to look at her mom, who was staring at her in complete and utter adoration, which seemed uncalled for. "Thanks, Mom."

Delia didn't know what there was to be proud of. She was, after all, a massive letdown. When you're raised to believe you're a powerful, magical person who will save your family from a life of humdrum normalcy, and you turn out to be just a humdrum normal person and not magical in the least, well, you'd expect people to be a bit disappointed.

But her people never were.

"I'm proud of you, too," Delia said. "Your face is all over town! And man, when you sell Halifax Manor, you'll be rolling in dough. Making bank. Money, money, money all the time."

Her mom laughed. "There's more to life than money."

"Thank God, because I don't have any."

Her mom sighed. "Sometimes I worry that you're still harboring a kernel of hope that maybe they're not wrong. That maybe witches are real and we're a magical family—"

"Believe me," Delia said with a grin. "I know they're nuts. I just don't care."

"I should never have let you grow up with all this witch nonsense. It's affected you. Don't tell me it hasn't."

Delia really and truly did not believe in magic. She was pragmatic in a way her mom had never been—the way *nobody* in her family had ever been. She'd realized at eighteen that there was no such thing as magic. And well, that was that. She was done with it. "How has it affected me?"

"Well, for one thing, you don't date."

"Neither do you."

"I was married once. That's how you came about."

Delia didn't remember her dad, but—

"Your father died under very natural circumstances."

A tree falling on you in the woods was about as natural as it got. Not exactly common though. And it was the same—natural but unusual—for all of the other folks who'd taken a chance with a Merriweather woman. Delia's grandfather had died before she was born in an unfortunate work accident involving faulty wiring, although Grandma Maddie claimed it was spontaneous combustion. Her next husband—an obviously not-very-good-botanist—had eaten bad mushrooms. The woman Aunt Thea had been sweet on was killed on a fishing trip.

By a flying fish.

As if she were sharing Delia's thoughts, Fiona cleared her throat and adjusted her scarf before giving her shoulders a little shake. "Unusual circumstances, all of them. But natural. Definitely not *super*natural. Don't listen to your grandmother. There's no love curse on the family."

"I know that. Some people are just unlucky in love. But either way, I simply don't have time for a relationship. I'm focusing on myself. Also, I don't know if you want to hear this, but I occasionally hook up on dating apps. So…"

Her mom raised an eyebrow. "Good."

Delia grinned slyly. "You could, too, you know."

"Don't worry about me," her mom said. "But you're young. You might want to consider something deeper than a hookup. I don't want you to be lonely."

"Are you lonely?"

"No. But I have you."

"And I have you," Delia said, squeezing her mom's hand. "And if I meet someone, I meet someone."

When she said the word *someone*, Max Halifax's incredibly handsome face rudely popped up in her mind. The way he'd stared at her as if she'd been a ghost. The way he'd awkwardly and formally offered his hand. And the way he'd kindly offered to fix the typo on her cards. Why did she always go for the weirdos?

"What are you smiling about?"

Oops. "Nothing."

"Have you met someone?"

"No! Of course not. When would that have happened?"

Her mom gave her a pointed look but moved on. "I want to discuss the house you staged."

Uh-oh. Delia's shoulders sagged, as all her creative juices oozed out all over the pink carpet. She probably shouldn't have played up the retro theme. "I can totally redo it if you want me to. Maybe the homeowners will agree to another open house?"

Her mom shook her head emphatically. "No, Delia. It was perfect. Absolutely perfect. At first I didn't know what to think. It was a bit wild, after all. And the first few people who came through just…" She threw her hands up in the air before laughing. "Well, they just didn't get it! But then a young couple came in, and they absolutely fell in love with it and offered on the spot."

"What?"

"The house sold! Well, pending approval, of course—"

Delia jumped up. "That's awesome!"

"And there's more," her mom said. "They were so impressed with the furnishings and touches inside the house, they want to consult you about bigger changes after the purchase."

"Really?" Delia squealed. "Because, you know, knocking out that half wall between the dining room and living room would really open the place up. And those fake beams across the ceiling, like, yuck—"

"I gave them your card."

Oh shit. "I really wish you hadn't done that."

"Why? I thought you'd be happy about it."

Delia grabbed her purse off the beanbag chair in the corner and fished out a couple of cards. "Look," she said.

Her mom looked at the card and handed it back. "I would have gone with a warm ivory over the gray."

"No. I'm talking about the typo."

"There's no typo."

Delia thrust the card back at her mom. "Look again."

Her mom took the card and read it. "Southern Charm Interior Decorating and Design." She handed it back. "Looks fine to me."

Delia couldn't believe her eyes. Her mom was right. There was no typo. "But—"

"Goodness, Delia. There's nothing wrong with your cards. What are you so worried about? Take a big stack of them to Becca's miscellaneous tea."

Delia dug the full stack of cards out of her purse and flipped through them all. Not a single one said *inferior*. Had she fever-dreamed the typo? She'd been in a fuzzy state. But Max had also seen the typo. He'd been the one to point it out.

"Did you ask Max about staging for his open house?"

"Not yet," Delia said, still confused by the cards. "I was so upset about these cards…"

Her mom looked at her like she was crazy. "That's literally what you went there for."

"I know. But the cards said *inferior* decorating and design—"

"Oh dear," her mom said, covering a smile with her hand.

"Max offered to fix it. He has a printer—"

"So, maybe he's not as big of an asshole as we thought?"

Maybe. But he'd shut a dang door in her face again. No matter how handsome he was or how helpful…

Something was off with Max Halifax.

CHAPTER SIX

Max was awakened by the low, bell-like chime of the doorbell. "Nikki!" he shouted.

"Yes?" Nikki said calmly.

Max jerked to see Nikki sitting on the dark blue wingback by the window. "How long have you been sitting there creepily staring at me like some kind of teenage vampire?"

"What else is there for me to do?"

"Besides packing? How about you get the door?"

Nikki rose, pulled at the sleeves of his white shirt, and muttered, "Yes, sir. Anything you wish, sir."

"Cut it out," Max said, standing. "I'll get it. Nobody's supposed to see you anyway. We've already had the one slipup yesterday with Delia in the antique shop."

Max rubbed the sleep out of his eyes as he headed for the foyer. Who the hell was ringing the doorbell?

With one hand on the doorknob, he glanced over his shoulder to make sure Nikki was out of sight. Then he opened the door to find the person he least expected to see. "Luc? What are you doing here?"

Luc smiled and held his arms open. "There's my wicked brother."

Max was almost at a loss for words. He hadn't seen Luc in nearly a year. But he was filled with joy. He and his younger brother were about as close as two people who rarely saw each other could be.

He held out a hand, but Luc pulled him in for a hug. It was awkward—Luc was a hugger, and nobody in the family had ever gotten used to it—but also, well, it felt wonderful.

"I see you brought luggage," Max said, squirming out of Luc's embrace. "How long can you stay?"

He motioned for Luc to come into the foyer.

"Well, the plan is for me to stay until the—"

Luc stopped speaking, and his eyes widened in surprise as he looked over Max's shoulder.

"Oh," Max said, trying to sound casual. "Nikki, this is my brother, Lucien Halifax. And Luc, this is Nikki. He's Uncle Hartwell's familiar."

For a moment Luc was totally silent. But then he looked at Max with a hint of a smile. "Since you're the oldest nephew, I'd say he's *your* familiar."

Max cleared his throat. "Yes, well. Technically."

Nikki timidly took a step toward Luc. "Can I take your coat?"

It took Luc a beat, but then he handed over his jacket. "Thanks."

Nikki draped the jacket carefully over his arm as if it weren't a piece of crap (Luc never visited the Stray Lands without hitting every thrift store within reach) and quietly headed down the hall.

Luc turned to Max immediately. "Really, Max? You're letting an imp walk around like a human?"

Max shrugged. "Uncle Hartwell was allergic to cats."

"That's a ridiculous excuse. But even so, Uncle Hartwell is dead. And you are *not* allergic to cats."

Max grinned, hoping to charm his brother. But of the two of

them, Luc was the charmer. He knew how it worked, and he wasn't falling for it.

With a sigh, Max ran his hands through his hair. "Honestly, it's been nice to have someone to talk to."

"Well, I'm here now," Luc said, putting a hand on Max's shoulder. "So, should we somehow undo whatever the holy hell was done to make *that*"—he nodded in the direction Nikki had gone—"possible?"

It wouldn't be hard, actually. But Max couldn't even imagine having Nikki and his smart mouth confined to the body of a non-talking cat, as appealing an idea as it might be at times.

Nikki, back from hanging the jacket, cleared his throat. How much had he heard?

"Can I fix you some tea?" Nikki asked, as if he hadn't heard anything, which meant he'd probably heard everything.

"Actually, Nikki," Max said, trying to use his normal voice even though nothing about this was normal. "If you wouldn't mind, some beer would be better. There's a six-pack in the small refrigerator in the utility room. Why don't you grab it and come hang out with us on the patio?"

Luc stared at Max like he'd lost his mind, and Nikki did the same, albeit for different reasons.

"Shit," Max said, because Nikki *couldn't* join them on the patio. Not as a human, anyway. "Make that the kitchen table."

Nikki nodded and went to get the beer.

"Listen," Max said when Nikki was out of earshot. "Nikki's fine. He's not like—"

Luc cut him off. "All the other imps? What makes you think that? He'd probably slit your throat if he could get away with it."

"I don't see how he's less likely to do it as a cat, honestly," Max said.

"He was bonded as a curse. He's got to *hate* witches. In fact, even imps who aren't bonded to witches hate witches."

Luc wasn't exactly wrong. While in the olden times, imps often entered willingly into symbiotic relationships with witches, relations between the two had soured since then. It was very rare to find a witch with a willing familiar.

Luc frowned. "Uncle Hartwell was a bit of a heretic, wasn't he? Maybe he was on the imps' side."

"I don't think there are *sides*, Luc. I just think our uncle was out in the Stray Lands too long." He gestured Luc into the living room, so they could walk through to the kitchen. "Let's go have a beer and talk."

Luc's head swiveled from left to right, taking everything in. "Wow. Lots of stuff."

"You have no idea."

Luc stopped in front of a wall of photos. "What is all this? Why does he have pictures of children hanging on the wall?"

"Nikki said he sponsored Little League teams," Max said. "I guess it helped him fit in."

"Little League? As in baseball?"

Uh-oh. Unlike Max, Luc hardly ever left Shadowlark. And when he did, he wanted to do everything. He was fascinated by the customs and traditions of the Stray Lands. "We're not going to have time to go to any ball games. Get that notion out of your head right now."

Luc frowned and followed Max into the large kitchen, where they settled at the table in the breakfast nook. "Nice view," Luc said, staring at the backyard through the bay windows. "Do you swim in the pool?"

"No," Max said.

"Why not?"

"I've been a little busy, and it's too chilly now anyway."

"Oh!" Luc said, spotting the hot tub. "Chilly enough for that?"

Max sighed. "I'm happy to see you, but are you going to tell me why you're here?"

Luc managed to tear his eyes away from the backyard. "I'm here at Morgaine's insistence," he said. "I'm to help you pack this place up, and, you know"—he winked and nodded toward the house next door—"spy on the neighbors."

Luc worked as a low-level investigator for the Magical Crimes Unit, which meant that he filled out forms and issued warnings based on tedious complaints filed by so-called victims of hexing. It wasn't really a job befitting a Halifax, but Luc wasn't especially gifted in the family skills and talents. It was, however, what his mother referred to as "respectable," and so Luc did it, although somewhat grudgingly.

"Morgaine thinks you're not taking this blue witch thing seriously," Luc added.

"And she sent *you* to help me be more serious?"

Luc grinned. "I know, right?"

"Nikki has been over there all morning," Max said, nodding at the Merriweathers' house. "And nobody is casting any spells. Seriously, Luc. They're clueless."

He paused for a moment as a tiny kernel of discomfort wormed its way into his consciousness. Should he mention how Delia breezed right past his deterrent spells?

Nikki arrived with clinking beer bottles. "Here we go. Icy cold."

Luc looked at Nikki as if the potted plant had just spoken. But then he shrugged and accepted a beer.

"He doesn't believe in blue witches," Nikki said, jerking his head in Max's direction.

"That's because they're fakes and charlatans," Max said.

Nikki put two bottles on the table and sat next to Max. "If you say so," he said, before draining half a bottle of beer and wiping his mouth on his sleeve.

Luc stared, wide-eyed. "You can drink beer?"

"When I'm in human form, I can do anything a human can do," Nikki said. "Although I prefer wine, honestly."

"You can do *anything*?" Luc asked.

Max didn't want to think of all the awkward places that particular topic could go. "She came into the shop yesterday," he said, changing the subject.

"Who?"

"The blue—" Dammit. He'd almost said it. "Cordelia Merriweather."

"Oh? What's she like?"

"I had cast a deterrent spell. And she didn't even break a sweat."

"Did you use your string? Maybe your knot came undone."

Commonly used spells simply required the utterance of a phrase, sometimes accompanied by a wand to direct the power. However, witches gifted at creating spells often used a talisman. Max's talisman was a string, and he was extremely good at making it do exactly what he wanted. Which was a good thing, because pointing a literal magic wand at things in the Stray Lands wasn't always feasible. "It did not come undone," he said, giving Luc a side-eye.

"So, maybe you cast a flimsy spell."

Nikki snorted and then quickly doused it by putting his beer bottle to his mouth.

"I don't do *flimsy* spells. And anyway, I also lit a deterrent candle. She waltzed right past it."

"Cordelia Merriweather isn't a stray, remember?"

"I know she's not a stray. But she's a magicless witch."

"She's a soundly hexed witch, but she's still a witch. And if rumors are correct, she's a blue one. That means she has—"

"Don't say it."

"Fairy magic."

Max tried to roll his eyes, but honestly, why *had* she been able to stroll past his deterrents?

"Don't forget to mention the other thing," Nikki said.

"Sorry," Max said. "I have no idea what you're talking about."

"What?" Luc asked. "What other thing?"

"Nothing," Max said, thinking that maybe he *should* turn Nikki back into a full-time cat.

"He became flustered and stupid around her," Nikki said. "More than usual, I mean."

Luc raised an eyebrow, and then the corner of his mouth curled up. He clinked his beer bottle against Nikki's and...

Holy hell. They're bonding.

"I felt a bit of attraction," Max said with a shrug. "And I wouldn't give it a moment's thought if Cordelia Merriweather wasn't a Cor witch."

"You don't seriously think it was heart magic?"

"I didn't say that—"

Luc laughed and leaned closer to Max. "Is she pretty?"

Delia's brown eyes didn't quite match her light blond hair. There was a very small gap between her front teeth, which was just enough of an imperfection to make her face even more interesting, especially when combined with the slightly crooked smile that bordered on a sexy snarl. She wasn't pretty in the classical sense of the word, but... "Yes. She's pretty."

"Maximus, my man," Luc said. "You're horny. And that's

because you never get laid. What do you say we get out your phone and swipe right a few times on Hot Cauldron?"

Nikki laughed, and Max shot him a dirty look. "The one and only time I did that, I came across the profile of my old Elemental Incantations professor," Max said.

"Was she stake-level smokin' hot?" Luc asked with a wink.

"Maybe in the eighteenth century," Max replied.

"Shame on you. That's ageism. But if you don't care for older women, maybe you should consider acting on that attraction you feel for Cordelia. I bet she'd go out with you."

Max choked, and Luc pounded him on the back.

"You can't be serious," he wheezed, standing up.

"Face your fears," Luc said, grinning.

This was going nowhere. Well, no, actually, it was going somewhere, and it wasn't any place Max wanted it to go. "Did you notice the grill outside?" he asked, knowing that Luc would immediately become interested.

"Ooh! Does it use gas?"

"I believe so."

"Let's grill some steaks," Luc said, eyes aglow.

Max laughed. "You've got a craving for blackened, burned steak? Or is it a hankering for raw meat? Because whenever you try to do this sort of thing without magic…"

Luc was undeterred. "Let's head to the store for some rib eyes. I mean, what could go wrong?"

"Do you know what propane gas is? Have you met fire?"

Luc just laughed. "Have you met *me*? Let's try something new. It won't kill you."

Max shook his head and hoped that was true.

CHAPTER SEVEN

"I just don't think it's an emergency, Mrs. Fleming," Delia said, squinting at the dirty windows. "Nobody who comes to the tea is even going to notice."

Delia bit her lip. She might be fibbing a little. The bay windows in Mrs. Fleming's formal dining room were so dirty you could barely see through them. And that was freaking weird because Mrs. Fleming claimed to have cleaned them less than an hour ago.

The doorbell rang, and Mrs. Fleming looked as panicked as a Baptist preacher caught in a liquor store. "Here," she said, thrusting a bottle of Windex in Delia's face. "Make them sparkle! That's probably just Amy at the door, but goodness, the guests will be here in under half an hour!"

Delia sighed. She wasn't Mrs. Fleming's housekeeper anymore, but dang, she'd decorated this place quite nicely, and the ugly windows were ruining the aesthetic. She accepted the Windex, grabbed some paper towels, and gave the windows a squirt. As she squeakily wiped them down, someone tapped on her shoulder.

"What the hell are you doing?"

Amy had a bag hanging off each shoulder and a gigantic pink box in her arms.

Delia made one last swipe at a streak and then nodded at a box. "What do you have in there?"

"Rosemary shortbread cookies, and you can't have any until you tell me why you're holding a bottle of Windex."

"She asked me to wash the windows real quick—"

"You should have said no!"

"I know, but, well, they were so dang dirty. I guess she's had a hard time finding someone to replace me."

"Not your problem. Also, you missed a spot," Amy said, squinting. "Several, actually."

"What?" Delia spun around to look at the windows, and Amy was right.

Mrs. Fleming put her hands on her hips. "Delia, you used to be so thorough. What in the world has gotten into you?"

"Who's cleaning your house now?" Delia asked, running a finger over the cherrywood sideboard. There was a light layer of dust all over everything.

"I haven't hired a new girl yet."

Amy, who was standing behind Mrs. Fleming, silently mouthed the word *girl* at Delia and grinned.

"I just dusted this morning," Mrs. Fleming said eyeing the trail Delia's finger had left on the sideboard. "And polished the furniture."

It sure didn't look like it. And what was really strange was that Mrs. Fleming and her quiet, henpecked husband, Norman, lived alone, and they just didn't make much of a mess. Their house had been one of the easiest breeziest houses to clean.

Delia wiped off the sideboard so Amy could set the box of cookies down. She hadn't noticed the dust when she'd set out the candlesticks, nor when she'd erected the beautiful magnolia-blossom arch made out of willow twigs.

"That is so pretty," Amy said, looking at the arch. In addition to the magnolia blossoms, it was strung with fairy lights and adorned with small silver pendant frames containing photos of the bride. She reached up to straighten one and yikes! A long spiderweb descended and dangled over the cookies.

Delia snatched a napkin and grabbed it, only to discover that there were several more. This was embarrassing. How had she not noticed them while she was attaching the photos?

"Mrs. Fleming," Amy called, setting down a stack of luncheon plates. "Are you sure you want me to use these plates? They're awfully stained, and some have cracks."

Mrs. Fleming stormed over and looked at the plates. Then she caught Delia plucking out spiderwebs, and her face screwed up and a flush worked its way up her neck like a gathering thunderstorm. Delia recognized a pressure cooker when it was about to blow, and she backed up.

Without another word, Mrs. Fleming stormed into the living room and began opening and slamming every drawer, as if searching for something. Whatever she was looking for, Delia sincerely hoped it wasn't loaded.

"Where is it?" Mrs. Fleming muttered, switching her attention to the couch cushions, which she tossed on the ground.

Delia grabbed Amy's arm and whispered, "Do you think it's hormonal?"

That was a private joke. Amy's mother said everything was hormonal, including her two-month affair with the propane delivery man.

But Amy wasn't laughing. "I doubt it."

Mrs. Fleming, who was busy feeling up the inside of a lampshade, shook her head. "Would you two please stop staring at me? Just get the decorations up and the food set out," she said curtly. "I'll handle this."

"Yes, ma'am," Amy said, wiping at a stained plate with a tea towel as if nothing too strange was going on.

Mrs. Fleming picked up a vase and peered inside before setting it down with a worried expression. Then she sighed in exasperation and rushed off in the direction of her bedroom.

"Want to help me assemble the charcuterie cones?" Amy asked, holding out a stack of crisp brown paper. "You can roll 'em, and I'll stuff 'em."

"I think I need to check on Mrs. Fleming first," Delia said. "What in the world has got her so upset?"

"Who knows?" Amy said. "But you don't need to get involved."

Delia didn't *want* to get involved, but she couldn't help herself. She had what Amy referred to as an unhealthy amount of concern and empathy. "I'll be right back."

Delia went down the hallway (she couldn't help but straighten three portraits) to Mrs. Fleming's bedroom door at the end. It was closed, but she could hear Mrs. Fleming. *And please get here soon!*

Delia knocked softly and spoke through the door. "Mrs. Fleming? Can I help in any way? I mean, I can just grab a feather duster—"

The door opened suddenly. "Help is on the way," Mrs. Fleming said, sniffing.

"You called a cleaning service? It's a little late for that—"

Mrs. Fleming rolled her eyes. "Delia, you're just exasperating," she said, scooting her out of the way. "Don't worry yourself. Just help Amy, and then the two of you can relax and enjoy yourselves like invited guests."

"We are invited guests…"

Delia followed Mrs. Fleming to the dining room, where the windows appeared dirtier than ever. "I just don't understand it," she said. "How is this happening?"

"There's a lot of dust in the air," Mrs. Fleming said. "Makes it hard to see clearly when you're cleaning."

Okay. It *was* autumn in South Texas, and there was a lot of pollen and whatnot floating around. She took a deep breath. There was always a logical explanation for everything.

The doorbell rang. Somebody had arrived ten minutes early, and nobody ever arrived early to a miscellaneous tea. Right on the dot was acceptable, but not a second sooner.

"Oh, thank God," Mrs. Fleming said. "That must be Mr. Halifax."

"Mr. Halifax?" Delia said. "As in *Max* Halifax?"

"Who else?" Mrs. Fleming said, heading for the door.

Max couldn't believe he was standing on Mrs. Fleming's front porch on a Sunday afternoon instead of setting steaks on fire with Luc.

"How often does this happen?" Luc asked. "Having to get involved in hedge witch affairs?"

"Way too often. It seems Uncle Hartwell served as some kind of keeper of the peace. He got involved in all their squabbles."

"Why?"

Max just shrugged. "Glutton for punishment?"

Luc laughed. "Well, you won't have to be involved in hedge affairs for much longer. Which means you're running out of time to make your move."

"My move?"

Luc waggled his eyebrows. "Cordelia Merriweather."

"I don't make moves—"

The door suddenly opened, and there stood Constance Fleming, looking as distraught as a witch could look.

"Oh, Mr. Halifax! Thank you for coming so quickly." She stepped out onto the porch, closing the door behind her. "Time is of the essence."

"We were literally driving by," Max said. "On our way to the Shop-n-Save to pick up some steaks."

Instead of apologizing for ruining a perfectly lovely afternoon, Mrs. Fleming thrust something in his face. "Look at this!"

It was a piece of fabric, frayed at the edges and—he wrinkled his nose in disgust—quite dirty. "What's growing on it?"

"I don't know," Mrs. Fleming wailed. "But it's ruining my tea!"

"Your tea?" Max said. "Did it fall into a teacup?"

Mrs. Fleming emphatically shook her head, and Max sighed in exasperation, knowing it wouldn't be that simple. Nothing in Willow Root ever was. "Iced? Hot? Herbal? What kind of tea, Mrs. Fleming? And how is it ruined?"

"A miscellaneous tea," she said.

"I don't know what that is," Max said. Then he lowered his voice. "Is it something magical?"

"It's a bridal shower," she clarified.

It was always surprising to see witches in the Stray Lands doing very unwitchy things like throwing bridal showers. "And this, erm, shower is being ruined somehow? By a dirty hankie?"

Mrs. Fleming suddenly narrowed her eyes and glared at him. The air became thick and electric. "Because of that witch," she spat.

"Which witch?" Luc asked with a little smirk that indicated he was enjoying himself entirely too much, confusion or no.

Mrs. Fleming had been so distraught that she hadn't even noticed Luc. But now she did, and she patted her hair and tried to collect herself. "Oh, forgive me," she said. "I'm Constance Fleming, lady of the house. And you are?"

"Luc Halifax, brother of the perpetually flustered."

"Pardon my poor manners," Max said, giving Luc a snide side-eye. "This is my brother, Investigator Lucien Halifax."

Luc held out his hand, and Mrs. Fleming grasped it. "Inspector? With the MCU?"

"Yes," he said. "Specifically, I'm with the Hexing and Cursing Division of the Magical Crimes Unit."

Mrs. Fleming looked as if she might faint. "Oh, dear Goddess, yes!" she exclaimed. "Violet will be here any minute. You can arrest her."

"Violet who?" Max asked. "And arrest her for what?"

Mrs. Fleming rolled her eyes. "Goodness, have you not been paying attention? Violet Wilson." She held up the piece of cloth, which looked even grosser than it had before. "And arrest her for this! She's hexed my house right before the shower."

"Why?"

"Because she's jealous. Why else?"

Currently, Max could think of two or three other reasons someone might want to hex Mrs. Fleming, but he kept them to himself.

"We used to take turns, you see, hosting miscellaneous teas. We both have lovely homes, but mine is quite obviously nicer, and I'm the better hostess. You can ask anyone and they'll tell you. Is it any wonder that most of the brides prefer to have their teas here?" She smiled and preened a bit by lightly smoothing some stray hair in place.

"What has that got to do with Violet?"

"She's furious."

When Mrs. Fleming said the word *furious*, she smiled a very wicked smile, and the hairs on the back of Max's neck stood up and took notice.

"I see," Luc said, indicating his had done the same. "But I'm not a cop. I can't arrest anybody."

"That's true," Max said. "He just inspects. Then he writes a report."

"Well, then, write a report!" Mrs. Fleming said. "I want Violet reported!"

"This isn't my jurisdiction," Luc said. "But if you believe you've been hexed—"

"Oh, I've been hexed, all right," Mrs. Fleming said. "My house is disintegrating as we speak. It's utterly filthy and getting filthier by the minute. The harder I clean, the worse it gets. And it's all because of this!"

Max and Luc both stepped back as she brandished the nasty cloth again.

"Violet was here last Tuesday when I hosted bunco night."

"I'm sure I can undo the hex," Max said.

With two fingers, he took the cloth from Mrs. Fleming. It vibrated with magic. He closed his eyes and summoned his power, which was always curled up in his belly, waiting for an invitation. He felt it rise, roiling up from beneath his diaphragm to expand in his chest. He exhaled slowly but deeply, feeling the magic exit his body. Still attached by a psychic string, Max could feel it searching, and his body tingled as the small trail of energy wriggled its way in and out of the cloth, skirting back and forth between the fibers, before finally seizing on the moment of ignition where the ordinary had shifted to extraordinary and the normal to paranormal...

There it is. The spark!

He shivered slightly, and with a barely perceivable quirk of his mouth—something irritatingly similar to the twitching of Samantha's nose in the sixties sitcom *Bewitched*—he doused the spark, thereby extinguishing the small yet exhilarating force behind the hex that was currently causing Mrs. Fleming so much distress.

He breathed in deeply, pulling the magic back into his body. And despite having full lungs, it literally took his breath away. Only after the tingling subsided and he could breathe normally again did he dare to open his eyes. (If he opened them too soon, they might literally be crossed with bliss, and that would be humiliating.)

"It's done," he said, shakily handing the now crisp and clean cloth back to Mrs. Fleming as if it were no big deal. As if *magic* were no big deal.

It absolutely was, though. A big deal. Every single time. And it was hard not to show his utter exhilaration over even this tiniest and most insignificant exercise of breaking a simple hex. Being a witch was everything to Max, and he damn well knew how special it was.

"Done indeed!" Mrs. Fleming exclaimed. "Thank you so much, Mr. Halifax."

"You're very welcome."

"Now," she said with a clap of her hands. "I absolutely insist that you and your brother come in for a cup of punch while you wait to interrogate Violet. She'll be here any minute to gloat over her handiwork."

"I don't think that's necessary," Max said.

"I'll type up a warning and drop it in the mail," Luc added. "That should handle it."

"Have a nice miscellaneous event," Max said as they turned to go.

The door behind Mrs. Fleming suddenly opened, and Max stopped in his tracks at the sight of Cordelia Merriweather. His heart fluttered a bit, which was annoying and curious.

"Hi, Max," Delia said, smiling.

"You know what?" Luc said suddenly, glancing from Max to Delia and back to Max with a devilish grin. "We'd love some punch."

CHAPTER EIGHT

Miscellaneous teas were predictable feminine engagements to be tolerated placidly, kind of like a pap smear. And they were supposed to take about as long. Nobody lingered at a tea. You congratulated the bride on her upcoming nuptials, you had some punch, you looked at the gifts, and you left. However, having two men at the shower was causing quite a stir. And since Southern ladies were compelled to make people feel comfortable at all costs, and Max, with his wide eyes and empty punch cup and obvious distress, was presenting a challenge they couldn't refuse.

It was getting quite crowded in Constance's house.

"Who is that young man with Max?" Grandma Maddie asked.

"The grapevine says it's his younger brother," Delia said. "Lucien Halifax."

Literally every conversation happening at the shower was about the Halifax men, and Delia felt bad for poor Becca, who stood at the mint and punch table accepting hurried congratulations from women who were clearly more intent on visiting with the two unexpected guests.

"Well, he seems more at ease than Max," Delia's mom said. "Maybe Max is the black sheep of the Halifax family. And good God, look at your aunts. They're lined up in front of those boys like wise men bearing gifts for baby Jesus."

Delia grinned watching Max turn down a cup of coffee, a saucer of pastel-colored mints, and, inexplicably, a fluffy pillow, offered by Aunt Aurora.

"Delia, you should put him out of his misery," her mom said.

Delia shook her head. "I'd have to get in line."

"Well, do it then. And convince him to let you stage the house. It's horribly dark and gloomy."

"It's grand and majestic. Just needs someone to lighten it up a little."

"Maybe Max needs the same thing," Grandma Maddie said. "Why don't you see if you can tackle both jobs?"

Delia just snorted. "Lightening up Max Halifax is a bigger job than I'm capable of."

"Well, you've done a wonderful job with this shower," her mom said. "It looks very nice in here."

"Aw, thanks," Delia said, noting with pride that it *did* look very nice. She squinted with a critical eye, hoping not to find a stray cobweb. Whew! There were none. The arch was as clean as a whistle. For that matter, everything was. The layers of dust were gone. She glanced at the bay windows in the dining room. Even those were sparkly and clear.

"Go talk to Max," her mom said. "Have confidence. You deserve to stage Halifax Manor."

Delia bit her lip and watched as Max juggled a handful of rosemary shortbread cookies and a newly filled cup of punch. Aunt Andi was busy stuffing a cloth napkin into the collar of his shirt, and he looked like he might die any minute. In fact, he appeared so terribly uncomfortable that maybe he'd appreciate a distraction.

She squared her shoulders. Halifax Manor could literally launch her career. She'd display her business cards in the fancy foyer—

The business cards! She needed to tell Max not to bother reprinting them. Oddly, it had only been the one that had a typo.

"Hold my punch," she said, handing her mom the cup. "I'm going in."

"Incoming," Luc said, with a casual nod of his head.

Max didn't need to look. He'd been painfully aware of Delia's presence since the moment he'd stepped through the door. And she'd been keeping an eye on him, which Luc seemed to find amusing.

The witches in attendance were well aware that something was up and that Max and Luc hadn't just stopped by for punch. The energy made his hair stand on end. There had been gossip, obviously, and they were eagerly awaiting the arrival of Violet. The strays were clueless, but did Delia sense that anything was off?

She wore a little pink dress with white polka dots and a pair of heels, and Max tried very hard to assume what he hoped was a normal facial expression as she headed his way, but the sight of her made him want to smile. And smiling for no reason at all was not part of his normal expression.

"Max," she said, reaching out with her hand. "It's just lovely to see you again. I hope you're having a nice time at the tea."

He swallowed and took her hand. It was warm, and for some reason, his cheeks heated up in response. He tugged at his collar. And when he went to speak, not a single thing came out. He quickly sipped some punch. "I'm having a great time," he said, recovering. "Have you met my brother, Luc? Your aunts were just insisting we look like twins."

"We don't look anything alike," Luc said, taking Delia's hand next.

"Oh, I definitely see a strong resemblance," Delia said, glancing from one to the other. "Very strong indeed."

"And now you've offended both of us," Luc said with a huge smile.

Delia's aunt Aurora said, "Don't be silly. You're both handsome devils and I daresay you know it."

"Delia was part of the pie brigade," Andi said. "But you might not remember because you only, you know, opened the door wide enough for us to slip the pie through."

"My apologies," he said. "I'm afraid you ladies caught me at an inopportune moment."

"I thought maybe you were ill," Aurora said.

"Or possibly that you'd been crying," Andi added. "Over your uncle."

Nope. Just chasing an illustrated hummingbird, freshly escaped from a bespelled copy of the Encyclopedia of North American Birds, *around Hartwell's library.*

"The pie was delicious," he said. "And Delia and I are acquainted. She came into the antique store yesterday."

"So," Delia said, locking her hands behind her back and looking them up and down. "Esther Martinez says you boys are from Chicago. Marian Knolls says it's Los Angeles or maybe even someplace more exotic like Minneapolis."

"People are talking about us?" Luc asked, clearly excited.

"Literally everyone," Delia whispered.

Luc's face broke out in a huge smile, because the idiot loved to be the center of attention. "We're from the Bay Area," he said.

Delia's eyes lit up. "Oh! I love the beach. Are we talking Corpus Christi or Rockport? Or maybe Galveston?"

"California," Luc said. "Specifically, near San Francisco."

Shadowlark was hidden in the mountains of Northern California. In fact, it was hidden so well that you couldn't find it on a map. And if you were a stray, you couldn't find it even if you were standing right in front of it, because it was magically cloaked.

"Oh, of course," Delia said, a slight blush rising up her cheeks. "I guess we Texans sometimes forget there's a rest of the world."

She put *the rest of the world* in finger quotes, as if maybe it didn't really exist.

"Well, Texas is big," Max said. The urge to relieve her embarrassment was overwhelming. "And wasn't it an independent nation at one point?"

"Oh, dear Lord," Delia said. "Don't get anybody here started on that. You'll have Gladys Pollan over there shouting at everyone to remember the Alamo. And yes, Texas *is* big. In fact, I've never been outside of it."

"That's not true, dear," Aurora said. "You've been to Louisiana. We took you to that witch festival in the bayou when you were about four."

"A witch festival?" Luc asked. "Did they have a permit?"

Max cleared his throat, and Luc's eyes momentarily widened in panic. He wasn't used to being around strays.

Luckily, nobody seemed to notice. Probably because Delia was laughing a little too loudly.

"She's kidding," Delia said, nodding at Aurora and rolling her eyes slightly. Then she grabbed Max's arm. "Let's go look at the gifts, shall we? I bet you're both dying to see which stoneware pattern Becca picked out."

"Don't be silly," Andi said. "Nobody cares about stoneware patterns. I'm sure the boys are more interested in the witch festival."

Luc clearly wanted to hear more but was afraid to speak. And honestly, Max wanted to hear more, too. "It sounds terribly interesting," he said. "Who organizes it?"

"Witches, of course," Andi said, looking at him like he was an idiot. "Specifically, witches who own bookstores. Like us—"

"Oh God," Delia said. "Are you sure you don't want to go look at—"

"It was muggy at the festival," Andi continued, completely ignoring Delia. "And the mosquitoes!"

Thea nodded in agreement. "Bigger than Texas mosquitoes even! But Delia made her first potion there."

The hair stood up on the back of Max's neck. Delia had been making potions as a child? "What kind of a potion?" he asked, aiming for casual.

Delia laughed again. "My aunt is good at pulling legs, and look at you two, encouraging her."

"She's so modest," Thea said. "It was just practice, but the head witch-lady said Delia showed promise."

"I'm sure it was just kids mixing up Kool-Aid for fun," Delia said. "It was a typical small-town festival with the face-painting and the sausage-on-a-stick-eating and the risking-of-your-life-on-a-Tilt-A-Whirling. That's all. No big deal."

"It wasn't Kool-Aid," Andi said. "And boy, you really didn't want to remove the newt's eye." She lowered her voice to a whisper and winked at Max. "I had to do it for her."

Delia clapped her hands together. "Who watched the Spurs game last night?"

"Did strays attend the festival?" Luc asked.

Max shoved his right hand in the pocket of his slacks and clicked the edge of his thumbnail against the nail of his index finger while silently mouthing *zingus butticus*.

"Ouch!" Luc said, turning to glare at him.

Max had just administered a not-so-gentle electrical current to his brother's ass—a little trick they'd cooked up as kids. It had been a while since he'd used it, but apparently it still worked just fine.

Luc's face quickly went from outrage to *Oh no, I did it again, didn't I?*

"Are you okay, honey?" Aurora asked.

"Muscle spasm," Luc mumbled, rubbing his right butt cheek.

"Did you ask if strays attended the festival?" Andi said. "Like cats?"

"Yes," Luc said emphatically. "Like cats."

"Yay! Let's talk about cats," Delia said, her face flooded with relief. "Will y'all be taking Nikki with you when you leave? Oh, and I'm talking about the cat. Not your cousin."

The electricity in the air shifted as Constance Fleming entered their little circle and interrupted the conversation. "Excuse me," she said to Delia, stepping in front of her.

Delia crossed her arms over her chest and raised a single eyebrow, but her lips were curled up in amusement, as if she was familiar with Constance's antics.

"Violet has arrived," Constance hissed into Max's ear. "I'm holding her in the laundry room."

What the holy hell did Constance expect them to do? Get out the thumbscrews and brank? "Mrs. Fleming, as we stated earlier—"

"I'll handle it," Luc said with a wink.

"Handle what?" Delia asked.

"Er…a plumbing issue. In the laundry room. Isn't that right, Mrs. Fleming?"

"Yes," Mrs. Fleming said, nodding her head vigorously.

Delia frowned slightly in confusion, but then she gave her head a little shake and carried on, as if things not making sense was a regular occurrence for her. "Max, there's something I need to talk to you about. A couple of somethings, actually."

His curiosity was piqued. "Oh?"

"These mints and cookies aren't going to do much in the way of filling your stomachs," she said, nodding at him and Luc—who was resisting Mrs. Fleming's yanking on his sleeve. "What do you say we head to a local café after Luc is done with the"—she glanced quizzically in the direction of the laundry room—"plumbing."

"That's nice of you, but we were planning to pick up a couple of steaks."

"No, no," Luc said, leaning toward them as Mrs. Fleming continued yanking him away. "Let's go to the café."

Max raised an eyebrow. Luc had been pretty damn excited about the grill. "You sure?"

"We can grill later. I've never been to a small-town café. What do you say we soak up some atmosphere?"

Max had had more than enough atmosphere for one day, but he was hungry. And burned meat didn't really do much for him. "Sure," he said. "Let's have some atmosphere."

"Oh, where I'm taking you, there's plenty of that," Delia said, grinning. "Just you wait."

CHAPTER NINE

Delia parked in front of the weathered building folks simply referred to as "the old hall" even though it hadn't been the Holy Name Parish Hall for over two decades (the *new* one was across the street).

Its white paint was peeling. The rickety front steps had a warning sign recommending that folks use the handrail. The porch had a definite tilt, but that didn't stop people from gathering on it, and today there were four old-timers standing in a circle having a post-lunch conversation. Delia knew it was a post-lunch conversation because all four were chewing on wooden toothpicks. Their heads were lowered, faces shaded by their cowboy hats and gimme caps, and they stared at their boots, nodding and grunting. Delia would bet ten bucks that the topic was whether the forecast called for rain.

In her rearview mirror, she watched as Max and Luc parked in the row behind her. Through the windshield of Max's car, she could see them staring up at the restaurant's faded sign above the porch.

Mourning Glory Café
All of the Comfort, None of the Death

Delia checked her face in the rearview mirror—lipstick still on—and grabbed her purse. She climbed out of her Kia just as

Max and Luc opened their doors. "I hope y'all are hungry," she called out.

Max looked around and self-consciously straightened his collar before running a hand through those rebellious locks.

"We're actually starving," Luc said as they walked up. "Thanks for inviting us to lunch."

"What is this place?" Max asked. "It doesn't look like a restaurant."

"Mourning Glory Café is a unique establishment," Delia said. "It specializes in one thing and one thing only."

"And what is that?" Max asked.

"Southern-style funeral food," Delia said.

"I'm sorry. Did you say *funeral* food?" Max asked.

"I did," Delia said. "Have y'all ever been to a small-town funeral?"

"I can't say that we have," Luc said.

"Well, everybody brings food to the church fellowship hall after the burial. And it's the best food you've ever had, but you can't act too happy about it," Delia said. "But here you can just enjoy the heck out of yourself without having to worry about looking like you're enjoying yourself. Now, follow me, and be sure and hold on to the handrail. The steps are rickety. Martha Bedford took a little tumble on them last week."

One of the men on the porch, Carl Snoga, quickly grabbed the door. "Thanks, Carl," Delia said, hoping they could breeze on past without having to chat, which was extremely unlikely.

"How's your granny?" Carl asked.

"She's doing great," Delia said, smiling but not stopping, because momentum was important in getting past Carl.

"That's good to hear," Carl said. "Be sure and tell her I said howdy and that Melba needs some more of that tincture for her aching joints."

Dang it. Delia couldn't just keep going now that Carl's wife and aching joints had been brought up. "I'll be sure and let her know. And I'm sorry if Melba isn't feeling well."

"She's been having a time of it," Carl said, shaking his head.

Melba had lots of health problems, and aching joints were the least of them. Carl had been her sole caregiver for many years, but recently she'd been attending an activity center, which gave Carl a break for a few hours every day. It was no wonder he wanted to spend them catching up with folks.

"Change in the weather, you know," Carl said. "It does a number on her. But I hear we'll be back in the upper seventies next week. Maybe even eighty."

Oh, dear God. He was starting to talk about the weather, and he could do that *forever*. Two people squeezed in around them as Carl continued holding the door, and suddenly he seemed to notice Luc and Max.

"Have you met the Halifax boys?" Delia asked, grateful to change the topic. "They're Hartwell's nephews."

Carl's eyes lit up, and he propped the door open with his booted foot—another person slipped in with a polite nod—and shook Luc's and Max's hands. "Pleasure to meet you," he said. "Sorry for your loss. Hartwell was a fine man."

Luc and Max said a simultaneously polite *thank you* and gazed longingly inside the restaurant.

"I guess y'all couldn't make the funeral," Carl continued.

"They're from California," Delia said, hoping the comment didn't make the brothers feel bad, because no, they hadn't made it to the funeral.

Carl nodded in understanding. "It's hard with families being all spread out the way they are now—"

Delia swatted at an imaginary fly. "Goodness, we'd better get on in, or Esther's place is going to fill up with flies."

"Oh heck," Carl said. "Sure enough. Y'all go on in. Sorry for holding you up."

"Don't be silly," Delia said. "It was good chatting with you."

"Yes, it was nice to meet you," Max said as they slid past Carl.

"Whew!" Delia said once they were inside. "He's a dear. And he's lonely. But you have to have an escape plan when he starts talking."

Miss Esther approached with a smile and open arms. "Delia, I haven't seen you in so long. Come here and give me some sugar."

Delia gave the older woman a warm hug. "I've been busy," she said. "And boy have I missed your cheesy grits."

"Technically, they're Helen Birch's grits," Miss Esther said. "It's a Methodist recipe."

"Whatever religion they are, they're delicious."

"And who are these young men?" Miss Esther asked, releasing Delia and homing in on Max and Luc.

"These are Hartwell's nephews."

Max held out a hand. "I'm Max, and this is my brother, Luc."

"Oh, bless your hearts," Miss Esther said, ignoring Max's hand and going in for a hug.

"Thank you," Max said, leaning in awkwardly and looking very much as if he were being assaulted. "And bless your heart as well," he added.

Miss Esther repeated the same thing with Luc, offering up a few more platitudes—she blessed their bones and their souls and even their britches—before scooting them off. "I'll have some sweet tea at your table in a minute."

Ice cubes clinked softly as two glasses of sweet tea appeared out of nowhere, and Miss Esther rubbed a small circle on Max's back with her large, warm hand. He wasn't used to being touched this way by an actual stranger, and it flustered him.

"I'll bring you some deviled eggs, hon. They'll make you feel better."

He wasn't feeling bad in the first place, but for some reason he just nodded and said, "Thank you, Miss Esther."

"What are deviled eggs?" Luc asked.

Delia raised her eyebrows. "Don't they have deviled eggs in California?"

Luc glanced at Max. "I think they're more of a Southern-style food," Max said, although of course you could get deviled eggs in California. But although Luc technically lived in California, he was hardly what you'd call a California guy. His life experiences were limited by the traditions and customs of Shadowlark.

"Well," Delia continued. "Deviled eggs are wickedly tasty. You're going to love them."

"So, this place serves ritual foods?" Luc asked.

"I guess you could call it that," Delia said, happily putting her napkin in her lap.

Luc leaned forward, intensely interested, as usual. "And why do you eat ritual foods without the rituals?"

"Because the ritual foods, as you call them, are freaking delicious," Delia said.

Luc leaned back, looking relieved. The refreshments offered at the last funeral they'd attended in Shadowlark had consisted of pickled boar hearts and goat livers, seasoned by salt collected from the tears of the mourners. Luckily, they hadn't gone for the spice de magnifique, which was just a pinch of the actual ashes of the deceased. And, of course, they'd been expected to wash it down with a disgusting fermented beverage made from Welsh onions and bitter gourds.

Funerals in Shadowlark were all about the suffering, and there was absolutely nothing comforting about them.

"Are you okay, Max?" Delia asked. "You look like you sucked on a lemon."

Before he could answer, a plate was set before him. "I'm just fine," he said, nodding at Miss Esther.

"Ooh," Delia said. "Here we go. Deviled eggs, pickled okra, and cheese straws. Dig in, boys."

"Pace yourselves," Miss Esther said. "I'll bring out more plates in a minute."

"Could I see a menu?" Max asked.

"Oh, honey, there's no menu," Miss Esther said. "I'll just fix you a plate."

"But how do you know what I want?" Max asked.

"I'm guided by the Spirit," Miss Esther said. "Don't you worry."

As she walked off, Luc stuck an entire deviled egg in his mouth before closing his eyes and groaning in bliss. Before Max could gently nudge him under the table over his disgusting table manners, Luc added another, resulting in *both* cheeks bulging obscenely.

Max risked a tiny glance at Delia and then had to hide a smile behind his napkin. Because it appeared she could also fit quite a bit in her mouth.

Max figured he might as well follow suit.

"Good, huh?" Delia asked.

All he could do was grunt.

"So, Max," Delia said, daintily dabbing at her mouth with a

napkin. "I hope you haven't gone to the trouble to print up more business cards."

Ah. She must have noticed they'd been fixed. He swallowed and took a sip of tea, pausing briefly because the tea was refreshing and delicious. "I'm afraid I haven't gotten around to it yet," he lied.

"Well, good. It was the weirdest thing. Only that one seemed to be affected. The rest were fine."

Luc glanced quizzically at them. "Max is printing business cards?"

Max shook his head slightly, "No. Apparently not."

Delia quickly grabbed her bag and began digging through it, pulling out lip balm, gum, tissues, and a phone charger, which she piled on the table. "Aha!" she said, finally extracting a small gold box. "I've got to stop carrying such a big bag. Pardon my mess."

She held the gigantic bag open and slid the small pile back into it before opening her little box and removing a business card, which she handed to Luc with a huge smile. "I'm an interior decorator."

Luc looked at the card and tried to hand it back.

"No, you can keep it. Who knows? Maybe you'll meet someone who needs a decorator."

With a slight grin, Luc slipped it into his pocket. "Thank you."

"So," Delia said, looking at Max. "That was one of the things I wanted to talk to you about. Now, for the other."

Max had no idea what she might want to talk to him about, but for some reason, he was excited to hear it.

"My mom tells me you're having an open house."

There had been paperwork and chitchat, but he wasn't entirely sure what he'd agreed to and what he hadn't. "An open what now?"

"An open house. It's where prospective buyers and agents stop by to tour the home and talk to the listing agent. It's a very effective way to sell a house. My mom says she talked to you about it."

Oh, crap. Fiona had said a *lot* of things, and Max hadn't really been interested in much of it. He wasn't worried about the house selling. It was a grand old place, and anyway, there were spells that would make it appealing to buyers. Easy spells.

"I honestly don't remember talking about it." He didn't like the idea of people—strays or witches—traipsing through the place. There were...things. And some of them were dangerous.

Delia's face fell. "Oh."

"I mean, I'm not saying I won't have one..."

Why? Why am I not saying I won't have one?

"Oh?" Delia's face brightened.

That's why.

"Well, if you decide to go with it, I wanted to talk to you a bit about staging. It really helps."

"I don't know what that is."

"It's where a decorator, and not an *inferior* one"—she winked, and his heart fluttered stupidly in response—"comes in and..."

"Decorates?"

"Yes," Delia said. "But in theory, the purpose is to bring out the best in a space in a way that still allows prospective buyers to imagine their own special flair and style."

"That sounds reasonable," Max said. "I'll take it into consideration."

"I'm so familiar with the house that it won't be a problem at all for me to go ahead and whip up a little design and proposal. What do you say?"

Cordelia Merriweather was a little pushy, and Max was

completely prepared to let her know he was not to be rushed into a decision...Until he looked into her eyes, which were brimming with excitement but, also, tinged with desperation.

"How much does it cost?" he asked.

"That depends on just how much you'll want me to do. I don't mind stopping by tomorrow, if you'll be home."

Yes, Cordelia Merriweather was definitely a little pushy. "I'll be home. Maybe around ten or so?"

They were interrupted by Miss Esther returning, holding a huge tray of plates. And behind her stood another woman with a huge tray of smaller plates and bowls. Delia sat back in her seat while a plate was set before her.

"Here you go, angel," Miss Esther said. "Buttered biscuits, greens, and pork chops. I also put a bit of chicken on there; it's not fried. It's the Lutheran kind with the cracker-crumb crust like Dee Campbell makes. And a few sides."

A *few* sides? Max watched in amazement as Miss Esther set down dish after dish after dish.

"Cheesy grits, green bean casserole, and macaroni salad!" Delia said, rubbing her hands together.

Next, a plate was set in front of Luc. "You've got brisket, slow-cooked beans, Ida May Bateman's creamy coleslaw, and Methodist funeral potatoes." The other woman set down a small bowl. "Oh, and green beans with bacon, of course."

"Of course," Luc said, grinning from ear to ear. A bit of drool had formed on his lower lip.

Finally, it was Max's turn. "And for you," Miss Esther said. "We've got King Ranch chicken casserole, the Catholic Daughters Mexican rice, some of Frank Medina's homemade sausage, stuffed corn bread—"

"You can stuff corn bread?" Max asked, licking his lips.

"Oh, honey. You can stuff anything. Watch out for the jalape-ños if you're not used to them. And save room, because the church crowd left just a bit of pot roast, and Betsy is back there plating it for y'all right now."

"There's no way we can eat all this," Max said.

"Speak for yourself," Delia replied.

Miss Esther rubbed his shoulder. "Feed your grief, honey. That's what I always say."

Max wasn't grieving. But he definitely felt like he was feeding *something*, because nothing in his life had prepared him for how badly he wanted to bury his face in this food.

"Oh, dear me," Miss Esther said. "I forgot the macaroni and cheese. And y'all look like you could do with some cucumber salad."

As she walked off, Luc whispered to Delia, "How does she know what we want?"

"Magic," Delia said, staring at a crusty, buttery chicken thigh.

Delia didn't realize that she'd probably just spoken the truth. Max definitely sensed magic around Miss Esther. Specifically, Corpus magic, which meant her magic would be of the body. Corpus witches were often healers, but also quite a few seemed to be cooks and chefs.

"God, I freaking love this chicken. I haven't had it since August Nixon died back in March." She sank her teeth into the chicken and appeared to have a somewhat sexual experience.

That little groan...

Max wiped his brow with a napkin, picked up a fork, and for the next few minutes, he ate. And when he thought he couldn't handle another bite, Miss Esther brought his second plate, and then he ate some more.

"So, tell me," Delia said, looking from Max to Luc. "What do you boys do in California?"

Luc pulled the napkin out of his collar where Miss Esther had tucked it. "I'm an investigator for the, um…well…" He looked to Max for help.

"Code violations," Max said. "He writes tickets for code violations."

That was basically true.

"Oh," Delia said. "I hope this isn't rude, but"—she leaned in closer—"that sounds boring."

"It is." Luc sighed.

Max knew that Luc would rather be doing what Max did. But Luc wasn't especially skilled in nullifying or undoing hexes, and anyway, as a Logos witch, he didn't get much choice when it came to what he *wanted* to do.

"And you?" Delia asked, looking directly at Max. "What do you do?"

"I deal in antiquities."

Well, he dealt *with* them, but that was a harder explanation and not one Delia would understand.

"Oh, like Hartwell! It must run in the family. You know, I'd love to go through the items in the shop. I'm sure there's so much there…"

Miss Esther's arm appeared in front of Delia, and she seemed to lose her train of thought.

"Texas chocolate sheet cake," Miss Esther said. "The pecans in the frosting are from the tree in my backyard."

Max took a small bite as soon as she set a piece in front of him, and he groaned embarrassingly when the fudge frosting, bumpy and lumpy with pecan bits, melted in his mouth.

"And some peachy cobbler for you, honey," she said to Luc. "You didn't look like the chocolate type."

"How did you know?" Luc asked.

Miss Esther just shrugged. "It's a gift, I guess. Now, then, can I scoop y'all with some Blue Bell vanilla?"

Everyone nodded with enthusiasm, and Miss Esther's helper appeared with a tub of ice cream and a scoop.

"I feel like a few people are staring at us because we're eating so much," Luc said as a scoop of ice cream was deposited on his warm peachy cobbler, where it immediately began to melt.

Delia glanced around the room. "Oh, they're all keeping up with us, believe me. But they *are* trying to figure out who y'all are. Once they do, they'll stop."

Actually, once they figured it out, they started coming over. A man named Ed Finkle approached first. "So sorry to hear about your uncle," he said. "I was in the Lions Club with him for, oh, I'd say right near twenty years."

Luc's eyes widened with alarm. "Did you say lions?"

Ed laughed heartily. "You've got a sense of humor, just like your uncle. I tell you what, I sure do miss him."

Next was Milton Ashrod, who'd apparently been Uncle Hartwell's auto mechanic. He was followed by Uncle Hartwell's dentist and some guy he went fishing with who pulled out his phone to share photos from their last trip to the lake.

Uncle Hartwell had been spry and handsome for a man his age, and he was smiling in every picture, especially the one where he held a huge fish.

"Quite a loss for Willow Root," the man said. "I'm sure it's much worse for you boys."

Max had only a few memories of his uncle. As a child, they'd visited several times, and he vaguely recalled going on a hike some-where, and when it started to rain, Uncle Hartwell had cast a spell that provided an invisible cover over their heads.

A knot formed in his throat. Everyone kept saying they were sorry for his loss, and now, for the first time, he realized he'd actually lost something. He'd lost the opportunity to collect stories. To form memories. To know his own uncle in the way these strangers had.

Finally, a plump, older woman came up. "I'm Shelly McBride," she said. "I was Hartwell's piano teacher."

"He took piano lessons? I noticed there was sheet music out on the piano in the parlor," Max said.

"He sure did. He started…" She looked at Delia. "How long ago?"

"Oh, I guess it's been about three years or so," Delia said.

In Shadowlark, the pianos played themselves.

"He'd only been taking lessons for a few weeks when he insisted on playing 'Here Comes Santa Claus' in the winter recital. Remember that, Delia?"

"Oh, I remember. Mostly because he invited me to attend. No offense, but I was pretty perturbed about it at the time." The smile on her face said otherwise, and she winked at Max. "He was the only adult performing, and I had to sit through various renditions of 'Jingle Bells' and 'Rudolph the Red-Nosed Reindeer,' and I did it stone-cold sober."

Max and Luc both laughed, and then they shared a glance.

This was our uncle?

"He actually got pretty good," Shelly said. "His favorite piece to play was 'Dream a Little Dream of Me.'"

With a sweet smile on her lips, Delia closed her eyes and started to hum the tune. Shelly's eyes filled with tears and then, damn it, so did Luc's. A tear slid down Delia's cheek as Max blinked furiously and tried to think of something—*anything*—else.

Miss Esther appeared out of nowhere. "You boys take these home," she said, setting foil-covered pans in front of them. "It's enough to get you through the next couple of days."

And then she squeezed Max's shoulder, patted Luc's back, and repeated the same thing everyone else had said.

Sorry for your loss.

And, unbelievably, as Max stood up and felt the warmth of the heavy foil-covered pan in his hand, the oddest sensation rolled through his overstuffed stomach, squeezed his heart, and settled just at the base of his throat before coming out as a croaky "Thank you."

He wasn't sure, but he thought that odd sensation might be what people referred to as *comfort*. It felt wonderful. And he hadn't even known he needed it.

Chapter Ten

Delia sat at the kitchen table with her tablet and design book. She opened a new design template, wondering how many rooms Max would let her stage. She labeled the template HALIFAX MANOR and felt a huge surge of pride and excitement. How was it possible that she was going to be freaking decorating the home of her dreams?

The surge of excitement quickly dissipated, replaced by grief. If Hartwell hadn't died…

No. Hartwell had been very supportive of her ambition to become an interior decorator. Most likely, he would have been her first client, although he was weirdly secretive and protective of certain rooms in the house. Like his study, for instance. And she'd never been allowed in the library.

The back door slammed, and Grandma Maddie came into the kitchen carrying a basket of freshly picked herbs and leaving a trail of dirt on the floor. "Fiona says you're going next door," she said.

"Yep. I'm meeting with Max to talk about the staging for the open house. I'm so excited! My mind is brimming with ideas—"

"Don't get carried away. It's just a staging," her mom said, coming in behind Grandma Maddie. She grabbed a broom and started sweeping. "Goodness, Mother. Be more careful. Delia did all this work tidying the house!"

"I didn't do that much." The truth was, Delia had given up a long time ago. Her grandmother and aunts just weren't the types to pick up after themselves. And worse, they seemed to thrive in a messy house.

"I'm leaving for a Chamber of Commerce meeting in just a few minutes," her mom said. "It's my first one, and I admit I'm a little nervous."

"You're going to be fine," Grandma Maddie said, placing a handful of herbs in a colander. "There is nothing a Merriweather woman can't do, and you, in particular, Fiona, are a force to be reckoned with."

Fiona's cheeks turned pink at the praise, and with a small smile, she walked over and grabbed a handful of herbs, shaking the dirt off onto a paper towel. "Who cleaned out the sink?"

Delia raised her hand. "Me."

The sink usually overflowed with dishes and things that shouldn't be anywhere near a sink. Yesterday there had been a frog blinking up at Delia from inside a Duke's mayonnaise jar. Delia had screamed and dropped an egg on the floor. The only explanation she could glean as to *why* there was a frog in the sink was that someone "might need him later." She hated to think what someone might have needed him for, so she'd quickly taken him outside, where she'd hidden him behind the rosebushes and warned him to stay put.

It ain't easy being green in a witch's house, little buddy.

"I put the dishes in the dishwasher is all," Delia said.

"It's nice to have room for the colander," Grandma Maddie said, sliding it beneath the faucet. "And I know just what Halifax Manor needs, if you're interested in an opinion."

"Oh! I'm interested. What do you think it needs, Grandma?"

"It needs a slide off the second-floor balcony right into the pool," Grandma Maddie said. "I told Hartwell a million times."

Delia started to list all the reasons that was a bad idea, but before she could, her mom changed the topic. "Max and Luc seem like nice boys. I haven't met the cousin yet, so I can't speak for him."

"I found them delightfully odd," Grandma Maddie said.

Delia's mom rolled her eyes. "Says the woman who pretends her family is a coven of witches."

Delia shot her mom a wicked glare. *Don't start...*

"Well," Grandma Maddie said. "We *are* a coven of witches. My mother knew it. Her mother knew it. And all the mothers who came before her knew it. And we even have the spell book to prove it."

"That nasty book we found in the library all those years ago? The one that called for boiling a baby?"

"That's the one," Grandma Maddie said.

"Grandma," Delia said. "We've been over this. That was a silly prank. It's no more magical than the crystal balls down at the Crooked Broom."

"Don't let your aunties hear you say their crystal balls aren't magical," Grandma Maddie said.

Fiona sighed. "We do not come from a line of witches. We come from a long line of delusional women."

"You're breaking my heart, Fiona," Grandma Maddie said, shaking her head.

"I'm heading out now," Delia said loudly. "And, Mom, you should probably head out, too."

Her mom crossed her arms over her chest and pursed her lips. But then she retied the colorful scarf at her neck and grabbed her purse.

Grandma Maddie came out from behind the kitchen island. "Take this tea to Max," she said to Delia. "I blended it myself. It'll help him chill out."

"Is it legal?" Delia asked.

"Of course it is. Just who do you think I am?"

"I know darn well who you are and what you grow in the garden and what you do with it, too. And you can't slip shit to people without their knowledge." Delia crossed her arms, raised an eyebrow, and tapped her toe in what she hoped was an impersonation of a mom doing some mom-ing.

Grandma Maddie looked up at Delia through her thick, round glasses and attempted to look chagrined. "It happened one time, and it was an accident."

"Uh-huh. That was quite the trip you took the Willow Root Green Thumb Garden Club on. Myrtle Wilson still thinks she talked to her dead dog."

"I gave that woman closure. But *this*," she said, holding up a little packet of dried herbs, "is just a bit of jasmine, fennel, basil, and lavender." She stuck it in Delia's hand and then suddenly tossed some herbs over her shoulder before shouting, "Amore!"

"Oh, dear God, Mother," Fiona said. "Stop it. You can't throw some herbs over your shoulder and shout a word in Italian and pretend it's a love spell."

Delia almost dropped the baggie.

"Why can't I?" Grandma Maddie said.

"For one thing, we aren't even Italian," Fiona said. And then she turned to Delia and yanked the little bag out of her hand. "Don't give that to Max."

"If there's no such thing as magic and love spells, why would you care?" Grandma Maddie said, grabbing it back and sticking it in Delia's bag. "And anyway, what would it hurt if Max were to drink a spot of tea and get a little frisky with Delia? For heaven's sake, let the poor girl have some fun, Fiona."

Max stared at the clothes hanging in the closet. He really needed to pack up Uncle Hartwell's wardrobe, but thus far, all he'd managed to do was shove his items over to the right side of the closet—just far enough to clear out space for his own stuff.

He'd noticed Nikki wearing some of Hartwell's things. They didn't quite fit, but Max suspected they brought him comfort. He'd been so close to Hartwell and was clearly grieving, while Max and Luc had barely known their uncle at all. And even if they had, Logos witches didn't grieve longer than seven days. Not outwardly, anyway. It was considered unseemly, no matter how close the relationship had been.

By the time they'd received word that Hartwell had passed, the funeral in Willow Root had already happened. Their father had seemed more angry than sad, although that might just be how sad looked on him. It was hard to know, since their father rarely showed much emotion at all. You could sense it, flowing somewhere beneath the surface, like a hidden river. But Armistead Halifax was a proper witch, and he kept his emotions in check.

Their mother, like Luc, wasn't quite as restrained. But Max was a Halifax through and through.

"Shouldn't you be getting dressed?"

Max practically jumped out of his house slippers before turning to face Nikki. "Holy hell, would you stop sneaking up on me?"

"I've never met anyone more easily startled," Nikki said, looking entirely too amused. "And I wasn't sneaking. I was just coming to say that Delia should be here any minute, and I don't think we have anything to offer in the way of refreshments."

Max hadn't thought of that. "She's just coming over to discuss decorating the place for the open house," he said. "I don't think I'm expected to provide refreshments."

Nikki laughed. "You do realize you're in Texas?"

"So?"

"At the very least you need to have a tin of cookies. Hartwell always kept them on hand in case anyone stopped by."

"And here I was thinking that choosing between gray and dark gray trousers was my biggest problem."

"It's a close second. Don't you have jeans? That's what people wear."

And imps, apparently. Because Nikki was sporting jeans, a black T-shirt, and a pair of cowboy boots. He looked ridiculous even if you didn't happen to know he was an imp.

"As a venator for the Concilium, my goal, wardrobe-wise, is merely to blend in. I'm supposed to avoid trendy clothing and colorful expressions."

Nikki clapped. "Well done on the drabby part. But you hardly blend in."

Max frowned. "Oh?"

"Those ugly gray pants you wear—"

"They're not ugly. They're corduroys. And they're perfectly fine."

"You look like you're wearing your dead uncle's clothes—" Nikki blushed. "Never mind. That would be me. But Hartwell dressed better than you."

Nikki brushed Max aside and started sorting through his clothes. Which was totally rude.

"Listen, it doesn't matter what I wear. Cordelia Merriweather knows this isn't a social call—"

Nikki snorted. "All calls are social calls. And here," he said, pulling a green sweater off a hanger. "Put this on. Women love a man in a sweater."

"Get out," Max said, giving Nikki a shove along with the direct order he couldn't refuse.

Nikki shrugged. "As you wish."

As soon as Nikki was gone, Max put on his comfortable corduroy trousers. He added a white button-up, which he tucked in... and then yanked out, because he had no problem being casual. He slid into his favorite loafers and headed for the stairs. But first he paused on the landing in front of a gigantic mirror. Nikki had told him it was a rare Mirror of Truth.

Max had never come across one before, so he decided to try it out. "What do you think?" he asked, feeling silly for talking to an inanimate object. It probably wasn't even magical. What did Nikki know?

A slow rumbling sound came from the mirror, and then it began to speak. "Not too shabby. Pretty fit, although you could probably firm up your middle."

Max allowed his pulse to return to normal before sucking in his stomach. "Thank you? I guess?"

"You need a haircut *badly*."

Max didn't appreciate the direction this seemed to be headed. "Okay. That'll do. I'm just going to—"

"I have not yet dispensed all of the truth," the mirror continued.

"Partial truth is fine. I'm good with it—"

"If you're asking about what to wear in front of the Blue Witch, I'd go with the J.Crew cable-knit."

"The green sweater in my closet?"

"Its color is *forest moss*, and it brings out the green in your hazel eyes. Women love a man in a sweater."

A very loud snort came from downstairs.

"I don't care about impressing a woman," Max said.

"Do you know what the difference is between you and me?" the mirror asked.

"For starters, you're a mirror—"

"I don't dispense lies. That's the difference."

Max turned and went back into his room, slamming the door behind him. Then he went to the closet, yanked the green sweater off its hanger, and put it on. Because while he definitely wasn't trying to woo Delia in any way, shape, or form, the truth was, he wasn't against looking somewhat attractive.

When he came back out, the mirror was once again quiet, and the doorbell rang just as he hit the stairs. He rushed down to the foyer, where he breathlessly opened the door, and what little wind he had was knocked right out of him.

Delia smiled brilliantly, and it was as if the literal sun was shining through his front door. He could feel the warmth spread slowly like honey from the top of his head to the tips of his toes. She wore a short black top with puffy sleeves that showed about two inches of smooth, silky skin above a pair of brown and black herringbone slacks. Her hair was slicked back into a ponytail, and golden teardrops hung from her ears. She held a briefcase in one hand and extended the other in a sharp and professional manner. "Howdy. I'm sorry if I'm a bit early. But I was just so excited to get started."

He took her hand—warm, small, and strong—and gave it a brief shake before stepping back and inviting her inside.

Cordelia Merriweather was all business, and Max suddenly felt silly for wearing the green sweater.

CHAPTER ELEVEN

Holy hot Jesus, the man looked good in a sweater. For one thing, it brought out the green in his eyes. For another, it made him look like a gigantic, soft, man-mountain of comfort and snuggles that she would definitely like to climb if she were not a professional interior decorator with a professional job to do.

But instead of commenting on how great the entryway would look with marble flooring, she said, "That color looks great on you."

Max looked at his torso, as if maybe he'd forgotten it existed, and then he looked back at her and blushed, which was freaking adorable.

"There's a bit of chill in the air," he said, as if sweaters needed explaining.

"It's supposed to warm up a bit tomorrow," she said, as if weather wasn't boring.

"Yes, well…" He waved his hand vaguely in the air. "Here's the house."

She obviously didn't need to be told that, and yet she looked around the foyer with what she hoped was a discerning and artistic expression on her face. After what seemed an appropriate amount of time, she said, "Shall we move into the living room?"

"Certainly," Max said. "After you. And I apologize for not knowing how this works."

"Don't worry, because I know what to do," she said, hoping he'd believe her.

"I realize it doesn't look like we've done much," Max said. "We've mostly been packing up the library and the shop."

"We'll definitely need to move most of this stuff out," Delia said, following him into the living room, where, on the couch, sat Max's cousin Nikki.

"Oh!" Delia said. "Hello again. I wasn't sure you were still in town."

Nikki's smile lit up his startlingly green eyes, and he came right over. "I'll be staying as long as I'm needed," he said, taking her hand in his.

Delia glanced around the room. "It looks like you're definitely needed. It must be so stressful deciding what to do with Hartwell's things."

Nikki brought her hand up to his lips and kissed it, and suddenly Delia had a dizzying moment of déjà vu. In fact, it was so strong that she swayed on her feet.

"Are you okay?" Max asked.

Nikki's brows furrowed in concern. "Do you need to sit down?"

Delia shook her head. "I'm fine. Thank you."

Goodness, but this was embarrassing. Not professional at all to get dang near knocked off your feet by a sudden wave of...

It isn't déjà vu.

"Oh my gosh. Nikki, we *have* met before!"

"Yes, of course," Nikki said. "At the antique shop, remember? I believe you bought a martini set."

Oops! She still hadn't paid for that. But that wasn't the encounter she was referring to.

The memory was fuzzy and cloudlike in the way that distant memories often were, but she distinctly remembered Nikki kissing her hand once before, and it had been right here in this very room. Only that absolutely wasn't possible. Because she'd been four or five years old at the time, and Nikki had been...

Exactly as he was now.

"No. Before that," she mumbled, scratching her head. "A long time ago."

"I think I would remember having met someone as lovely as you," Nikki said.

She ignored that obvious bit of delightful nonsense, because this was serious. And weird as hell. "No. I was a little girl at the time."

Max looked at her oddly.

Shoot. What was she thinking? That absolutely couldn't have happened. "I'm being silly," she said, suddenly doubting herself. "It must have been someone else. Someone who looked very much like you."

"Ah," Nikki said. "Another relative perhaps."

"Yes," Max said. "That must be it."

So maybe she wasn't going crazy. "Whew! For a moment there, I thought I'd lost my marbles."

Nikki laughed. "I'd say your marbles are fully intact. Nothing to worry about."

"How strange that Hartwell had this whole family I never knew about. And it's so unfortunate, because—"

"I'm so sorry to interrupt," Max said. "But Nikki was supposed to be at the shop to help Luc nearly half an hour ago."

"That's right," Nikki said. "I should get going."

He smiled at Delia and headed toward the laundry room, which had an exit to the garage.

"Would you care for some coffee?" Max asked.

Delia nodded, still feeling a bit unsettled, and followed Max into the roomy, bright kitchen, where she was overcome by even more memories, because Hartwell's house was brimming with them.

Goodness, she missed that man. And boy, oh boy, did she love this kitchen.

The layout was what she now recognized as distinctly French in design. Its massive island was centered squarely in the middle of the room with long countertops running on either side. In front of the bay windows sat a table, and even though there was a formal dining room, this nook was where they'd always settled for teatime.

"You're smiling," Max said.

"I am?"

"Hugely."

"I was just remembering how Hartwell and I used to have tea, right at that table."

"Really?"

"Yep. All the time." She sighed and set her briefcase on a chair. "I can't imagine anyone else living here. In Hartwell's house."

"Yes, well," Max said, getting down a can of coffee. "That's the way of things, I guess."

It was. But Delia didn't have to like it.

Max started reading the directions on the coffee can, which was something Delia had never seen anyone do. She covered a smile with her hand as she watched him dump whole beans into the filter.

"You need to grind those first," she said.

"Grind them?" he asked, looking around the kitchen. "With what?" He reached for the blender on the counter.

"Oops. No, not that. You're obviously not much of a coffee drinker, so how about tea? Grandma Maddie sent me over with a special blend."

Max looked massively relieved. "Tea sounds great."

Delia grabbed Hartwell's copper teakettle, quickly filled it with water, and set it on the stove. Then she stepped onto a small stool next to the counter and reached for the Portmeirion teapot on the second shelf, but she was about an inch too short.

Max stepped up behind her, so close she could feel the warmth from his body and inhale the very scent of him: soap, old books, and something dark and sweet and mysterious. And as he reached for the teapot, his body momentarily pressed against hers, making her skin tingle and her head swim.

"Let me," he said.

At the moment, Delia thought she might let him do absolutely anything.

The teapot was chipped, so Max went to grab a different one.

"Nope. That's my favorite," Delia said.

She had a favorite teapot at his Uncle Hartwell's house? Max was once again reminded that his uncle's relationship with the Merriweathers clearly went beyond notions of fairies and blue witches.

He set the chipped teapot on the counter and took a step back, which broke the physical contact between him and Delia, something he deeply regretted. With every fiber of his being, he wanted to continue touching her.

Obviously, he'd been attracted to women before. Logos witches might not do love, per se. But they did everything else. He knew what it was to want someone in that particular animalistic way. He was familiar with lust and desire, but this was somehow different. And because he was a logical witch, he had to ask himself *why.* What was different about it? And what was causing it?

Hexed or not, Delia was a Cor witch. A direct descendant of

Lucinda Merriweather, just as he was a direct descendant of Wilmot Halifax. You didn't have to believe in fairies and blue witches to recognize the possible danger. Magic was not 100 percent predictable, which was the one irritating thing about magic.

"I chipped that teapot when I was about ten years old," Delia said.

"You did?"

Delia smiled her adorably crooked and quite possibly dangerous smile, and Max's insides fluttered stupidly. "Hartwell and I were having a very fancy teatime, and I'm afraid I was an overly zealous pourer. I felt just awful when it happened, but Hartwell said it gave the teapot character. He said he liked imperfect things." She stepped down from the stool. "That's probably why he liked me."

She shooed him out of the way and pulled the drawer open like it was her own kitchen, and extracted a mesh tea strainer. "Anyway, it was basically my pot after that. We poured tea after school whenever I'd had a bad day or whenever I'd had a particularly good day, and on rainy days, of course, and sad ones, too. Like if I hadn't been invited to a birthday party—"

"Who wouldn't invite you to their birthday party?" Max asked, feeling ridiculously stunned by the fact. And also a little outraged on Delia's behalf, which didn't seem like a logical reaction at all.

"There were lots of things I wasn't invited to."

"Ah, well. Kids can be mean sometimes," Max said, shaking his head. "I think that must be a universal truth."

Delia nodded and then stared at him as if sizing him up. Finally she said, "I'm not sure if you picked up on this, but my family believes they're a coven of witches."

She paused, continuing to stare at him unnervingly. Was this a test? Did she know what was going on? Had she pegged him as a descendant of the very witch who had hexed them?

"Why aren't you laughing?"

"Laughing?"

"Everyone laughs."

"I guess I'm just—"

"At a loss for words? Well, believe me. I know it's nuts. But you know what? It doesn't hurt anybody."

"You think it's nuts?"

"Well, yes, of course I do. Don't you?"

Holy hell, she really had no idea. She didn't *believe* any of it. She wasn't trying to break a hex. And the scarlet creeping from her cheeks all the way down her neck and across her chest…

Stop looking at her chest.

She was deeply and painfully embarrassed, and he hated it. He hated it because it *was* true. They were witches. Witches were real and wonderful and magical and the Merriweathers were not a part of that world and never would be, and she believed her family to be delusional.

A knot formed in his throat.

"Aren't you going to say something?" she asked.

He had to swallow the knot first. "I haven't been around them all that much, but I find your family to be delightful. And my uncle obviously thought highly of you."

That was true, and the relief on her face damn near did him in.

Delia's eyes started to mist, and she quickly began spooning tea into the strainer.

Max cleared his throat and leaned against the counter. "You know your way around this kitchen better than I do."

"Well, I've been in it more than you have," she replied, carrying the pot to the table just as the kettle whistled. "Can you grab a couple of mugs?"

He'd been a child when the adults—his father and his uncle—had a falling-out. There hadn't been much he could do about it. But he hadn't *stayed* a child. Maybe he should have visited Uncle Hartwell. He'd never even heard his side of the story. Hell, he hadn't really heard his father's. All he knew was that Hartwell had somehow shamed the family and had been shunned as a result. Wasn't that the real reason he'd spent the past thirty years in the Stray Lands?

He retrieved the mugs, and soon he and Delia were staring at each other while waiting for the tea to steep.

"Don't feel bad," she suddenly said. "California is a long way from Texas."

Was he that transparent? He'd always thought he was pretty good at keeping a blank face. "My father and Uncle Hartwell were estranged. It's unfortunate, but as a result, Luc and I didn't have much contact with him."

"Ah. Well, families are weird. These things happen."

Delia poured tea into their mugs, and Max simply nodded. Because she was right. Families were absolutely weird.

"It never really bothered me, to tell you the truth. I didn't think of Uncle Hartwell all that much. But now, after coming to Willow Root, I really wish things had been different. I would have liked to have gotten to know him."

Delia pushed a mug in front of him. "Well, estrangement or not, you were his nephew, and I'm sure he loved you."

Max stared at his tea as the warm steam floated up to his face, bringing a rich floral aroma and tickling his nose. Logos witches didn't profess feelings of love. He knew his parents cared for him and Luc. And of course he and Luc were fond of their parents. But they'd never even lived together as a family, and they'd never said they loved each other, because what was the point of it?

"You know," Delia said, stirring sugar into her tea. "I never heard the back door close. Did Nikki leave?"

Nikki had most likely gone straight into the laundry room, where he'd transformed into a cat before making an exit through the cat door. He was probably lounging about by the pool.

"And I didn't hear a car leave," Delia added, craning her neck toward the laundry room, where a door led to the garage.

"Oh, he likes to walk," Max said quickly.

"It's got to be at least three or four miles, if not more, to the antique shop—"

"He walks quickly. Gets in his cardio that way."

"Oh," Delia said. A tiny little line appeared between her eyebrows as she pondered this. Obviously, it didn't sound quite right to her. And then there was the whole recognition thing. Like, what the hell? He'd have to talk to Nikki later. Just how reckless had he and Uncle Hartwell been to have allowed Delia to see Nikki in human form all those years ago?

"Tell me about staging," he said. "I know nothing, and I'm sure you wouldn't approve of my very stark and bachelor-style digs back in Shadowlark."

That was the truth. He was hardly ever there. Why bother adding personal touches? And he really didn't care about staging this place, except it gave him a good excuse to spend some time with Delia. Because of the hex. Not because he *wanted* to spend time with her.

"I've never heard of Shadowlark," Delia said. "Of course, I've never been to California."

"There's not much to it," he said.

Just a city run almost entirely on magic.

"Well, when you've never been outside the state you were born in—"

"There was the trip to Louisiana for the witch festival," he said with a small grin.

Delia blushed. "Yes. Well, that was a long time ago. I'd love to go somewhere exotic."

"I travel the world for my job. And although it's not all it's cracked up to be—I'm almost always traveling alone—I admit that it's pretty exciting."

"Oh, I'd love to hear about your travels," Delia said, leaning in. "And thank you, by the way, for not acting weird about the witch festival in Louisiana."

His grin automatically expanded into a full-blown smile. "Now, why would I act weird about a witch festival in Louisiana, where you excelled in potion-making?"

"I threw up on the Tilt-A-Whirl," she whispered. "If you're wondering what happened to the so-called potion."

Max laughed. "I've never ridden a Tilt-A-Whirl, and you're not doing much to sell me on the idea."

Although riding a Tilt-A-Whirl with Delia at a witch festival sounded like something he might very much like to try.

And why was that? Again, he wondered if maybe this woman was influencing his emotions in some strange way. Not purposefully, maybe. But he felt something. And he didn't hate it.

"So," Delia said, sitting up straight and adjusting the neckline of her blouse, which had dipped deliciously low during their conversation. "What do you say we talk color swatches?"

"I'd say I don't know what that is."

Delia chuckled, and then she reached over and squeezed his hand. "Thank you," she said softly. "For being so kind."

The knot was back in his throat. If Delia knew who he was and why he was really here, she wouldn't be thanking him at all.

CHAPTER TWELVE

The little bell over the door of the Crooked Broom jingled cheerfully, but inside it was deathly quiet. And Delia knew why.

It was an ambush.

"Yoo-hoo!" she called. "Where are my aunties at?"

She thought she heard some giggles by the counter, so she headed that way, trying to steel herself for what she knew was coming, which would nevertheless startle her senseless.

Where were the customers? There were usually at least one or two, since the Crooked Broom was the only thing resembling a bookstore within seventy-five miles. There was also a huge herbal area, thanks to Grandma Maddie. Lots of locals bought the lovingly prepared tinctures, teas, and aromatherapy blends. And of course there were always plenty of buyers for the candles and art and cheap toys and gadgets. Need a back scratcher? You could find it at the Crooked Broom. Need a candle that would ward off demons while boosting your chances of winning the Texas Lottery? They were by the register.

Delia arrived at the counter—*heavy breathing/giggling/shushing*—and timidly drummed her fingers against the glass. That was all her family needed to hear, and they sprang up like snakes from a can, shouting *Surprise!* As for Delia, she screamed at the top of her lungs while clutching her chest, as was her custom.

"Oh, wow!" she gasped after she'd somewhat caught her breath. "You got me! Again! Which is stupid, really—"

Before she could finish her sentence, she was smothered by hugs and kisses. And over her grandmother's shoulder, she noticed that Gertie Scott and Bethany Howard had been hiding behind the counter as well and now stood awkwardly grinning and holding the items they'd apparently been about to purchase.

"Did we surprise you?" Andi asked, brushing confetti out of Delia's hair.

"You know you did!"

"Such a startle reflex on this one!" Grandma Maddie said, pinching Delia's cheek. "It's so gratifying."

"Y'all look pretty dang happy with yourselves," Delia said.

"That's because we are," Aurora said, handing Delia a small bouquet of yellow flowers.

Delia buried her nose in them as Gertie came around the counter. "Happy Birthday, Delia. I came in here to buy some herbs, but what fun that it turned into a party."

"Same," Bethany said. "Only I came here for your grandma's witch hazel ointment."

The bell over the door jingled again, and Misty Herrera entered the store, pushing a baby stroller. "What's going on?"

"It's Delia's birthday," Bethany said. "And it's a surprise party!"

Constance Fleming rose slowly from behind the counter, knees creaking loudly in protest. "I hardly call it a party when you're tackled and thrown behind a counter while trying to purchase candles," she said. "That's some crappy customer service, if you ask me."

"Nobody did," Grandma Maddie said pleasantly. "And good Goddess, Constance! Your knees creak louder than the gate in my garden. I insist you take some of this devil's claw and turmeric balm."

She set a jar of joint balm next to the candles on the counter, and Constance eyed it warily.

"On the house," Grandma Maddie said.

Constance huffed a bit but then dropped the little jar in her bag. "Thank you. And happy birthday, Delia."

Misty pushed her stroller up to the counter, and everyone made the appropriate sounds at the drooling baby inside. "How old is little Miles now?" Delia asked. "I swear your baby shower wasn't all that long ago."

"He's nearly nineteen months," Misty said. "And what about you?"

"Big three-O," Delia said. She did some hurried mental math. "Or rather, I'm three hundred and sixty months old."

Misty laughed. "I hit that milestone last month. How did we get here? It seems like we were in high school only yesterday, and now I'm pushing a stroller and picking out kitchen drawer handles for my brand-new house, and you're busy..." Misty looked Delia up and down. "What is it you're up to lately? Cleaning houses?"

"She's an interior decorator," Aunt Andi said loudly. "Maybe she could help you with those kitchen drawer handles?"

"Hold on," Delia said. "I have a business card—"

The bell over the door jingled again, and everyone turned to see who else had shown up.

It was Max, followed by Luc. And Delia's heart, which had finally settled down, started hammering again. Goodness, there was something about that dark, unruly lock of hair hanging over Max's eye that had her fight-or-flight reflex primed and ready, as if it recognized some hidden part of Max as being inexplicably dangerous.

And I like it.

Aunt Andi hurried over. "Welcome to the Crooked Broom," she said with a fair amount of drama. "We have anything and everything you might need for your health and happiness."

Max's eyes flitted over the shelves of lucky candles and sparkling crystals and sloppy stacks of T-shirts and rows of coffee mugs and refrigerator magnets. Delia felt her cheeks getting warm, but then she remembered how Max had reacted when she'd told him about her eccentric family, and she relaxed.

"Thank you," he said. "This is a very interesting shop."

Good choice of words, but also, the genuine expression on his face indicated he might even mean it.

"Have a pumpkin spice muffin," Grandma Maddie said, sticking a platter in front of their faces. "It's Delia's birthday."

Delia hadn't noticed the muffins until now. They smelled delectable, and she grabbed one right after Max and Luc.

"You didn't mention your birthday was today," Max said, taking a huge bite of his muffin.

"She doesn't like anyone making a big deal out of it," Grandma Maddie said.

"That's true. I don't," Delia said. "And, as usual, everyone ignores me."

"It's her thirtieth!" Andi said, as if it were a badge of honor or a huge accomplishment that didn't consist of merely continuing to eat, breathe, and sleep for another year.

"The big three-O," Misty Herrera added, stepping up and eyeing Max and Luc curiously.

"The tarot cards are on sale in her honor," Andi said. "Fifty percent off."

The tarot cards had been fifty percent off as long as Delia could remember.

"But not the cat ones," Aurora clarified. "They're new and not on sale."

"The cat ones?" Misty asked, curiosity clearly piqued. "I collect anything and everything with cats on it."

"It's the Meow Moon deck," Andi said, pointing. "On the shelf behind you. The cards are so cute, they're practically frameable."

No, they were not frameable. They were horridly tacky. Delia quickly held out a business card to Misty. "And speaking of frames and art, I can help you choose the right accents for your home."

Misty took the card and looked at it with a smug grin, and Delia had the horrible feeling she'd missed a misprinted one and Misty was about to read it out loud in front of everyone: *Southern Charm Inferior Decorating and Design*. But instead, she just stared at it before handing it back. "I'm afraid my budget won't allow for an interior decorator."

"It's more affordable than you might think," Delia said. "And since I'm just starting up, I'll even offer a discount."

"No thanks," Misty said. "But I was wondering what you'd charge to do my outside windows? They are such a mess!"

Was she freaking kidding? "I don't do windows anymore."

"Don't be silly, Delia," Mrs. Fleming said, coming around the counter. "You did mine on Sunday."

"That was a special circumstance," she said. "I'm an interior decorator now."

Suddenly, Max cleared his throat. "Delia, I stopped by today hoping you'd have time to see me without an appointment. I was so impressed by your ideas for Halifax Manor that I'd like to get started right away."

He looked her dead in the eye before smiling at Misty.

"Of course," Delia said. "My day is pretty much free—"

Grandma Maddie coughed loudly.

"I mean, I think I might be able to squeeze you in."

"You're decorating Halifax Manor?" Misty asked, mouth agape.

"She's professionally staging it, so I can sell it," Max said.

Misty snatched the card back from Delia and looked at it again. "I'm sorry," she said. "I've got to run. I'm having a dinner party tonight. And honestly, I can't even remember what I came in here for."

She turned and pushed her stroller out the door, leaving Delia to wonder what she'd done wrong. Misty was always unpredictable in her behavior. One minute she was warm and the next cold.

She shrugged and looked at Max, who was rocking back on his heels with his hands clasped behind his back. His eyes narrowed as he watched Misty make her hasty exit.

"Max, give me just a few minutes to get my stuff together, and then I'll see you back in my office. It's, um, in the stockroom. Just until I can afford a place."

"I hope you don't mind that I've come along," Luc said. "I'm curious as to what you've got planned for the manor."

"Feel free to ignore any and all of his opinions," Max said.

"Are you crazy?" Delia said. "Another opinion is always welcome."

That wasn't necessarily true, but Delia couldn't stop smiling.

Something told her that these two weren't going to be sticklers for details like color schemes.

As Delia went to the stockroom to prepare for their meeting, Max mindlessly ran his fingers across the spines of some books. Who was that woman with the baby? He didn't like the way she'd stared at Delia's business card, as if she was surprised it didn't have a typo. Could it be that she was the witch who'd hexed her? Because she *had* been a witch. She wasn't very powerful, but he'd sensed a bit of magic hovering around her.

"You need to ask Delia what she's doing for her birthday," Luc said, holding up a T-shirt that said ALL MY HEXES LIVE IN TEXAS. "Strays always have some kind of celebration."

"Morgaine called this morning, and she's insisting that we not let Delia out of our sight until midnight. I guess we could just send Nikki over there…"

Luc refolded the T-shirt and put it back on the shelf. "I wonder if there will be cake and presents? That sounds way more fun than a Shadowlark birthday."

In Shadowlark, birthdays were celebrated properly, by calling forth the names of your ancestors in a sun chart ritual that made sure your soul was still aligned with your destiny.

Words floated their way from the counter. Words like *world-famous lasagna…gooey chocolate volcano cake…cutthroat game of Pictionary…margaritas.*

Max swallowed. Partly because his mouth was suddenly salivating—what was a gooey chocolate volcano cake?—and partly because it sounded like the Merriweathers were definitely planning a party. Chocolate evoked its own kind of magic on witches with feminine energy, and if you added alcohol and an edge of competition... Well, if Delia really *did* have a bit of fairy magic, sparks could fly.

What if, while drunk on margaritas and enraged by Pictionary, the chocolate-fueled coven accidentally broke the hex?

No. Breaking the hex would have to be intentional. They'd need an actual *spell*. And they didn't have the book. Even if they had the ability to do magic, they didn't know how. The items on the shelves in front of them attested to that fact. There was absolutely nothing in here that contained even a hint of—

"Max," Luc hissed. "Come here."

Max rushed over to where Luc had wandered to the end of the aisle. And all of a sudden, the hair stood up on his neck. His chin vibrated and his lips tingled as a wave of magic—wild and unhinged—rushed over him. "What the hell?"

Luc pointed at a basket of small, crooked, knotty twigs.

"Whoa," Max whispered, running a hand lightly over the innocent-looking twigs.

"Can you feel your face?" Luc asked. "Because I can't feel my face."

"It's the twigs," Max said.

"Is my tongue swollen?" Luc asked, sticking it out.

Max took a few steps back. "Come over here before you literally choke."

Luc walked away from the basket of twigs. Then he opened and closed his mouth a few times and poked at his cheeks. "You don't think those are wands, do you?"

"Where would they have gotten them?"

"I don't know."

"I'm not sure we should let these women gather tonight," Max said.

"I don't see how we could stop them."

Max rubbed his chin. "Maybe a small curse or hex?"

"Aren't they hexed enough?"

"It would be short-term. Just to get us safely to tomorrow, when we can tell Morgaine that Delia has turned thirty without breaking the hex."

"What do you have in mind?"

"Maybe horrible hives?" Max asked, pulling the string from his pocket. "We could make it look like an allergic reaction to herbs. Or maybe just a light *gastro-oh-no* curse for Delia."

"What kind of a monster gives a woman diarrhea on her birthday?"

True. But what could they—

"Boys! There you are."

Aurora had rounded the corner of the aisle, and Max quickly shoved the string back in his pocket.

"Yes, here we are," Luc said. "Right by the magic twigs. Where did you get those, by the way?"

"Oh, those old things?" Aurora looked over her shoulder at Andi, who was walking their way with Delia. "Andi, where did we get these sticks?"

"Down by the pond," Andi said. "The old willow tree."

"That's probably the most magical spot in Willow Root," Aurora said.

She was right, of course. That absolutely was the most magical spot in Willow Root. The tree was fed by the ley lines, and it was where the magic tidings were dispensed every Hallowtide. But how would the Merriweathers know that?

"It's just a silly rumor," Delia said.

"I don't know what the sticks could possibly be used for," Andi added. "But I figure they're good for something. We're practically giving them away, but nobody wants to buy them."

"I'm not sure that those should be for sale," Luc said.

"I keep telling them that," Delia said. "Who would buy them? Unless maybe it's to tie them up with some country twine and place them on a fireplace mantel, maybe with some pretty candles. You know, bringing the outdoors in and all that. And speaking of decorating, I'm ready for y'all to come on back."

"But first," Andi said. "We'd like to invite you to Delia's birthday party tonight."

"What?" Delia said, her face aflame. "Listen, guys. You do not have to come—"

"It's my world-famous lasagna," Maddie said.

"You don't want to know what it's famous for," Delia said. "And seriously, if you're busy—"

"It's famous for being *tasty*," Grandma Maddie said. "And for the one time it ended up on the ceiling."

"But we still had enough in the pan to feed the firemen," Aurora added.

"The firemen?" Luc asked.

"Small mishap with the oven," Maddie said. "But don't worry. It shouldn't happen again."

"Thank you for the invitation," Max said, still toying with the string in his pocket. "But Luc and I—"

"Would love to come," Luc said, smiling brilliantly.

Delia smiled, too, but it was a nervous smile. "It'll be quite the party, then. Now, come on back to the stockroom and we'll talk color schemes."

CHAPTER THIRTEEN

God, why? Why had her nice, relaxing evening turned into such an anxious tummy-twister?

"I don't know what you're upset about," her mom said, running a brush through Delia's hair. "Didn't you say they were perfectly nice young men?"

Delia winced as the brush caught on a tangle. Why the heck was her mom brushing her hair like she was ten years old? She grabbed the brush. "They are. But do they have to come *here*? And on my actual birthday?"

She'd planned to wear stretchy pants while stuffing her face with lasagna and cake before passing out on the couch. A perfectly awesome birthday.

"Do you have any clean Spanx?" her mom asked.

Jesus. She was *not* squeezing herself into Spanx on her freaking birthday. Not even for Max Halifax.

"They're going to talk about witchcraft," Delia said, wringing her hands.

"Of course they will," her mom said.

"I've already warned them, but I doubt they're really prepared." Max had seemed perfectly understanding about it. But, well, it was going to be a lot. "Max is going to think they're nuts."

"Of course he will. But he's coming to see you, not your grand-mother and aunts."

"Says who?"

"Says your mother, who, despite being an old hag, is well aware of how these things work."

"I'm not looking to hook up with Max, Mom. I just want to decorate his house."

The little thrill that traveled up and down her spine when she mentioned Max's name said otherwise, and Delia bit her lip.

"Whatever you do, don't let him up here. If he sees this room, he'll definitely change his mind."

As if the downstairs was any better. It was cluttered and dusty and looked like a Halloween store had exploded in their living room. And it looked like that year-round.

"Maybe he won't notice."

"Delia!" Grandma Maddie yelled. "You'd better get down here before the boys arrive!"

Two grown-ass men. Definitely not boys.

"Coming," she shouted.

She ignored her mom's sighs as she put her hair in a sloppy bun and started digging in the drawer for lip gloss. Was the yellow baby-doll dress with white daisies and a big off-the-shoulder ruffle too short? Too babyish for a thirty-year-old?

"Delia! They're here!"

Shit. She abandoned the lip gloss, ran out of her room, and flew down the stairs, because it would probably be best if she was the one to open the door—

Too late.

The welcome wagon of witches had lined up, and Max and

Luc were already being forced to run the gauntlet. All five feet of Grandma Maddie had over six feet of Luc Halifax in a choke hold of a hug, sauce-covered wooden spoon hovering precariously close to the back of his head. The aunties were on Max, all talking at once and petting him as if he were a particularly mortified puppy. Their heads bobbed like clucking chickens as they complimented his appearance and commented on the weather and offered him wine and beer and appetizers Delia didn't think anyone had actually prepared.

He smiled awkwardly, said thank you repeatedly, and glanced above their heads to where Delia stood at the bottom of the stairs.

Their eyes met, and *oh my*. Delia had to place a hand on her tummy to calm the herd of butterflies that always seemed ready to take flight whenever Max was around.

He ran a hand through his incredibly disobedient hair, which bounced right back into its preferred position of flopping sexily over his left eye.

A couple of the butterflies in Delia's tummy started to actively flutter.

"Dinner smells delicious."

"Thanks for inviting us," Luc added.

"It's Maddie's lasagna you're smelling," Andi said.

Grandma Maddie held her spoon up. "World famous! I once made it for a king."

"Oh?" Max said.

"I'm sure you've seen his photo," Grandma Maddie said.

Delia's mom rolled her eyes. "She's talking about Stanley Samson. He's the bloated face on the billboard when you first drive into town."

"Oh!" Luc said, snapping his fingers. "The Insurance King!"

"Auto, home, *and* life," Grandma Maddie said proudly, as if anything less than a three-way bundle was an embarrassing disgrace. "We used to date. But I broke it off before anything could happen to him."

"Pardon?"

"Nothing," Delia said.

They'd had exactly one date, and Grandma Maddie hadn't been the one to break it off. Stanley had taken her to the Catholic church picnic, where she'd won an ice chest in a raffle that was big enough to hold an entire deer carcass. That had all been well and good, but then a casual conversation at a craft booth selling decorative kitchen witches had turned into a heated discussion about the Inquisition and the Catholic church. Stanley had been forced to take Grandma Maddie home, ostensibly before she could burst into flames.

"We brought you flowers," Max said, thrusting a bouquet of bedraggled supermarket flowers at Delia.

"Oh, how sweet," Delia said, looking for the nearest vase. "You didn't have to bring me flowers, but I'm sure glad you did."

Andi grabbed a milk bottle Delia had painted in the third grade, dumped out the dead wildflowers Grandma Maddie had collected in early summer, and stuffed the bouquet in it. "There now. Isn't that lovely?"

The cuckoo clock went off, startling everyone, including those who should know better. It was a witch clock, supposedly from Germany, and on the hour (every hour, which is why nobody should be surprised), a miniature boy and girl emerged from the clock's tiny door, chased by a witch on a broom.

"Yay! It's the witching hour!" Aurora said. "Let's head to the kitchen."

"The witching hour is midnight," Delia's mom said, following her. "You can't say every hour is the witching hour just because you like to say it's the witching hour."

"I can say whatever I want," Aurora said over her shoulder.

Delia grabbed two long-stemmed glasses from the dry bar and blew the dust off them. Then she held them out to Luc and Max. "You're going to need these."

Max was finding it hard to concentrate, what with all the delicious smells and the steam rising from the pots and the herbs dangling from the ceiling and his brother wearing an apron that said WITCH, PLEASE.

Delia, in her short dress that rose up when she reached for dishes in the cabinets, wasn't helping. "Is that knife sharp enough?" she asked.

Upon entry to the kitchen, Max had been handed a knife, a tomato, and an ironically accurate apron that said SON OF A WITCH. He looked at the knife in his hand. "I haven't used it yet."

"Well, you let me know if it's dull," she said. "I'll switch it out with another equally dull knife from that drawer behind you, and we'll all act like I accomplished something."

"That makes no sense," Max said. "But if I know anything, it's how to follow orders."

"What I meant is that despite endlessly whining about dull knives in this house, nobody has ever actually sharpened one," Delia said with a shrug.

"Some people are fixers," Aurora said. "And we are not those people."

"We are bemoaners," Maddie said with a smile wide enough to

make Max wonder if she'd ever actually bemoaned anything in her life.

The dizzying level of activity made his head spin. There were pots bubbling over, water streaming from the faucet, drawers opening and slamming, and all of it enshrouded in a constant chorus of women excusing themselves or asking each other to move their asses. And it was messy! Sauce and cake batter were splattered everywhere. The pile of dishes in the sink would give the Leaning Tower of Pisa some stiff competition. And one half of a lasagna noodle clung for dear life below the light switch, where Maddie had thrown it to see if it was done. Its other half was on the floor, and nobody seemed especially interested in picking it up.

His fingers itched for the string in his pocket. Two or three knots was all it would take to tidy the place up, but obviously, that was out of the question. He could at least sharpen the knives though.

When nobody was looking, he quickly pulled out the string, and then, while concentrating on the knives in the drawer behind him, he tied a knot and muttered, "*Infini acuti*."

There. Those knives would never be dull again.

"Hakuna matata to you, too, dear," Andi said, reaching past him for a dish towel. "But you'd better get started on that tomato, or we'll never eat."

Max didn't cook. Like, ever. In Shadowlark, it wasn't necessary. There were dining halls, and if you really wanted to use your own kitchen, well, you uttered a few spells. He couldn't actually remember ever having diced a tomato by hand, but he grasped the theory well enough. He visualized the process as if he were about to cast a spell, and then he made the first slice. It was ridiculously rewarding, so he did it again.

"Good job," Aurora said, patting his arm.

He couldn't help but smile at the childish praise. He probably looked as stupid as Luc, who'd been gleefully grating way more cheese than anyone could ever possibly need with embarrassing and unbridled enthusiasm.

Andi pointed at a little speaker on the bar. "What's your favorite poison, boys?"

Luc paused in his cheese grating. "Not that I would ever attempt to poison anyone. But, if I were, I think I'd go for belladonna. It's potent. Doesn't take much—"

Max tried to laugh as if Luc were joking and ended up choking instead.

"Settle down, cowboy," Maddie said, pounding him on the back. "And I disagree, Luc. I wouldn't go for the quick method. Too suspicious. I'm a fan of plain old arsenic. Slow and steady wins the race."

Now it was Delia's turn to laugh too loudly. "Grandma Maddie is teasing. She's never poisoned anyone." She stared intensely at her grandmother, eyebrows raised in question.

"I'm a henbane girl, myself," Andi said. "I think the slow onset of madness could be fun. But when I said poison, I meant music." She pointed a frosting-coated spoon at the speaker on the windowsill. "What do y'all like to listen to?"

"Shouldn't the birthday girl choose?" Max said quickly, before Luc had an opportunity to suggest something bizarre like underground Cerridwen grunge, which was popular among a certain sect of young witches.

"I'm a Swiftie," Delia said.

"Taylor it is," Aurora answered, handing a spoon to Delia. "Sing it, girl."

Delia handed the spoon back. "I'm not doing wooden-spoon karaoke in front of Max and Luc. Not while they're sober, anyway."

"Whatever you say, dear," Aurora said, dangling the spoon in front of Delia's face.

The intro to a song started up, surprisingly loud and clear for such a small speaker, and Delia grinned. "You're not going to goad me into singing with *that* song," she said. "I'm not exactly feeling twenty-two."

Aurora held up a finger. "You can't resist this one," she said, finding a new song on her phone. "It's going to take you back to high school."

A different melody rang out, and Delia snatched back the spoon. "I hate that you're right, Aunt Aurora, and I apologize to everyone for what is about to happen," she said, talking over the opening stanza. She waited a bit, took a deep breath, and was soon singing—quite off-key—about being on a balcony in the summer air, something to do with Romeo and Juliet.

Singing wasn't Delia's forte, but nevertheless, she was mesmerizing. Watching the emotions float across her face was like watching a slideshow of anything and everything that made a person feel *good*. And the sound of her voice—off-key or on—had the effect of a siren, pulling him in…

He shook himself. Sirens were not what they seemed. And Romeo and Juliet hadn't ended well.

Everyone clapped as Delia finished with a very dramatic bow. And for some reason, Max's heart was beating erratically in his chest. Delia might not be doing anything to him intentionally, but she was definitely doing something to him. Oddly, Luc seemed unaffected. He was busy looking through Aurora's playlist, as if he were going to—

"Luc's next," Aurora said, as Delia handed over the spoon.

Oh shit. Max's face flushed. His stomach lurched. And he wasn't even the one about to sing. But someone had to be embarrassed for Luc, and it was almost always Max.

"I think I know this one," Luc said. "But someone needs to sing with me."

"A golden oldie from KC and the Sunshine Band," Aurora said, and with a touch of her finger, the music started playing.

Max accidentally locked eyes with Aurora, which was unfortunate, because it apparently gave her an idea. "We might need a little help with the chorus," she said, gyrating her way over to Max. "Come on now, let's do a little dance and make a little—"

"Oh no," Max said, carefully making another slice in the tomato. "I don't know the words."

Aurora spun and then bumped him on the butt. With *her* butt. "Loosen up, sweet cheeks!"

Not only were Max's cheeks not loose (it might require medication to release the tension), but he'd nicked himself with the knife. And it was a deep nick. He quickly applied pressure to the wound with his apron, so as not to draw any attention, but Thea saw it. He'd bled all over the cutting board.

"Medic!" she screamed, and Andi ran to get the first aid kit.

A few seconds later, he was covered in women when Fiona walked in, took in the scene, and asked, "What on earth did you do to him? And just how many Merriweathers does it take to apply a bandage?"

"He cut himself with one of our stupid, dull knives," Delia said.

That wasn't true. It was actually pretty sharp, thanks to his spell. He'd cut himself because he was stupid and had never diced a tomato before.

"That bandage is too big," Fiona said, digging through the kit.

"Oh, it's fine—"

"Aha!" Fiona said, holding up a more appropriately sized bandage. "Follow me into the parlor, where the lighting is better."

She grabbed Max's hand (none too gingerly, considering it was the one with the injured finger), and dragged him into the parlor, where the lighting, if anything, was worse. She sprayed his finger with an antiseptic, which burned like hell, and then swiftly applied the bandage.

"Thank you for being so nice to my mother and aunts," she said softly. "And to my daughter, too, for that matter."

"There's no need to thank me for that. I'm sure I speak for both of us—myself and Luc—when I say it's we who should be thanking you and your family for your hospitality."

Fiona shook her head. "They're eccentric. It's uncomfortable for many people. For most people, actually. And it's embarrassing for Delia when the witchy talk starts up. But you and Luc just go with the flow and brush it all off. Believe me, not everyone does that."

He didn't know what to say. He remembered Delia telling him about the birthday parties she hadn't been invited to as a child. Surely the strays found them to be more than eccentric. But Nikki had told him that the local hedge witches scoffed at the Merriweathers and their witchy proclamations, too. With the exception of Maddie and her sisters, nobody believed the Merriweathers were witches.

Fiona looked around the room, eyes flitting over the cobwebs hanging from the crooked chandelier and the comical cauldron sitting in the fireplace, before coming to rest on the countless family photos gracing the top of the dusty baby grand piano in the corner. "This house is its own little island of crazy, insulating love, but it can be…"

She frowned, as if searching for the word.

"I imagine it can be isolating, as well," Max said, trying to grasp the idea of being banished to a world where nobody would ever quite accept you.

"Yes. Poor Delia has felt lonely at times."

"I'm sure she has," Max said. "But I was talking about you."

Fiona smiled. "I'm going to go check on the cake."

Max looked at the bandage on his finger as Fiona walked away. If another Merriweather thanked him for being nice or kind or understanding, he was going to shrivel up into a ball of tightly wound shame.

He looked at his watch. The evening had flown by, and luckily, he only had to keep an eye on Delia for another few hours.

CHAPTER FOURTEEN

I t could have been worse. Yes, Max had bled everywhere, and yes, there had been talk of witchcraft. But Delia's mom had been good at steering the conversation back to real estate or interior decorating, and once Grandma Maddie started regaling Max and Luc with stories about Hartwell, witchcraft had finally fallen off the radar. But when it *had* been brought up, Max and Luc hadn't seemed taken aback in the way most people were.

"Dinner was delicious," Max said, leaning back on the parlor sofa and patting his stomach. "I don't think I could eat another bite."

"And the way it was all prepared was just so fabulous," Luc added. "I mean, it was really remarkable."

Some guys lived entirely off Hot Pockets. But with Luc and Max, it seemed to go beyond that. It was like they'd never even *seen* a home-cooked meal. Aunt Andi had had to show Luc how to use a cheese grater, and then, after Max had finally finished dicing the tomato, Luc had literally tossed the salad, like *up in the air*, and only about a third of it had made it back into the bowl.

"I hope you have room for cake," Delia's mom said, coming out of the kitchen. "Because it's coming, whether you're ready or not."

"Volcano cake?" Delia asked.

"Yes," Fiona said, holding up a roll of paper towels. "This will offer minimal protection, but I suggest y'all cover up as much as is practical."

"Is it literally going to erupt?" Luc asked, rubbing his hands together in glee. "Because that would be amazing."

"No," Fiona said. "But it's going to make a holy mess, nonetheless."

"And it's decadently delicious," Delia said.

Max politely accepted a paper towel, and then he looked at his watch. He'd been doing that ever since dinner, as if maybe he had somewhere else to be.

"Well, this is all great fun," Luc said. "We don't do volcano cakes in our family. Or any cakes, for that matter."

Delia knew that some people didn't do holidays for religious reasons. Maybe Max and Luc came from a family like that. "Do y'all not celebrate birthdays?"

"We do," Max said. "But we're not much for cake and singing and whatnot."

"So, no party? No celebratory dinner? No cake?" Delia's mom asked.

Luc crossed his arms. "Max likes to have a Dumb Supper, which is incredibly boring."

"I'm sure it's not dumb," Delia said, even though she absolutely believed it would be incredibly boring if Max spent the entire time looking at his watch, which was what he was doing again.

Luc snorted. "No, it really is."

The doorbell rang with a chime that played "Ding Dong! The Witch Is Dead," which made no sense for a house full of witches, but Grandma Maddie was like someone who collected rooster knickknacks. She just couldn't help herself.

"That's probably Amy," Delia said, standing up. "She couldn't make it for dinner but said she'd swing by for cake."

Just as she reached for the door, it opened, and Amy burst in. Actually, a shit ton of electric-blue balloons came in first, but Amy immediately followed.

Delia swatted the balloons out of the way to reach her friend. "You didn't have to do that," she said, absolutely meaning it. The last thing this crowded house needed was helium balloons.

"I really did," Amy said. "Arla Rogers sent them to Marisol's baby shower, and Marisol's cousin has a latex allergy and started breaking out in hives. I'm basically a hero."

"Thanks?" Delia said, struggling to drag the balloons all the way inside the house.

"But wait, there's more!" Amy was a big fan of paying it forward, also known as regifting, so Delia braced herself for the white elephant. Last year she'd received duck-shaped earrings and a "rodeo-scented" candle that smelled like literal bullshit.

"Ta-da!"

Delia stared incomprehensibly at what Amy held in her hands. There was a word for the thing, and it was a simple one, but Delia's brain couldn't produce it.

"Do you love him?" Amy asked.

Delia's mouth finally connected with her brain, and she was able to put a name to the butterscotch ball of fluff with a pink potbelly that Amy held out in front of her. "You... got me a dog?"

"It's a puppy," Amy said, as if the correction was necessary. "Somebody left the poor thing in the parking lot of the Shop-n-Save."

"Well, why don't you keep him then?"

"I asked Mr. Guerrera, and he didn't just say no. He said *hell no*."

Mr. Guerrera owned the little house Amy rented.

"Don't worry," Amy said, rubbing the puppy behind his ears. "If you don't want him, I'll simply take him to the pound."

Willow Root didn't have a no-kill shelter. Amy knew exactly what she was doing.

"Hand the stinker over," Delia said, taking the little fluff ball and melting the minute warm puppy breath hit her cheek.

His stubby tail wagged furiously, as if *stinker* were a compliment.

Amy smiled. "Thanks," she said quietly. "I know puppies are a hassle. But I just couldn't leave him there. He's completely innocent. I mean, it's hardly his fault someone dumped him in a parking lot."

"You've got a good heart, Amy Cotter."

Amy stopped short at the sight of Max and Luc.

"Be nice," Delia whispered. "Grandma Maddie invited them."

Max stood up. "Hello. I'm Max, and this is my brother, Luc."

"And you're the cranky girl from the tea," Luc said. "Nice to see you again."

Amy didn't say anything in response, until Delia poked her.

"Charmed," Amy said, and Delia suspected the only reason she didn't follow it up with a middle finger was because it was Delia's birthday.

"Okay, well," Delia said. "You and the little pee-puddle-meister are just in time for cake."

"He needs a name," Delia's mom said. "Something respectable."

"Are you saying Pee-Puddle-Meister isn't respectable?"

Her mother crossed her arms.

Before Delia could try out any names, the cake procession

entered the room, led by Grandma Maddie, whose face glowed in the light of the gigantic taper candles that had been swiped from the dusty candelabra on the mantel and stuck into the cake, because who needed plain old birthday candles when you could have gigantic, dripping columns of wax?

Everyone began singing "Happy Birthday" at different speeds and in different keys, and then they noticed the puppy, which further complicated matters, and by the time the last voice died out (Aunt Thea, a full five seconds behind everyone else), Delia was getting a little itchy to blow out the candles before the entire house burned down.

"Don't forget to make a wish," Grandma Maddie said, setting the cake platter, dripping chocolate on all sides, down on the coffee table in front of Delia.

Delia fought to control the puppy as she leaned forward to blow. But first she closed her eyes.

Please let Southern Charm Interior Decorating and Design be a success.

She blew, the flames went out, and everyone cheered as if she'd done something grand, which pretty much summed up her role in the family. When she, along with every other member of her class, had graduated from high school, the witch brigade had treated it as if she were top of her class at Harvard or Yale, instead of right smack in the middle of the one hundred and twenty-two graduating seniors of Willow Root High. Like, literally, her ranking was sixty-one. And that didn't typically land you on the college track. But that was okay, because every harebrained scheme Delia tried was a sign of her brilliant (!) entrepreneurial (!) spirit (!) and was insanely celebrated, despite each venture's repetitive lack of success.

But this one was going to be different. She could feel it.

"Delia, this will be your best year ever. I just know it," Grandma Maddie said, cutting into the soft, gooey confection with a plastic knife and then smooshing it onto a paper plate.

"Better late than never. Right?" Delia said.

Aunt Aurora kissed her on the cheek. "There's nothing wrong with being a late bloomer."

"You didn't get your training bra until you were thirteen," Aunt Thea added unhelpfully, squeezing herself between Max and Luc on the sofa.

"I wonder," Aunt Andi said. "In regard to training bras..."

Oh, dear Lord. "Aunt Andi, let's not—"

"What is it we were supposed to be training our breasts to do?" Andi continued.

Aurora stuck her chest out. "These babies are highly trained."

"Honey, those tits are retired," Andi said.

"Retired from what, though? That's the question."

"Pictionary!" Delia hollered. Because it was definitely time to change the subject. "Let's team up."

"I was enjoying the titty talk," Luc whispered.

"Shh," Max said, shaking his head. "Shame on you."

He looked at his watch again. It was kind of becoming a habit, but even though he was having a good time—or maybe *because* he was having a good time—the evening was exhausting. It was hard to feel good about being a spy in his gracious hostesses' home.

What was he even doing here? Nobody was breaking any hexes. That much was clear.

"Here we go," Delia said, dropping the Pictionary box on the table and blowing off the dust. "We obviously haven't played it in a while."

Thea lifted the lid. "The twins can't be on the same team."

"Why not?" Andi and Aurora asked simultaneously.

"Because y'all cheat."

Curse-laden denials erupted in a chorus of indignation.

Maddie poked him in the ribs. "They don't technically cheat," she said, nodding at Andi and Aurora. "They just have weird twin energy and can read each other's minds."

"That's why they need to be separated," Thea said.

"We don't do a weird twin thing," Andi protested.

"We're just exceptionally skilled artists," Aurora added.

"Ha!" Fiona said. "One of you draws a squiggly line and the other shouts *baguette!* or *convection oven!* and it's always right. Meanwhile, I'm over here stuck with Delia screaming *jack-in-the-box!* when I've expertly sketched a drawbridge."

"Hey!" Delia said. "That was last year, and you need to get over it. Also, that did not look like a drawbridge."

"Fiona, you're with Andi," Maddie said.

"Fine," Delia's mom said. "But only one or two rounds. I'm leaving for a Realtors' conference in Austin early in the morning."

"Just one or two rounds," Grandma Maddie repeated. "Thea, you're with Aurora. Amy and Delia make a team, obviously. And we'll let Max and Luc be together. That's four teams, which is perfect."

"What about you, Grandma?" Delia asked.

"I'm here to break up the fights."

The twin aunts drained their glasses, licked chocolate off their forks, and stared each other down. The rules were briefly explained. Along with Delia, Thea, and Amy, Max would draw whatever the little card told him to, and hopefully, Luc would be the first to guess correctly.

"Y'all ready?" Delia asked. "The first subject is in the *difficult* category."

It figured. Nervously, Max picked up his tiny pencil, and Delia passed him the card. He shielded it with his hands while taking a quick peek and then smiled confidently, tingling with anticipation. Because this was going to be easy.

As soon as the tiny hourglass was flipped, he frantically began to draw a hangman stick figure, complete with *X*s for eyes and a lolling tongue.

"Dead man!" Luc shouted. "Hanging man! Murder!"

Max nodded enthusiastically, noticing that everyone else had stopped drawing, probably because he was doing such a bang-up job. How could they compete?

"Watch the gesturing," Maddie warned.

"Sorry."

This was definitely more fun than a Dumb Supper, which was a ritualistic meal where all participants ate in total silence while waiting for a dead ancestor to show up. Max insisted on Dumb Suppers for his own birthday celebrations, because he preferred silence to awkward conversation, which was the only kind of conversation his parents knew how to have.

He quickly added squiggly lines coming out of the stick figure's torso, and then he scrawled out a seven-day calendar, coloring in the square that stood for the sixth day—

"Black Friday!" Luc yelled.

Max threw the pencil down. "Yes!"

As he high-fived Luc, he glanced at the other drawings and realized that clearly, Black Friday in the Stray Lands did not refer to the capture, torture, and disembowelment of Symon Shevenko by Anglican witch hunters.

Maybe Pictionary wasn't such a great idea.

What if they did something a little quieter and calmer as they approached the countdown to midnight? He tapped Delia on the shoulder, and she looked up at him with a bit of chocolate on her lower lip.

"Would you like to head over to the manor to talk more about the staging?" he asked, hoping he sounded casual and light and not at all like someone who wanted to lick chocolate off Delia's lower lip. "I was thinking we might go ahead and include the kitchen and dining room."

Her eyes lit up. "Of course! Let me grab my stuff."

CHAPTER FIFTEEN

As Delia followed Max around Hartwell's pool toward the French doors on the patio, she had to admit she was a tad disappointed that Luc and Amy had tagged along. And that was stupid, because Luc was freaking staying at the manor, and it wasn't like Max had invited Delia over for a glass of wine. He'd simply invited her to go through the staging plans, which made perfect sense with an open house coming up soon.

"Here we are," Max said, standing at the door.

"Yes," Delia said. "Here we are. All four of us. Ready to go in and talk about staging."

"I don't want to talk about staging," Amy said. "I just hate Pictionary." She poked Luc in the shoulder. "What kind of tequila do y'all keep in the house?"

"I don't know if we keep *any* tequila in the house," Luc said. And then he looked at Max. "Do we?"

Max laughed, reaching for the doorknob. "We're hardly party central over here."

A blast of extremely loud music smacked them all in the face when the door was opened. Max covered his ears, and Delia stared at the scene in front of them, which consisted of a random man, line dancing (alone), in the living room of Halifax Manor.

She looked at Max and Luc, both of whom were shaking their heads.

"Who is that?" Amy asked, just as the dancing cowboy turned around.

"Oh my goodness. It's Nikki!" Delia said. "We should have invited him to dinner."

Nikki, seemingly as startled by their appearance as they were by his, quickly killed the music. And then he stood there, red-faced and flustered, in his full cowboy getup (ten-gallon hat, pointy-toed boots, and belt buckle the size of Texas), shuffling from foot to foot. "I'm so sorry," he said. "I wasn't expecting you home this early, and with company, at that."

"Clearly," Luc said, not even remotely attempting to hide the humor in his voice.

Someone needed to rush in and save Nikki, who looked like he was going to literally wither away from embarrassment. "Who doesn't love to crank the music up and dance like nobody's watching when nobody's actually watching?" Delia said. "We've all done it. And honestly, Nikki, you were doing it pretty well."

Nikki grinned. "I do think I'm getting the hang of it."

Max cleared his throat. "Is that Uncle Hartwell's hat?"

Nikki nodded, looking just as silly in the hat as Hartwell had. Grandma Maddie used to tease Hartwell about how you could always tell a real Texan by the way he wore his hat.

Amy walked right on over to Nikki and eyed him up and down, which was rude, even for Amy.

"This is our cousin Nikki," Max said.

"So many nephews," Amy said. "And we've never met any of you before now."

"Amy!" Delia said, absolutely aghast at her friend's manners.

Amy looked at Delia and shrugged. "It's true."

Luc cleared his throat and stepped in between Amy and Nikki. "You know, I've always wanted to learn to line dance."

Delia said a quick prayer to Whoever Was in Charge of Awkward Moments and gave Luc what she hoped was a grateful smile. "It's easy. Let's all do it. It'll be fun!"

"Fine. Whatever," Amy said.

Delia grabbed Max's arm. "Come on, cowboy."

"Oh no. I don't think so—"

"It's a law in Texas," Delia said. "If a line forms, you have to jump in." She pointed at Luc, Amy, and Nikki. "And we're forming a line, so..."

Max seemed to dig in his heels. "I do not think that's a law."

Amy grabbed his other arm, and before Max could protest in earnest, they pulled him into the center of the room, squeezing him in between the two of them.

Nikki turned the music back on, and everyone started moving. Luc was struggling to follow along, but he seemed hell-bent on picking it up. Max, however, was barely shuffling his feet.

That was unacceptable, so Delia gave him a poke and a little shove when it was time to scoot to the left. Max rolled his eyes, but he did, indeed, start scooting. And then he turned (the wrong way, but hey, he did it on the beat), gave a kick, clapped his hands, and slid to the right with everyone else.

"You've got it, Max," Nikki hollered.

Max's cheeks had gone crimson, but a hint of a grin tugged at his lips.

"There you go," Delia said, yanking him to the right. "Now two steps to the left..."

Max fell in sync, and his grin turned into a smile. Those little laugh lines around his eyes were incredibly sexy, and since Max was such a serious sort, Delia bet they were also pretty rare. When his eyes locked on hers and his smile deepened, it felt as if it was just for her. But then Amy bumped into Max, and he bumped into Delia, and the domino effect took over with Luc and Nikki. Max started to laugh, and the deep, melodious sound of it seeped into Delia's very bones, tickling her rib cage until she was laughing, too.

"Come on," Max said, grabbing her hand. "You can't stop now. Not when I'm getting so good at this."

The unruly lock of hair had found its way back over his left eye, and the right one gave her a little wink, which set a herd of butterflies loose in her tummy and made her heart flutter in her chest like it was literally trying to escape.

Delia's cheeks were pink. Her breasts were heaving. Her hips swayed, and oh…yeah…that little hip thrust. Max liked that. In fact, he liked it so much that he once again lost his footing while dancing and just finished the song while basically flopping around like a fish out of water.

Delia patted him on the shoulder. "You did great."

"Really? Because I feel like a slow learner when it comes to dancing."

"You are a slow learner," Luc said. "Delia is being nice. Also, I might add, she's showing some favoritism."

"Are you begging for praise?" Max asked. "Because that's pathetic."

Luc grinned and shrugged.

"You did great, too," Delia said, rubbing his arm. "You boys must have dancing in your genes."

They did not, in fact, have dancing in their genes, but they grinned stupidly anyway. At least, Luc was grinning stupidly. Max figured his face was probably doing something similar.

Delia turned her attention back to him. "Max, you seriously did so well that I think we can tackle the two-step next. That'll make you a real Texan."

Even though he doubted there was anything in the entire world that would make him a so-called real Texan, the idea of being pressed up against Delia for a few minutes was very appealing. However, it wasn't a great idea, considering he was a Halifax and she was a Merriweather, and he was basically here to make sure they never regained their magic, which made him feel like a bad guy, even though he wasn't.

He hadn't hexed the Merriweathers. He wasn't responsible for what his ancestors had done.

And Delia isn't responsible for what hers did, either.

"Let's not forget our mission," he said. "Color schemes. Measuring. That sort of thing."

Luc shook his head. "This is why nobody likes you."

"It's probably just one of the reasons," Amy said. "But who cares? I'm still wondering where y'all keep the tequila."

"We keep it in the liquor cabinet, like normal people," Nikki said. "Who's up for margaritas?"

"You're going to make margaritas?" Luc asked. "Can I watch?"

"Sure," Nikki said. "Although I'm warning you. I've never used the blender before."

"This sounds disastrous," Max said.

Delia linked her arm through his like it was the most natural thing in the world. "Amy," she said. "Why don't you go help with the margaritas?"

"I sure hope you're not trying to get rid of me," Amy said. "Because—"

"Go away," Delia said. "You're a distraction for my student."

"Message received," Amy said, turning to make her exit. "With disapproval though," she added over her shoulder.

Holy hell, he'd never felt so conflicted in his life. He shouldn't flirt and dance with Delia. For one thing, he didn't know how to do either of those, and for another, it just seemed like it wasn't a decent thing to do, under the circumstances.

"You ready?" Delia asked. "We're going old-school with George Strait. This one is easy to learn on."

"I'm not really sure if we should—"

"Take off that stuffy blazer, cowboy," Delia said with a wink.

Max removed the blazer with the speed of lightning, which embarrassed the part of his brain that was still functioning.

"Whew! You worked up a sweat line dancing, didn't you?"

Actually, no. It wasn't the exertion that had sweat dripping down his back. Delia just seemed to have his entire body in some sort of uproar.

"Well, don't worry," Delia said. "This is going to be a slow, calming activity."

Max doubted that immensely.

The sound of a fiddle floated through the air, and Delia turned to face him. She put her left hand on his right shoulder and then laced the fingers of her other hand through his. "Now, then. Put your right hand on the small of my back."

He did, and then, without thinking, and as if it were the most natural thing in the world, he pulled her close against him.

"Whoa," Delia said, putting a bit of distance between them. "Let's save some room for Jesus."

"Sorry."

Delia smiled. "No worries. You've never done this before, so how would you know how to do it?"

"Lead the way, Miss Merriweather."

"Actually, you're supposed to lead, but we'll get to that in a minute."

That was too bad. Because right now he'd follow her anywhere.

CHAPTER SIXTEEN

The way Max pulled her against his hard, hot body had Delia very much wanting to abandon one of her dancing tenets, which was that you didn't let anyone properly feel you up until at least the second or third dance.

Had he done it on purpose? Did he want her pressed up against him as much as she wanted to be? Or was it just him not knowing what to do?

He looked down at her, his hazel eyes simmering behind the rogue lock of dark hair, and said, "I think I like this better than line dancing."

"We haven't actually started yet."

Liar, liar, pants on fire. Something has definitely started.

"Okay. What do we do first?"

"This will be easy," she said, hoping it was true. Because it was actually going to take some concentration and restraint on her part. "It's basically two quick steps, followed by two slow steps. Like this."

She started counting steps while moving accordingly, and Max immediately lowered his gaze to stare at their feet. "No, no," she said. "You always look at your partner's eyes. Your feet will be fine without your attention."

"That might be hard. I'm a bit of a perfectionist, I'm afraid."

"There's no perfection expected here," Delia said. "Just have fun."

Good Lord. How were these loose, casual words pouring out of her mouth when her insides were practically on fire?

Max stared into her eyes with an adorable amount of concentration, and she somehow lost count...while counting to two. "Oops," she said, fumbling her way right onto Max's toes. "Just who's teaching who here?"

Max steadied her and laughed. "I actually think I've got it. You're right. It's not that difficult."

He leaned over and began counting softly in her ear, and if honey and velvet had a baby, it would be Max's voice. Goose bumps broke out on every inch of her skin as she shivered delightfully.

Max was now leading, smooth as silk, and Delia forgot all about leaving room for Jesus. She pressed her cheek against his chest, and his hand inched just a tad lower, past the small of her back, which technically wasn't the proper placement, but now wasn't the time to criticize form. In fact, if he wanted to let that hand slip even a little lower, she wouldn't complain.

"How am I doing?" Max asked.

"Oh, you are doing just fine," Delia said, hoping she didn't sound as hungry and breathless as she felt. Because she was not going to make out with Max Halifax. Even though it *was* her birthday, and God knew she sure as heck deserved some fun, it simply wouldn't be professional. But dancing? And maybe a little flirting? There were no rules against that.

The blender started up in the background, but Delia barely heard it. Somehow, the world had shrunk to just her and Max.

"I'm going to have to get your butt to a honky-tonk before you leave," she said. "With a little practice, you'll be able to spin me around the floor."

"I don't know about that. Slow dancing is more my speed."

Delia brought both of her arms up to wrap around Max's neck, and they stopped two-stepping and started swaying gently back and forth, like two hot and bothered kids on the gym floor during prom.

The song ended, but Max pulled her even closer. "One more?"

"Maybe even two," Delia said, letting her eyes drift to his lips.

With comedic timing, the margarita crew crashed their party. "Are we interrupting anything?" Luc asked with a smirk.

"We were just dancing," Delia said, letting go of Max and yanking her dress down. The dang thing had ridden up when she'd had her arms around Max's neck.

Amy narrowed her eyes. "It's the *just* that gives it away."

Max's face turned all sorts of interesting shades of pink. "Delia was teaching me how to two-step."

"That wasn't the two-step," Amy said. "That was a one-step, as in, one step away from some lips connecting."

Nikki handed Delia a margarita with a knowing smile. "You look like you could cool off a little."

"Nikki, where did you get these obnoxious glasses?" Max asked, taking the margarita by its cactus-shaped stem and hoping the icy drink would cool him down.

"None of your business," Nikki said.

Not only was it Max's business, but it was probably his credit card. It seemed that for every box he packed up, Amazon delivered another one. Uncle Hartwell had clearly indulged Nikki's retail hobby, probably out of guilt. And Max couldn't exactly blame him.

The more he got to know Nikki, the more he realized just how limited the poor imp's world was.

How would it feel to literally never go anywhere other than this house or the shop? Well, Nikki did roam about as a cat, but it seemed the only place he ever went was the Merriweather house next door.

Max had to figure out how to break the spell on Nikki.

Delia took another healthy sip out of her cactus glass and choked. "That's got quite the kick," she sputtered.

Max patted her firmly between her shoulder blades as a loud *beep!* came from the kitchen.

"That's the microwave," Nikki said. "We're making some queso. It was Hartwell's favorite indulgence."

"I'll grab the chips," Luc said. "Come on, Amy."

Amy rolled her eyes. "I guess I'll pretend the two of you are helpless and can't handle some plates." Then she bowed dramatically and added, "I shall get the plates."

Max felt his cheeks heating up again. Having an audience for his and Delia's...whatever this was...was humiliating.

"This is turning into birthday bash number two," Delia said. "Although, really, we should be talking about the staging."

Ah, yes. The staging. "We'll move the furniture out of this room soon. I think I'll take it all down to the shop and see if maybe we can sell it."

"That would be great," Delia said. "And I might even buy some of the smaller things for my business."

"It's yours," Max said. "Take whatever you want. And I absolutely refuse payment."

"Oh, I couldn't possibly—"

"Hartwell would want you to have it."

He knew that was true. He could practically *feel* Uncle Hartwell's wishes in that regard, which was silly, because he wasn't sentimental, and he definitely didn't believe in ghosts. But he knew, without a doubt, that Delia was welcome to any and all of it.

"Oh, and don't forget the chipped teapot," he added. "It's yours, after all."

Delia's eyes had gone misty. "Thank you," she whispered.

"You're welcome," he said, quickly taking a peek at his watch, so his own eyes wouldn't do something dreadful, like leak.

"Should we leave?" Delia asked suddenly. "Because either you're dying to get to bed or you've got a nervous tic. You keep looking at your watch."

Luc came out and set a basket of chips on the coffee table. "Max is the human embodiment of a nervous tic."

Max crossed his arms. "I am not. And I'm sorry for checking the time. It's a habit, I guess. But I'm absolutely not ready to call it a night. You can't go to bed before midnight on your birthday."

"Delia's thirty now," Amy said. "She should have been in bed two hours ago."

"We'll see how long these jokes last with you turning thirty next month," Delia said to Amy with a grin. "And, Luc, you should have seen your brother two-step. Nothing nervous about it."

"I saw part of it," Luc said, dipping a Texas-shaped tortilla chip into a thick, yellow, cheesy sauce before cramming the entire thing into his mouth. "It made me uncomfortable."

"It made us all uncomfortable," Amy added. Then she downed at least half her margarita and shuddered. "Brain freeze."

Nikki sat on the couch next to Amy, and the puppy jumped up and put its little paws on his leg. Nikki recoiled comically, and Amy narrowed her eyes. "You have a problem with dogs?"

"Several," Nikki said.

"Have you had an incident?" Delia asked. "Like, did a dog bite you when you were a kid or something?"

"Or something," Nikki said.

Max needed to steer the conversation in another direction, because of course Nikki didn't like dogs. He'd probably been chased up trees by them. "I honestly don't know how you all are stuffing your faces with more food. I couldn't eat another bite after Maddie's delicious world-famous lasagna."

"If you think that was good, you should have been over a few nights ago for our fabulous Blue Moon Non-Baby Vegetable Soup," Delia said. "Because it might give the lasagna a run for its money, if I do say so myself."

"Did you say non-baby?" Luc asked, chuckling softly. "Like, do you have to go out of your way to make soup without a baby in it?"

Delia raised an eyebrow. "Laugh all you want, because I know it's hilarious. And also, it's not really soup," she added with her eyes twinkling like fireflies.

Those eyes did a number on Max. "Oh?"

"It's a potion," she whispered dramatically.

That perked his ears up.

"I don't know why I whispered that," Delia added. "God knows my family will tell anyone who'll listen."

"I'm all ears," Luc said, smiling casually and glancing at Max. "Tell us about this potion."

"You asked for it," Delia said. "So, during every blue moon, we try to break the so-called hex that was placed on our family."

Max nearly dropped his margarita.

"And how do you do that?" Luc asked, a little too quickly. "Is there a, um…"

Max scooted to the edge of his seat and finished his brother's question. "Recipe?"

"Oh, heck yes, there's a recipe. It's part of the so-called Blue Moon Spell on page thirty-two."

Max sure hoped his face wasn't mirroring Luc's, because Luc's mouth looked like a train tunnel. He cleared his throat. "You have a book of spells? Wherever did you find such a thing?"

"Oh, the library, of course," Delia said, rolling her eyes as if it were a joke.

Max relaxed. There was no way in hell that the book of keys had been sitting on a shelf in the Willow Root Public Library. It was probably some kind of silly, harmless book written by a stray or a charlatan that the Merriweathers had innocently come across—

"Somebody left a note on our doorstep conveniently telling us exactly where to find it," Delia said.

Or not.

"Do you know who?" Luc asked, apparently finding his voice again.

A funny, squirmy, uncomfortable feeling wormed its way into Max's gut, and he and Luc looked at each other.

Could it have been Hartwell?

"Of course not," Delia said. "And it doesn't really matter. It was a just stupid prank, played by stupid people who think they're funny and clever."

Max could totally see someone pulling a prank on the Merriweathers. Maybe they'd taken a cookbook and created a silly new cover.

"What's the title of this book?" Luc asked. "And can we see it?"

"It was probably something obvious like *Magic Spell Book*," Max said. "Am I right?"

"I can't even remember the title," Delia said. "It's engraved into a nasty old cover, and it's not in English."

Uh-oh.

"Grandma Maddie says it's Latin, although it could be *pig* Latin for all I know."

Clavis Hexicus. Definitely not pig Latin.

"And you...consume this potion?" Luc asked.

"Oh, you better believe it. And I have to admit, it's some pretty decent soup."

The original hex had called for a blood sacrifice. The key to unlocking it would require something equally dire. Whatever you'd end up with after concocting the potion, nobody in their right mind would call it soup.

CHAPTER SEVENTEEN

Maybe she'd said too much. Because it seemed she'd finally crossed the threshold into freaking Max and Luc out. Why had she mentioned the stupid soup?

The puppy whined and started to squat in a very threatening way, right there on the nice rug.

"No!" Delia said, lunging for the little rascal.

And dear Lord, she shouldn't have lunged. Because her back had been a bit wonky ever since moving that furniture for the open house, and now it was seized up. "Oh shit," she said, wincing.

"Are you okay?" Max asked.

"No," Delia said. "Not really. Can somebody put the puppy out before he piddles on the rug?"

"Too late," Amy said. Delia opened one eye to see that yes, it was, indeed, too late.

Nikki hopped up. "I'll go grab a towel."

"What's wrong?" Max asked. "Are you in pain?"

"It's my back," she wheezed. "It seizes sometimes. Like a spasm. It's an old cheerleading injury."

Amy grabbed a pillow and stuffed it behind Delia before gingerly assisting her in sitting up. "You were *not* a cheerleader. That's embellishment to the nth degree."

Delia let out a huge breath, forced herself to relax, and raised an eyebrow at Amy. "I did some cheers in my day."

"We were members of the pep squad," Amy said to the men. "We had shitty little pom-poms that were not even a quarter the size of real pom-poms—"

"Speak for yourself," Delia said. "I was pep captain, and I had a big set."

Amy snorted. "Yeah, yeah. You were the envy of us all. But your so-called athletic injury was sustained while—"

"Okay, okay. Enough. Nobody needs to hear how I tripped over my shoelace and fell down the bleacher steps."

"It was the best cartwheel you ever did," Amy said, touching her margarita glass to Delia's.

"It was the only cartwheel I ever did."

"That sounds terribly painful," Luc said.

"Is there anything we can do to help?" Max asked.

Amy drained her margarita and set the glass on the table. "Help me get the old girl up. I'll take her home and put her to bed, and she'll be just dandy in the morning."

Nikki came back in with a towel and started dabbing at the spot on the rug. "Calling it a night so soon? On Delia's birthday?"

There was something about Nikki that gave Delia the impression he was a bit lonely. "I wish you had come to dinner, Nikki. Shame on your cousins for leaving you behind."

"Oh, it's quite all right," Nikki said. "I'm kind of a homebody."

"Well, next time I'm going to insist that you join us. As for tonight, once my back pulls this trick, it's usually time for some rest and a heating pad. And thanks for cleaning that up. I'm rather horrified. We're terrible guests."

"Don't be silly," Nikki said. "You're delightful guests. And I wonder if the hot tub might be good for your back?"

Actually, Hartwell's hot tub had been her go-to for back therapy for years. She was slightly suspicious it was the reason he installed the thing. "That is so nice of you to offer. But I'd hate to keep y'all up any later than I already have."

Luc sat up, looking particularly interested. "I've been dying to try the hot tub ever since I got here."

Delia looked at Max (caught him glancing at his watch again) and was surprised when he said, "Me too. Let's do it."

"We'll have to go change into our swimsuits," Delia said. "If you're absolutely certain you don't mind, that is."

Max gave her a perfectly wicked grin that assured her he didn't mind seeing her in a swimsuit one little bit. "Sounds perfect. And we'll do the same."

The guys helped her up, and then she very carefully followed Amy to the backyard, where the wispy clouds floating across the face of the moon created shadows that danced around like drunken party girls.

"Oh, no," Delia said, looking at the glowing windows of their house next door. "They're all still awake."

If she went over there to change, she'd come back with an entourage of old ladies in bathing suits.

Amy shrugged and began peeling off clothes. "I'm just getting in the tub in my underwear."

Delia chewed on her lip, noting that Amy was sheathed in the confident body armor that only drunk girl energy could provide. Unfortunately, Delia was not.

"Seriously?" Amy said, reading the situation correctly. "It's dark, and we'll leave the tub lights off."

Delia winced as the muscle in her lower back spasmed. Trying to squirm into a swimsuit would be difficult, and the hot tub was literally right in front of her.

Amy started the jets up. "Come on," she said. "This will make you feel better."

Delia's bra and panties were about as modest as the bikini she'd bought over the summer. Which was to say not modest at all, but one was deemed suitable for public and one wasn't, and for no reason that made any sense. It was silly to feel weird about it. Especially since she'd gone skinny-dipping in Willow Pond at least a million times in her youth. "Okay," she said, slipping the little dress over her head before she lost her nerve.

Amy held her glass up. "Huzzah!"

Delia tried to kick her left boot off—no way she could bend over and wrench it loose—but it was too tight. "I can't believe I'm doing this," she said. "I'm a professional interior decorator, at a client's house, and I should probably look and act like a professional."

She tried to give the boot another kick, but just as she lifted her foot, something warm and fuzzy tickled the back of her knee. She startled, but before she recognized that it was just the cat, she lost her balance.

No, no, no... Her arms went into useless windmill mode as she fell backward onto a chaise lounge, landing with a soft thud.

"You're really nailing the professionalism," Amy said, giving a thumbs-up. "I mean, seriously. Doing great."

Delia opened her mouth to make a snarky comment, but she couldn't think of one, and when she took a deep breath, her back seized up again.

"Uh-oh," Amy said, rushing over. "Do you need help?"

The last thing Delia needed was a drunk girl trying to help her up. "Don't touch me. I've got it."

Only she didn't, because she couldn't sit up.

New plan: she lived here now. Right here on this chaise lounge.

"Should I get help?" Amy asked.

Delia did *not* want Amy to get help. She was going to get up by herself, and she was going to do it before Max, Luc, and Nikki came out.

"Blink once for yes and twice for no," Amy said. "Or maybe it's the other way around. Once for no and twice for yes. Honestly, the fact that I already can't keep it straight doesn't bode well for our communication going forward."

"I can do this. Just give me a minute."

"Okay. Try not to think about how three super-hot guys will be coming out the door any moment now."

The cat jumped onto the chaise next to Delia's face, whiskers twitching. "This is your fault," she said, and it nuzzled her chin before scurrying off.

Max sat on Hartwell's bed watching Luc pace back and forth. "Do you really think Uncle Hartwell found the book?"

"He was literally famous for finding impossible-to-find magical objects," Luc said. "Books, in particular. If anybody could have gotten their hands on *Clavis Hexicus*, it would have been him."

Luc was right. Hell, there was even a framed picture of Uncle Hartwell hanging in Shadowlark's Museum of Heroic Feats, and in it, he was holding the only known copy of *Vacate Et Scire*, the spell book of Merlin, himself. It had been hidden in a tunnel beneath the ruins of Tintagel Castle, protected by nine hexes and eleven spells, all of which Hartwell had broken.

Hartwell should have been hailed a hero and rested on his laurels, retiring to a life of luxury in Shadowlark. Instead, he'd chosen to come to the Stray Lands to watch over a baby born beneath a blue moon. Why?

Max got up and wandered to the window. He'd always imagined his uncle standing right here, in this very room, looking out this very window, bitter and lonely. But it seemed nothing could have been farther from the truth.

Had Hartwell diced tomatoes in the Merriweathers' kitchen while music blared and pots overflowed? Had he played games in the parlor? Had he oiled a squeaky hinge on occasion in Maddie's overgrown garden?

Max suspected he had. He *hoped* that he had.

"Uncle Hartwell found the book," he said. "I'm certain of it."

Luc joined him at the window. "Okay, let's say he had the book. Why would he give it to the Merriweathers?"

"I can only assume he was hoping Delia would break the hex."

Luc's eyes grew wide and round. "But—"

"Treason of the highest order," Max said. "He went against the Concilium."

Laughter came from the doorway, where Nikki had been standing for who knew how long. "Treason of the highest order," he mimicked.

Max glared at Nikki. "It's not funny."

"Sorry," Nikki said. "But you Logos witches take yourselves so seriously."

Max's blood started to boil. No matter what Nikki said, it *was* treason of the highest order. It was awful. It was embarrassing.

"Listen, Luc," he said, ignoring Nikki. "It doesn't matter. What we have to focus on now, at this moment, is fulfilling *our* mission. We stick with Delia until midnight."

"Yes, yes," Nikki said with an impish grin. "By all means, continue with your important duties, which, so far, have consisted of margaritas and dirty dancing. Tell me, how do you handle the huge responsibility that has been placed upon your shoulders? And should I warm up some more queso?"

Max rolled his eyes. But Nikki was kind of right. This whole thing was ridiculous. Even if the Merriweathers had the book (and he was pretty sure they did), Delia clearly didn't know how to break the hex. Hell, she didn't even believe in it.

"I don't suppose you have any swim trunks we could borrow?" Luc asked.

"Sorry. They don't make them for cats."

"Oh. Right. What was I thinking?"

"Can't you two just conjure up some trunks?" Nikki asked with a smirk.

"Conjuring is Big Magic, and way overkill for swim trunks," Max said. "And besides, we don't have time for it."

"Well, in that case," Nikki said with a huge smile, "feel free to borrow some of Hartwell's. They're in the bottom drawer."

Max opened the bottom drawer and dug past socks and handkerchiefs and other old-man oddities like suspenders until he found—

"Oh no," Luc whispered.

Max looked at Nikki. "Did he have anything else?"

"No," Nikki said. "I'll leave you two alone so you can don your important battle gear."

CHAPTER EIGHTEEN

Oh, dear Lord, the patio door opened, and Delia was still flat on her back on a chaise lounge wearing only her underwear and a pair of cowboy boots. Amy had made several attempts at getting her up, but Delia's back was spasmed into a knot, and knowing that the guys were going to appear at any moment hadn't done a dang thing to release the tension.

Luc peered down at her. "I'd say you're feeling no better?"

"Oh my God," Amy said, bug-eyed. "What are you guys wearing?"

Delia glanced below Luc's waist and stifled a laugh, despite her pain.

"It's all Hartwell had," Max said, stepping next to his brother and right into Delia's line of sight. And oh boy. She'd never thought it possible for a man to do a Speedo justice, because in her opinion, Speedos didn't *deserve* justice, but here Max was, stepping up to the plate. The man knew how to deliver.

"Are you okay, Delia?" Max asked.

For a moment there she'd forgotten all about her back. "I fell when the cat startled me. And now I'm afraid I can't move."

This was absolutely mortifying.

"It's just a spasm," she added through gritted teeth. "I'll be fine in a few minutes. Y'all just go on about your business."

They did not go on about their business. In fact, Max and Luc crossed their arms and commenced to proper staring, as if she were a five-thousand-piece puzzle that needed to be solved, and all the pieces were the same color. Amy, for her part, took a swig of her margarita, causing an icy, cold drop of condensation to slip off the glass and land right between Delia's boobs.

Delia sighed heavily. "This is the worst birthday ever."

"No, it's not," Amy said. "Remember your tenth birthday, when your aunties sent everyone home with cemetery dirt tied up in little handkerchiefs instead of goody bags?"

"They did what now?" Max asked.

Delia rolled her eyes. "They thought it would bring good luck or something," she said. "Goodness, y'all know my family is nuts."

"It started a satanic panic down at the Baptist church," Amy said. "They convinced the mayor to cancel trick-or-treating that year. Totally sucked."

"There are several old ladies still spitting over their shoulders when they see me," Delia said.

"Oh, Delia, they've always done that," Amy said.

"Amy," Max said. "Pull her boots off. I'm going to carry her to the hot tub."

"I don't know about that," Delia said. "For one thing, I'm probably a bit heavier than I look."

Actually, that wasn't true. She was probably exactly as heavy as she looked, and it typically didn't bother her one bit, because she loved her curves. But having Max throw *his* back out while in the process of trying to hoist Delia into a therapeutic hot tub wasn't how she ever wanted to hot-tub with Max.

Max smiled confidently. "Pretty sure I can handle it," he said, bending over and gently sliding his arms underneath her as Amy yanked the boots off. "Wrap your arms around my neck."

She'd already had her arms around Max's neck once tonight and was more than happy to do it again, although she was suddenly very conscious of the fact that she was in her underwear. But come to think of it, she was wearing more than Max.

"You shouldn't bend over like that. Use your legs."

"I've got this," Max said.

Delia held her breath and tried very hard not to be deadweight while Max slowly straightened. It was a relatively painless process, and he pulled it off with nothing more than an adorable manly grunt.

He smiled at her, as if to prove it was no big deal, and walked to the hot tub. Despite the warmth of his skin, she was hit with a small shiver.

"You've gotten chilled. You should have sent Amy in for help," he said, frowning.

It wasn't the night air making her shiver. It was Max. He was broad and firm and solid and all of the things most men who wore Speedos never were, and she was enjoying the feel of him, muscle spasm or no.

"Here we are," Max said. "Let's get you in front of a strong jet. You need that knot pounded out."

Boy, did she ever.

Max managed to set Delia down without dropping her, and then he sat down, sucking air through his teeth as the hot water frothed against the sensitive skin of his abdomen.

"These jets are hitting the spot," Delia said, easing her head back and closing her eyes. Then she blindly held out a hand. "Drink."

"You didn't bring your margarita out," Amy said. "But I'm still dry. I'll go get it."

"Maybe Nikki can bring it when he comes out," Delia said.

"He won't be joining us," Luc said, getting in the tub with a splash. "He doesn't do water."

"So, that's dogs and water he doesn't get along with," Amy said. "I'll go in. I need to freshen my drink anyway."

As Amy walked away, Nikki slinked out of the shadows. He sat next to the tub and dipped a paw in. Then he shook it, sending droplets right into Max's eyes.

"Shoo," Max said.

Nikki didn't shoo. Instead, he slowly turned—tail in the air—until Max was staring at a puckered, pink asshole. It felt intentional, so Max splashed Nikki, who then turned on him and hissed.

"What are you planning to do with the cat when you sell the house?"

That was the question, wasn't it? "I'm not sure," Max said. "We'll figure something out."

Nikki suddenly produced an eerie, low growl. For a moment, Max thought Nikki was growling at *him*. But the cat was looking at the puppy, who was headed their way at a drunken trot.

"I'll go stick him in the laundry room," Luc said, climbing out of the hot tub and wrapping a towel around his waist. "And maybe I'll help Amy whip up another blender of margaritas while I'm at it."

He took the little dog into the house, leaving Max and Delia alone in the hot tub. Max cleared his throat. "I enjoyed dinner with your family. Thanks for inviting us."

"Well, thank you for being such a good sport."

Max waved a hand. "I mean it. I enjoyed having dinner with them. You have no idea how lucky you are to be surrounded by such an adoring family."

"What about your family? Are you guys close?"

Max made a derisive little sound through his nose. "My mother and father don't live together. Our family is nothing like yours."

"Oh, I'm sorry they split up."

"It's not what you're thinking." He took a deep breath. "This is probably going to sound weird to you—"

"Max, my family thinks they're a coven of witches. Nothing you can say is going to sound weirder than that."

Max laughed. "You haven't heard it yet."

"Lay it on me."

"My parents never married."

"So? There's nothing wrong with that."

Max wiped a wet hand over his face and through his hair, which was now probably completely out of control. "In my family, relationships are strictly business. They're formed for the purpose of procreation and protecting bloodlines and—"

"I'm sorry. Did you say bloodlines? And procreation?"

His mouth was apparently just as out of control as his hair. Why was he divulging private information? "I know it must sound strange to you."

"Yes, it does. I mean...like arranged marriages?"

"Not marriages. Partnerships."

This was probably incomprehensible to Delia. But after the dancing and the hugging and the skin-to-skin contact, and considering the moon and the stars and the steamy heat of the tub and the way her eyes were locked onto his...

It just seemed some things might need to be said.

"I don't believe in romance," he blurted.

Delia sat up straighter and furrowed her brow. "What do you mean you don't believe in romance? What about love?"

"It's not a very logical emotion, and I don't believe in that, either."

Delia laughed, as if she expected him to join in, but then she stopped. "You're serious, aren't you?"

"Yes."

There. It was out in the open. She had to know this flirting that had been going on between them (if that was what it was) wasn't going to lead to anything more.

"Honestly," she said. "That's kind of a relief."

"Pardon?"

"It's nice to meet someone else who isn't looking for marriage. Good Lord, it's all my friends talk about. Finding the right person to spend the rest of their lives with blah, blah, blah."

"So, you're not...?"

"Looking for a boyfriend." Delia shrugged. "I don't want one. We Merriweather women like to be independent. But back to your family, they sound fascinating. They actually seem stranger than mine, which is really saying something."

"I'm thrilled you find me so interesting," Max said.

"I really do!" Delia said. "So, if you don't mind me asking, who raised you?"

"Our parents shared responsibilities. They live in the same building."

"Well, that's convenient. And you know what? Maybe both of our families are a little off-kilter. But at least they love us, right?"

Max looked down. His family didn't love him in the same way that Delia's loved her. At least, not so demonstrably. When he looked up again, Delia's eyes were closer than ever, and maybe it was the steam or maybe it was the margarita, but they were absolutely *sexier* than ever.

"You know," she whispered. "They think I'm a blue witch."

"And just what is a blue witch?" Max whispered back, curious to hear her definition.

"It has something to do with a birthmark on my ass," she said, with a totally straight face. But then she burst into giggles. "Can you believe it? I mean, all this insanity over a birthmark on my ass."

"What does it look like?"

Was he flirting? He couldn't tell. And from the expression on Delia's face—a grin and a raised eyebrow—she probably couldn't tell, either.

"Well, I can't give a good description, because seeing it takes a trick with two mirrors. Now, what about you?"

"What about me?"

"Tell me something crazy or unique about yourself."

"I already did. My parents—"

"No. About *you*."

Max rested his arm on the edge of the tub. "I can touch my nose with my tongue."

Delia laughed as he demonstrated. "That's a useless skill, and yet I'm mightily impressed."

Max smiled slyly, thinking that it wasn't entirely useless, and then he noticed Delia's cheeks had turned pink, possibly from the steam and heat.

And possibly not.

"And what else?"

"I can speed-read."

"Ooh, nice."

"And I'm good at rhyming."

She laughed. "As in, my name is Max and I'm here to say..."

"I'm a wizard with words. I didn't come to play."

He couldn't keep a straight face, and they both started laughing. "Well, let's just say I'm adequate at rhyming," he added.

"I can't rhyme, but I won a hot-dog-eating contest once."

"How many did you eat?" he asked.

"Not saying."

"Oh, come on. You can't tease a guy like that. How many did you get down?"

"You'll think poorly of me."

"I saw you stuff two eggs in your mouth at the Mourning Glory Café, and it only made me respect you more."

"Eleven."

He raised an eyebrow. "Just eleven? I'm...I mean...I'm trying not to be disappointed."

"I was only nine at the time."

"Okay, well—"

"The trophy is in my room. Maybe I'll show it to you sometime."

Max cleared his throat and ran a wet, shaky hand through his hair. It wasn't every day a girl invited you to her room to show off her hot-dog-eating trophy. "You know, if we were to combine our skill sets, we'd be unstoppable."

Delia laughed. "But unstoppable at what?"

Max shrugged, grinning.

"I think you're pretty remarkable," Delia said. "You're obviously smart. You're well traveled. You're established, so to speak, and just inherited a freaking gorgeous house. And I'm a thirty-year-old woman with a birthmark on her ass who can eat a lot of hot dogs and lives with her grandma."

She had no fucking idea how special she was. She was a blue witch! He was certain of it. Uncle Hartwell had obviously thought so, too.

"Oh, Delia," he whispered. "You are so incredibly special. You have no idea."

"That's what they say," she whispered back.

Her eyes seemed to darken at the same moment that a cloud drifted in front of the moon, and he was helplessly trapped by her gaze, as if she were the moon, and he, an endless ocean at the mercy of its pull. Feelings rushed over him and through him like rolling tides, one wave after another, washing away every shred of dignity and ounce of control…

Delia's eyes dipped down to his lips, and damn it, he was going to kiss her. He knew it as surely as he knew the sun rose in the east and set in the west. It was an undeniable fact.

Delia's eyes reflected the same certainty, and with a mixture of excitement and lust and wonder and…*dread?*…he touched his lips to hers. And oh, they were as warm and full and soft as he'd hoped they'd be. Steam billowed up around them as he tilted her head, urging her mouth open with a questioning brush of his tongue.

She accepted without hesitation, producing the most tantalizing little moan in the process. Her fingers tangled in his wet hair, and then—

"Woot! Margaritas are here!"

They separated with a splash—hearts pounding and gasping for breath—as Amy and Luc made their way back to the hot tub, carrying drinks and wearing smirks. They might not have actually witnessed the kiss—it was dark and the tub's lights hadn't been turned on—but they clearly knew they'd interrupted something. Again.

"Dang," Delia said softly. "Talk about shitty timing."

Was it? Or was it *good* timing? All he knew was that he'd lost himself for a minute. Like completely and totally lost himself. It couldn't be heart magic. Could it?

"Feeling better?" Luc asked Delia, easing himself back into the water.

"Yes, much," Delia said, taking a margarita from Amy and glancing at Max. "Much revived," she added with a wink.

Max could see her pulse pounding at the base of her throat. She'd been just as turned on as he was.

He looked at his watch. In just three minutes, his mission would be accomplished.

"Am I supposed to feel like shit about this?" Luc whispered. "I mean, Uncle Hartwell clearly wanted Delia to break the hex—"

"Shh," Max said. "None of this is up to us. None of this is *because* of us."

"What are you two whispering about over there?" Amy asked, teetering at the edge of the hot tub.

"Come on, Amy," Delia said, offering a hand. "Get in the tub. It feels great."

Amy got in with a splash, nearly upending her drink.

"Careful," Delia said, and then she looked across the patio. "Dang, y'all left the door open. The dog is out again."

Nikki, who'd been contentedly sitting next to a potted plant, was up and hissing. He arched his back, and the puppy, who wasn't too keen on social cues, wagged its stump of a tail and rushed over.

"Uh, we should probably put the puppy back in the house," Max said.

"Oh, I don't know," Luc said. "Let's not, and see what happens."

Nikki took his eyes off the puppy in order to glare at Luc, and the puppy, taking advantage, circled around and wet-nosed Nikki in the ass.

Nikki was weird, but he wasn't *that* weird, and he spun instantly, hissing and clawing at the puppy's twitching nose.

Nikki might not be making it out with his dignity intact, but the puppy was at greater physical risk. Recognizing this, he yelped and backed up until his hind feet flirted with the edge of the tub.

"Oh dear," Delia said. "Amy, grab him!"

Amy grabbed, missed, and the puppy went in with a splash that seemed unnecessarily huge for such a small animal.

Margaritas were upended as everyone grabbed for the dog. Luc and Amy bumped heads and produced a duet of stunning profanity, while Delia splashed around, blindly feeling for the puppy, who was somehow evading her with a frantic figure-eight doggy paddle through the frothing water. Max got his hand around one of the rascal's front legs and pulled him over. The mutt wriggled something terrible as he was lifted out of the water, but Max managed to hand him to Delia, who immediately cradled him against her breast.

Next to the tub, Nikki gloated, tail twitching.

"Bad kitty," Delia said.

Max gathered the empty margarita glasses bobbing in the water and glanced at his watch. Less than a minute to go.

"You've lost your bandage," Delia said, pointing at his finger.

She was right. The tomato-dicing wound was bleeding again.

Delia held out a cocktail napkin. "Take this."

Goddess, she was a sight, sitting there in her underwear with mascara dripping down her cheeks while clutching a wet, shivering puppy. His insides literally felt as if they were melting.

"Thanks," he said, reaching for the napkin. But he wasn't fast enough, and just before he could snag it, a single drop of blood hit the roiling water.

"Max," Luc said. "It's midnight."

CHAPTER NINETEEN

Delia leaned over to pick up Splash (aptly named after last night's hot tub fiasco), who'd been napping beneath her desk in the stockroom. He yawned and snuggled against her chest as she mindlessly rubbed between his little ears.

She'd come to the Crooked Broom to work in peace and quiet—it was closed on Sundays—and she'd lost herself in plans for the manor. How had three hours zoomed by so quickly?

Easy answer: time flies when you're having fun. And Delia was having so much fun with her work that she could barely control herself. Those floor-to-ceiling windows in Hartwell's library! She nearly cackled with glee over what she wanted to do to them.

She couldn't wait to show Max. And that reminded her of the things she still wanted to do to *him*.

Maybe she'd close her eyes and replay last night's kiss. Again.

Her phone chimed with an email before she could even get started. She didn't have notifications set up for her personal email, so it had to be her business account. She checked, and oh! It was from Misty!

Dear Delia,

I talked to Scott, and we've decided there's enough money in the budget for a modest project. I'd love to talk to you about our front porch, entryway, and maybe even the living room.

It's so dated, and now that we've got a toddler, I just don't see how any of our dreams will be accomplished without professional help. Can we meet up?

Misty

Yes! She would love to work some magic on Misty's cookie-cutter house.

She quickly set Splash down and typed a response—How about today?—before leaning back in her chair again, smiling so hard that it made her cheeks hurt. Before long, her mind drifted back to Max and the hot tub. Had it been professional behavior? No. But they were both adults, and it was just a kiss.

Like hell it was.

Her phone chimed again, and this time it was a text from Amy. How are you feeling this morning?

Delia responded that she was feeling freaking awesome, because she was. Like, incredibly, incredibly awesome. Her back was fine. You'd never know she'd tweaked it. And all morning she'd been accosted by one brilliant design idea after another (if she did say so herself, and she did).

She stared at her phone, waiting for Amy to text back. It rang instead.

"Hey, Amy. What's up?"

"That's what I was going to ask you," Amy said. "I left before you last night, and it occurs to me that you might have gotten laid, and I wouldn't even know."

Max's chest popped into Delia's mind, slick and wet from the hot tub. She bit her lip, remembering how the steam had turned his cheeks ruddy. And how his eyes, ringed by damp, dark eyelashes, had lowered to her lips right before—

"Oh, my God. Did you?" Amy asked. "Did you sleep with Max?"

"Not that it's any of your business, but no, I did not. I left right after you. Took Splash home and dried him off."

"Did you say Splash? Because that's perfect. Let's dress him up for Halloween. All he needs is a little top hat, a guitar, and a life preserver."

Okay, so that was actually kind of cute. And maybe if Delia had a puppy on her lap, the neighborhood kids would be less likely to throw eggs at their house on Halloween night.

"Do you want to grab some brunch at the Prickled Pear?" Amy asked. "That's actually why I called."

The thought of a prickly pear mimosa made Delia's mouth water. But she really wanted to keep working. "Can I get a rain check? I'm in my office, and I'm about to start on a new project."

"That sounds fancy and professional. You'd never know you were sitting in a broom closet."

"It's a stockroom."

"Well, have fun working on the Lord's day, you despicable heathen. If you need me, I'll be at the Prickled Pear, sucking down mimosas as God intended."

"Amen," Delia said. "Chat later?"

"You bet."

Delia hung up and cracked her knuckles. Time to get back to work.

"What about this one?" Nikki yelled from behind the counter of the antique shop.

Max didn't even look to see what Nikki was asking about. His string was already dangling from his fingers. Softly, he muttered:

Seal these boxes
Off at Last
With this knot
My spell is cast

He pulled the knot taut and watched the packing tape fly from one box to another, efficiently sealing them up. Then he turned to Nikki, who held a pink dish. "That looks like a candy bowl," he said. "Where did you find it?"

"It was in the pile of undetermined things. Should I go ahead and pack it? I don't think it's hexed."

"How the hell would you know if it was hexed?"

Max hadn't gotten much sleep last night. And the little he had managed to snag was fitful. His dreams had been weird (and erotic), and he'd tossed and turned in agony until the morning sun and a cold shower had finally put him out of his misery.

Nikki just shrugged. "You said it's a candy bowl, and I took you at your word."

"I'm sorry for snapping at you. I'm tired, and also, I just can't shake the feeling that something is...*off.*"

"Oh, I think that's just guilt," Nikki said. "Because after last night, the hex is pretty much sealed. Delia and her family will never get their magic back."

Max pinched the bridge of his nose and counted to ten, so as not to continue snapping at Nikki. And then he said, "I've got nothing to feel guilty about. I didn't hex the Merriweathers."

"Being logical about whether or not you *should* feel guilty doesn't really have much to do with whether or not you *do* feel guilty. It was your family who hexed them, and if Delia had managed to break the hex, you would have had to rehex them. If you're a decent person, you might have some feelings about it, logical, or otherwise."

Max didn't want to examine his feelings too closely. What was the point? But he couldn't stop thinking about that kiss. And his total loss of control. "I'm wondering if it's possible that..."

Nikki came around the counter. "What?"

"Nothing. Never mind."

"Max, what is it? What are you wondering?"

"Do you think that maybe the hex wasn't quite all it was cracked up to be? Like, is there a chance that it didn't work as well as it should have? I know you saw the kiss—"

"Is that what's bothering you?"

"I lost control of myself. And I've *never* lost control of myself before." He swallowed loudly. "It felt almost like magic."

Nikki chuckled. "Magic schmagic. You experienced plain old-fashioned attraction. Accept it. It's nothing to be ashamed of."

Maybe Nikki was right. Only it hadn't felt like mere attraction. Not last night in the hot tub, and not on any occasion prior. Unless, of course, you were going by the scientific definition of attraction, in which case, the object being attracted had no say in the matter and just mindlessly flung itself at the source of the gravitational pull.

"Do you think it's possible that she was, you know...?"

"Leaking magic? No. I don't think so. Not *witchy* magic anyway."

"Well, what about fairy magic? You claim to know about fairies. Could it have made me feel that way?"

"Fairy magic is playful, and it's often humorous. There's almost always a joke of some sort attached to it. And honestly, a Logos witch cross-eyed in bliss, with little cartoon hearts floating above his head, is pretty hilarious."

Max rolled his eyes. It hadn't been *that* bad. "Maybe I should invite Delia over for dinner now that the hex is sealed and the fairy magic has run out. See how I feel around her?"

Nikki nodded solemnly, but the twinkle in his eye said he wasn't taking any of it very seriously. "Oh yes, by all means. Test that theory with a nice romantic dinner."

"I don't know why you find this so amusing."

Nikki placed a hand on Max's shoulder. "Trust me, Max. It's not Cor magic or fairy magic or any kind of magic drawing you to Delia. You just really like her. And from what I can tell, she likes you, too."

Max shrugged Nikki's hand off his shoulder. "You know, it's hard to accept advice from someone when you've seen them lick their own—"

The bell over the door jingled, and Luc walked in. "You forgot to lock that again," he said.

Oh shit. This was why magic in the Stray Lands was dangerous. What if someone had come in and seen a bunch of boxes taping themselves shut?

"I imagine you've been somewhat distracted this morning," Luc added.

"Just busy."

"Nothing to do with the kiss, then?" Luc asked with a knowing grin.

Max glared at Nikki. "Why can't you keep your trap shut?"

Nikki shrugged. "I don't know. It might have to do with the hundred-plus years I was stuck with merely a meow to express myself. And you never told me what to do with this bowl, by the way."

The bowl looked like any light pink Depression-era glassware you might find in your granny's china cabinet. But Max took it from Nikki carefully, because granny items were sometimes similar to honey badgers in that they looked sweet, but could absolutely rip your throat out.

He held it against his chest, closed his eyes, and called his power, shivering as it unfurled and tingled its way to the surface of his skin before branching out to surround the candy bowl.

His pulse sped up until it pounded in his head, filling it with thunderclouds.

Oh, yes. It's dangerous.

His magic swirled around the bowl, nipping and teasing and searching. Was it enchanted? Was it hexed? He caught a whiff of its intent—something sweet and sickly and dark.

"Oh, I don't like the way you just shivered," Nikki said.

"This bowl is definitely magical. But I don't know *what* it is. I have to categorize it. Nullify it or unhex it." He sighed. "Get me the catalog."

Nikki retrieved a gigantic book from a shelf and dropped it in front of Max with a loud thud. "Why can't witches just use the internet like everyone else?"

"Because even though it would be wonderful to simply type *magical candy bowl* in a search bar, you can't hide anything on the internet. There are watchers on the internet, you know."

"I doubt they're witches. You people are still impressed by the technology of pocket calculators."

"Did you just say *you people* to me?"

"Sorry. I thought you identified as people."

"Let me concentrate."

With Luc and Nikki peering over his shoulder, Max flipped through the pages to get to *B* for *bowl*. The book was endless, of course. Like, literally. It didn't matter that it appeared to be six or seven inches thick. You'd never get to the end of it, no matter how long you flipped pages.

Eventually, he found it. "Oh, this is awful," he said. "Anyone who eats candy from this bowl will develop an infection of the molar that will lead to an abscess requiring a root canal."

Nikki grimaced. "That's horrible. Who thinks this shit up? Oh, never mind. It's witches."

CHAPTER TWENTY

Pots simmered on the stove—magically stirred by wooden spoons—and Max opened the oven door to peek at the roast. Delia would be here in less than an hour. She'd accepted his invitation readily, and he was curious to see if sparks still flew between them now that Delia was truly and completely magicless.

"You've got to be kidding," Luc said, strolling into the kitchen. "She's going to know you didn't cook this dinner."

"I most definitely *am* cooking this dinner," Max said. And then, to demonstrate his culinary skills, he picked up a tomato and a knife. "I'm about to make the salad."

"Don't maim yourself this time."

"I'll try," Max said, noting his wound from yesterday's attempt.

"What's your end goal here, by the way?" Luc asked, sticking his finger in chocolate soufflé batter that was gently folding itself.

"Good question," Nikki said from a seat at the table.

Max jumped, nearly nicking his finger. "Holy hell, can you please not do that?"

"Do what?"

"Suddenly make an appearance out of thin air."

"I've been sitting here for ten minutes."

"Oh? Well, maybe you should try doing it more like a human—breathing, blinking, et cetera—and less like a fucking gargoyle."

"I'm assuming you've never met a gargoyle. They can be quite lively, you know."

"There's no such thing as gargoyles," Max said.

"If that's what you choose to believe—"

"And you need to vacate the premises." Max made a careful slice in the tomato. "I'm talking to you, too, Luc."

"Fine," Luc said. "Mr. Escamilla, down at the hardware store, invited me to a rodeo on the outskirts of town. Would you like to come along, Nikki?"

Max looked up from the tomato. "Luc, Nikki can't."

"Oh shit," Luc said. "I'm so sorry. I forgot again."

Nikki shrugged. "It's fine. I'll just scoot out the kitty door. It's a nice day to lounge by the pool."

"It's not really fine," Luc said, stating the obvious.

"No, it's not." Max sighed. "And I was wondering about something. Do you think the key to breaking the curse on Nikki is in the book that Uncle Hartwell gave to the Merriweathers?"

"Surely he'd have broken the curse if it were," Luc said. "Do you know if he looked, Nikki?"

Nikki turned to gaze out the window. "He looked," he said quietly.

"Oh. Well, that's too bad," Max said, exchanging a look with Luc. Did Nikki realize he'd just admitted that Hartwell had delivered the missing *Clavis Hexicus* directly into the hands of the Merriweathers?

Luc gave a subtle shrug. *It didn't do them any good.* And then he cleared his throat. "So, I see you've got candles, wine, and chocolate soufflé. Is this an attempt at romance?"

"Don't be silly," Max said. "Logos witches don't—"

"Do romance," Luc finished. "But does Delia know that? I'd hate for her to misinterpret this. She's not familiar with our motto."

Nikki shook his head. "Mens omnia cor."

"That's right," Luc said. "Mind over heart. Love is a weakness."

"Luc, it might surprise you to know that Delia also isn't looking for love," Max said. "She was very clear about it. Her career is what she's focused on."

"Max is right," Nikki said. "Delia isn't looking for love. But it's not really because she wants to focus on her career. It's because of the hex."

Max set the knife down. "What's the hex got to do with it?"

"Do you really not know?"

Max and Luc looked at each other blankly.

"There was a secondary curse piggybacked onto the original. Hartwell didn't believe it was intentional, if that will make you feel any better."

"What are you talking about?" Max asked, putting down the knife.

"Well," Nikki said, rising from his chair. "When Wilmot hexed the Merriweathers, he apparently didn't want Lucinda to fall in love with anyone else, and those emotions were inadvertently attached as a secondary hex."

"What exactly are you saying?"

"Anyone a Merriweather falls in love with tends to..." Nikki dragged a finger across his throat dramatically.

Max gasped. "They fucking *die*?"

"It's technically just a theory," Nikki said. "Now relax and enjoy your dinner."

Once again, Delia sat at the kitchen table with her tablet and design book. The meeting with Misty had gone really well. They'd shared

tea and chatted, and before long, Delia had understood *exactly*
what Misty wanted. Initially, there had been an awful lot of talk
about cats—Misty, after all, was carrying a cat clutch purse and
wearing kitten heels—but eventually Delia had understood what
it was that Misty loved about cats. They were sleek, smart, and yet
incredibly warm and comforting.

Delia could create that environment easily. In less than fifteen minutes, she'd gathered a few examples of furnishings that evoked the feel
of, well, a cat. And she'd done it without a single cat-shaped pillow.

Cozy Luxe was the style. The design called for muted colors
with warm accents—minimalist, yet soft and fluffy. And it turned
out the budget wasn't small at all, and Misty wanted furnishings,
art…the whole shebang.

She checked the time, and her tummy's resident butterflies took
flight when she realized she was supposed to be at Max's in fifteen
minutes for dinner.

She shook off the notion that it was anything other than a business dinner (hard to do with last night's kiss still burning on her
lips) and opened the file on her tablet for the Halifax Manor project. It was smart. It was logical. It was a perfectly reasonable staging design, and she was pretty sure Max would go for it.

Easy peasy.

And then she quietly clicked on the project she'd worked on this
morning, the one called Dream Design, and sighed in bliss when
it popped up.

She shouldn't have spent so much time on it, and she'd probably never show it to Max. But it was good practice. Only it hadn't
felt like practice; it had felt like her freaking *life's work*, and every
moment had been a treasure.

She'd given herself permission to pretend Max was a client who wanted her to design the living spaces in Halifax Manor for *him*. Not so he could sell it but so he could live in it.

He traveled a lot, so he'd want a place that required little upkeep. But she also knew he'd need a place to actually come home to. A refuge. A hideaway for his studious, introverted self to be rejuvenated and nurtured. What she'd ended up with was a home that was distinctly masculine and simple—Max was a no-nonsense kind of guy—but also incredibly inviting.

She'd pretended she had carte blanche. And that meant a warm travertine marble in a soft, toasted ocher for the entryway. She could practically *feel* the sigh he'd make as soon as he set foot on it—finally home from some exotic place. He'd kick off his shoes and drop his bags before heading to the kitchen for a warm cup of tea. And the kitchen! Good Lord, she'd replaced that nasty tile on the countertops with more marble, except for the island, which she'd topped with red oak butcher-block wood. It would age beautifully. And in the bedroom—

The back door opened and slammed shut, and Grandma Maddie came in carrying bags of groceries. Delia hopped up to help.

"I've got it," Grandma Maddie said, waving her off. "The twins are right behind me with the rest."

Andi and Aurora burst in on her heels. "It's fondue night, Delia!" Andi said. "We have at least ten pounds of cheese in these bags."

"And chocolate!" Aurora added. "It's time to don our stretchy pants!"

"Actually," Delia said. "I'm going next door for dinner. I'm leaving Splash here, and I'm counting on y'all not to poison him with chocolate."

"You can count on us," Grandma Maddie said. "And what fun to have dinner with Max and Luc!"

"And probably their cousin," Delia said. Although she was sincerely hoping it was just going to be her and Max.

"It's so odd that we haven't met the cousin yet," Grandma Maddie said. "The poor boy doesn't seem to leave the house."

"Maybe we should invite them all over?" Delia said.

"Oh yes," Aurora said. "There's enough fondue for everyone."

"Judging by the sweater Delia's wearing, she doesn't mean tonight," Grandma Maddie said.

Delia looked down, like *way* down, practically to her navel. "Yikes!" she said, grabbing the neckline and yanking it up.

"Don't do that," Grandma Maddie said. "You've got cleavage from here to Dallas. Be proud. Also, don't pretend that you didn't know what you were doing when you put it on."

Delia grinned, because she had absolutely chosen the sweater on purpose. It was black and tight and low-cut and it looked dang good on her. She'd paired it with her favorite jeans (the ones with the rhinestones on the back pockets that her mom said were tacky), which she'd tucked into black boots.

"I have more of that special tea," Grandma Maddie added with a wink.

"I don't think that will be necessary," Delia said. "But thank you."

Grandma Maddie stopped unpacking groceries and came over to the table, staring at Delia through magnified eyes that looked uncharacteristically serious. She took Delia's hand in hers and gave it a little squeeze. "Listen, I don't want you to worry about that silly curse."

Oh Jesus. "Believe me, I'm not," Delia said. "Because there isn't one. Merriweather women have had a bit of bad luck, for sure, but I'm not the slightest bit worried."

Her grandmother got even closer, until they were practically nose to nose, and stared deeply into Delia's eyes. "Yes, you are."

Delia giggled, and it sounded ridiculous and quite possibly telling, because while she didn't believe in a curse, there was simply no getting around the fact that most of the people Merriweather women fell in love with tended to suffer unfortunate deaths. The universe was sometimes a bit of a bitch, but Delia liked to think it wasn't intentional.

"Grandma, I love my life, and I want to focus on my career. That's it. That's the whole story."

"Don't let a curse dictate your happiness."

"I'm not."

"Show it who's boss."

"Don't need to."

"Kick it in the balls by falling madly in love—"

The door opened and slammed shut again, and Delia's mom walked in.

Grandma Maddie gave Delia's hand one last squeeze and scurried back to the groceries.

"Is that the proposal for Halifax Manor?" her mom asked.

Delia picked up the tablet. "Oh. Well, kind of—"

Fiona peeked over her shoulder. "Oh, dear God, Delia? What is all this?"

"Nothing," Delia said, frantically trying to pull up the other file. The one for the staging. "Seriously, I was just messing around."

Her mom snatched the tablet out of her hands and studied it.

"Mom, really—"

"This is not for a staging."

"I know. I have that in another file."

"But these are some mighty impressive upgrades that will increase the value of the home. I think you should show this to Max. In fact, send it to me, and I'll work on an upgrade impact report. He might actually want to do some of this. It'll help the home sell, and he can recoup a percentage of these costs."

This was not what Delia had expected to hear. "Really?"

"Yes, really. You, my darling daughter, are an amazing interior designer."

Grandma Maddie smiled at Fiona. "And *you*, Fiona Merriweather, are an amazing mother and Realtor. I'm proud of the both of you."

There was a moment of silence as Grandma Maddie wiped at her eyes.

"Well, I didn't mean to start all this," Fiona said. "I just came by to say goodbye before I head to Austin. I'm a little bit nervous. It's my first conference."

"You're a Merriweather," Delia said. "And that apparently means you're exceptional and unstoppable. So, go kick some Austin real estate ass, Mom."

"I think I will," her mom said. "And you go next door and do the same with your proposal."

CHAPTER TWENTY-ONE

There is no way you cooked this dinner," Delia said, unabashedly licking the last bit of chocolate soufflé off her fork. It was the first chocolate soufflé she'd ever had, and she was a fan. "Fess up."

Max sat across from her—he'd set a lovely table in the formal dining room—and pretended to look offended. Which was adorable.

"Cooking is just following instructions," he said. "And I'm good at that."

Delia narrowed her eyes at him. "Uh-huh. But when it says to fold something or grate something or braise something, you have to know what that means. And I watched you try to dice a tomato, remember?"

"I do have access to the internet, you know."

Delia sat back (her jeans were already killing her) and crossed her arms over her chest. The action bumped her cleavage up a bit, and she was delighted to see that Max noticed. At least, she assumed that's what made his cheeks turn pink and his left eyebrow disappear beneath that unruly lock of hair.

"Let's see. I know this didn't come from Hank's Café. It's too good. And while the roast could be the work of Miss Esther at the Mourning Glory, she wouldn't know a chocolate soufflé if it bit her on the ass. So, if this wasn't takeout, who did you get to come over here and cook it? I mean, that roast melted in my mouth. The potatoes were a buttery dream come true, and the green beans were somehow steamed to perfection. Oh! And the gravy! Don't tell Grandma Maddie, but it put hers to shame."

Max looked so dang pleased with himself that for a minute Delia had to consider that maybe he'd actually cooked the meal. But no. There was no way in hell he'd done it himself.

"Cordelia Merriweather, you saw the dirty dishes in my sink as proof."

Had he said *Cordelia*? "Did you just call me by the official name on my birth certificate?"

"It's a very pretty name. I heard your grandmother use it."

Delia narrowed her eyes. "It's been a long time since I've been sent to the corner to think about what I've done, and I doubt you were there at the time."

"Oh? Well, I obviously heard it somewhere. Maybe from Uncle Hartwell."

Delia considered this. "He did use it on occasion."

"Well, there you go. Shall we have a look at that proposal?"

"Sure. Would you like to move to the living room? I left my bag and tablet in there."

Max wiped his mouth on a napkin and stood up. "I'll meet you in there. Let me get these dishes to the kitchen."

"I'll help—"

"No. I insist."

Well, okay then. If a man wanted to clear the dishes off a table, Delia sure as hell wasn't the woman to stop him.

She went into the living room and pulled out her tablet, still amazed by the fabulous dinner and trying to interpret it all. There hadn't been any overt flirting, although Max's hazel eyes had dipped repeatedly to her lips, which was somehow less personal than when he gazed directly into her eyes through those thick lashes. His gaze was so disorienting that she'd forgotten to chew once or twice.

They'd talked about his travels (his favorite country was Greece), and the house, and Willow Root's upcoming Fall Harvest Festival, and her meeting with Misty, but they had *not* talked about the kiss. Were they just going to pretend it hadn't happened?

Max came into the room with two cups of tea.

"That was fast. When did you have time to steep tea?"

"It's your grandmother's blend, and I started it earlier," he said, taking a seat next to her on the sofa. "Now, show me what you've got."

Delia took a big sip of tea and wiped her sweaty, nervous hands on her jeans. Then she opened the file on her tablet. For the next few minutes, she showed Max her plans to remove Hartwell's very eclectic furniture, accessories, and art and replace them with neutral modern pieces that would show off the attributes of the manor. Max listened attentively, and he didn't bat an eye when she showed him the quoted price.

"Let's do it."

"Great," Delia said. "And there's something else I wanted to talk to you about, if you're interested, that is."

Max moved closer to her. "I'm interested," he said softly.

Delia cleared her throat and opened her Dream Design file. "Sometimes, with older homes such as this one, folks choose to do some minor upgrades in order to improve the home's appeal and, possibly, its market value. Things like flooring, paint, countertops, and the like."

"Oh, I don't think that's necessary—" His eyes came to rest on the simulated image of Hartwell's living room, and he became very still before finally shifting his weight in order to get a closer look.

"Delia," he said. "This is stunning."

"Thanks."

"You are unbelievably good at this."

"I did earn an associate's degree—"

"This is natural talent." He leaned over the tablet. "I didn't know that a room's decor and furnishings could make me"—he swallowed—"*feel* something."

Delia's heart sped up. "What do you feel?"

"I don't know how to describe it." He seemed to struggle for a moment to come up with the right words. "It's almost as if this is exactly what I'd want if I wanted an actual home. Only I never would have known it before now."

Those words were like a cartoon arrow straight to her heart. *Zing!*

"It's almost like magic," Max said softly.

Was he attempting a little joke at her expense? She couldn't tell. But honestly, she didn't really care. Because she'd just achieved an interior decorator's dream. Someone had looked at her design and seen a space they'd call *home*.

Max didn't typically care about his surroundings. His apartment in Shadowlark was sparse and utilitarian and perfectly functional. But *this*—he stared at Delia's plans for the kitchen—did something weird to him. For one thing, it made him want to cook. Like, really cook. And he wanted to do it while barefoot and sipping red wine and listening to music. He wondered what she'd do with the library. And the bedrooms upstairs.

"And you say I can recoup some of the investment?"

"I'm not going to lie. I don't know how much. And it would mean postponing the open house. But my mom says she can produce something called an upgrade impact report, and it'll give you a good idea."

"Sounds good to me. Should we go upstairs next?"

"Oh, I wasn't going to stage the upstairs. I was just going to have you empty it all out as much as possible. I mean, this is a big freaking house."

He totally understood that. And yet…

"I guess I just really want to see what you'd do with it."

The smile on Delia's face was dangerously rewarding. He was probably going to end up redoing the entire house if it meant she'd keep smiling like that.

Delia stood. "Let's go, then."

Max nodded and led the way to the staircase.

"You know," Delia said. "When I was a kid, Hartwell never let me play on the stairs. He said he kept monsters in the bedrooms."

Max snorted, because judging by some of the things he'd found in the house, that was a distinct possibility.

"He was also weird about his study," Delia said. "I've never been in there."

And same story.

"But I've been in Hartwell's home gym," Delia added as they hit the landing on the second floor. She pointed to the door at the end of the hall. "After my six terribly long months as a dog groomer, I did a short stint as a personal trainer. Hartwell and Amy were my only clients. And since there's no gym in Willow Root, we used Hartwell's equipment."

"Why did you give that up?"

"It turns out that Amy cries a lot when you make her exercise, and since I'm a softie, I'd reward her efforts with a weekly trip to Mourning Glory Café. She and I both gained ten pounds, and she gave me a bad Yelp review. Hartwell, however, was a champ."

Max shook his head, grinning. "I get the feeling that Amy doesn't care for me all that much."

"You and almost everyone else. Don't worry about it."

Max shrugged. Unbeknownst to Delia, Amy was a hedge witch. And it wasn't unusual for hedge witches in the Stray Lands to be resentful of the Logos witches in Shadowlark.

"There are three bedrooms up here. Four, if you count the gym," he said, opening the door to Uncle Hartwell's exercise room.

Delia looked around at all the exercise equipment. "Hm. I'd absolutely love to make this into a serious gym. But we should probably just turn it into a bedroom for the open house. What do you think?"

Max appreciated the home gym. But Delia was probably right. "I trust your opinion."

Delia went straight to the stair-step machine. "This one is my favorite," she said. "It's so fun."

She pushed some buttons and started stepping. "Good for the glutes," she said, winking over her shoulder.

The attraction from last night was still there. If anything, it was even stronger. Listening to her talk about her work with such passion, and seeing her massive talent, had only deepened his desire. It wasn't just her crooked grin, her curvaceous figure, and her playful personality drawing him in. It was her mind and intellect, too. He had it bad for Cordelia Merriweather—for every last bit of her—and there was no magic involved. No fairy magic. No witchy magic. Just real feelings that a Logos witch wasn't supposed to have.

Delia hopped off the machine, fanning her pink cheeks with her hand. "Whew! I'm definitely not dressed for this. Do you like to work out, Max? I mean, you're from California. I bet *everyone* has a gym membership in California."

"Actually, I—"

"You're about to crush my image of California, aren't you?"

He laughed. If she only knew.

"I have no gym membership. I do boring daily calisthenics like push-ups, pull-ups, and crunches. And I use some free weights. That's about it."

"Well," Delia said as her eyes roamed his body. "It works for you."

She was flirting. And he was enthusiastically soaking it up. Because why not? They were neither one interested in a relationship, and he would be leaving soon anyway. In the meantime, there was no reason they couldn't enjoy each other's company. "I was recently told my middle could use some firming up—"

By a mirror.

"Whoever told you that is a liar. Your middle is fine from where I'm standing." Delia ran her hands over her hips and across her belly. "I'm definitely the softie here. But looks can be deceiving. I bet I can do a hundred sit-ups, even in these jeans. And I'm more flexible than you might think."

Max swallowed. *Is it hot in here?*

"Soft looks good on you. But I don't believe you can do a hundred sit-ups in those jeans."

Delia dropped her bag on the ground. "Did you just issue a challenge to a Merriweather woman?"

"I believe I did. Yes."

"Ha! I accept. But only if we make it a competition."

"You're on."

"We'll see who can get to a hundred first," Delia said, sitting on a mat.

Max immediately stripped down to his undershirt, dropping his flannel shirt on the floor.

"No fair," Delia said. "Now you're in a thin T-shirt and I'm in a sweater."

"All is fair in love and sit-ups." Max stretched and flexed. "What are the stakes?"

"Since you're going to need it after you lose, how about a shoulder rub?" Delia asked. "The kind that makes your toes curl."

He might have to throw this thing, just for the opportunity to make Delia's toes curl. He stretched out his legs and clasped his hands behind his head, and Delia did the same. "Ready, set, go!"

CHAPTER TWENTY-TWO

Seventeen, eighteen...

She had never done a hundred sit-ups in tight jeans before.

Nineteen, twenty...

She'd made it to twenty!

Twenty-one, twenty-two...

This was a mistake.

Twenty-three...

She was going to die.

"You're slowing down, Merriweather."

Twenty-four...

"Oh yeah? Pretty sure you just farted."

He hadn't, but she hoped the comment would knock him off his game.

It did not.

Dear Lord, her tight jeans were forcing all her fat upward whenever she came up. Would it eventually come out of her ears and eyes? Like one of those squishy dolls whose eyeballs popped out when you squeezed their middles...

Max's white T-shirt was drenched in sweat. She was wearing a sweater, for God's sake. So, it wasn't really cheating when she lost count and decided to just follow whatever numbers Max was spewing, even though he was going twice as fast as she was. Her plan was to just scream *one hundred!* whenever Max did. Only louder and a millisecond sooner. And then she'd have those big hands squeezing down on her shoulders. Hell, even if she lost, she got to put her hands on *his* shoulders, so really it was a win-win, and who cared how many sit-ups she did.

Only, there was one little problem. She couldn't do even one more. "I quit," she called, plopping down on the mat, arms and legs splayed out like a starfish, gasping for air.

"Keep going," Max grunted. "Eighty-five, eighty-six…"

"Okay," she said, not moving a muscle. "One thousand billion sixty-seven…one thousand billion twenty-two…"

"That's not even in ascending numerical order."

Max finished the last few while Delia tried to ignore his grunting and sweating and flexing muscles and flat, taut stomach and the fact that he was going up and down and up and down.

"One hundred," he said quietly.

He did not sprawl. He sat with his arms wrapped around his knees, not even breathing hard and staring at her with the one hazel eye that didn't have a dark lock of hair hanging over it. And smirking! Jesus. That smirk.

"I did pretty well, considering I tweaked my back yesterday," she said.

"That's probably true, but unless you're in pain, you should finish what you started."

She looked at him, and he seemed dead serious, which was hilarious considering she had quite possibly perforated an organ.

Max got right in her face. "Come on. You can do it. And I'll even hold your feet for you."

Fine. She bent her knees and Max held her feet down as she sat up, hands clasped behind her head until she and Max were nose to nose. Her gaze dropped to his lips.

"Eighty-six," he said. "Because I'm giving you the benefit of the doubt."

She wanted to stick her tongue out, for various reasons, but somehow refrained. Instead, she inelegantly grunted and forced herself to curl up again, but this time was easier. The little break must have done some good, because it almost felt like there was an invisible hand pressing against her back, supporting her. She was done in a matter of seconds.

"One hundred," Max said officiously. "I knew you could do it."

He didn't let go of her feet, nor did he scoot away.

"Well, I guess you technically won," Delia said breathlessly (because she was horny but also because she was out of breath). Her fingers itched to sink into those shoulders.

"Let's call it a tie," he said.

Wait. What? Was this his way of escaping the awkwardness of having to be on the receiving end of a shoulder rub?

"I'm thinking I need to take my own advice," he said, leaning in closer.

She swallowed. "Oh? And what advice is that?"

"To finish what I started"—his eyes dropped to her lips—"last night in the hot tub."

His eyes darkened. His nostrils flared. And Delia lost what little restraint she had as soon as his lips were on hers. Her hands roamed from his firm shoulders to his soft hair.

She parted her lips, and he wasted no time getting down to business, framing her face with his hands and tilting her head to thoroughly invade her mouth. And before Delia's irritating inner voice could start up its nonsense about professionalism, her knees drifted open, and she let Max firmly press her down onto the mat.

The man was definitely intent on finishing what he'd started.

What a thrill it was to give in to emotions without an ongoing subconscious stream of thought and analysis.

Lizard Brain, take the wheel.

Only it didn't feel entirely thoughtless. He was very much thinking about how badly he wanted her and how much he liked her. Every moment with Delia felt like an adventure. And that was saying a lot for a guy who spent his life hunting down rare magical items all over the globe.

The tight jeans that had given Delia so much trouble felt amazing beneath the palm of his hand as he caressed her hips, and she made a little moaning sound that encouraged him to go lower, so he did. The rhinestones on her pockets tickled his palms as he cupped her ass.

She yanked his T-shirt out of his corduroy slacks and ran her warm hands all over his bare back, giving him goose bumps.

He broke the kiss long enough to pull his T-shirt off, and then Delia fiercely pulled his face back to hers. But before they locked lips again, he took a moment to just look at her. To soak her all in. Her brown eyes were hooded and lustful, her lips were swollen from his attention, her blond hair was a mess, and the sight of it all sent a wave of desire over him with such force that it literally moved his body. He rode it, pressing himself against Delia, and she responded by wrapping her legs around him.

Oh fuck, yes. He grabbed one of Delia's hands and pinned it above her head while running his other hand beneath her shirt. She arched her back to receive his touch, and he dropped his mouth to her neck, feasting and exploring as his hand went higher...

"Oh, Max," Delia said breathlessly. "This feels so good."

He cupped her breast, and it filled his hand perfectly: plump and round and everything dreams were made of. He squeezed it lightly, and then he pulled the cup of her bra down just enough to get to her nipple, which he rolled between his fingers. His mouth literally watered, and she pressed on his head, urging him to lower.

He licked his lips and—

"Max, I hear something."

He lifted his head. "What?"

"Is someone pounding on the door downstairs?"

He listened, but all he heard was the pounding of his own heart, which was desperately trying to escape his chest at the moment. They stared at each other silently, breathing heavily, but all was quiet.

"Shall I, um, continue...?"

Delia arched her back. "Oh, yes. Please do."

Max was ready to oblige, but then he heard it. And it wasn't even a knocking. It was definitely a pounding. "Shit," he said, wondering who it could possibly be.

"Should you go answer it?"

Was she kidding? No. He definitely should not. "It's probably just kids. They're bothersome as hell."

"That's probably our fault," Delia said. "They pester us because of the witch stuff, and they pestered Hartwell by association."

"Well, they'll go away," he said, dropping his gaze back to Delia's exposed breast.

"Maximus!" a woman's voice called from downstairs.

Max froze.

"Who is that?" Delia asked, showing signs of both annoyance and panic.

This couldn't be happening. "It's my mother."

"Your *mother*?"

Max hauled himself off Delia, adrenaline rushing through his veins. The door had been locked, but clearly that had been no trouble for Dorcas Golding, who would no doubt be on her way up the stairs in a matter of minutes. What was she doing here? Max couldn't even remember the last time his mother had made a trip to the Stray Lands.

Delia was still on the mat, eyes wide, cheeks pink, chest heaving… "You, um, might want to put that away," he said, pointing at her breast.

That spurred her into action, and she was on her feet in no time, adjusting her bra and pulling her sweater down. "Did you know she was coming?"

"No," Max said, grabbing his flannel shirt off the floor. "You just stay up here. I'll get rid of her."

"Get rid of her? She just flew in from California!"

"You're right," Max said, putting his shirt on. "Anyway, it's stupid to ask you to hide."

"No shit."

"Everything will be fine."

"Of course it will. We're adults. Goodness, Max."

"It's just that, well, you haven't met my mother."

Delia brushed some dust off her black sweater. "Well, I'm about to. So, get a grip."

Max headed for the door, then stopped and turned to face her. "You might want to prepare yourself. My mother is…weird."

That was an understatement. Dorcas Golding almost never

ventured outside of the Shadowlark science lab where she studied genetics, and when she did, it wasn't for a quick trip to the Stray Lands. She was clueless about social norms and customs outside of the witching world and would no doubt appear exquisitely and painfully strange to Delia.

Delia laughed. "Are you serious? After meeting my relatives, you still think yours can compete in the weird category?"

Max looked her straight in the eye. "Yes."

CHAPTER TWENTY-THREE

Dang it. Max had his flannel shirt on inside out. Delia went to tap him on the shoulder, but he took off down the stairs before she could. When he got to the bottom, she heard him say, "It's both of you? You *both* came?"

Delia hit the bottom step shortly after, and sure enough, there were two people standing in the middle of the foyer. The woman, who Delia presumed to be Max's mom, was dressed all in black, including a gorgeous vintage hat perched stylishly on top of her platinum-blond head. Like Max, she was tall and lean, and Delia recognized those cheekbones immediately.

The man, who was surely Max's dad, wore a long dark coat and carried an umbrella, even though there wasn't a cloud in the sky. "Is that any way to greet your mother, Maximus?"

"Sorry—"

"I've missed you, too," Max's mother said, rolling her bright green eyes and then suddenly catching sight of Delia. And if Delia looked even half as disheveled as Max, his mom knew exactly what they'd been doing. Well, maybe not *exactly*, since it involved sit-ups. But she'd get the gist.

"This is my interior decorator," Max blurted.

God. Why were men so hellishly awful with introductions?

Delia held out her hand to Max's mom. "I'm Delia," she said. "From next door."

Max's mom looked at Delia's hand as if it were a snake, but eventually she accepted it. "Did you say *Delia*?" she asked, giving a limp shake. "From next door?"

"Yes, ma'am—"

"Yes," Max rudely interjected. "As I stated, she's my interior decorator." He waved an arm in his parents' general direction. "And these are my parents, Dorcas Golding and Armistead Halifax."

Delia raised an eyebrow at Max. If he kept referring to her simply as his interior decorator (instead of friend or neighbor or even just plain old Delia) less than ten minutes after being inside the left cup of her Aphrodite Fuller Figure Bra, she was going to have no choice but to raise the other eyebrow, too.

"Pleasure to make your acquaintance," Max's dad said.

Delia immediately saw where Max had inherited his broad shoulders, dark wavy hair, and somewhat formal manner of speaking. "Likewise," she said, feeling almost as if a curtsy were in order.

Next, Mr. Halifax awkwardly patted Max on the back, eyes drifting over the curling tag at the back of his neck, and then Ms. Golding came really close to kissing Max on the cheek, stopping just shy of actual skin contact.

Max responded to this bit of weirdness by nodding. "To what do I owe the pleasure of this visit?"

"Have you checked your phone, Maximus?" his mother asked. "Morgaine has been calling."

Max immediately began patting down his pants. "Where's my phone?"

"You're lucky Morgaine didn't come in person," Mr. Halifax said.

Who the heck was Morgaine?

Max ran his hand through his unruly hair, and then he looked down and noticed the side seam of his flannel. His cheeks turned bright red, and he looked as if he'd be relieved if the sky opened up and swallowed him whole.

But there was no such luck, and it seemed he was going to stupidly stand there and let his parents linger indefinitely in the foyer, wearing their coats and holding an umbrella. Delia hated to jump in as hostess—not her house, not her parents—but somebody had to.

"Why don't y'all come on in and have a seat," she said. "Can I take your coats?"

Dorcas and Armistead looked relieved that they were actually being invited in, and they followed Delia and Max into the living room.

"Let's go fix some tea," Max said. "Mother, Father, we'll be back in a bit."

Mother? Father? Is that what he calls his parents?

Max grabbed Delia's arm and dragged her into the kitchen, where she immediately turned on him. "Max, you're being weird. And rude. Goodness, this reminds me of the night we met. What's gotten into you?"

His frantic eyes softened when he looked at her. "I'm so sorry. And I know. I know that I'm being strange, and this is all horrific—"

"It's not horrific. It's a visit from your parents. Why are you acting as if the firing squad just showed up expecting tea before they execute you?"

He took her hand and kissed the inside of her wrist. "I need you to know that I thoroughly enjoyed what we just did upstairs. You're a beautiful and amazing woman, and I honestly can't believe that what happened actually happened. But after a cup of tea, I'm going to need some time alone with my parents. Is that okay?"

Something weird was going on, and it was quite possible that Max's family *was* even stranger than hers.

"Of course it's okay. But…"

"But what?"

"Listen. I'm not sure what you're hiding, *Maximus*, or who the hell Morgaine is or why she was calling you," she said. "But, you'd better not have a wife and kids."

At that Max's serious expression dissolved into a surprised grin, and then he began to laugh. He took her hand and kissed her wrist again. "Believe me, I don't."

And something inside Delia—probably her dang heart—*did* believe him. "Okay," she said. "Let's heat up the tea—"

"I already did it," Max said, cramming something in his pocket.

"When?"

"Come on," he said, grabbing a small tray out of a cabinet. "Help me get the tea served. And then, if you don't mind—"

"I'll leave," Delia said. "So you can have a nice visit, or whatever, with your folks."

"Thanks. And again, I'm sorry—"

"Oh, and look," Delia said, picking up his phone from where he'd left it on the counter. "Your parents were right. Whoever the hell Morgaine is, she's called you like a million times."

Max watched as Delia poured tea for his parents. He was overwhelmed by feelings like pride (look at this beautiful woman who seems to like me!) and defensiveness (if they only knew who she was) and fear (because they were probably figuring it out).

Also, he wasn't used to seeing his parents together. It was unnerving.

"How was your flight?" Delia asked, sitting next to Max.

"Perfectly horrible," Dorcas said. "We came out in a horrid little shop—"

"Tea?" Max said, grabbing the pot and starting to pour. Because holy Hecate, his mother and father had traveled through the portal.

"The flight was fine," his father said with a small smile. He was a tad more comfortable in the Stray Lands than Max's mother was. But what had brought them here?

Max shivered at the thought of Morgaine calling him over and over...Something had definitely happened. Something bad.

"You're Max's interior decorator?" Dorcas asked. "What on earth does he need one for?"

"My mom is his real estate agent," Delia said. "And I'll be staging the manor for an open house and possibly doing some upgrades to improve the market value."

His mother chuckled and glanced at Max. "Oh, Maximus. Really?"

Max cleared his throat. "Delia's very talented."

"And you're from next door?" his mother said, turning her attention back to Delia.

"Yes," Delia said. "We've been neighbors of Hartwell's since shortly after I was born."

His father gasped. "*Cordelia* Merriweather?"

"Yes," Delia said, smiling. "How did you know?"

Shit. Shit. Shit. Shit. "I'm sure Uncle Hartwell mentioned you," Max said quickly. "Now, then, everyone, let's drink up."

"My grandmother grew these tea leaves herself," Delia said. "So, cheers."

His parents froze—teacups almost to their mouths.

Delia looked puzzled, and then she drained her cup, as if attempting to prove it was safe. "Don't worry. There's nothing weird in it." She furrowed her brow before adding, "Probably."

His parents took what were obviously fake sips of their tea before setting their cups down. "Max, we need to talk," his father said.

"In private," his mother added.

Delia had no idea what was going on, so this had to be hurtful. No wonder she'd thought he was rude upon meeting her. He'd probably acted just as bizarre.

"It was, uh..." His father appeared to search for words. "Nice to meet you, Cordelia Merriweather."

Max was shattered. Delia was the epitome of Southern politeness. And it was completely genuine. What must she think of his family? What must she think of *him*? "Delia, let me walk you out—"

"Don't be silly," she said, and the unfamiliar sharpness in her tone cut his heart in two. "I'll let myself out."

She stood, and Max half expected her to storm off. He would have. But instead, Delia smiled warmly at his parents. "If y'all are going to be in town for long, I'd be happy to show you around. Just let me know."

And then she turned and walked out, leaving Max to face his parents alone.

As soon as the door shut, his father was on him. "Maximus, what on earth are you thinking?"

"He's bewitched already," his mother said. "What else could explain this?"

"Nobody has bewitched me. You're being ridiculous. The hex is sealed, and the Merriweathers are magicless."

"Are they?" his mother asked.

"There was a fluctuation in the Source," his father said. "Morgaine is beside herself."

Weather events could sometimes cause a fluctuation in the Source. Magnetic shifts. Major events like an earthquake, even. But it was usually felt by everyone.

Max frowned. "I didn't feel anything. Did you feel anything?"

"Well, no," his father said. "But the high priestess is probably more sensitive than we are."

"What does this have to do with me?"

"Are you not listening?" his mother asked. "Morgaine thinks the hex might have been broken."

Max almost laughed. "That's not possible. Delia has not been out of my sight."

"Obviously," his mother said wryly.

"I don't know what caused the fluctuation," Max said. "But the hex wasn't broken."

"I'm a historian, not a physicist," his father said. "But Morgaine is adamant that the Merriweathers are somehow responsible."

Max crossed his arms and frowned.

"We are *so* disappointed in you, Maximus," his mother said.

His father clucked his tongue. "Maybe it's just as well that Max has become, erm...*close* with this woman. If she's broken the hex—"

"She hasn't," Max said.

His father sighed. "If she has, we'll have to rehex them."

Max ran a hand through his hair. "If that were true, we'd need to have a discussion. But believe me—"

"Who is that?" his mother suddenly asked, looking over his shoulder.

Max turned to see Nikki—eyes as round as saucers—standing in the doorway to the library.

Max's father was on his feet in an instant. "Please don't let that be what I think it is."

Max stood, arms out to calm his father, who was already reaching for his wand. "Let me explain."

"Is that...?" His mother gawked. "Hartwell's imp? In *human* form?"

Nikki stepped back into the library and closed the door.

"Uncle Hartwell was terribly allergic to cats," Max said. "He let Nikki assume that form in the house and shop, and over the years they became friends."

"Friends?" his father asked incredulously.

"Maximus, have you gone insane?" his mother asked. "You came to Willow Root with a mission to make sure the Blue Witch didn't break the hex, and not only did you fail, but we walked in to find you...fraternizing with her!"

"Okay, hold on a minute—"

"This is not like you," his mother said. "Not like you at all."

"How would you know?" Max said. "Neither of you have spent enough time with me to have a clue as to what I'm like."

His father shook his head. "Gibberish. We know who we raised you to be."

Max rolled his eyes. He was raised by cold Logos nannies in cold Logos nurseries before being sent off to a cold Logos school.

"We've walked in on a disaster," his mother said. "What else could go wrong?"

CHAPTER TWENTY-FOUR

The next morning, Delia pushed open the door of the Crooked Broom and set the dog down. "Now, don't you dare piddle," she said. "You've been a good boy all morning."

The place felt weird for some reason. There was the usual pleasant smell of dried herbs and candles. But there was also something else. Something she couldn't quite put her finger on that was similar to that eerie, electric sensation you got when lightning was about to strike.

"Oh, Delia!" Grandma Maddie said, rushing over with wild eyes. "Do you have magic, too?"

Grandma Maddie's boundless hair was dancing as if it had literally come alive. And she looked, well, fantastic. Her cheeks were pink, and her skin glowed.

Delia ignored the question, because of course she didn't have magic. "Grandma Maddie, are you using a new moisturizer?"

"Delia, the hex is broken!"

Delia really wasn't in the mood for crazy right now. Not after last night, when she'd literally been about to have what probably would have been the best sex of her life, only to have Max's parents show up. And if that wasn't bad enough, Max had then turned weirder than shit. Rude, even. And she was kind of pissed. Definitely confused. So, she didn't need any more confusion or weirdness.

Thea, Andi, and Aurora bounded around the corner of the candle aisle. Their eyes were just as huge as Grandma Maddie's, and they seemed out of their minds with excitement. "Delia! Come back here," Aurora said. "Wait until you see this."

"See what? Goodness, what is all the fuss about?"

She followed her aunts, and...*No freaking way.*

The willow sticks—the same ones that had been sitting on the shelf as if anyone would buy literal sticks—were floating. Levitating. Hovering over the basket as if waiting for something.

This had to be a trick. "How are you doing that?"

"It's magic!" Thea said.

"Hold on, you crazy old ladies," Delia said, narrowing her eyes and trying to spot whatever was making the sticks look like they were floating. "Y'all got me good. Is it invisible string?"

"It's not a trick," Grandma Maddie said. "And that's not all."

"Show her the herbs!" Aurora said.

"And the crystals!" Andi added.

Delia looked at the packets of dried herbs on the counter. And then she looked again. "Are those *blooming*?"

"Yes!" Grandma Maddie said. "They were all properly dried, but now they're covered in bright blooms. And look what happens when I do this."

Grandma Maddie waved her hand over the herbs, and they changed colors.

"Am I high?" Delia asked.

"How would we know that, dear?" Aunt Aurora said.

"I mean, did y'all slip something into the coffee? Have you drugged me?"

"It's not drugs, silly," Grandma Maddie said. "It's magic. Just look at the crystals."

Delia turned to see shelves of glowing crystals. And they weren't glowing just a little. They were full-on glow-in-the-dark-you-could-read-by-them glowing.

"They hum, too," Andi said. "It's quite lovely."

"Okay," Delia said. "This is nuts. Either on purpose or by accident, y'all have drugged me and drugged yourselves and—"

"That's initially what I thought," Thea said. "Because it wouldn't be the first time, would it?"

"Oh my Goddess," Grandma Maddie said. "It was just a little peyote, and it was just the one time. You act like I poisoned you."

Thea shot Grandma Maddie a look that said she had 100 percent been poisoned. "Anyway, listen, Delia. The books balanced."

As an accountant, Thea did the books for the store. And it gave her fits and spells because the books *never* balanced. It would take an act of God or...magic.

"Are you sure?"

"Yes. Every single column added up and each page balanced perfectly."

That wasn't anything Delia thought would be the result of a hallucination. And really, none of them looked like they were on drugs. They looked, well, pretty dang put together. Spry. Healthy. Glowing.

None of it made sense, but Delia knew one thing immediately. They needed to flip the sign until they could figure this shit out.

The bell over the door jingled, and Delia realized with dread that it was too late. And for some reason, she knew who it was before she even turned around.

"Oh, boys!" Grandma Maddie said. "We have the best news!"

"Oh shit," Max said.

Luc grabbed his arm. "Mother and Father were right. She broke the hex."

"Don't jump to conclusions."

Magic had definitely been unleashed. But there were explanations beyond the hex having been broken. Maybe another witch had done this. Maybe the shop was under a spell. Someone had enchanted it.

Delia rushed over. "Follow me," she said, dragging him to the counter where a bunch of herbs were strewn about. As she ran her hand over them, they bloomed and changed color.

"Do you see that?" Delia asked.

Max nodded, and Delia's eyes widened in response. She threw her arms up in the air. "So, we're all high?"

"I don't think—"

"There must be hallucinogens in the drinking water. Do you think the entire town is tripping?"

No. He did not think that. Max could understand this theory, but it seemed unlikely. Even though he desperately wanted to believe it. "Is it just in the shop?"

Delia bit her lip. "Well, when I woke up this morning, the kitchen was clean. I mean *really* clean. I don't think I hallucinated that."

"Maybe someone just cleaned the kitchen," he said.

Delia looked at him like he was nuts. "Nobody ever cleans the kitchen."

"I don't know what's going on here," Max said. "But we should probably lock the door, so no one else walks in."

Delia's eyes widened even more. "Oh God. Yes. I meant to do that. Thanks."

As she rushed off, Max grabbed Luc. "I need to call Morgaine. And I need to do it in private."

"Do you really have to?"

"I don't see how I can avoid it. And anyway, she already thinks the hex is broken. There's no hiding it. Can you stay with the Merriweathers?"

"Of course. But, Max, how did this happen? And what are we going to do?"

"I don't know. But don't let them out of here. They have no control of themselves."

"You're not going to rehex them, are you?"

Max shook his head. "I don't even know how. My specialty is *un*hexing things."

He went to the door, where Delia was waiting. "Where are you going?" Her voice held more than an edge of desperation.

"I just have to step out for a minute. Luc will stay here with you."

"Do you have to?" Her hands were shaking. The poor woman was terrified, and it tugged at Max's heart like an anchor. He wanted to wrap his arms around her and assure her that everything was going to be okay. But he couldn't do that. Because if she *had* somehow broken the hex . . .

"Luc is going to take good care of you while I'm out. Try to relax."

"How am I supposed to do that?"

He leaned over and kissed her forehead.

"Oh," she said, the tension in her face melting away. "That actually helped."

Holy Hecate. What was he going to do?

CHAPTER TWENTY-FIVE

The antique shop smelled like fish.

"Oops," Nikki said, holding a can of tuna. "I didn't think you'd be back so soon."

Normally, Max would be irritated by the smell. But he had bigger fish to fry, so to speak, than a can of tuna.

"I think Delia broke the hex," he said, stopping at the counter. "But for the life of me, I don't know how."

A smile took over Nikki's face. "Really? That's great!"

"No, it's definitely not." He ran his hands through his hair. "When did she do it? We were with her until after midnight."

"Well, then I'd say she did it when we were with her," Nikki said simply.

"I don't see how. But there is definitely magic happening at the Crooked Broom."

"Maybe it's enchanted?"

"I don't think so. You can tell just by looking at them. They're spilling magic all over the place. I've got to call Morgaine."

Nikki made a hissing sound that raised the hair on the back of Max's neck.

"I know. But I'm hoping I can convince her to just leave the Merriweathers alone."

"She's not going to agree to that," Nikki said.

Nikki was probably right, but Max had to try. "I'm going to the back. This requires more than a phone call."

"She's not coming here, is she?" Nikki looked incredibly close to becoming feline. "There's a portal back there. I know there is."

"No. I'll use the bowl."

"The bowl? Why can't you just do a video call? Why must witches be so dramatic?"

"Shut up, Nikki."

Max didn't care that he'd just given Nikki a direct order. He needed to steel himself for a conversation with the high priestess, and he didn't need Nikki asking a bunch of stupid questions for the sake of mere annoyance.

He passed through the black curtains that led to the back of the store, where, yes, there was a portal to Shadowlark. There was also a bunch of other stuff that shouldn't be messed with, including the apparitium bowl.

Nikki was right; witches *were* dramatic. And traditional. But mostly, they used the old ways because they were secure.

He filled the bowl with water. Then he grabbed his rarely used wand and gave it a swirl.

To Morgaine Gerard I wish to speak
Her guidance now is what I seek

It was corny. But it worked. Within a few seconds, Morgaine's face appeared, transparently floating above the bowl. Her image was soft and misty, but her stern expression was anything but. Was she beautiful? Yes. Was she scary as hell? Also yes.

"The hex was broken," she said, skipping any and all formalities. "When you ignored my calls, I had to send your parents."

"Yes, thanks for that—"

"How did you let it happen? You were supposed to be monitoring the Blue Witch at all times."

"I was. I did. And she never cast a spell. She never made a potion. She never did any of the things that could possibly break a hex—"

"Who says she played by the rules? Were you waiting for her to whip out a cauldron?"

"Well…"

Yes. Basically.

Morgaine laughed, and it turned her face into something vicious. Max, who hadn't said anything remotely humorous, winced.

"You're in danger, Maximus. That's why I sent your parents. You cannot be alone with that witch. Do you hear me? It's possible that you're already compromised. Your mother told me about the little party they walked in on."

Max took a deep breath to calm himself down. He was not about to be told who he could or could not be alone with, but also, could she be right? His head began to swim, and he almost forgot why he'd wanted to speak with her in the first place. "Morgaine, I'd like to request a hearing with the Concilium. I think we need to reevaluate the punishment in regard to the Merriweathers. They mean no harm to anyone."

The air in the room chilled, and ice formed on the surface of the bowl. Max shivered and took a step back as it cracked and disappeared in a cloud of steam.

"The punishment fit the crime. And it's an eternal sentence. This is not up for discussion, and I am denying your request for an audience with the Concilium."

"But why—"

"You have a new mission, Maximus."

Dread filled his belly.

"You and your family are tasked with rehexing the Merriweathers. And if you are unsuccessful, the status of the Halifax name in regard to the Logos line will be reconsidered. After all, it was a Halifax at the center of this mess to begin with."

"How dare you? My family has given everything to the Logos line and to Shadowlark. My father is an esteemed Logos historian. My mother is a respected geneticist who devotes herself to keeping the line strong. And Uncle Hartwell was a celebrated—"

"Hartwell Halifax was a fool who couldn't take simple orders, and I suggest you *not* follow in his footsteps."

Max was literally shaking with rage, but he couldn't let Morgaine see it. "The hex is centuries old, and it calls for a blood sacrifice. Surely you can't mean for us to perform a blood sacrifice."

"The hex is a Halifax hex. It's your responsibility, and no one else's."

"We'll need time."

Time to figure a way out of this.

"You have until Hallowtide."

"But that's in less than two weeks—"

"No buts, Maximus. And stay away from that witch."

Morgaine's face evaporated, and Max slumped into a nearby chair.

Nikki emerged from a shadow, where he'd been hiding and listening to the whole thing. "Max, what are we going to do?"

For some reason, the *we* in Nikki's question gave him a bit of encouragement. He, Nikki, and Luc were of one mind.

"I don't know," he said. "But we'll think of something."

"Max—"

"I won't allow them to be rehexed."

Nikki smiled. "I knew you wouldn't," he said softly. "Hartwell said so."

Delia sat on the floor in front of the glowing crystals, clutching Splash to her chest. She would prefer to go back to her office, where there would likely be fewer things flying around, or at least *appearing* to fly around. But she was afraid to leave her grandma and aunties alone.

How long would this last? With the exception of the one or two times she'd pretended to inhale in high school or caught second-hand highs at concerts, she'd never done drugs. And she'd certainly never done anything hallucinogenic.

It felt absolutely nothing like she'd thought it would. Was she supposed to be this self-aware? When would she start feeling euphoric? Where was the spiritual enlightenment? Wasn't she supposed to meet Jesus?

A willow twig smacked her in the head. "Ow!" Were hallucinations supposed to *hurt*?

Aunt Thea tapped her on the shoulder and nodded at the twig. "That's your wand, dear."

Andi and Aurora danced by, round hips gyrating suggestively to Santana's "Black Magic Woman." "Delia!" Andi said. "Grab it! Grab your wand!"

Aurora held up a stick of her own. "We all have them. They've been sitting in that dusty basket all this time!"

Delia didn't believe for a minute that the stick tapping on her head was a magic wand, but she grabbed it anyway. It was better to hallucinate holding it in her hand than to hallucinate herself into a concussion.

It was warm and tingly and vibrated just a bit. And for some reason, it calmed her.

"Try it!" Andi said, pointing her stick at a bin of stuffed animals. "Abracadabra!"

Little stuffed owls and black cats took flight, and Andi cackled in delight.

Aurora pointed her stick at some folded tapestries. "Hocus pocus!"

The tapestries unfolded themselves and rose into the air, and magical flying carpets were added to the mix.

Someone banged noisily on the shop's door, so she was now hallucinating an angry customer.

"Oh, it's Amy," Grandma Maddie said. "Somebody go let her in."

Luc stood up. "No, don't let her—"

Too late. Grandma Maddie had dragged Amy in, and Amy's jaw immediately dropped.

"Oh no!" Delia said. "You're hallucinating, too?"

"Holy shit," Amy said, wearing a huge grin. "What have you done? And when did you do it?"

"I had coffee this morning," Delia said. "And I thought Grandma Maddie put something in it. But now I'm not so sure. Because I'm tripping. You're tripping. Is the whole town tripping?"

"This is literally the best rave I've ever been to," Amy said, starting to dance with Andi and Aurora.

"Max is back," Luc said, opening the door again.

"What would a party be without a party pooper?" Amy said.

Max sighed. "Luc, I told you not to let anyone in."

Luc shrugged. "I didn't do it."

"It's not just *anyone*," Aunt Thea said, attempting to mount a broom. "It's Amy."

Amy made a heart shape with her hands at Thea.

The broom was now between Thea's legs, hiking up her pumpkin-patterned skirt and exposing her chunky thighs.

"I'm sorry, Thea," Luc said. "But I'm going to have to take that. There are rules and regulations about riding brooms, particularly indoors."

The broom slipped effortlessly from between Thea's thighs and floated right into Luc's hand.

Delia's brain began trying to logic its way out of what she'd just seen, but it gave up almost immediately. "What the actual fu—"

"Ladies," Max said. "You're coming with us. We'll explain everything when we get you home."

"But should we drive?"

"No, you most definitely should not," Max said.

"Or operate heavy machinery," Luc added solemnly.

"Amy, you can take the aunts. Delia and Maddie, you're going with us," Max said, eyeing the dog.

Delia was still staring at him, trying to snap herself out of it, when he suddenly waved his hand in the air, and everything that had been flying around the room dropped to the ground at once. The lights went out. The ceiling fans stopped. All was still and quiet.

"Max, did you just—"

He winked at her. "Pretend you didn't see that."

CHAPTER TWENTY-SIX

"Can I get you something, Delia?" Max asked, watching with concern as she stared blankly from an overstuffed armchair in the Merriweathers' living room. Luc had somehow convinced Maddie and the aunties to lie down, as they'd literally entertained themselves into a stupor, and now it was just the three of them—Luc, Amy, and Max—trying to reason with Delia.

"No. I just want it to be tomorrow already, because it occurs to me that I might be dreaming."

Amy looked up from the romance novel she'd plucked off Maddie's nightstand and waved Max over. "She's not going to listen to you. Why should she?"

"Fine," Max said. "Maybe she'll listen to you."

Amy snorted. "Good try. You know I can't talk about—"

Delia held up a finger, and everyone quieted. "What I'm wondering, though," she said, "is when exactly did this start? Max, did we really do sit-ups and make out on the floor in the exercise room? Or did I dream that?"

"I'm sorry. What did she just say?" Amy asked, dropping the book.

Luc looked up from the handheld vacuum he'd been irritatingly turning on and off. "Sit-ups? Really, Max?"

"Yes," Delia insisted. "I dreamed that Max and I did sit-ups, and then he kissed me senseless while rubbing himself all over me and—"

"Delia, that's quite enough," Max said.

"No," Luc said, shaking his head emphatically. "That is not nearly enough. What else happened?"

"Well," Delia said, raising an eyebrow and putting a hand to her mouth as if preparing to share a secret. "I could feel everything right through his corduroys."

"Oh my God!" Amy screamed, standing up. "There is no way you'd have a sex dream involving corduroys. That means it really happened! And you didn't even tell me."

"It *was* a dream. And it was a really good one," Delia said. "I only wish I hadn't dreamed that his parents arrived."

Luc lost it in a coughing fit. When he recovered, he turned to Max. "Mother and Father showed up in the middle? This just keeps getting better."

"What's wrong with corduroys?" Max asked.

"Oh, it was *fun*," Delia said, turning her big brown eyes on Max. "Can we do it again?"

"She's punch-drunk," Luc said. "This is awesome."

She absolutely was. Sometimes surges of magic could make a witch loopy. Inebriated. And Delia was a chatty drunk.

Delia's birthday was Saturday. Why did this all start up today? Magic was pure energy. And the hex was like closing a valve. If the valve was opened, the magic should have flowed immediately.

"Amy, have you known all along about the hex?" Max asked.

Amy stood up. "It's not like they ever stop talking about it. But most people didn't believe them. Not strays and not witches." She jutted her chin out. "I did, though. I always believed them."

"You're a good friend to Delia," Max said softly.

"Please don't be nice to me," Amy said. "You're a Shadowlark witch. And I'm just a little old hedge witch, right?"

"It's not like that."

"It very much *is* like that. And now, if you'll excuse me, I'm going to make some tea."

Amy promptly turned and left the room, and Luc pulled Max over to the window. "Listen, Max. What happened between you and Delia can't happen again. You realize that. Right? She's broken the hex."

Max pinched the bridge of his nose. "If I was bewitched, don't you think I'd know it?"

"No."

How would she have done it? She didn't know how. Max plopped into an armchair and avoided eye contact with Luc. He just needed a moment or two to think.

Amy came in and set a tray of mugs on an end table. "How long do you think she's going to ignore reality?"

"I don't know," Max said. "Why don't you try to talk to her?"

Amy glared at him. "Are you kidding?"

"Why would I be kidding at a time like this?"

"This isn't Shadowlark, you dummy. We hedge witches are gagged. If I try to say anything about the hex to Delia, or even speak of witchcraft in any serious way, I hiccup uncontrollably."

Holy hell, she was right. How could he have forgotten how hedge witches in the Stray Lands were unable to talk about witches or magic around non-magical people? But Delia was no longer magicless. Maybe… "Have you tried now that the hex is broken?"

Amy opened and closed her mouth a few times, but it took a while for her to produce an actual sentence. "Are you saying that I might be able to actually talk to Delia about the hex? That I can tell her that she's a witch and her family isn't crazy?"

"Why don't you try?"

Amy closed her eyes, and when she opened them again, they were shiny with tears. "You have no idea what this means to me."

Delia took small sips from the mug Amy handed her. She was feeling so warm and cozy that she barely heard Amy and Max talking. And that was another reason to believe this was all a hallucination. *Max and Amy were talking.*

"Feeling better?" Amy asked, kneeling in front of her.

"Maybe a little," Delia said. "How about you? Are you still hallucinating? Or did I dream that, too?"

"Nobody is dreaming or hallucinating."

"Ha! I saw things flying around the room back at the Crooked Broom. Herbs were blooming, and crystals were glowing."

"You're a witch," Amy said. And then she fanned her face and forcefully exhaled. "Shit. That felt like a dam just burst. Whew! I mean, oh my God! I said it!" She jumped up and grabbed Max by the lapels of his blazer. "Did you hear that? Not a single hiccup!"

"Max," Delia said. "What's wrong with her?"

Amy launched herself at Delia next, grabbing her by the hand and yanking her to her feet. "I've been wanting to tell you since we were kids. You have no idea—"

"Ha ha," Delia said, although her voice was a bit shaky. "You've crossed over to the dark side with the rest of my family."

"You're a witch," Amy repeated.

This was becoming tiresome. "Listen, Amy, I've had a long day, and it's barely noon. So, if we could stop with the witch nonsense, that would be great."

Amy frowned and looked around the room, as if seeking

inspiration. Her eyes finally landed on the mug still in Delia's hands. "Is that tea too hot for you?" she asked, as if they'd been having a perfectly normal conversation.

Irritation wormed its way up Delia's spine, and when that happened, it always chose her mouth for an exit. "Damn it, Amy. I don't care about the tea—"

"Let's give it a stir." Amy blinked her eyes, and the tiny spoon Delia had set on the end table delicately floated its way up and into the mug, where it began to stir, creating a tiny whirlpool.

Delia shook her head. "What just happened?"

"I'm a witch, too, Delia."

"Oh, for crying out loud. Are you all crazy?"

"I know this is a lot," Amy said. "Especially since I've never mentioned it before now—"

"Ya think?" Delia said. Her head pounded. Her hands shook. How was any of this possible?

"I couldn't tell you before," Amy said, gently taking the cup and setting it down. "Because all the witches of Willow Root are under a gag spell when it comes to talking about witchcraft with anyone who isn't a witch. Not that you aren't a witch, because you are. But you were hexed—"

"Hold up. Did you just say *all the witches of Willow Root*? As in, plural? A plurality of witches?" It seemed there was a word for that, but for the life of her, Delia couldn't think of what it was.

"That would be a coven," Max said. "And, yes, there is one in Willow Root."

"Even if that were true—which it's not—what do you have to do with all of this?"

Max sighed, and then he twitched his mouth in a way that bordered on adorable, and the fireplace roared to life.

Delia shot across the room. "What the hell?"

Amy crossed her arms. "Not all that impressive for a Halifax, but okay."

Delia put a hand to her chest. "Are you trying to tell me everyone in Willow Root is a witch?"

"Of course not," Amy said. "That's silly."

"It's just about two percent of the population, according to the latest census," Max said.

"Oh my God! Stop! Seriously. I don't know what your game is, but I'm done playing."

Max held out the stick from the store. "Try it."

"Try what?"

"Magic, of course. A spell. An intention. Whatever you want. Use your wand."

"This is not a wand," Delia said, glancing at the stick in his hand. "And anyway, I wouldn't even know what to do."

Not that she *wanted* to know what to do. Also, this was stupid.

"I've cast a spell of protection on the room," Max said. "It's safe for you to experiment. And since this wand is *your* wand—"

"And how do you know that?"

"It chose you," Amy said. "It's your wand."

Delia warily eyed the stick.

"As I was saying, since this wand is yours, all you have to do is point it with intention. Nothing complicated, of course. But you should be able to lift a cushion or adjust the fire or open the blinds—I suggest you *don't* open the blinds, by the way—stuff like that."

Tentatively, she took the stick from Max. "I feel so silly." She looked at the book Amy had been reading. Could she flutter its pages?

"All you have to do is think about what you're trying to achieve," Max said. "And then project it through your wand."

Delia took a deep breath and pointed the wand at the book.

"You can speak your intention, if you wish," Max said. "It might be easier."

Nope. She wasn't making this any stupider than it needed to be.

She homed in on the book, and the wand began to vibrate. Her hand and wrist felt pleasantly warm, and that sensation slowly began to creep up her entire arm. Oddly, this caused little to no anxiety. She thought... *Flutter.*

The book's cover lifted.

"Oh my God, did you see that?" Delia said. "It freaking moved!"

"That was very good, Delia!" Amy said, clapping her hands.

"Can I try again?"

Max smiled. "Absolutely. And this time, maintain your concentration until the task is complete. Don't give up."

She squared her shoulders. She looked at the book. She pointed the wand. She projected her thought... *Flutter.*

It started slowly. One page, then two, and three, slowly turning. And then it picked up speed. One after the other, the pages began to flutter. Soon they were a blur. A rush of exhilaration lifted Delia's hair, and—

"Whoa," Max said. "That's enough."

The book slammed shut, and the rush was gone.

"Holy shit," Delia whispered.

Max smiled at her, and the pride that went coursing through Delia's body wasn't magic, but it dang sure felt like it.

Chapter Twenty-Seven

Max's mother paused mid-sip with a cup of tea. "You left your brother over there? What if she tries to bewitch him, too?"

Max rubbed his temples. He, Luc, and Amy had spent the night at the Merriweathers, just to make sure no harm came to them. Max had rushed home first thing this morning to deal with his parents.

"Mother, she hasn't bewitched anyone, nor is she going to bewitch anyone." He hoped that was true. He pushed a paper plate over to Dorcas. "Here. Have a brownie. Luc and Amy made them."

Luc and Amy had stayed up late making brownies while Max had sat in front of the fireplace, trying to figure out *how* and *when* the hex had been broken. And this morning, bleary-eyed and exhausted, he still had no idea.

"Who's Amy? And what are brownies?"

"A brownie is a type of goblin, I believe," Max's father replied. "I don't know who Amy is."

Max pointed at the plate. "Brownies are chocolate cake squares, and Amy is Delia's best friend. She's a witch."

"You mean she's a hedge witch," his mother said, eyebrow raised.

"I've been informed that that is an offensive term."

Dorcas flared her nostrils as she inhaled, but she didn't say anything and commenced sipping her tea.

Logos witches considered hedge witches to be slightly inferior, mostly due to their limited power, which was, of course, a result of the restrictions placed upon them by the Concilium.

"Luc and Amy are bringing the Merriweathers over in about an hour."

"Whatever for?" his mother asked.

"Maybe we should just keep them at their own house until we can figure this hex out," his father said. "Morgaine says we only have until Hallowtide."

"We're not placing the Merriweathers under house arrest," Max snapped. "And anyway, I want to work with them here, at Uncle Hartwell's house. It's heavily protected with charms, and things are less likely to go awry."

"Work with them? Why?" his mother asked.

"At the very least, they need some control. They'll out the witching world otherwise."

"Not if we keep them contained."

"In this town, if the shop remains closed, or Maddie misses a Green Thumb Garden Club meeting, or Thea misses her Zumba classes—"

"What is Zumba? It sounds like dark magic."

"It's some kind of dancing, I think."

He tried not to smile as he remembered Thea bumping into him with her ass while he'd tried to dice a tomato. Smiling was considered a suspicious activity by his parents.

"Listen, as I was saying, if we try to tuck them away from now until Hallowtide, people will notice."

His mother frowned, but she didn't say anything more.

"Hartwell seems to have quite a few books that might be useful to us as we figure out how to rehex the Merriweathers," his father said. "And, of course, I brought the most important book with me."

Armistead held up the *Halifax Book of Hexes*—the same one Max had once seen as a child—and it was just as creepy now as it was then.

"Surely you're not going to try to use the original hex," Max said.

"No, of course not. It's archaic. I don't even understand most of it, and it calls for a—"

"Blood sacrifice."

His father cleared his throat and stirred his tea. "I'm sure there's a way to cast a perma-tempus hex without having to kill someone."

"Goodness, Armistead. Let's hope so," his mother said.

"The whole thing is ridiculous," Max said. "For one thing, we are required to follow the laws of the nations in which we reside. Murder is illegal. And the Merriweathers are a family of harmless women—"

"It's concerning that you consider them harmless," his father said simply. "And I have no intention of breaking any laws. But we must find a way to do what we've been told to do, or—"

"Or what?" Max said. "I mean, what are they going to do to us?"

"Oh, believe me, Maximus," his mother said. "There are things they can do."

"I asked Morgaine if we could appeal to the Concilium—"

"Maximus, don't be so dense," his mother snapped. "The Concilium does whatever Morgaine tells them to do."

"Dorcas is right," his father said. "You're hardly ever in Shadowlark. But things have changed. You don't go up against a Gerard."

Delia woke up with a headache and rolled right into Amy, which was something that hadn't happened since high school. She groaned and closed her eyes.

"How'd you sleep?" Amy asked.

"I don't know," Delia mumbled. "I had the weirdest dreams."

"Were we witches?"

Delia opened her left eye and squinted at Amy. "How did you know?"

"It wasn't a dream, Delia."

Delia kicked off the covers and sat up like a rocket, headache or no. Her eyes darted all around her bright pink room, which looked the same as ever. She got up and hurried to the window, and the front lawn looked the same as ever, too.

But when she looked back at Amy's earnest-yet-clearly-entertained-by-Delia's-crisis face, it hit her.

It's real.

Her head started to spin…

"Whoa, whoa, whoa there," Amy said, getting up and grabbing Delia by the arm. "Do you need to lie down again?"

"No," Delia said, forcing herself to stop shaking. "I'm fine."

"That might be a stretch."

"No kidding."

"So, how did you do it?" Amy asked.

"How did I do what?"

"Dummy, you broke the hex!"

"It wasn't me. Promise."

Amy sat back down on the bed, and Delia sat on the tiny vanity stool.

"Seriously," Delia said. "We made soup like we've done during every blue moon. That's it. We didn't stick any babies in it. We didn't spill anyone's blood. At no time did any ghosts appear."

"Well, somebody did it."

Delia plucked a tissue off the vanity and blew her nose. "I feel… crazy?"

"You're not. Believe me."

"Tell me everything," Delia said. "How long have you known that I'm a witch?"

"I think it was around the third grade when I first heard the rumors."

"People talk about us? Like, other people here knew we were witches?"

"Nobody really believed it. I mean, *I* did. But everyone else just thought..."

"That we were nuts."

Amy nodded, looking a bit sheepish. "I hiccuped every single time I tried to tell you."

Delia sighed. "You hiccuped a lot."

Amy shrugged. "I tried to tell you a lot."

"That must have been pretty rough on you."

Amy walked over, picked up a hairbrush, and began working what was apparently a gigantic rat's nest of a knot out of Delia's hair. "It's been lonely having to hide a part of myself from you. I mean, we've always done everything together."

"And now we can do witch things together," Delia said, reaching back and squeezing Amy's hand. "Although I don't really know any witch things to do."

"There's a coven meeting tomorrow. Y'all should come."

"Really? That sounds...scary? But I feel like I've got so much to learn. For example, *ouch!* Use a lighter touch, will you?"

"Sorry."

"What I'm wondering is, who hexed us? And why?"

"I have no idea who hexed you. But I've heard rumors as to why—"

A loud crash downstairs interrupted the conversation. Delia

looked at Amy, and then the two of them jumped up and sprinted out the bedroom door and down the turret tower stairs. When they arrived at the bottom, they were met by a very harried Luc—shirt untucked, hair sticking up, sweat dripping down his scruffy face— yielding a freaking wand like he was on a movie set.

"Stay back," he shouted.

Delia and Amy froze as an end table crashed into the recliner. Andi and Aurora stood in the doorway to the kitchen, looking very apologetic.

Luc waved his wand and said something completely unintelligible, and the furniture righted itself.

"Sorry," Andi said.

"You didn't do it on purpose," Grandma Maddie said, coming in from the kitchen with a platter of pancakes. As she set them on the table, the light bulbs in the chandelier popped, one after the other, raining glass on the table.

"There went some perfectly good pancakes," she muttered, removing the plate.

"Maddie, we need to teach you how to rein it in," Luc said. "You're popping light bulbs everywhere you go."

"I can't help it," Grandma Maddie said. "All I have to do is open my mouth to speak and—"

The light bulb in the lamp on the sideboard popped.

"Everyone, go get dressed," Luc said. "We'll head to the manor, where, hopefully, Max can help you all get some control of yourselves."

The aunts filed silently by, and when Maddie passed, she patted Delia on the cheek. "Good morning, dear."

As soon as they were out of the room, Luc collapsed into a chair, looking totally spent.

"What was with the furniture?" Amy asked.

"Whenever Andi and Aurora argue, the furniture starts fighting. I've never seen anything like it."

"Yikes! We'd better go get dressed," Delia said. "Before the entire house falls apart."

Just as they turned to go, Luc touched Delia's arm. "You know that book you mentioned?"

"Were we talking about books?"

"Yes. You got one from the library with the Blue Moon Spell…"

"Oh my Lord. That silly old thing?" The look on Luc's face, combined with her current unbelievable reality, made her change her tune. "Oh shit. You mean it's a real spell book?"

"I'm certainly thinking it might be," Luc said.

"It's in the kitchen with all the other cookbooks," Delia said. "Just to the right of the stove."

Luc's mouth dropped open. "In the kitchen with all the other…" He shook his head as if getting rid of cobwebs.

"Well, all we use it for is making soup," Delia said. "Just made sense to keep it there."

CHAPTER TWENTY-EIGHT

These are our parents," Max said as the Merriweather women gathered in the foyer. "Armistead Halifax and Dorcas Golding."

"Oh my goodness!" Maddie exclaimed, rushing over to Max's mother as if they were old friends. "It is such a pleasure to meet you. I'm Madora Merriweather, and these are my sisters, Aurora, Andromeda, and Theadora."

Thea nodded, while Aurora and Andi curtsied clumsily, as if they were meeting royalty.

"And this is my daughter, Fiona."

Fiona waved shyly.

"And my granddaughter, the Blue Witch Cordelia, whom I think you've already met."

Delia's cheeks turned bright red, and Max wasn't sure if it was because she'd just been referred to as the Blue Witch Cordelia or because she was remembering the circumstances under which she'd met his parents.

"We absolutely adore your sons," Maddie continued, in a gushing tone. "Truly, we do."

Dorcas put a hand to her chest, as if this were shocking news. And really, it probably was. Expressing adoration was an outlandish concept to a Logos witch.

"Oh, absolutely," Aurora said. "We love them to bits."

"You have done an excellent job raising such wonderful young men," Thea added. "You must be so proud."

A little color rose in their mother's cheeks, and there was a hint of a smile on her lips. "Well, now, I guess they are rather fine, aren't they?"

It was as if the concept had never occurred to her.

Behind Thea, Fiona stood quietly, looking shell-shocked. Max walked over to stand next to her. "How are you doing?"

"Max," she whispered. "I just arrived home this morning, and all hell had broken loose. I've seen some...things. Is it true?"

"That you're a witch? Yes. Yes, it's true. Surely you noticed something while you were in Austin?"

"Oh yes. I nearly burned my hotel down by cursing the thermostat in my room. And by cursing, I'm ashamed to say I called it a ducking pathetic waste of space on the wall, only I didn't say ducking. And then it burst into flames."

"Did it warm up the room?" he asked with as straight a face as he could muster.

A small smile unfurled on Fiona's pale face. "Oh yes, it did. Quite nicely. And you should probably go retrieve my mother before she gives your parents a heart attack. I understand, from Amy, that you Halifaxes are..."

Max raised his eyebrows. "That we're what?"

"High class," Fiona whispered.

"I was certain you were going to say assholes," Max whispered back.

Fiona smiled. "I didn't want to quote her directly."

Delia touched his arm, and when their eyes met, something settled neatly in his chest like a missing puzzle piece, and he'd never felt so whole. A small voice in the back of his mind, however, tried to raise an alarm.

Watch yourself. She has her magic back.

She had puffy eyes, and her hair was messy, which made her all the more endearing.

"Where is Amy?" he asked.

"She went home for a bit with Splash. She said she'll be back around lunchtime. And don't worry. Amy explained about the gag. I realize you couldn't tell me that you knew we were witches."

Max swallowed. Delia didn't realize that only the hedge witches were gagged. He should speak up and tell her the truth, but...

"Let's all head to the library," Luc said, and they started moving that way.

Maddie squeezed Max's arm. "Thank you for teaching us the ropes. How lucky are we that you're here?"

"Yes," Max said, swallowing with difficulty. "So lucky."

As they stepped into the library, Max tried to get everyone's attention by clearing his throat. But there was a lot of chatter, and no one heard him. "Can I have everyone's attention, please?"

The answer was apparently no, because the racket didn't noticeably simmer down. Max sighed, and then he directed his gaze at a huge stuffed owl perched in the corner. He twitched his mouth, and the owl screeched loudly and fluttered its wings.

Everyone froze.

"Just a bit of necromancy," he said with a wink.

"Show-off," Luc quipped.

His father puffed out his chest. "That's my boy."

In the newly minted silence, Maddie's knees gave way, and she landed inelegantly into a chair that was, thankfully, directly behind her.

A light bulb in the nearest lamp exploded. "Pardon me," she said.

"You are pardoned," Luc said with a small, formal bow that made Maddie blush.

"I admit that I don't even know where to start," Max said.

Maddie smiled encouragingly at him. "Don't be nervous. We're your eager and trusting students."

"With a shit ton of questions," Delia added. "So maybe we should start with those."

This was going to be a tightrope act. Because they would definitely have a lot of questions, and he had no intention of answering all of them. The one he was dreading the most was—

"Who hexed us?" Delia asked.

He'd grappled with it all night. If he told the Merriweathers that it was his ancestors who'd hexed them, would Delia trust him enough to accept his help now? In the end, he didn't want to risk it.

"We'll be getting into that later—"

"Why not now?" Delia persisted.

Max wiped a bit of sweat off his forehead.

"It was someone who'd been bewitched by your ancestor, Lucinda. As I said, it was a long time ago. Water under the bridge, as they say."

"What does that mean?" Thea asked. "What does it mean for something or someone to be bewitched, as opposed to hexed or cursed?"

Of course, it would be practical, analytical Thea who would want to know the difference. "Well, bewitchment involves getting your subject to do your bidding, often by manipulating their feelings."

"Like with a love spell?" Thea asked.

And there it was. The first spell mentioned by a Merriweather was a love spell.

"Well, yes," Max said. "They're forbidden, by the way. For that reason."

Maddie's eyes grew huge, and Max swore she mumbled the word *oops* before saying, "Really? It seems pretty harmless to encourage love among people."

"I think," Delia said, "that it's kind of like how we talk about consent. You can't consent to anything if you're bewitched, because you're not fully in control of yourself."

"Oh goodness," Maddie said. "Then I would never want to bewitch anyone."

Max believed her. He risked a glance at his parents, and their expressions told him they were not convinced. Not in the slightest.

"Shall we start with the basic principles of magic as it relates to the physical realm?" he asked.

Andi raised her hand, waving it back and forth.

"Yes, Andi?"

"Are vampires real?"

"Are you...? Did you just...? I'm sorry, did you ask about *vampires*?"

"It's a perfectly reasonable question," Aurora said. "Witches are real. So, why not vampires?"

"Witches have always been real," Max said incredulously. "In fact, the theory is that all humans were once witches. But demons led most astray—"

"Demons are real?" Delia asked. "Are they evil?"

"Of course they are," Luc said. "They're demons. But vampires? That's absolutely bonkers."

"Well, what about werewolves?" Maddie asked.

"What about them?"

"Are they real?"

Max covered his eyes with his hand and took two deep breaths to collect himself. "No. No, there is no such thing as werewolves."

"How about were-tigers?" Thea asked.

Maddie raised her hand. "Or were-elephants?"

"There are no shape-shifters whatsoever," Max said. "They do not exist. The idea of a human shifting into an animal and back again is ridiculous."

Nikki poked his head in. "It's not *that* ridiculous."

Luc grinned at Nikki. "But you're not a human, now, are you?"

The women gasped, and Max sighed. Apparently they were going to let it all hang out. Lay it all out on the table, so to speak. Except for one crucial fact: the Merriweathers were hexed by the Halifaxes.

Nikki smiled, enjoying the attention. "No, I'm not human. But I *am* somewhat of a shape-shifter."

The women squealed in delight as Nikki crossed his arms and leaned against the doorframe with a smirk.

"At most, you're a lesser demon," Max said. "Don't get too full of yourself."

"Nikki, what are you exactly?" Delia asked, eyes narrowed.

Nikki bowed dramatically. "I am an imp."

Nikki was enjoying this way too much. But it was rare that a magical creature was ever allowed a Big Reveal, so Max let him have his moment. And sensing Nikki's desire for drama, the ladies obliged with raucous applause.

"I am the familiar of Hartwell Halifax," Nikki continued. "And of Magnus Halifax, and of Basil Halifax before that, and of Patience Halifax before that—oh wait, no, I forgot about Thaddeus—"

"Aren't familiars typically cats?" Thea interrupted.

"They are," Nikki replied.

Delia gasped. "Oh my God. You're Hartwell's cat!"

Nikki smiled warmly, took Delia's hand, and kissed it. "Hello, Delia."

Delia jumped out of her chair and hugged him. "I knew it. I knew I'd met you before."

"Yes, you naughty thing," Nikki said with a grin. "You kept Hartwell on his toes, constantly barging through the back door without knocking."

Delia squeezed Nikki until Max thought the imp's eyes might pop. "Sorry."

"Don't be. That brief interlude got me through the next twenty-five years, until you barged into the shop, past the closed sign and the deterrent spell, and we were able to speak again."

"Oh, Nikki," Delia said. Then she turned to Max. "Why can't you let him talk to other people?"

"It's too risky," Max said. "He's not human. He can only assume this form in the manor or the antique shop."

"Do you like being a familiar, Nikki?" Maddie asked, shooting Max a side-eye.

"That's a story for another day," Max said. "Let's move on to another topic, shall we?"

"Can I ask Nikki one more question?" Fiona asked.

Since she hadn't asked *any* questions, Max nodded.

"What do you look like when you're not a black cat or a ridiculously handsome man?"

"Imps are too horrid to be seen by human eyes," Luc said. "Our minds can't even process it."

"I'm not sure that's the reason, but okay," Nikki said.

Thea's hand shot up. "Excuse me, Max. But are there fairies?"

"I think I'll have to say yes to that one."

"I knew it!" Delia said. "I've always had a soft spot for fairies. Making fairy circles in the garden was one of my most favorite childhood activities."

Andi raised her hand and shouted, "What about elves? Do they exist?"

"No," Max said.

"Ghosts!" Aurora said, snapping her fingers.

"Open to interpretation."

"BIGFOOT!" Maddie shouted, as if she were on a game show.

"Now you're just being silly."

Why was he smiling? For the life of him, he didn't know.

CHAPTER TWENTY-NINE

M ax kept Delia in the library while everyone else followed Luc to the living room. And she was glad, because she desperately wanted to be alone with him. Being close to Max was the only thing making her feel sane. Which was crazy. Because the man was a freaking witch! Or maybe a warlock. Good Lord, she didn't know what he was.

"This is a safe room," Max said. "Uncle Hartwell has it very well protected. There's nothing you can do here that could result in your own harm."

"What about Grandma Maddie and the others? Can they hurt themselves or someone else?"

"Father is casting protection spells as we speak. And Luc has gotten pretty good at dodging the occasional exploding light bulb or flying chair. I think everyone will be fine."

"I still have so many questions. Like, why isn't any of that stuff happening around me?"

"We haven't discovered the nature of your magic yet," Max said. "As for the other questions you might have, I thought we settled the Bigfoot thing."

"Hardly! But let me ask a few more. Was Hartwell also a witch? Or, rather, a wizard? I mean, what do you call yourself?"

Max, seated on the leather ottoman, leaned in. "I prefer witch.

And yes, Uncle Hartwell was also one. Most witches are women, although obviously, not all."

"Who are the others?"

All last night, she'd tossed and turned, remembering various times when things hadn't been quite right. Like, for her entire freaking life, it seemed that something was somewhere it shouldn't have been. Then it wasn't. Something happened too quickly or too perfectly, and explanations didn't quite make sense, or everyone in the room suddenly stopped talking.

"I don't know all of the local witches. But I've met a few besides Amy. They're probably all people you know."

"Are there witches *everywhere*?"

Max reached out and took her hands in his. "Wherever there is a magical source, you'll find witches. Ley lines run beneath Willow Root, and one of them feeds the old willow tree on the banks of Willow Pond. I suspect that's where your wands came from."

"I can't believe this has been right under my nose, and I never knew."

"We'd like to keep it that way. I need to help you and your family gain control before you out the entire witching world. Did you notice your backyard?"

Their backyard, usually a mess of weeds and sticker burrs, had literally bloomed overnight. It was now a jungle of tropical blooming plants, butterflies, and songbirds. "I'm pretty sure that was Grandma Maddie. It's totally harmless."

Max looked pretty tired this morning. His wavy hair was even more rebellious than usual, and he hadn't shaved. The more she focused on how his stubble was darker and more concentrated in that tiny little rivet of his chin dimple, the more she felt her insides stirring in a very pleasant way.

Max suddenly sat up straighter. "What are you doing?"

"Pardon?"

"You're doing some magic. I can feel it."

Well, this was mortifying. She wasn't doing anything on purpose.

Max closed his eyes and became very still. "It's retreating now."

"To where?"

"Inside you. And that's where it should stay until summoned."

"I don't know how to summon it."

"Obviously. And until you learn, it'll occasionally rush out on its own whenever you become...excited." He brushed a bit of imaginary lint off his shoulder, and color appeared on his cheeks.

There was a loud thud in the other room, followed by raucous laughter.

"Okay," Max said, sitting up straighter. "We're going to discover the nature of your magic. We'll do an exercise we typically do as children, when our magic is first waking up. You'll need to lie down, flat on your back."

Delia sat on the floor. "You're not going to make me do sit-ups, are you?"

Max laughed. "No. I promise."

She lay down on the plush, woven rug and looked up at Max, feeling overwhelmingly curious but also totally and completely safe.

"Have you heard of Reiki?" Max asked.

"Yes. There's a practitioner who comes into the Crooked Broom every so often. It has something to do with energy, right?"

"Exactly. I'm going to use something similar to try to find your granum, which is a tiny spark of magic. I'll see if I can turn it into a flame. And don't worry. It should feel rather pleasant."

"Go for it. Many men have tried and failed."

"Pardon?"

"Just joking."

Max smiled deliciously. "I was raised in a matriarchal culture, Delia. Believe me, I know where it is."

Delia fanned her face and looked at the ceiling. She 100 percent believed that Max knew where it was.

Max sat on his butt and crossed his legs. Then he held his hands over her body, fingers splayed, eyes closed. "Relax."

"Do I close my eyes?"

"If you want to."

She did.

"Breathe in and out," Max said softly. "At first you'll feel my power…"

She opened one eye and watched as Max's hands hovered over her chest and then down over her tummy, and *whoa*. Something warm and electric moved just over the surface of her skin. It tickled slightly, but not in an irritating way, as it darted this way and that. It felt curious. And as Max had predicted, it was pleasant.

"I'm searching for your granum." He opened one eye and grinned. "You'll know when I find it."

She closed her eyes again and let Max's magic go wherever it wanted.

"Oh," Max gasped. "It's there. I can feel it."

She could feel it, too. And it was becoming a little more than pleasant.

"Imagine my hands as magnets," Max said quietly. "Let's see if I can get it to move."

Oh, things are definitely moving.

Something inside her was following Max's hands like an obedient puppy.

"Your magic is checking mine out," Max said. "It's a flirty little spark."

She concentrated, trying to grab hold of the energy buzzing around hers.

"Hey," Max said. "What are you doing?"

She didn't know, but she was doing *something*, and it felt awesome.

Max suddenly sucked air in through his teeth. "Delia—"

She had it. Him. His magic. Whatever. She began to throb in a familiar way, and her hips rocked against her will.

Max began to breathe even heavier. "Delia," Max gasped. "You need to stop."

She didn't want to stop, but also, she didn't know how.

"Pull it back—"

Something crashed loudly in the other room, and Delia sat up with a start. And then, just like that, her power, which she'd apparently unleashed in a fury of lust, just kind of slowly slithered down an imaginary drain to hide itself in horny shame.

"Sorry," she said, not really knowing what she was apologizing for.

Max exhaled and ran both hands through his hair, making it stand on end. "You, uh…that was…"

The library door slid open, and Luc poked his head in. He raised an eyebrow and took a couple of steps into the room. "Wow. What just happened in here?"

Max's pupils looked larger than average. "Nothing."

Luc raised an eyebrow. "Amy is here with lunch. And the dog. Also, the twins got into it, and the chandelier attacked a table lamp, but it's all good now."

"Thanks," Max said. "We'll be out in a moment."

Luc started to retreat and close the door, but then he seemed to hesitate and left it open.

Delia glanced at Max, expecting to see a grin on his face. But instead, his eyebrows were drawn into a contemplative scowl.

Delia's magic was *querious*, like his own. It wasn't exactly rare, but it wasn't common, either.

Most magic exited the body through a wand or talisman to *do* something. But querious magic was on a mission to *find* something. He used his to find a hex's path, so he could undo it. But it could also be used to find someone's weakness. Or desire. Or any number of things.

It would come in handy for a Cor witch.

"Is everything okay?" Delia asked. "Did I do something wrong?"

Not intentionally. Of that, he was certain.

He smiled and stood, offering a hand to Delia. "You surprised me a little. That's all."

"Oh Lord. Was it weird? What I did?"

He tried to chuckle, but it came out as a gross kind of gurgle, and he cleared his throat instead. "Not weird. Just uncommon. We'll talk more about it later. As for now, I'm starving. Let's go see what Amy brought."

Together they went to the kitchen, where the others were gathered around Hartwell's table.

"Check out this spread," Aurora said, cramming an olive into her mouth. "Amy does the best boards."

Max's parents entered the room. "We were summoned," his mother said. "Is there a problem?"

"No. But there's lunch," Maddie said. "This is Amy. She brought all this food. Now, y'all sit down and let us fix your plates."

"We can service ourselves—"

"Sit," Maddie said, pressing Max's mother into a chair.

"This is how they do it here," Luc said, patting her back. "Don't offend them."

"What is all this?" Max's dad asked, gesturing to the gigantic board piled high with crackers, meats, cheeses, and spreads.

"Charcuterie," Amy said. "It's my business. And since I'm pretty much out of magic, I had to do this shit by hand."

"You created this without magic?" Max's mother asked.

"Yes. And believe me, Hallowtide can't come soon enough."

"What is Hallowtide, dear?" Aurora asked.

"And how can you be out of magic?" Delia asked. "What does that even mean? And anyway, I saw you use magic yesterday, remember? You made the spoon stir my tea."

"You're right. And it was the last bit of magic that I had."

"You used the last of your magic for *me*?" Delia asked incredulously.

"What else was I going to do with it?" Amy said. "It was worth it to see the look on your face. But as I was explaining, every year at Hallowtide, we poor little hedge witches gather at the willow tree to receive whatever piddly ass amount of magic the Concilium has decided we can have for the year."

"Now, now," Max's father said. "It's a proper amount."

"A proper amount for what?" Amy asked.

"This all looks absolutely delicious," Max's father said, ignoring Amy's question.

Delia pointed at a little bowl. "Is that the pumpkin hummus I've been waiting all year for?"

Amy nodded. "I also made the pumpkin fig spread you love. It's going on all my fall boards."

Good. They'd moved past the discussion of tidings, which were always a somewhat touchy subject for witches in the Stray Lands.

"Pardon me, Amy," Fiona said, very politely. "But who is the Concilium? And why do they limit your magic?"

Alas, they had not moved past the discussion of tidings.

"The Concilium is the so-called governing body. And they don't just limit my magic. They'll limit yours, too. And it's so they can have more for themselves."

"That is not true," Max's father said sternly, and discomfort wormed its way into Max's belly, even though there was nothing to feel uncomfortable about. Magic was regulated in the Stray Lands because it had to be.

"Shadowlark has spoken," Amy said with an eye roll. "End of discussion."

"Can we just eat?" Max asked. "I think we're all tired and hungry."

His father dipped a cracker in the pumpkin hummus and plopped it in his mouth. "Oh my, this is delicious. Dorcas, try it."

Maddie handed Max's mother a plate loaded with cheeses, dips, olives, grapes, crackers, and pretzels. "Try the fig jam with a piece of cheese. It's a party for the mouth."

Dorcas nibbled at a cracker smeared with fig jam and then took a dainty bite of cheese. She chewed slowly, almost cautiously, and then said, "Oh my. Amy, you hedge witches are brilliantly resourceful."

Amy gasped. "Did you just call me a hedge witch?"

Max's mother looked surprised. "It's what you are, and you just said so yourself—"

"Of course I can say so myself!" Amy said. "But *you* can't say it."

"Amy," Luc said. "Maybe this is a discussion for another time."

"Why?" Amy said. "The Merriweathers need to know how things work around here. Don't they? And the truth is that the witches of Shadowlark withhold magic from the rest of us—"

"It's not withheld," Max said, trying to sound calm. "It's regulated."

"Ha," Amy said. "And they call us hedge witches. As if we were simply born without the ability to do Big Magic."

"This is exactly the kind of talk that influenced Hartwell," Armistead said, pushing his plate away. "I will not listen to it."

"What is she talking about?" Maddie asked, looking at Max.

"Magic is a limited resource. Shadowlark is considered the Cradle of the Craft. It's where our libraries and vaults are. It takes an immense amount of magic to protect it. Also—and I assume Amy knows this—it simply isn't safe to do Big Magic in the Stray Lands."

Delia looked indignant. "The Stray Lands? Are we considered strays?"

"That's not a bad word," Luc said. "Strays are simply non-witches. They're people who strayed from the Source. And no, you are not one."

Max's father rose from the table. And as he passed, Max could have sworn he heard him say, "For now."

CHAPTER THIRTY

Max couldn't believe this was Halifax Manor. In just one week, and with just a few upgrades, the place had been transformed. The countertops looked amazing. In fact, the entire *house* looked amazing.

"Are you really going to let someone else move in here?" Luc asked.

Was he? Because he could somehow see himself in this kitchen, doing all kinds of kitcheny things. The butcher-block island made him want to grab a knife and dice a tomato while blaring music and sipping wine and dancing with Delia and—

"Maximus," his mother, said, coming in from the living room. "There have been odd people here all day! Making all sorts of horrible noise and an even bigger mess, for the sole purpose of what, exactly?"

"To make the home more appealing to buyers," Max said simply, choosing not to mention that it seemed to be making the home more appealing to *him*.

"That's the silliest thing I've ever heard," Dorcas said. "There are spells for that."

Max shrugged. Until recently, he would have had zero qualms about using them. But now it seemed like cheating.

His mother rolled her eyes. "And you could even use magic to do all this physical labor in a fraction of the time and without any mess."

That was also true. But Max kind of liked watching the craftsmen work. Most of them were friends and acquaintances of Delia's. "You do realize that the people in the Stray Lands need jobs with which to support their families?"

Dorcas looked slightly confused, as if Max had spoken in another language.

"Anyway," Max continued. "The painters are just finishing up the trim outside. They'll be gone soon. And then Luc and I are headed to a local coven meeting."

Dorcas looked astonished. "Why would you want to do that?"

"Constance Fleming invited us," Luc said. "Since I work for the Hexing and Cursing Division of the MCU, she asked me to put the fear of the Goddess into the local witches. They've been illegally hexing each other over mundane things like showers and volleyball tryouts."

"Why must Maximus attend?"

"Because as representatives of Shadowlark, it would be bad form to turn down an invitation," Max said.

Also, he was hoping to lose Luc after the meeting and go somewhere he and Delia could be alone for five fucking minutes. Even if she was able to bewitch him, she certainly didn't have the intent. And he trusted his own ability to keep himself safe. After all, he'd felt it when her power had crossed the line, hadn't he?

He was a skilled and powerful witch. There was nothing to worry about.

"I didn't come in here to discuss local matters," Dorcas said. "Your father has called us to Hartwell's study."

"What does he want to talk to us about?" Max asked. Anxiety clenched his gut. Hopefully, it wasn't—

"The Merriweathers, I presume," Dorcas said. "Let's hope he's figured out a way to rehex them, so we can all return home."

Max and Luc had worked with the Merriweathers for the past week, and they'd made huge gains in controlling their abilities, which were as unique and quirky as the Merriweathers themselves. It was exhilarating to watch them discover their own power. It was, well, magical.

As they followed their mother to the study, Max and Luc looked at each other. *What are we going to do?*

They entered the study to find their father slouched behind the desk with a stack of books piled so high that it threatened to tumble over.

Armistead stood up and walked to the window, and for the first time, Max realized his father was aging. His hair had gone completely gray, and there was a stoop to his shoulders that hadn't been there before.

"It's been a very long time since I've been here," he said, picking up an old, framed photo of two young men.

Luc smiled. "Is that...?"

"Me and Hartwell. Yes. It was right before he was sent on his first mission, in search of the Sicilian demon stones."

"Did he find them?" Max asked.

His father looked almost offended. "Of course he did. And he had to fight two demons in the process."

"Those were the good old days for venators," Luc said. "All Max has ever had to fight is traffic."

"That's not true. I had to fight an old Russian woman for cursed nesting dolls once."

But Luc was right. Max's hunting of rare magical items mostly involved antique stores, flea markets, and bazaars. Occasionally, he was sent to handle an actual emergency with a hexed item (he'd never forgive whoever had hexed that porta-potty at Burning Man), but typically, he was responding to rumors, reports, and good old-fashioned hunches.

"Oh yes," Nikki muttered from where he sat in a leather armchair situated in the corner. "The good old days for the venators."

"Pardon me?" Armistead said, looking clearly startled, because he'd probably been unaware of Nikki's presence. "If you have something to say, please don't mumble."

Nikki stood. "All I'm saying is that witches no longer have to steal magical items from demons and the like, simply because there are none left to steal."

"Did you say *steal*?" Armistead said. "What nerve!"

"What would you call it? Those were Sicilian demon stones, not Sicilian witch stones."

Max was used to Nikki's opinions by now, and honestly, they seemed less extreme to him than they had in the beginning. But his father wasn't used to it, and he huffed and puffed and turned various shades of purple before saying, "Collecting dangerous magical items is for everyone's protection."

Nikki waved a hand. "It's for the protection of witches. Shadowlark witches in particular."

Luc and Max looked at each other expectantly, because their father wasn't going to let that one slide. "Now I know where my brother got all his strange ideas," he said. "From an imp!" He pulled out his wand. "It's time to put an end to this nonsense."

Luc stepped in front of Nikki, who had stealthily moved toward the door, and Max rushed over to their father. "Hold on. Don't do anything rash."

"It was Hartwell who acted rashly by giving this creature a voice."

Nikki had one hand on the doorknob, ready to bolt.

"Father," Max said. "You're upset."

Armistead, triggered by the accusation that he was emotional, began sputtering and fuming in earnest—a perfect demonstration of being emotional—until he finally said, "How my brother ended up in this Goddess-forsaken town, separated from his family and his own kind, disgraced, and dying all alone, I will *never* know. And the idiot did it by choice!"

Nikki stepped out from behind Luc. "He was not disgraced; nor did he die alone," he said through clenched teeth, his bright green eyes flaring dangerously.

Armistead lowered his wand. Max moved closer, just in case he'd need to take hold of his father's arm.

"He didn't die alone," Nikki continued. "Because I was here with him."

Oh, holy hell. The narrative was that Hartwell had died alone in the house, but of course Nikki had been there.

Max went to touch Nikki's shoulder, but Nikki moved just outside of his reach. Then he walked over to Hartwell's desk and opened a drawer.

"That's empty," Luc said. "I packed up everything in Uncle Hartwell's desk."

Nikki raised an eyebrow at Luc and then effortlessly removed the drawer's false bottom, revealing several leather-bound books. He handed them all to Armistead. "These are his journals. Believe it or not, I think he'd want you to have them."

"You've read them, haven't you? You insolent—"

"I have not," Nikki said. "Hartwell forbade it. He said there were things in it an imp shouldn't know."

"I guess he hadn't totally lost his mind then." Armistead put the journals on the desk with an air of reluctance—it was obvious he wanted to read them on the spot—and picked up the *Halifax Book of Hexes.* "I called you in here, because we must discuss rehexing the Merriweathers. It seems nobody has done a perma-tempus hex in the last hundred years or so. And they all have that problematic element in common."

"Blood sacrifice?" Max asked, dread pooling in his belly.

His father nodded.

"Maybe we shouldn't even be researching perma-tempus hexes," Luc said. "I mean, nobody wants to come out and say this, but it's dark magic, isn't it?"

Everyone in the room seemed to hold their breath until their father finally answered. "It doesn't specifically call up the dark forces. But it's an uncomfortably blurry line. Unfortunately, we only have a week until Hallowtide. We have to figure something out, and I want everyone's mind in the game. If we fail, I fear the consequences will be…unpleasant."

Their mother shivered, and for the first time, Max wondered exactly why she'd come. After all, she wasn't technically a Halifax.

"Well, on that not-ominous-at-all note," Luc said, "I'm afraid Max and I are running late. We really must be off."

Nikki followed them out of the study, and as soon as the door was shut behind them, Max turned to face him. "I want to thank you for taking care of our uncle."

Nikki looked shocked for a moment, but then he said, "Oh, well, it was…"

"You were his family in our absence. I know you comforted him as best you could."

Nikki swallowed loudly.

"You were loyal, faithful, and devoted. In ways you weren't

required to be. And you have my gratitude. I promise, I will do whatever it takes to free you of this bond. Do you hear me? You deserve to be free, and I won't stop until I figure out a way."

Nikki didn't say a word.

And then Max did something that he could never have imagined doing when he'd first walked through the front door of Halifax Manor.

He gave Nikki a hug. And it was a long one.

"I can't believe the coven meeting is at Constance Fleming's house," Grandma Maddie muttered as they parked across the street and watched a group of three go in.

"I guess we were bound to have our first witchy disappoint-ment," Thea said, staring out the windshield. "Isn't that the high school volleyball coach?"

Delia pressed her nose against the window. "Yes, but more sur-prisingly, isn't that the Methodist minister's wife?"

Fiona sighed. "I'd always assumed covens met in the woods. Beneath a full moon. Something romantic like that."

"What have you got against a nice cul-de-sac?" Andi asked.

"I'm a Realtor," Fiona said. "I love a good cul-de-sac. But this is…"

"Underwhelming?"

"A bit."

Relief washed over Delia as Amy pulled up behind them in her minivan. They wouldn't have to go in alone. "I think we're over-dressed," she said, watching Amy get out of her van wearing jeans and a Willie Nelson T-shirt.

Grandma Maddie had insisted on pulling a big trunk down from the attic. To Delia's horror, she'd pulled out six dusty, moth-eaten robes in crimson red. She claimed they'd belonged to their ancestors and had insisted they all put them on for their first official coven meeting. Luckily, the matching pointy hats were so holey and misshapen as to be unwearable.

Amy tapped on the window and waved. "Y'all coming in?"

Grandma Maddie opened her door, and then they all spilled out like clowns from a clown car. Amy stood there, gobsmacked.

"They're the cloaks of our ancestors," Grandma Maddie said. "Aren't they grand?"

"They're something, all right," Amy said, winking at Delia. "This is going to be great."

When Constance opened the door, her mouth dropped.

"Trick or treat," Delia said.

Constance yanked them all inside. "Goodness gracious, get in here before the neighbors see you!"

As was often the case when the Merriweathers arrived on the scene, all conversation in the room stopped.

"So, it's true then?" Joyce Gonzales finally said. "The Merriweathers are witches?"

"Since you just said it in front of them, I'd say it's true. The Merriweathers are witches," Mona Henning said.

"Oh!" Joyce squealed. "You did, too! Mona, you said it. Out loud!"

"Well, what do you know?" Constance said. "I never believed it, myself. But here you are. And since none of us are sneezing, burping, gagging, or coughing—"

"Or hiccuping," Amy added.

"Then the Merriweathers must be witches."

A chorus of uncontrollable chatter broke out, and Delia was overwhelmed by the enormity of the secret. How deep it had gone. And for *how long*.

Constance clapped her hands sharply. "I need everyone's

attention. I know this is all very exciting, but we need to start our meeting. Take a seat, please!"

They all sat, and a light bulb in the small Tiffany lamp on the end table burst, making everyone jump. "Oops," Grandma Maddie said. "Pardon me."

A few titters traveled through the room, but a stern look from Constance settled them down. Aunt Thea raised her hand.

"Yes, Thea?" Constance said.

Aunt Thea pulled a piece of paper out of her bra. "I have a few questions."

"We have an order to our proceedings. I'm afraid you'll have to wait."

Thea tucked the paper back in. "Carry on."

"First of all, a warm welcome to the Merriweathers," Constance said. "How delightful to have you join us."

Everyone clapped politely.

"Would you like to stand up and tell us a bit about yourselves? That's what we do when witches from neighboring covens come to call."

Delia's family looked at her, so she stood up. "Well, y'all know us. So I don't think we need to introduce ourselves. And this is Willow Root, so you know our business, and I don't think we need to get into that, either. But somehow I've accidentally broken a centuries-old hex on my family, and we have no idea how it happened. If anyone has any ideas, we'd love to hear them."

"Oh, well, dear," Constance said. "I doubt any of us can possibly know. The Halifax brothers will be here in a few minutes. Maybe you can ask them."

Max and Luc, of course, didn't know the answer, either. But Delia was thrilled to hear they were coming. Maybe she and Max could sneak away later. They hadn't had a moment to themselves since that bit of time in the library.

"Are the Halifaxes going to teach us new hexes?" Joyce asked.

"No, of course not," Constance said. "They're going to tell Violet—I mean *everyone*—why hexing is not allowed."

Violet rolled her eyes so far back in her head, it had to be painful.

"In unrelated news," Constance continued. "I regret to inform everyone that I received an official letter from the desk of the high priestess, the benevolent and honorable Morgaine Gerard. It seems we will not be receiving our full tidings at Hallowtide this year."

The room erupted in gasps and groans of disappointment, and Amy stood up. "They can't do this to us."

"I'm afraid they can," Constance said. "It's not up to us—"

"But why isn't it?" Amy said. "The willow tree is ours. Why does Shadowlark have to be involved at all?"

"For one thing," Constance said. "We don't know how to harvest the tidings of the Great Willow. That is not a secret divulged to us, and it is for our own good—"

"How do we know it's for our own good? How do we know *anything*? We in the Stray Lands are intentionally kept in ignorance."

"Again, it's for our own well-being. Ignorance is bliss, as they say," Constance replied.

"How is it in our own best interest to withhold magic from us?"

Constance banged her gavel. "Again with all of this, Amy? Goodness, I'd hoped you would have outgrown this nonsense by now. Shadowlark protects the Craft. And part of protecting the Craft involves regulating magic in the Stray Lands. Dear Goddess, do you want to start a witch hunt? Did your mother not tell you about the Burning Times, when they burned witches at the stake?"

Constance's voice had become so shrill that Delia hardly heard the doorbell.

"There now," Constance said, taking a deep breath and rearranging her hair. "That must be the Halifax brothers."

Max and Luc didn't receive the same hospitable welcome they'd enjoyed at the miscellaneous tea, and Delia understood why. The women were understandably upset about the tidings. And why wouldn't they be? Delia didn't know much about the workings of the witching world, but the inequality was hard to ignore.

As soon as Max and Luc had given their little speech about hexing, Max made his way over to Delia. "Icy reception," he said.

Delia didn't want to add to the chill, but she was starting to understand that there was quite the divide between Shadowlark witches and the witches of the Stray Lands. "We were told about the tidings just before you got here."

"What about the tidings?"

"The high priestess says they will be smaller this year."

Max frowned. "Did she say why? Never mind. She wouldn't."

"I guess you know her pretty well?"

"Not really. I mean, she's the high priestess, after all. It's not like we hang out. And quite frankly, she's terrifying."

"Why was she calling you that day that we, you know, worked out together?"

"Just some Shadowlark business."

Luc walked up with a paper plate full of finger sandwiches. "I wouldn't be talking Shadowlark business right now. I sense it isn't a very popular topic."

No kidding. And across the room, Amy was glaring at Delia as if she were consorting with the enemy.

CHAPTER THIRTY-ONE

Amy sat cross-legged on Delia's bed. "Why did you invite them to join us? Seriously. It's ladies' night at Ice House Sixty-Seven. Not bring-a-bad-witch night."

"They're not bad witches," Delia said. "They're helping my family. And anyway, why did you invite them to stay for the junior coven meeting if you didn't want to spend any more time with them?"

"Because I'm the junior coven leader, and because I wanted to extend their suffering. Telling a coven full of adult witches that they're not going to receive their full tidings is nothing compared to telling four fifteen-year-olds, one of whom was on her period."

"There are only four kids in the junior coven?"

"No. There are only four kids whose moms make them come to coven meetings."

"Oh my goodness. I think I'd have given anything to go to a junior coven meeting when I was a teen."

"Ha! Our meetings are fairly pathetic. And I wanted Max and Luc to see just *how* pathetic. Outdated handbooks that teach you how to light a candle with nine energy-preserving steps. Jesus Christ, these kids have lighters. Why would they need to take thirty minutes to make fire?"

"That seems pretty lame. What did Max and Luc think?"

"They were shocked. I could tell. Luc seemed downright upset. And he taught them how to do it in one step."

"See? Maybe they're not such bad guys, after all."

"They're from Shadowlark, Delia. They are literally *the* bad guys—with a capital B—as far as I'm concerned."

"I can't believe that," Delia said, holding up a little black skirt. "What do you think of this?"

"It's slutty, and I love it."

"I can wear it with my midriff ruffled top and those boots that come above my knee."

"It's going to fluster the hell out of Max."

Good. That's what Delia was going for. Max was freaking adorable when he was flustered.

"Just bang him and get it over with," Amy said. "Get him out of your system. Then he can go back to Shadowlark, and we can all get back to normal, only with even less magic than usual."

Delia didn't think anything in her world would ever be so-called normal again. But as to the other part, well, she'd been trying to get Max alone for an entire week, all to no avail. It was freaking weird, but it seemed like every time they had a chance to sneak away, Luc popped up. Or Max's mom or dad. And of course, her family didn't have any concept of boundaries, so they were always around, too.

"I don't know how far things will go tonight," she said, holding the little black skirt against her hips and eyeballing herself in the mirror. "But I'm hoping we can at least find some time to be alone later."

"Was that hint directed at me?"

Delia grinned. "Take it however you'd like, but mostly, it's Luc I want to lose. He follows us everywhere!"

Amy crossed her arms over her chest. "I wonder why."

"I don't know, but maybe you can distract him, if you know what I mean. Dance with him or something."

Ice House Sixty-Seven was basically a gas station with a bar in the back. It got its name from the farm-to-market road where it was situated. The jukebox was loaded with pure honky-tonk gold, and the nachos were loaded with pretty much everything. "You know," Delia added. "Max is a good two-stepper. Maybe Luc is, too."

"They probably give them bizarre dance lessons in Shadowlark. There aren't too many men, so I suppose they get a good amount of practice at a *lot* of things."

Delia remembered how, during their magic training, Max told her he was raised in a matriarchal culture. *Believe me, Delia. I know where it is.*

"Holy shit. What are you thinking about? You're blushing."

Whew. Was she? Or was it just hot in here? Time to change the subject. "You know, I've been thinking. Why isn't our magic limited? My family didn't get tidings, and yet we seem to have plenty."

"I suspect that you received the amount your ancestors had at the time they were hexed. Back then you could use all the magic you could muster. The more skilled you were, the more powerful you became. And the more powerful you became, the more magic you called. That's still how it works in Shadowlark. But here in the Stray Lands, we line up like Oliver Twist with our dirty little hands out, grateful for whatever they dole out."

"That's awful."

"I know that Max and Luc seem nice enough, Delia. Truly. But I don't trust them. And you shouldn't, either."

"Just because they live in Shadowlark?"

"They literally live in an ivory tower. What are they even doing here? It's all very suspicious, if you ask me."

"Have you ever been to Shadowlark?"

"Have I ever...?" Amy shook her head. "Listen, you don't get it. Nobody but Shadowlark witches go to Shadowlark. Only Logos witches live there. They think they're like royalty, but they're a bunch of weirdos, if you ask me."

"That's not nice, Amy."

"Listen to me. Shadowlark looks after one thing, and one thing only. And that's Shadowlark."

That didn't seem like Max or Luc. Or Hartwell, for that matter. "I wonder why Hartwell didn't live in Shadowlark?"

"I've been wondering about that myself," Amy said. "And you're not going to like what I've concluded."

"What? What have you concluded about Hartwell?"

Jesus, she was already feeling defensive. But Hartwell was the closest thing she'd ever had to a grandfather, and she'd loved him dearly.

"Well, he showed up in Willow Root—presumably from Shadowlark—right after you were born. And moved in next door. So, what do you think?"

Delia gasped. "Do you think he was spying on us?"

"And don't forget Nikki. How long has the neighborhood stray been lounging on your doorstep?"

Delia plopped down on the bed, stunned. Because, sure enough, the black cat, which she now knew was really Nikki, had been around as long as she could remember. "How long do cats live?" she asked.

"You look pretty stupid right now," Amy said, laughing. "And yeah, I suspect Nikki has been spying on you for your entire freaking life, and y'all were just over there feeding him tuna and whatnot the whole time."

"But why?" Delia asked. "Why would they be watching us?"

"That's the question, isn't it? It probably has something to do with the hex. And it's one of the many reasons you shouldn't trust Max."

Delia chewed on her lip. Even though it would be easy to be paranoid and start looking at things through Amy's lens, she just couldn't do it. Maybe Hartwell had kept a few things from them. Like the fact that he was a freaking witch and so were they. But she couldn't—wouldn't!—doubt his love for them. If anything, she'd always felt he was protecting them.

Surely, Max was doing the same.

Max slammed the car door. "Come on," he said to Luc. "We don't have much time before we're supposed to meet Delia and Amy at the ice house."

"Hold on," Luc said. "One more thing—"

"Luc we're already late."

"I can't stop thinking about it, Max. The witches here have so little power already. Why is Morgaine reducing their tidings? What has happened that Shadowlark needs more magic than it had last year? Or the year before?"

Max held up a hand. "I know you're worked up. But don't jump to conclusions."

"What other conclusions can I jump to? I don't think the magic hoarding has as much to do with Shadowlark as it does with Morgaine and her endless appetite for power."

"Okay, I admit that something is going on, but you've made a pretty huge jump, and I don't want to continue speculating. Now come on, there's not much time until I'm supposed to hook up with Delia."

"Did you say *hook up* with Delia?"

"Yes. And I'd like to take a quick shower first."

Luc grabbed Max's sleeve. "Think about what you're doing."

"You're the one who just said the witches here have very little power."

"You know damn well that all the magic the Merriweathers had before they were hexed has come back to them. And back in those days, the Merriweathers were powerful witches."

Max gave his head and shoulders a quick shake. Surely, they could talk about this later? "Let's get inside."

They hurried to the back door, where they accidentally woke up Nikki, who was in cat form and curled up next to a potted plant.

"Oops, sorry," Max said, feeling stupid for saying sorry to a cat, even if it was Nikki.

"The door is locked," Luc said. "Do you have a key on you?"

Max reached into his pocket. "I wonder why they locked the door."

Luc shrugged. "Mother is fairly terrified of being in the Stray Lands."

"Yeah," Max said, inserting the key. "Why is she here? It's weird. The hex really doesn't concern her at all."

"Maybe she's concerned about us," Luc said. "Because if we don't figure something out to appease Morgaine, there are the unpleasant consequences Father spoke of."

Max frowned. "The key won't turn."

"Let me try," Luc said, taking the key and inserting it into the lock. He frowned. "That's weird. Why doesn't it work?"

Max twitched his mouth. "Now try."

"Still locked."

Nikki was doing figure eights around his ankles. "Go through the cat door, would you? And then let us in."

Nikki put his head against the small flap he typically used to enter the house, but it didn't move. He looked up as if to say *See? It's why I'm out here.*

Max closed his eyes for a moment, and he immediately felt the magic. "Someone has put a spell on the locks."

Luc frowned in confusion. "Why would they do that?" His expression quickly morphed into one of alarm. "Do you think Mother and Father are okay?"

Max walked around to the patio and tried the French doors, just for kicks. They didn't budge. "I'm sure they're fine. Father seemed a little upset earlier. Maybe he's being extra cautious. Let's try a window."

The first one they tried lifted right up.

Luc climbed in, and Nikki hopped easily through the window next. Max was a little less graceful about it, but he made it inside, where it was eerily quiet.

"Maybe they went out?" Luc said.

"How? They don't have a car." The lights were on in the kitchen, but the rest of the house was dark. "Mother," Max called.

Silence.

"I don't like this," Luc whispered.

Nikki, who'd gone into the laundry room to transform, returned to the kitchen, fully clothed. "They shooed me outside for no apparent reason about twenty minutes ago. And when I tried to get back in, the cat door was locked."

Luc furrowed his brow and headed for the stairs. "Father?"

Max followed, and by the time they got to the top of the stairs, they heard ghastly moaning coming from one of the bedrooms. "Oh no," Max said. "They're hurt!"

The first thing Max thought of was Morgaine. He didn't know why, but his blood ran cold. "Luc, do you have your—"

Luc whipped out his wand. "Let's go," he said, somehow sensing the same threat.

They sprinted down the hall, fueled by fear and adrenaline. Max threw the door open and...

He and Luc froze in their tracks at the horrible sight before them. "Oh my Goddess," Luc gasped.

"What in fresh hell is this?" Max said, trying desperately to wrap his mind around the sight of his parents—*naked*—in bed together, before desperately trying to unwrap it.

"Now, Max," his father said, running a hand through his hair and looking somewhat insane. "It's not what you think it is."

"It isn't?" his mother asked, clutching a sheet to her breasts. "What do you suppose he thinks he's seeing?"

"I doubt they were taking a nap," Nikki whispered, poking his head in. "Just in case that's what anyone was thinking."

"Well, we were just," their father stammered. "Having sex! So what?"

"Oh, is that so, Armistead?" their mother asked, jerking the sheet away. "That's all we were doing?"

"Great. Look what you've done," their father said, looking at them. "She's miffed."

"What did we do?" Luc asked. "You're the ones who have been...sneaking around!"

"We'll be downstairs in a few minutes," their father said. "Now kindly get out."

Ten minutes later, Nikki poured tea—there was no way he would miss out on this conversation—while Max and Luc stared at their parents, now, thankfully, dressed.

"Was this a onetime thing?" Luc asked.

"No," their father said, while their mother stood stiffly next to him, wringing her hands.

So, it wasn't a matter of them just losing their minds while alone in the house. Was it possible this was a weird *regular* thing? "How long has this been going on?" Max asked.

"Oh," his father said with a sigh. "How old are you again?"

"I'll be thirty-four in May."

"About that long, then."

Luc gasped. Nikki snorted. And Max was just dumbfounded.

"But you never even lived together. We never saw you say more than two sentences to each other. It was just *Here are the boys* or *Send the boys back in three days* or *Thank you for taking the boys.* I mean, how—"

"Our relationship would be frowned upon," their father said. "We're Logos witches, Max."

"Your . . . relationship," Max said.

"We're in love, Maximus," their mother said. "Sorry to be such a disappointment to you and Lucien, but we admit it. We're weak."

"Shameful," his father said. "Can you still find any small amount of respect for us?"

"For being in love?" Max asked. "Maybe. But for spouting that *mens omnia cor* crap at both of us for our entire lives when you didn't even believe it yourselves? Well, that's going to take some getting over."

"We would prefer to keep this in the family," Armistead said.

"Oh, are we a family now?" Luc asked. "Now that the two of you have come out with your so-called relationship?"

Dorcas dramatically brought a hand to her chest. "Lucien, we have always been a family."

"No, we have not," Max said. "Not a *real* one, anyway. For example, we've never cooked together in the kitchen—"

"Why on earth would we?" Dorcas asked.

"We've never played games," Luc added. "And we've never sung into a wooden spoon or danced—"

Dorcas laughed. "Now you're just being silly. That's not what wooden spoons are for, and we dance together every solstice at the Festival of Darkness."

"You've never thrown wet noodles against the wall," Max interjected. "And we've never had cake." He knew he sounded childish. But quite frankly, this situation made him feel quite childish, so how else was he supposed to sound?

"Well," Dorcas said, looking incredibly flustered. "I guess we can have dinner together tonight. And I can throw things against the wall, if that's a particular custom you'd like to observe. I don't know about a cake…"

Max sighed, trying to imagine his family eating and laughing and playing together. It would be a disaster, and why was he even longing for it? What the holy hell was the matter with him? "Forget we said anything."

"Speak for yourself," Luc said.

"We can eat at the table together tonight," his father said. "What time should we gather?"

"We will not be gathering," Max said, trying desperately to get his emotions under control. "Luc and I have been invited to an ice house."

"An *ice house*?" Dorcas said. "Is it made of ice?"

"I sincerely hope so," Luc said. "Delia and Amy didn't say."

Their parents rose from the couch at the same time. "Do not go out with Cordelia Merriweather," Dorcas said.

"Maximus, I agree with your mother," Armistead said. "It isn't safe."

"What do you mean by that?" Max asked.

"You know what he means by it," his mother said. "You're either bewitched or you're on your way to being so."

"I most certainly am not. If I were, I'd be in love with Delia or in the process of falling in love. And I am neither of those things." He swallowed. Because he was very much *in like* in a way he never had been before. "And anyway, Delia hasn't cast a love spell. She doesn't even know how."

He looked to his brother for help. "Tell them, Luc."

Luc sheepishly lowered his eyes.

"You've got to be kidding," Max said.

"It's just that we don't know how Delia broke the hex," Luc said. "And yet, clearly, she did."

"This is utterly ridiculous—"

"Delia is Cor, Max. I like her as much as anyone. Well," he added with a devilish grin. "Maybe not as much as *you* do. And I just think a little caution is called for. But no worries. I'm happy to chaperone."

Max stared at his brother, speechless. He felt downright betrayed. And confused. And exhausted. And the only person he wanted to talk to about it all was the one person he couldn't talk to about any of it.

Delia.

Dorcas pulled something out of the pocket of her bathrobe. "I made this for your protection."

"Mother, I don't need such a thing, believe me."

"Keep it in your pocket," she said, pressing a tiny silver tube, about the size of a bullet, into his palm. "I made the scroll myself. Pounded it out of willow bark and inscribed it at exactly three minutes past three, while facing the north, and then I called an owl and invoked the Spirit of Lillith, just for good measure."

"I really hate that you went to all that trouble on my account," Max said, pulling the tiny scroll out of the tube and squinting. "I mean, I definitely don't need it, and anyway, I can barely read it."

The words slowly came into focus.

Protection now is what I seek
From feelings that might make me weak
Erotic inklings wither fast
With this knot my spell is cast

"Mother, this looks less like a protection charm than a curse meant to make me impotent."

"Whatever works," she said. "Be sure to tie your knot and recite each line three times, then, here"—she pulled a tiny mandrake root out of her purse that vaguely resembled a woman's form—"stomp on this, and grind it into the ground."

"Holy hell, Mother."

"And then spit on it before covering it with dirt."

Luc leaned in, entirely too amused. "It's very subtle."

Their mother inhaled so severely that her nostrils pinched, and Max stuck the stupid thing in his pocket just so he could get out of there.

CHAPTER THIRTY-TWO

Max was late, and Delia doubted he was ever late. So, something must have happened.

She took a sip of her beer and set it down on the Ice House's rickety table. She tried to tell herself it was nothing. Maybe he had a flat. Maybe he took a little nap and overslept. Maybe—

"Jesus. He's like ten minutes late," Amy said. "Settle down."

"I'm totally settled," Delia said. "And it's nearly twelve minutes."

Amy squeezed the juice from a lime wedge into her bottle of beer before poking it all the way in with her finger. "You're not usually such a nervous Nellie."

Amy was right. But Delia couldn't shake this horrible sense that something bad was about to happen. And what if it was about to happen—or had *already* happened—to Max?

No, no. That was stupid. Nonsensical. Plain old dumb.

"I'm sure you're right. Maybe he dribbled toothpaste on his shirt and wasted five minutes trying to get it out only to discover that you could still see it when it dried, and so then he tried to find another shirt, but he had fallen behind on laundry and ended up having to iron one that he never wore specifically because it required ironing. I mean, that could happen, right?"

"That was a lot. You are a lot right now. In fact, you are a hot mess. And believe me, I can't stand that term. It's overused. But it is you. You are it. And that can only mean one thing."

"What?"

"You really like him. And I hate it."

Delia took a big gulp of beer and wiped her mouth. "What if...?" She crossed her legs and nervously bounced her foot.

"You're killing me, Smalls. What if what?"

Delia leaned in, lowering her voice. "What if he forgot? Because I'm, you know, not that important to him."

"Believe me. You're the best thing that ever happened to that dork. Do you think he regularly goes out with witches in thigh-high boots?"

"For a minute there, I thought you said *bitches*, because I keep forgetting that I'm actually a witch."

"You're not supposed to say that in public. How are the lessons coming?"

"The lessons are going great. I've developed quite a bit of control. So has the rest of my family. But Max said it will probably take years for me to reach my full potential, and I'm cool with that. But I'm just not sure, well, this is embarrassing..."

"What?"

"I'm not sure what I'm supposed to use my magic *for*."

Amy snorted. "That decision isn't actually as big as you think. Because, eventually, you're going to have to receive tidings like the rest of us. And then you'll have fun choices to make like should I ration my tidings so that I can use magic to stir my coffee every morning for a year? Or should I choose to blow it all in one shot and simply give Karen Williams a really bad case of back acne right before the prom?"

Delia gasped.

"Don't judge me. She started that rumor that I made out with Reggie, the boy in the mascot suit who always smelled like feet and wet dog."

"I remember—"

"And I didn't have much impulse control when I was seventeen. Honestly, I can't believe I managed to hold on to my magic until May."

"You should be ashamed. Is that why she wore that ugly green shawl of her mom's over her backless gown?"

"I felt kind of bad about it when I saw her."

"Good."

"Listen, some of these older ladies can be dangerous," Amy said. "Unlike teenagers, they're patient, and revenge is like fine wine to them. They'll hoard magic for years to see a plan through. Don't think for a minute that Violet's hex on Constance was a spur-of-the-moment thing."

"That reminds me," Delia said. "Did you know that Misty Herrera hexed *me*?"

"What?"

"Yes! I was getting ready to leave the coven meeting, and she pulled me aside and confessed! She said she was always jealous of me, because my family talked so openly about being witches and people whispered that I was a blue witch. And every time I started a new business venture, she hexed it! That's what happened with my business cards."

"That bitch."

"Well..."

"Don't you tell me you've forgiven her."

"I kind of have. She was so remorseful and couldn't stop saying she was sorry. She was *crying*, Amy."

"You're too nice."

"You're probably right. But anyway. It seems like such a waste to use magic in that way. It could be used for such wonderful things."

"No shit," Amy said simply. "In Shadowlark, everything runs on magic. Nobody there lifts a finger, and it's all under the guise of doing so-called important work."

Delia thought of the dinner Max had prepared. "They can use magic to make fancy meals?"

Amy laughed. "Of course. Even I can use magic to make a fancy meal. But I could only do it a few times a year before becoming completely drained. And that's what it feels like, by the way. When your magic starts to dwindle, you literally don't *feel* well. Which is all the more reason to simply not use it." Amy frowned and picked at the label on her beer bottle. "We're magical beings, Delia. We're meant to have magic coursing through our bodies in the same way we have blood coursing through our veins. We're meant to do big, beautiful things with it. Or heck, maybe we're meant to do awful, horrible things with it. Either way, it's ours. And they took it."

Delia bit her lip, no longer wanting the loaded nachos they'd ordered. Could she believe Max when he said everything Shadowlark did was to protect the Craft and the witching world?

"I just can't stop being mad about it," Amy said.

"I'm not sure you should stop being mad about it. In fact, I'm kind of getting mad about it."

Amy's head jerked up. "Really?"

"Yes, really. I mean, how dare they?"

Amy picked up a nacho. "Doh. Look what the cat dragged in."

Delia spun in her seat, and as soon as her eyes landed on Max, all of her outrage disappeared. He'd stopped in the doorway, and it seemed to take a minute for his eyes to adjust to the dim lighting of the Ice House. But when they did, they locked on to hers immediately. And then he walked just as straight and fast as he could, blowing past the two couples two-stepping on the tiny dance floor, weaving in and out of the tables until he made his way to her.

She stood, but he didn't even look at the boots or the rest of her sexy outfit. He just took her in his arms and held her, squeezing her so tightly that she could barely breathe.

"Are you okay?" she wheezed. Because there was something desperate in the way he held her.

"I am now," he whispered. "It's been a long day. And I just want to talk to you about it."

Luc stepped around them and pulled out a chair. "Beer," he said. "I'd very much like a beer."

"Do I look like a barmaid?" Amy asked. "And does this look like a classy place with barmaids? You have to go to the counter and order."

"Actually, do they have anything stronger than beer?" Luc asked.

Max finally let go of Delia, and when they sat, he reached over and held her hand beneath the table, which literally made her knees weak.

"Like tequila?" she asked Luc.

"Yes. I need something to completely wipe my memory."

Amy rose from her chair. "You're speaking my language. I'll go get a round of shots."

"We walked in on our parents," Max said as Amy walked off.

"You walked in on them doing what?" Delia asked. But when she saw the look on his face, it hit her. "Oh my God. You didn't."

"I keep closing my eyes," Luc said. "And there it is. Permanently imprinted on the insides of my lids."

Max shivered. "We just didn't think they *did* that."

"Did what?" Amy said, returning to the table with four shot glasses.

"They walked in on their parents having sex," Delia said.

Luc grabbed a shot glass with each hand and downed one, followed by the other.

"Okay, so I guess someone doesn't get a shot," Amy said. "Also, did you two think you were brought to your parents by owls, or what?"

"No," Max said. "But we're Logos, remember?"

He picked up a shot glass, dumped the tequila down his throat, and then started coughing. Delia pounded him on the back.

"Oh shit. That's right," Amy said. "Here, take the other one."

Max did, making a little less of a show this time, merely wincing as it went down.

Amy elbowed Max. "But you still bang, right? And believe me," she said, winking at Delia, "there's a lot riding on your answer."

Delia tried to kick Amy under the table but missed.

"We just thought," Luc said, "that our parents, you know—"

"That they used a turkey baster?" Amy said.

"Amy, that's not appropriate," Delia said, but good grief, she wanted to laugh. Like so, so bad.

"No," Luc said. "But we thought they only did it twice."

Delia couldn't hold it in anymore. She started to laugh, and then Amy started to laugh, only she was more obnoxious about it, and then finally, Max started to laugh, too.

Luc continued looking shaken. "This isn't funny."

"This traumatic moment you're experiencing," Delia said. "Most of us went through it in grade school. And I'm so sorry for laughing, but y'all are so stinkin' cute with your outrage."

Max squeezed her hand, and then he looked at her lap and

280   CARLY BLOOM

seemed to finally notice her short skirt and boots. When his eyes finally made their way back to hers, they were dark and simmering.

She leaned toward him and whispered, "Do you like the boots?"

"Very much. And right now I'm wondering if they were made for dancing."

"I think they were made for a few things, and dancing is definitely one of them."

There were so many questions to ask. But at the moment, all she wanted to do was dance.

Max was getting better and better at the Texas two-step, and this song had him spinning Delia across the room with wild abandon. Maybe they'd stepped on each other's toes a few times. And they'd bumped into a big, brawny guy wearing a T-shirt that said COME AND TAKE IT (Max had assured the man he didn't want it). But, by Goddess, they were dancing, and their troubles seemed farther and farther away with every step.

"Whew!" Delia said as the song ended. "Should we rest our feet and grab a drink?"

Before Max could answer, somebody started a new song on the jukebox. And it was the same one he and Delia had danced to on the night of her birthday.

She smiled up at him. "I don't think we can sit this one out."

"Oh, we definitely can't," Max said, pulling her close.

This is our song.

They swayed together gently, and all the previous clumsiness vanished as if they were one body. He bent his head and inhaled her hair, intoxicated by the scent of her. The feel of her. The very essence of her. And it made him hard. There was no way she didn't feel it.

"Oh, Max," she said, lifting her face to his.

His heart thudded in his chest as her dark brown eyes dipped down to his lips.

It was an invitation he couldn't refuse, and he kissed her with as much restraint as he could muster, because they weren't exactly alone.

Delia wasn't having it. She bit his lower lip in an invitation to go for it, right there on this shitty little dance floor in front of all these people.

Such a public display was unheard of in Shadowlark. But why the hell should he care? He'd already danced like no one was watching. He might as well make out like no one was watching.

He accepted her invitation with a brush of his tongue, and for the next few moments, he completely lost himself in her lips. But then someone tapped him on the shoulder.

He broke the kiss and saw Amy shaking her head. "Somebody is going to tell y'all to get a room," she said. "I'm saving you the embarrassment."

Delia's cheeks turned bright pink. "Shoot. Sorry. I don't know what came over us."

"Well, whatever it was, bring it back over to the table before Mabel turns a hose on you."

"A hose?" Max said.

"Mabel owns this place," Delia said. "She's been known to break up both fights and overly amorous activities with a water hose from the kitchen."

Before Delia could turn to follow Amy, Max leaned in. "I want you," he whispered in her ear. "So badly."

"Do you think we can lose those two?" she asked, nodding at the table.

"Absolutely. Where should we go?"

"We can go to my place. We'll have to be quiet though. Unless you want a cheering section outside the bedroom door."

Max laughed. "I don't think our families could be any more different from each other."

They made their way to the table, where Luc was busy tossing back another shot of tequila. "Max!" he shouted, slamming his glass on the table. "Isn't this the best ice house ever? I'm a little disappointed it's not made of ice, but nothing's perfect."

Luc was beyond buzzed. He was drunk.

"Luc," Max said. "Maybe you should slow down."

"Hell no," Luc grumbled. "I'm just getting started. I'm not anxious to go back to the sex house. What if they're doing it right now?"

Delia touched Luc's arm, preventing him from getting more tequila to his lips. "Your parents are adults. And, Luc, they're in love. Isn't that wonderful? I mean, really. It is. Try to be a grown-up about it."

"She doesn't get it, Max."

Max shook his head. "She's kind of right. Aren't you at least a little bit happy for them?"

"No. I'm embarrassed for them."

Max looked at Amy, who was watching the conversation with an amused expression. "Do you think you could get my brother home safely? Delia and I are going to head out."

"Yes," Amy said, rolling her eyes. "Totally not surprised."

"Thanks," Delia said, lunging across the table to give Amy a hug.

"What?" Luc said. "You're leaving?"

"We're headed for Delia's," Max said.

Luc leaned over, and in a loud stage whisper, he said, "Do you have the charm?"

"What charm?" Delia asked.

"He's talking nonsense," Max said, standing up and offering a hand to Delia. "Are you ready to go?"

Delia took his hand, but she was looking at Luc with concern.

"Don't worry," Amy said. "I'm cutting him off. Mabel always has a fresh pot of coffee back there."

Delia sighed, but then she squeezed Max's hand. "Let's go, then."

As they turned to walk away, Luc grabbed Max's arm. "Don't forget that you have to say it"—Luc belched loudly—"three times."

CHAPTER THIRTY-THREE

They ran across the yard and slipped into the house, tripping over somebody's shoes and knocking over a plant before they reached the stairs. Giggles were somehow restrained as they climbed up, repeatedly telling each other *shh* as they made their way to the first landing and crept past Maddie's bedroom door. Then up they went, around and around, to get to Delia's bedroom in the tower.

"Brace yourself," she said. "It's pink."

"Pink's not a bad color—"

Delia opened the door.

"Oh. Wow."

"I told you to brace," she said, pulling him all the way in.

"That's a round bed," Max said, staring.

"Yep. And that's a jar of quarters on the nightstand."

Max raised an eyebrow in question.

"It vibrates," Delia said, grinning hugely.

Max wanted to ask why Delia had a vibrating bed, but he was in the Merriweather house, so why *wouldn't* there be a vibrating bed?

She'd been driving him crazy all night with boots that went all the way up to well, there. And a short little skirt and an even shorter top that showed off her smooth, toned skin. He'd dreamed of running his hands over every inch of her since the small taste he'd gotten in Uncle Hartwell's exercise room.

Delia fell back on the bed. "There's no mirror on the ceiling. Just a poster of One Direction."

Max lay down next to her. "This is none of my business, but why does your room look like...?"

"Like it belongs to a fifteen-year-old girl?"

"Well, yes."

"Because it once belonged to a fifteen-year-old girl. And she got stuck in a rut. Saw no real future for herself outside this little town and this bizarre house and this Pepto Bismol room."

"And what about now? Is she still stuck in a rut?"

"No," Delia said. "She's a freaking witch, and she's decorating your house, and her future is unbelievably bright."

Max grabbed her hand and squeezed it. "I'm stupidly excited about the plans for the house."

He loved the Italian marble that was going in the foyer. He couldn't wait for the new cabinets to go in the kitchen and for the whole place to be lightened up with the colors Delia had chosen. And her plans for the library—his favorite room in the house—were breathtaking. No more hiding the floor-to-ceiling windows behind drab, dark curtains. No more stuffy furniture and dark paneling. It was going to be a welcome refuge from the outside world. A light and airy room where he could disappear for hours and—

What was he thinking? Halifax Manor wasn't his. Not really. The new owners of the house would be enjoying the library. He'd be going back to Shadowlark, where everything looked like everything else because it made the magic work more smoothly.

Delia rose up on one elbow. "Do you trust me with your house?"

"Yes," he whispered. Because he did. "I trust you with everything."

He felt the little charm, heavy in his pocket. And he knew right then that he'd never use it. He didn't need to. He was under a spell, for sure. But his feelings were absolutely real. And he *did* trust Delia.

"Oh my gosh," Delia said, sitting up. "That reminds me. The draperies arrived for the main bedroom. And the new light fixtures for the dining room. I'm thinking maybe—"

Max yanked her back down. "We can talk draperies and light fixtures later. Right now we have other things to do."

He rolled her over and kissed her. Hard. And she ran her hands through his hair, turning it into a tangled mess, and he didn't care. Delia could do whatever she wanted with him, and he wouldn't utter a single protest. His heart pounded, and he realized, for the first time in his entire life, that he didn't need to shield it.

Mens omnia cor, my ass.

He let it go. Set it free. Opened himself up. And the rush of emotions nearly overwhelmed him. A small sound escaped his lips, an embarrassing whimper of a thing, and he realized he was holding in a sob.

"Are you okay?" Delia asked, breaking the kiss and looking deeply into his eyes.

He wanted to look away. He *should* look away. But he didn't.

"Oh, Max," she whispered. "My sweet Max."

He kissed her before he could fall apart, before he did something truly embarrassing. And his magic started to rise, along with a part of his body that was distinctly more physical, and he realized he could channel that crushing energy into something else. Something sexual.

"Delia," he said. "I'm going to want you to keep those boots on."

"Oh yeah?" she said, running one up the back of his leg.

Yeah, definitely. He wanted to feel them on his bare skin. He rose up on his knees and unbuttoned his shirt, and Delia immediately ran her hands all over his chest and belly. His magic responded, like an obedient animal, and he had to quell it.

Down, boy.

Otherwise, he might literally destroy the room. It would make the twins' fighting furniture look like battling cotton balls.

He pressed Delia down onto the mattress, and her hair splayed out around her head like a halo, although she didn't look much like an angel at the moment. She gazed at him through brown eyes that simmered with a deep, shimmering lust while licking her lips, plump and swollen from his attention.

She fumbled with her top until she had it pulled up over her breasts, which rose and fell and practically spilled out of the lacy black bra that he somehow knew she'd worn just for him. He kissed the rounded tops, so smooth and soft, and when she moaned desperately in response, he thought he might come undone.

There were other things that needed undoing, like her bra.

His hands slipped beneath her, searching for the abominable clasp...

"Isn't there a spell for that?" Delia asked.

"There are as many spells for that as there are sixteen-year-old male witches, and not a single one of them works," Max said, fumbling with the tiny hooks.

Aha! He got it. The joy of victory.

Delia pulled her top over her head before slipping out of the bra and...

He was going to die of happiness. This was bliss. Nirvana. Heaven, if he believed in such a thing. He brushed his fingers across her nipples, and she arched her back and grabbed his hair, pulling him closer until he licked her nipple gently. It hardened beneath his tongue, inviting his lips to close around it.

He suckled gently at first, and then harder, while Delia continued making a mess out of his hair, moving her hips in a desperate way that was driving him crazy.

He could worship her breasts for hours and never grow tired of it. If this was religion, he wanted more of it. "Take me to church, Delia."

Every inch of Delia's skin hummed and tingled as if she were a freaking neon sign buzzing and blinking *Take Me!* Good Lord, she'd never wanted to claw a man's back before, but as soon as she got Max's shirt off…

"Delia, that's a delightful skirt, and it's given me a good tease all night long, but it's time to get rid of it."

"Okay—"

In one swift motion, he had the skirt off, and Delia was lying there wearing only a pair of black panties and black thigh-high boots.

Max's nostrils flared. That lock of hair hung dangerously over one eye, and the one she could see was downright simmering. The bed shook as he crawled to her. "Open your legs," he said softly.

She did, and Max leaned in, rubbing his cheek and chin—bristly with a five-o'clock shadow—across her inner thigh before dragging his lips across her skin.

It was so unbelievably hot, and she was ready to beg him for more, when he broke the contact and all she could feel was a whisper of hot breath on her panties. He paused there—so close—before moving on and giving her other thigh the same treatment. By the time he got back to where her thighs met, she was trembling.

Max forced her legs to open wider. And then, with a single finger, he gently moved her panties aside. His breath grazed her for just a moment, but then he pulled away, his eyes glued to the most private spot on her body. She swore she could *feel* his gaze.

He glanced up, and her cheeks warmed from the longing desperation on his face.

He looked hungry.

He lowered his head and delivered a whisper of a kiss, right where she so badly needed it, and for the next few minutes, which somehow seemed to both stretch out and pass by at a dizzying speed, he explored her thoroughly, building her pleasure to a roaring crescendo, only to bring it back down, over and over again.

Max, moaning, seemed to be just as lost in sensations as she was.

Something stirred in her belly, and she recognized it as what Max called her spark.

As her pleasure grew, so did the spark. Soon it filled her completely, until there was no separation between self and spark. They were the same.

Max's ministrations became more urgent. His moans more desperate. And Delia couldn't help it. She pulled his hair, because she was riding higher and higher with no end in sight, but desperately needing to get *somewhere* to find her release.

She rode a swell, all the way to the top, balanced briefly on its precipice, and then...

She shattered. Fell apart. And her magic rushed outward with such force that Max looked up, startled and gasping for breath.

"Delia, can I—"

"Oh God, yes," she said, already hungry for more. "What are you waiting for?"

"I was just waiting for you to maybe recover a little—"

"Come here," she said, sliding her panties off. "I don't want to cool off and catch my breath. I want the opposite of that."

The man knew how to take an order. He was on her in an instant, kissing her deeply. His hand went between her legs, and then he guided himself in. "Oh, Max," she gasped.

He sent ripples of pleasure through her body, and she wrapped her legs around his waist, moving so he'd feel the leather of her boots on his bare skin.

"Oh, yes," he said. "That's what I've wanted. Oh, fuck yes."

He stared into her eyes with each thrust, watching her as if he needed to see what he was doing to her. How crazy he was making her. How high he was taking her.

She hadn't known another orgasm was possible—the first one hadn't entirely left her body—but as he went faster and harder, she felt herself climbing up another wave. And then another. And then she called his magic.

She didn't mean to. She didn't even know how she'd done it. But it came. And Max's eyes grew wide with surprise as she pulled his very source from him, fast and swift.

"Don't stop," he begged. "Don't stop. Take everything. It's yours."

Just as she reached her highest wave of pleasure, Max cried out, pouring himself into her. Their magic collided, and the rush was so intense that time seemed to stand still, just for a moment, and then she crashed into a place of pleasure so deep and strong that her mind simply disappeared, and she was nothing but ecstasy itself.

Slowly, she came back into her body, languishing in the heaviness of Max resting on top of her, apparently spent.

"I don't know what just happened," he said. "But I'm still so high on you that I don't care."

He didn't say anything else until morning.

CHAPTER THIRTY-FOUR

Max awoke to the sensation that his entire body was vibrating. Was it magic?

No. Something hummed mechanically, and he smiled, realizing it was the bed.

"Hello, sleepyhead," Delia said, her face appearing above his.

Everything came back to him, and he grabbed her, pulling her close. "How long have you been awake?" he asked, with his voice bleating like a sheep's because of the bed.

"About half an hour. I thought maybe the good vibrations would finally get you up."

"They did." In more ways than one.

His mind was still groggy, and his body held the peculiar achiness that followed a night of really good sex, but he was also oddly energized.

"How do you feel?" Delia asked.

"Like I could bench-press an elephant."

"Same. Why do you suppose that is?"

The bed stopped vibrating—the quarters must have run out—and he felt less silly speaking. "I think something happened last night."

"Oh, it happened all right. Twice for me."

He grinned, feeling stupidly accomplished.

"Is sex between witches...? Is it always like that?" she asked.

"Not in my experience. It's like our magic—"

"Melded."

Yes. That was it.

"It got all tangled up," Delia said. "And I think it's still tangled."

Should he be alarmed? He didn't know. But more importantly, he didn't care. Everything about this felt right. Everything about *Delia* felt right. For the first time in a long time—possibly forever—he felt settled. Content. Like lying on a round bed in a pink room with a blue witch was exactly where he was supposed to be.

He'd grown up being terrified of falling in love. Absolutely terrified. And falling in love with a Merriweather? Well, that was the stuff of nightmares.

And it was all lies. Screw that "mind over heart" stuff. He didn't care if it was his family's motto. Mind and heart *together* definitely felt better.

"What do you have going on today?" Delia asked.

"More packing, I'm afraid."

"Can't you just use magic? Amy says you Shadowlark witches can do stuff like that."

He wasn't sure, but he thought he detected a tiny bit of bitterness in her tone.

"Amy is right. But many of Hartwell's things aren't exactly ready to be tossed in a box. He collected all kinds of magical items, and some of them are dangerous."

It got a little quiet between them, and it wasn't exactly a comfortable silence. He felt compelled to fill it. "And, of course, in the afternoon, they're ripping up the tile in the foyer. It's crazy to watch all of this being done without magic. And there's a lot to do between now and the open house."

"Yes," Delia said. "And then you'll be going off on some grand adventure."

She smiled brightly, as if she were happy that he'd be going off on some grand adventure, but it didn't reach her eyes, and a heaviness settled in Max's chest. It pressed the air out of his lungs and made his heart feel like it was trapped in a vise.

"Don't look so sad," Delia said. "You can come back and visit any old time you want. And, anyway, you don't do romance, remember?"

Was that still true? It seemed that everything had changed. His parents, of all people, were in love. And *mens omnia cor* was crap.

"Neither do you," he said, testing the water. "You're happy being single, right?"

"You betcha," she said, rising from the bed and pulling the sheet with her.

But he saw it. The way her eyes darted upward—just for an instant—when she'd answered. And he tried not to smile, because Delia had just told a little fib.

"Now, get your pants on, mister," she said. "I guarantee you there are kitchen witches downstairs ready to smother us with pancakes. And I apologize in advance for any crude remarks from my grandmother."

He fought off a blush as he lay there, heart flip-flopping in his chest while completely exposed (in more ways than one), wanting to say so many things but somehow struggling to come up with even a single word that could come close to expressing how he felt. All he knew was that nothing was really as it seemed, and he was tired of pretending it was.

"Delia," he said. "What would you say if I told you that I might want to try a little romance?"

He hadn't necessarily expected to be smothered in kisses (okay, maybe he had), so when Delia literally backed up as if he'd just grown a second head, he was stunned.

"What's wrong?" he asked. "Was that too soon? Am I moving too fast? I'm sorry... I've never done this before."

"Max, I can't," Delia said. "You don't understand."

She was right. He didn't. He didn't understand a damn thing about what he was feeling or how he was supposed to express it. But he'd clearly done something wrong,

"There's a curse," she said. "On my family. In addition to the hex."

Holy hell. He remembered the dreadful secondary curse that Nikki had told him about.

"You'll literally die," Delia stammered. "I mean, I didn't use to believe it. I thought it was just bad luck. But if the hex was real, the curse might be, too. So put your damn pants on and get out of my house."

"Delia, listen—"

"Don't you *Delia, listen* me." She took another step back, as if she could kill him just by mere proximity. "Not only should you get out of my house, but you should go back to Shadowlark, and stay there. Like right this minute." She picked his pants up off the floor and threw them in his face. "Go! Let Luc handle the rest. And your parents. But you get your butt on the first plane, or however the hell you people travel, and get away from me before you..."

She started to cry. Softly, at first. But it progressed to full-on blubbering at a rapid pace. And it was quite a sight. Mascara ran down her cheeks, snot dripped from her nose, and it was really... fucking adorable. Also, was she trying to tell him she had feelings for him? Real feelings?

Is she falling in love?

He reached for her, but she dodged him. "Max, get out!"

No. He was not going to do that. He yanked her back onto the bed. She looked appropriately stunned, so he kissed her. And then he rolled her on top of him, squeezing her tight.

"Stop it!" she wailed into his chest.

He loosened his grip, and she raised her head to look him in the eye. "Max. I'm not kidding." She wiped her nose on the sheet. "You'll croak."

"I will do no such thing. I promise."

"No, listen. Something's happening. I have feelings that I've never had before, and maybe it's just because my world is changing and I'm kind of out of my mind, or maybe I'm just really super horny because, you know, look at you. But also, maybe not. Maybe this is real and serious and something I can't stop. So please get out of here."

He held a tissue to her nose. "Blow."

She did, but then she pushed on his chest, struggling to get away.

He grabbed her wrists and held her still. "That curse was broken with the hex."

Delia stopped struggling. "What?"

"Nikki said Uncle Hartwell believed it was a secondary curse, attached to the hex. So it's gone. Disappeared with the hex."

Delia sat up, and the sheet slipped down, giving Max a view that he truly appreciated. "So, Hartwell knew?"

"He was trying to figure everything out. I'm pretty sure he's the one who left the note about the library book. He *wanted* you to break the hex."

Delia gasped. "I knew it. I just knew Hartwell was trying to help us. But, Max…"

Max gently dabbed around her eyes with a tissue. "Yes?"

"What kind of monsters hexed my family?"

After such exhilaration, this question simply crushed him.

It was time to discuss the history of their families and how they were intertwined. He started to step into his pants, because this wasn't a topic to address while naked.

Delia obviously wasn't expecting an answer to what she thought was a rhetorical question, and she slipped into his shirt with a small smile. "I smell bacon. Do you?"

Max smelled it, too. And he was hungry.

But first things first.

As he pulled up his pants, the charm fell out of his pocket.

"What's this?" Delia asked, picking it up.

He held his hand out, hoping she'd drop it in his palm. "Oh, it's nothing. A silly thing my mother gave me."

"It's kind of cute," Delia said, rubbing a finger over it. "Is it magical?"

"It is, but it's really nothing—"

"It looks like some kind of charm."

"Yes," Max said, simply and truthfully. "Like I said, it's silly."

It wasn't something you'd find on a fancy bracelet, but the charm was still pretty. "What's it for?" she asked, turning it over in her palm.

"Protection."

A tiny scroll of paper fell out of its end. "Protection from what?" she asked, trying to unroll it.

"Here," Max said. "Let me stick it back in—"

"Hold on," Delia said, squinting at the tiny lettering. "Let's see what the powerful and masterful Maximus Halifax needs protection from."

"Delia—"

She spun around playfully to keep the scroll out of Max's reach and started to read.

Protection now is what I seek
From feelings that might make me weak
Erotic inklings whither fast
With this knot my spell is cast

She frowned. "I'm sorry, but is this protection against, like, romantic feelings?"

Maybe all Logos witches carried such charms, kind of like how some religious people carried medals or pendants of saints.

She waited for an answer while Max finished buttoning his pants. But when he looked her in the eye, she didn't like what she saw. Not one bit.

"Listen. It's a stupid thing. Like I said, my mother gave it to me."

The words Max had just spewed formed a neat little trail, but for a moment Delia struggled to follow it. Then, all of a sudden, it became very clear, as if an arrow had just appeared, suggesting that Delia leap straight to a horrible conclusion.

"Wait a minute. Is this protection against *me*?"

"It's only because you're Cor—"

Max stopped talking mid-sentence and his mouth formed the perfectly round circle of someone who was thinking *Oh shit*.

"What does that mean?"

Max ran a hand through his hair and sighed. "Don't read too much into this, but it's the name of your line. Cor witches have been known to practice heart magic. But since you're not doing that, this is a silly conversation."

He was right. She absolutely wasn't practicing heart magic. She didn't even know how!

But wait a minute. She didn't really know *anything*. Like, she didn't know how she'd broken the hex. And hadn't her ancestor bewitched someone? "How do you know I'm not practicing heart magic?"

Max laughed, but it was a nervous laugh. "Delia, I only crammed this charm in my pocket to avoid an argument with my mother. And then I didn't give it another thought. I didn't even activate it."

Oh, dear God. This was awful. Max's feelings seemed to have developed rather suddenly, hadn't they? "Maybe you should have activated it."

"Are you honestly saying you've bewitched me?" This time he laughed in earnest. "Delia. Unless you know something I don't, I refuse to even consider the possibility. Now, hand me my shirt. Surely, you aren't going to make me face the kitchen witches while half-naked."

Delia slipped his shirt off and handed it to him. "I haven't done anything on purpose."

"Well, then, there you go." He dropped the little amulet into the wastebasket in the corner. "I'm not bewitched. End of story."

Delia bit her lip, wanting to believe him. But she kept coming back to the question of whether he'd actually *know* if he was bewitched. "How did I break the hex, Max? I'd feel a lot better if I knew that. Because apparently I do magic without knowing—"

He put his finger to her lips, hushing her. And then he slid that finger under her chin, tilted her face to his...

Maybe I'm the one who's bewitched.

She let him kiss her, and oh, how he kissed her. It was with the single-mindedness of a man who wanted to possess her heart, body, and soul.

Or maybe of a man who is freaking bewitched out of his mind.

She should pull away. But she couldn't. So she surrendered to the passion—not of the body but of her whole dang heart—melting into him, savoring the tease of his tongue, the brush of his fingers, the caress of his breath on her cheek.

After he'd completely destroyed her with that kiss, he framed her face with his hands and stared deeply, penetratingly, into her eyes. "See?" he said. "There's nothing more to say."

She shook her head, removed his hands from her cheeks, and took a step back.

Max sighed. "I'm in complete control of myself. I know who I am, and who you are, and how I feel. Do I seem bewitched to you?" His eyes traveled her face, as if it were a map and his life depended upon reading it correctly.

"Honestly? Kind of."

He clenched his jaw, and she sensed he was losing his patience. "Since you're so knowledgeable, how does a bewitched person behave?"

"I suspect that a bewitched person would undergo a personality change. And you have."

"That's because I'm happier. *You* make me happy, Delia."

"You sound bewitched, Max. You really do!"

"I sound like I'm quite possibly falling in love, which has nothing to do with a spell and everything to do with how you make me feel."

"If I told you I'd bewitched you on purpose, what would you say?"

"I'd tell you I didn't fucking care. That I want to be with you, no matter what it takes. That I'd give up anything and everything in order to do so, and you're probably going to say that makes me sound bewitched."

That was exactly what she was going to say.

"Max," she said. "I don't think we should be alone together again."

"Delia, don't do this." He ran a hand through his hair, making it look as wild as his eyes. "Are you kidding me?"

She had to do it. At least until she knew for sure how heart magic worked and whether she was practicing it without even knowing it. "I wish I was kidding, Max," she said softly. "You have no idea how much."

Max opened his mouth as if he were going to say something more but thought better of it. He silently buttoned his shirt, stepped into his shoes, and left.

CHAPTER THIRTY-FIVE

Nikki was right. The fates did love a good twist. How was it that after denying himself love for his entire life, he'd finally allowed it in only to have it yanked away because of, well... love?

He trudged through the damp grass of the Merriweathers' lawn, dragging his shoelaces because he hadn't bothered to tie them, and opened the gate that led to the manor's backyard.

They were watching him. He knew they were. He could fucking *feel* it.

Those poor women. The way they'd greeted him with knowing smiles, plates heaped with mountains of food, kisses on the cheek... Andi had called him a stud muffin, and everyone had laughed and said the bats frolicking in the attic had kept them up all night—*wink, wink.*

Oh, how their faces had fallen when they'd finally noted his silence. And then Delia had come down the stairs with her puffy eyes and red nose, and Max had sensed the tide turning. The women gave him wary looks, ready to take Delia's side. Hell, they probably would have torn him limb from limb if they thought he deserved it, and he loved them for it.

That's what real families did. They protected their own.

But Delia had said three little words—*it wasn't him*—and their expressions had turned to pity. They'd hugged him silently, one by one, before he'd made a sad and hasty exit, tripping on a garden gnome in the process.

Slowly, he walked past the pool, past the hot tub, and across the patio. His plan was to sneak into the house quietly. The last thing he wanted was to run into his family right now. He wanted to hole up in the study and go over the Blue Moon Spell again. It was a dreadful thing, and he didn't see how Delia could have cast it—accidentally or otherwise—but somehow she *had* broken the hex.

Quietly, he slipped inside. But before he could even close the door, Luc appeared in the kitchen doorway. "Oh, good! You're home. There's coffee, and I also whipped up a hangover potion, if you need it as badly as I did."

Max shook his head. "No to all of it."

"Oh, shit," Luc said, taking a step toward Max. "What the hell happened to you? You look awful."

"Thanks."

"You're welcome. But seriously. What's wrong? Besides you obviously having spent the night with a Cor witch."

Max clenched his fists. "She's not just a *Cor witch*. She's Delia."

"Whoa, Max. First of all, I know that. Sorry. I was just kidding. Kind of. And second, I should warn you—"

"Maximus!" Dorcas pushed Luc out of the way to emerge from the kitchen. "You're just in time for breakfast."

"I'm sorry. What did you say?" He'd never heard the word *breakfast* come out of his mother's mouth. But then again, he'd never seen her wearing an apron while holding a...

Is that a spatula?

"This is what I tried to warn you about," Luc said.

Armistead poked his head out. "Hurry up, boys. Before the pancakes get cold."

Luc shrugged. "It's a disaster zone in there."

Max allowed himself to be led into the kitchen, where it was, in fact, a disaster zone. Pancake batter was splattered all over the stove. Dishes were piled high in the sink. Eggshells littered the countertops. And yes, there was a literal mountain of pancakes sitting in the middle of the table.

Luc placed a hot mug of coffee in his hand. "She didn't really cook this herself."

"Well, now, give your mother some credit," Armistead said. "She came very close. Very close indeed."

"I boiled the water," she snipped. "I filled the pot, set it on the burner, and turned it on."

"Yes," Nikki said, emerging from the pantry with a jug of syrup. "Dorcas boiled water to, you know, boil the pancakes, I guess. Who knows? I never really figured it out."

"Hush, imp," Dorcas said, but she was grinning. "I was going to make deviled eggs. Luc says they're delicious."

Armistead put his arm around her, and Luc produced a gagging sound.

"You don't want to know what she thought deviled eggs were," Luc said. "Stopped her just before the screaming started."

"I scrambled them instead," Nikki said, gesturing to a plate of light and fluffy eggs. "Oh, and I set the table with Hartwell's good dishes. He used them for special occasions, and I think he'd approve."

Max stared, slack-jawed. He never could have predicted walking in on such a scene. And on any other day it would have amused him immensely. But not today. He was wrecked. "I'm afraid I'm not hungry."

"Of course you are," his mother said, yanking on his arm. "Come to the table."

He was dragged to a chair, where he obediently sat, but only because he was too tired to fight about it.

Suddenly, jazzy music filled the air. "Ooh," Nikki said, nodding his approval at Armistead. "Billie Holiday. Excellent choice."

Armistead smiled, and everyone began passing dishes. Someone plopped a pancake on Max's plate. Someone else dumped a heap of eggs next to it.

"So, how was the ice house?" Armistead asked.

"What?" Max could readily hear the words, but he was having a hard time understanding anything. He'd never felt pain like this. It was the stuff of sappy Stray movies.

A breakup. I'm going through a breakup.

"We're supposed to have light conversation during mealtime," Dorcas said. "That was your father's attempt at it."

"And then after," Luc said, cramming half a pancake in his mouth. "Maybe we can play some games. That's how they do it at the Merriweathers'."

"I doubt you know enough curse words to do it like they do it at the Merriweathers'," Nikki said. "But Hartwell did keep a deck of cards. Maybe a little gin rummy would be nice."

"Yes," Armistead agreed. "And then we need to have a serious conversation. I've read through Hartwell's journals. I've learned some things. I'm ready to delve into the hex—"

"Nobody is rehexing the Merriweathers," Max said. "And I don't want any conversation, light or otherwise. So could you all please just shut up?"

"How unbelievably rude," Dorcas said. "Max, what has gotten into you? You're behaving oddly."

He wasn't about to discuss why he was behaving the way he was. And he couldn't handle another word from anyone. Not a single one.

He set down his fork, raised his hands in the air, and closed his eyes...

"Oh no, you don't," Luc said.

"What?" Nikki asked. "What's he doing?"

"He's about to initiate a Dumb Supper," Luc said. "Father, stop him."

"But it's not even suppertime," Nikki said. "It's breakfast. Is that what makes it dumb?"

"Maximus," Armistead said. "Stop this right now."

Max had no intention of stopping. A Dumb Supper would render everyone at the table mute. At which point, Max might scarf down a pancake before going, well, literally anywhere else. "I invoke the ritual of my ancestors," he said loudly. "For it is their wisdom I seek in silence."

He quirked his mouth, and a plate flew out of the cabinet and landed on the table next to his mother. Because you couldn't have a Dumb Supper without setting a place for the dead.

Next, the saltshaker levitated gracefully before upending itself over the spare plate, spilling its contents in a heap. Because you couldn't set a place for the dead without giving them a way to communicate.

They wouldn't communicate, of course (because they were dead), but you had to follow these steps to get to the good part, which is where his family would shut the hell up.

"Shit, shit, shit," Luc said. "Max, cut it out."

The chair at the place setting yanked itself out, offering a seat to the dearly departed.

"Is this really necessary?" his mother said. "I thought you wanted a family meal."

"Yes," his father said. "With living relatives."

"Someone please, tell me what's happening," Nikki said.

"He's about to mute us," Luc said. "We won't be able to speak until the meal is over. It's completely obnoxious—"

"Muta cena!" Max said.

Everyone fell silent, except for Billie Holiday, and Max quirked his mouth and made her shut up, too. His father cleared his throat, opened his mouth, and a small, strangled sound came out. He slapped his hand on the table in irritation.

"I've never seen this before," Nikki said, clearly impressed.

The spell obviously didn't work on imps, which was unfortunate.

Luc shrugged and started shoveling eggs into his mouth. Dorcas drained a glass of orange juice, produced a small, feminine burp, and strummed her fingers on the table, ignoring her food. Armistead chewed with the fury of one who couldn't wait to kill his firstborn son.

"This is delightful," Nikki said. "I see the appeal. I really do. As one who went decades—no, make that over a century—unable to speak, I must say it's somewhat nice to see the tables turned."

Suddenly, the curtain behind Dorcas waved, even though the windows were closed. The lights above the table flickered and then went out entirely.

"Max, did you do that?" Nikki asked.

Max shook his head. The hair stood up on the back of his neck as the table began to vibrate. He could feel an energy in the room, one that hadn't been there before.

Luc dropped his fork, and it clattered to the ground. Max

followed his brother's stunned gaze to the ceremonial plate, where something was quite clearly written in the salt:

133.4 MER

"What is that?" Nikki asked.

"That's a library call number," Max blurted. And then he put a hand to his throat, because the mute spell usually lasted either until the ceremonial plate was removed from the table, or an ancestor—

"Holy hell," he said. "I believe Uncle Hartwell came to breakfast."

❦

Delia sat at the kitchen table with Splash in her lap, crying into her untouched oatmeal and staring at her phone.

"What does it say?" Amy asked, biting into a piece of bacon.

"Thanks for coming so fast," Delia said, sniffing.

Amy raised an eyebrow. "Really? That's what it says?"

"No, Amy. That's what *I* said. To you. Because you got here so fast. Stop being stupid."

Amy gasped dramatically. "Did you just call me stupid?"

Grandma Maddie set down two mugs of coffee. "There's no name-calling in this house. You girls stop fussing."

Delia's mom brushed a lock of hair out of Delia's face. "Listen to your grandmother, honey. I know you're upset. But Amy is our guest, and you're being rude. She's here because she loves you. We all love you."

Delia looked at Amy. "Sorry."

"No problem. And I guess I was being kind of stupid. But, for reals, what does Max's text say?"

"It says *I need to see you*. And I don't know how to respond."

"I know what I'd say, which is *yes please come here right now and bury your head between my thighs and we'll work the rest out later.*"

"Dear God, Amy," Fiona said. "You're so crass."

"Mom, remember. Amy is our guest—"

Fiona made a little sound with her lips that was just shy of a raspberry.

"And anyway, Amy," Delia continued. "You don't understand."

"I understand that you have definitely not given the dumbass a love potion."

"But—"

"Listen. There are plenty of reasons you shouldn't be seeing Max. But that's not one of them."

"How do you know that? How do you know I haven't inadvertently cast some spell?"

Amy poured cream into her coffee through the paw of a little kitten pitcher. "Spells don't work like that. Potions don't work like that. You can't just make them or cast them without knowing it."

"How did I break the hex, then?"

"Okay, I admit that's a weird-ass mystery. But the bigger mystery is why it's so difficult for you to believe that this man might actually have feelings for you."

"He had a protective charm, Amy. Do you know what it feels like to discover the man that you might be falling in love with has a charm? To protect himself from *you*?"

Amy laughed. "Well, seeing as how he gave you two orgasms, one of which you claim was an out-of-body experience, I'd say his shitty little charm didn't work."

"Oh dear," Andi said. "I think we might have heard that one."

Delia's cheeks grew warm, but there was no point in trying to have a private conversation in this house.

"I don't know…"

"He's into you. And not just physically. I mean, for crying out loud, Delia. The man got new countertops."

"But I'm *Cor*, Amy."

"Yeah, yeah. Cor witches supposedly practice heart magic. And Logos witches are supposed to be logical and super smart, and yet look at Max and Luc. Dumb as rocks."

"But—"

"No buts," Amy said. "For the millionth time, you didn't put a spell on Max."

"Agreed," Grandma Maddie said, adding a spoonful of brown sugar to Delia's oatmeal. "Eat."

Delia took a small bite while watching Amy slather a biscuit with gravy. It occurred to her that she didn't know what kind of witch Amy was. "If I'm Cor, and Max is Logos, what kind of a witch are you?"

"Me? Oh, I'm Corpus. It means body. There are also Animus witches, and that means soul. Logos is logic, so basically it means mind. And you know what Cor is. Together we're body, heart, mind, and soul. It sounds cheesy, right?"

"I think it's fascinating. And I guess that's why you feed people? Because you practice magic of the body?"

Amy scowled a bit and then looked up at Delia. "I honestly never thought about it. To me, our so-called lines are like silly team names. Or like when you go to summer camp and are split into groups like the Pintos and the Garbanzos."

"Your mom is a nurse. I'd think healing would be a type of body magic, too."

Amy was quiet for a moment. "You could be right. But we hedge witches have so little magic to work with that it honestly doesn't matter. We can't do Big Magic, and that's why my mom doesn't even bother with it anymore."

"Max says that's for the protection of everyone in the Stray Lands," Fiona said. "If witches attract attention to themselves, things become dangerous."

"Oh yes," Amy said, with an edge of sarcasm. "The threat of the dreaded witch hunts. That's what they use to control us."

Amy was about to get worked up, so Delia turned the conversation back to her. "Listen. It's weird that Max is suddenly so into me. I mean, look at me."

"I am," Amy said. "You're super hot."

"He's traveled the world. I've only been out of Texas once. I live with my grandmother. His mother hates me. And, Amy, he freaking told me point-blank, to my face, that he does not believe in love or romance, and now, all of a sudden, he's head over heels."

"That's adorable."

"No, it's not. What if it's not real?"

Amy rolled her eyes. "Delia, it's as real as anything."

"Do you know the details surrounding our family and the hex that was placed upon us? Max told us that our ancestor bewitched someone. Have you heard the story? Know any details?"

"Who, me? A poor little hedge witch? All I know is that supposedly your great-great-great-great-whatever nearly brought down Shadowlark. So, yay for the Merriweathers! You're fucking heroes, if you ask me."

CHAPTER THIRTY-SIX

"It's all connected," Armistead said, pointing at the books and journals laid out on the long table in front of the window in Hartwell's study.

"Father, did you get any sleep at all?" Luc asked from the couch where he'd been passed out for the past three hours.

"Not much," Armistead said. "And I don't think Max did, either."

Actually, Max hadn't gotten *any* sleep. He'd been reading non-stop, ever since they'd returned from the Willow Root Public Library, where nestled next to a book on extraterrestrials, they'd found the missing *Book of Cor*.

Every witch line had a book chronicling its history and the nature of its magic. But the *Book of Cor* had supposedly been lost in a fire in 1792.

Just another lie.

Max ran his hand through his hair at the same time his father did, and they shared a brief, tired smile.

"Is there truth to *any* of our history?" Max asked.

"Of course there is," Armistead said. "But one thing I know as a historian is that we never know as much as we think we do. There's always an agenda. And as the old saying goes…"

"History is written by the victors," Max said, quoting Winston

Churchill. "And Cor magic, or heart magic, as we often call it, isn't anything at all like what we've been told."

"It isn't?" Luc asked, rubbing his eyes and accepting a mug of coffee from Nikki, who nobody had even seen enter the room.

"Cor witches do not practice magic *of* the heart," Armistead said. "They practice magic *from* the heart."

"What's the difference?"

"All their magic has love at its core," Max explained. "They're incapable of doing anything that goes against that basic principle. They couldn't bewitch anyone even if they wanted to."

Luc sat up straighter. "So, you were right, Max. You weren't bewitched by Delia."

"I know that, you idiot."

"And likewise," Armistead said, holding up a worn, faded journal. "Our ancestor, Wilmot, could not have been bewitched by Lucinda Merriweather."

Max stared at the journal. "Is that Wilmot's? Really?"

"Yes. It was in the hidden drawer, mixed in with Hartwell's personal journals." Armistead glanced at Nikki. "Thank you, by the way."

Nikki's eyes widened, as if a thank-you from Armistead Halifax was the most shocking thing he'd ever heard. "You're very welcome," he said, sitting in a nearby chair.

"Oh, I, um, do not think we'll be needing you anymore," Armistead said. "You may leave."

Nikki bristled, but then he stood and quietly exited the room.

"Father, was that really necessary?" Luc asked.

Armistead shrugged and then turned his attention back to Max. "Did you know that Wilmot was a venator just like you? Runs in the family, I guess."

Max shook his head. "I never knew that."

"He met Lucinda while traveling through the Stray Lands, and according to his journal, they fell in love. This wasn't a situation that pleased the family, obviously."

"Another thing he and I have in common," Max muttered.

Luc came to stand by Max. "Does this mean that the hex on the Merriweathers was *not* a Halifax hex? Because surely Wilmot didn't hex someone he loved."

Armistead carefully opened the creepy *Halifax Book of Hexes*. "Yes, I believe it's a Halifax hex. But there's something very strange about it."

"Oh?" Max said, adjusting the blinds to allow more sunlight into the room.

"I don't know how much you boys remember from your academy days, but try to knock the cobwebs out of your skulls and ask yourselves if magic can be destroyed."

"Magic is energy," Max said, incredulous that his father had asked such a simple question. "It cannot be destroyed."

"Exactly. And typically, a hex that takes away magic—"

"Really only redirects it back to the Source," Luc said. "So what?"

Armistead wiped away a bead of sweat from his temple. "None of us felt a fluctuation in the Source. It would have been a rush of magic. We should have felt *something*."

Max pinched the bridge of his nose as hazy ideas floated throughout his hollow-feeling head, refusing to connect in any cohesive way. "Delia had to have broken the hex before midnight on the night of her birthday," he said, hoping his train of thought was going somewhere specific. "And yet magic didn't start happening until two days later."

"Maybe it was more of a leak than a rush?" Luc suggested.

Armistead ran his fingers over a brittle page of the open book. "I can't tell where the magic actually went in this hex. Somewhere in here it should say *fons omnium rerum*. The hex should have sent the Merriweathers' magic back to the Source."

Max scanned the hex—there were so many words, and most of them were in Latin—but that line should be in there. He didn't see it, and if his father, who had no doubt pored over every single word, didn't see it, then it wasn't there. "Where did the magic go?" he asked. "Because it had to go somewhere."

His father planted a knobby finger on the page, just beneath some very small print—so small that Max had to squint. "Secretum alveus?"

"That's a secret something, isn't it?" Luc asked. "Sorry, I only know the basics in Latin."

Armistead looked to Max, and he shrugged sheepishly.

"Secret reservoir," Armistead said. "The magic was diverted to a secret reservoir, created specifically for that purpose. And I'm theorizing that it was heavily reinforced. So much so that when the hex was broken, the magic merely *leaked out*, as Luc suggested. Until eventually whatever held it weakened to the point of collapse."

"Morgaine felt it before the point of collapse," Max said. "She sent you and Mother here before things started going haywire with the Merriweathers."

"She felt the leak," Luc whispered. And then, in a louder voice, he added, "I have no idea what that means."

"I suspect it means that Morgaine is the reservoir," Max said.

And that was insane. It meant she had literally stolen magic.

"Yes!" Luc said. "That's where I was headed. Also, holy shit."

"The hex goes back to way before Morgaine was born,"

Armistead reminded them. "I'd say a closer truth would be that the entire Gerard monarchy is the reservoir."

Morgaine Gerard had only been the high priestess for the past three years. But before that it was her aunt, Minvera Gerard. And before that, it was her grandmother, DeLilith Gerard. Max didn't really know how far back the monarchy went—history wasn't his strong suit—but he could think of only two or three high priestesses who were not connected to the Gerard family.

Armistead nodded at the small stack of Hartwell's personal journals. "My brother left a theory behind. Your mother is in the library following its promising trail."

Their mother was a geneticist for Shadowlark. With such a small gene pool—and yes, there were jokes about it—it was important to keep track of the various families and their lineages. That's what prevented the jokes from becoming reality.

"She's researching the Gerards' lineage?" Max asked.

Armistead flinched slightly. "Keep your voice down."

"Who's going to hear?"

Armistead glanced at the door Nikki had recently exited. "You never know."

"Father, really," Max snapped. "Stop it."

"Maximus," Armistead said quietly. "He is bonded to our family, but he is an imp. Do not ever forget who he serves."

"Demons," Luc whispered dramatically.

Max nearly channeled Delia with an *oh good Lord.*

"The two of you are being fairly dramatic, aren't you? There are very few demons left. And the ones who are still around have little power."

"Well, speaking of power," Armistead said. "We'll need all we can get. Hallowtide is in four days. And the high priestess herself is coming to dispense the tidings."

"What?" Max and Luc said together.

"And also, presumably, to witness the rehexing of the Merriweathers," Armistead said.

"We're not going to do that," Max insisted.

"Correct," Armistead said with a sigh. "But we need a plan for what we're going to do instead."

"Before we start any plans, I'm going to the Merriweathers."

"Wait—"

"Father, the *Book of Cor* belongs to them. We need to return it."

Luc smiled. "Yes, and it also proves you're not bewitched, which is something Delia would no doubt appreciate knowing."

Their father shook his head. "Listen to me. I'm presuming that Morgaine knows the history of Lucinda and Wilmot. She knows that their power was stronger when they were together."

Max swallowed, remembering how amazing and strong and powerful he'd felt after making love with Delia. Were *they* more powerful together?

"Morgaine feels threatened. She's desperate. I would try to stay away from Delia until after we've come up with our solution. Otherwise, it could put all of us, including the Merriweathers, in even more danger than we're already in."

His father was right.

Delia sliced into a tomato and tried not to think about the night Max had cut his finger. She succeeded by thinking about the kiss in the hot tub instead. She tried to reverse course and go back to the tomato…

The back door opened and slammed shut. "Delia!"

"In here, Mom."

Fiona rushed into the kitchen, high color on her cheeks and a smile on her lips. "I just came from the manor—"

"Nope. I'm not talking to Max. You can forget it. I don't want to make any possible enchantment or bewitchment or whatever the hell you call it even worse."

"I wasn't going to talk about Max."

"Oh."

"But he was there. He and his dour parents were holed up in Hartwell's study, and when they finally came out, I got the grand tour. And oh, Delia! It's beautiful. Absolutely beautiful. It's hardly the same house. And I just can't believe…Well, don't get me wrong. I had faith in you, Delia. I did. But I didn't know just how talented you were. How utterly gifted. I just couldn't be prouder."

Delia waited for the swell of satisfaction to rise in her chest. To be *pleased as punch*, as her grandmother would say.

But she felt nothing. Because dang it, she'd found true love. But even though she no longer had to worry about it being ripped from her grasp by a falling tree or a flying fish or a poisonous mushroom, she couldn't hold on to it. Being a Cor witch meant never knowing if someone's love for you was real.

She might as well still be cursed.

"Thanks, Mom. I'm glad you approve of the house. Hopefully, it will bring in a good offer."

And then Max can go back to traveling the world, and I'll go back to, well, not traveling anywhere.

"Max's dreadful parents didn't care one iota about any of it. But Max sure did. The way he ran his hands over the butcher-block island, you'd have thought he was a chef instead of a man who couldn't slice a tomato."

Great. Back to the tomato.

"He looked dreadful, by the way."

Delia couldn't imagine Max looking dreadful. "I hope he's not getting sick."

"I suspect he's heartsick."

Of course he was. He was bewitched. She'd done that to him.

"Did he ask about me?"

"Only to boast about your skills in regard to the house. He was beaming with pride."

Delia went back to dicing her tomato.

"It's odd, isn't it?" her mother asked.

"What's odd?"

"Well, if he was bewitched, wouldn't he be over here night and day? Begging you to let him in or, God forbid, holding a boom box on his shoulder? I'd think a spell would compel him to do that, at a minimum. And yet, instead, he's simply next door, refusing to shave or, judging by the bags beneath his eyes, get any sleep. All while respecting the hell out of your boundaries."

Delia stopped slicing. That *didn't* sound like someone who was bewitched.

The back door opened and slammed shut again, and in walked Grandma Maddie and the twins. "Hello, Delia! We came home for lunch," Aunt Andi said.

"How are you dear?" Grandma Maddie asked, stopping to touch Delia's cheek.

"I'm fine. Truly."

Aunt Aurora dug around in her bag. "Look. I brought something that should cheer you up."

In Aurora's hand were five beautiful opaque stones. "My goodness. Are those opals?"

"Well," Aurora said in a low voice. "Not real ones. But the box said they're fairy stones. First you make a little circle. Then you make a little wish. You've been so sad, I thought maybe you could use them."

"What a lovely idea," Grandma Maddie said. "We need our Delia to cheer up. After all, Hallowtide is only four days away. Our first ceremony! We must all be at our best."

"Oh, absolutely," Andi said. "When we're standing at Hallowtide, arm in arm with our sisters in the Craft, we'll know we've finally arrived."

Grandma Maddie looked at the stones in Delia's hand. "If you spit on those, they'll be even brighter. They'll attract more fairies that way."

Delia knew that it was supposedly fairy magic that had allowed her to break the hex. But the truth was, she didn't know how she'd done it or even *if* she'd done it. It was kind of hard to believe in fairies, and even harder to believe in fairy stones that were probably made of plastic.

But she took them and slipped them into her pocket and did her best to smile.

"We just want so desperately for you to be happy," Aunt Andi said.

She knew that. And sometimes it was a heavy burden to bear.

CHAPTER THIRTY-SEVEN

Children walked up and down the sidewalks in costumes, trick-or-treating with their big orange buckets. Normally, Halloween was a huge event for the Merriweathers. Grandma Maddie and the aunties loved nothing more than handing out candy and saying *boo!* while cackling on the porch. But what the kids didn't know, and what the Merriweathers hadn't known until recently, was that there was another holiday celebration happening every year in Willow Root. A celebration of witches.

Hallowtide was here.

Grandma Maddie set a huge bowl of candy on the porch, and a little boy in a superhero costume ran up and stuck his hand in. "Don't be greedy," Grandma Maddie said. "We need to make sure there's enough for everyone."

"Okay," the boy said, dropping a couple of pieces back into the bowl.

"Brendan, what do you say?" his mom called from the sidewalk.

"Thank you," Brendan said before sprinting off.

His mom waved. "Nice costumes, ladies!"

They weren't costumes. They were the robes of their ancestors, and this time they'd been dry-cleaned so they didn't smell like mothballs.

"Time to go," Fiona said, pulling the deep crimson hood up

over her hair. Her eyes were bright. Her cheeks were pink. And Delia didn't think she'd ever seen her mother look more beautiful.

"We're waiting for Amy, remember?" Delia said.

"Speak of the devil," Grandma Maddie said. "She's pulling up now."

Amy got out of her van, and Delia gasped.

"I know," Amy said, lifting her robe to reveal a pair of beat-up Doc Martens. "It's too long. I keep meaning to hem it."

"No, Amy. You're freaking stunning." Amy's dark hair, which she usually wore in braids, pigtails, or a sloppy bun, spilled loosely over the shoulders of her black velvet robe in long, sensuous waves. Delia squeezed her hand. "You look glorious and powerful. Like a badass witch."

"If only it were true," Amy said, blowing a bubble with her gum.

"I hope we don't make fools of ourselves in front of Priestess Gerard," Grandma Maddie said.

"It's so weird that she's coming," Amy said.

"She doesn't usually come?" Delia asked.

"Heck no. None of us have ever met the woman. Honestly, it makes me uneasy."

"Everything makes you uneasy, dear," Thea said. "It's why you're sometimes so difficult to get along with."

Amy nodded as if that made perfect sense.

"We're not supposed to get in line to receive tidings, right?" Grandma Maddie asked, peering out from her hood through her large glasses. "I don't want it to be like that time we got in line at the Catholic church."

"Max said we probably won't be offered tidings."

"Yeah," Amy said. "You've still got magic. I can't see the high priestess letting you have any more."

"That's right," Aurora said. "It's kind of like that Catholic wedding. We're just going for the celebration."

Grandma Maddie nodded. "It had better be a good party. I've been waiting my whole life for it."

Andi came around the corner with tiki torches. "We can use these to light our way to the park."

Delia held up her phone. "I'll just use this."

Andi's face fell in disappointment.

"Never mind," Delia said, holding out her hand. "I'll take the dramatic tiki torch."

Grandma Maddie clicked her heels together, and the light bulb on the porch burst. "Damn it," she said. "I was trying to light the torch."

Thea wiggled her ears—a skill Delia had found endlessly entertaining as a child—and all the torches roared to life.

"Good job, Auntie," Delia said.

The magic willow tree where tidings would be dispensed was at the city park, which was only a few blocks away. They headed in that direction, blending in with the costumed kids and parents. Or at least they tried. Blending in had never been a strong suit.

"Look, Mom," a little boy whispered. "It's the witches."

They passed Halifax Manor, with its For Sale sign on the lawn. "Do you think Max will be at Hallowtide?" her mother asked.

"I don't know," Delia said. "I guess he has no real reason to be there."

"You're a reason."

Maybe so, but the truth was, Max hadn't been by even once since she'd ordered him to stay away. Was that because he was bewitched and had to do as she'd asked? Or was it because he *wasn't* bewitched? It was impossible to know, and that was the problem.

In just a few short minutes, they arrived at the city park.

"Oh no," Andi said, pointing at the cones and barricades at the entrance. "It's closed."

A figure came out of the shadows, and Delia recognized Sheriff Ruby Shepherd. "You've come for tidings?"

"We have," Delia said, shocked out of her mind.

"Happy Hallowtide," the sheriff said, removing a cone and letting them pass.

"And to you!" Grandma Maddie said cheerfully.

The trail was a pretty one, winding through trees and following a small creek. Up ahead were whispers and the sound of footsteps. Delia couldn't help it. She was getting excited. And when they came to the end of the trail, the sight before them took her breath away.

In the clearing was a roaring fire, and it was surrounded by robed women, all chanting and swaying in unison. And floating among the branches of the willow tree were thousands and thousands of fireflies, blinking yellow and gold.

Her mother squeezed her hand.

"Do we just go join the circle?" Thea whispered.

The chanting stopped abruptly, and a tall figure approached. "Witches, let us welcome the newest members of your coven."

The woman pulled back her hood, revealing a face almost too beautiful to be real.

"Priestess Gerard," Grandma Maddie said in a small, timid voice. "We are so happy to be here and to be included in this—"

"Bow," the priestess said.

There was a slight pause, and Delia heard Andi whisper, *Oh shit*, before all manner of bowing and curtsying and creaking knees commenced.

Priestess Gerard pushed Delia's hood back. "Ah. Here you are. Our esteemed Blue Witch who broke the unbreakable perma-tempus hex!" She leaned in, and Delia saw a glimmer of something ugly in her eyes. "And you did it right at the last possible moment, didn't you?"

"Um, I guess? I don't actually know."

"Come," the priestess said. "I've prepared a place of honor for you and your family."

They followed Priestess Gerard past the silent women. Next to the fire was a circle made of stones, leaves, and flowers.

Priestess Gerard gestured toward it. "Step inside, won't you?"

"Oh, isn't that lovely?" Thea said. "Like a fairy circle."

It was lovely. And yet they hesitated…

"I said step inside."

Delia didn't care for the icy tone of the priestess's voice, and she shivered as she entered the circle first. Everyone silently followed, but the priestess put her arm out in front of Amy. "Not you," she said. "You're not a Merriweather."

Amy looked at Delia, brows furrowed, but remained silent. And Delia knew for absolute certain that something was very wrong.

"There now. That was easy, wasn't it?" Priestess Gerard said.

The circle sparked and popped before bursting into flames, causing the Merriweathers to squeeze in closer as the other witches gasped and murmured.

"Be careful," the priestess said, smiling at them. "Those robes are flammable."

Delia had no idea what was going to happen next, but she didn't like how warm her ankles felt. And that's when four hooded figures stepped out of the shadows and into the clearing.

"We've come, Priestess."

Oh, dear Lord. That was Max's voice. Delia stared at him as hard as she could, but he didn't lift his hood or look in her direction.

"Oh, goody," Priestess Gerard said. "We're all here."

Max didn't like the looks of this.

"Come, Maximus," Morgaine said, holding out her hand.

For just a split second, Morgaine's face went from beautiful to monstrous, but so quickly that you might miss it or doubt you'd seen it. Max accepted her hand and stood next to her. "Getting enough beauty sleep, Morgaine? You look a little tired."

"My...fatigue...will soon be alleviated. Thank you for being concerned."

Max forced a smile, but he felt Morgaine tense. She knew something was up.

"Ladies," Morgaine called, and then she looked at Max. "And gentlemen, of course."

Max nodded. "Of course."

"I'm afraid I have a bit of bad news."

The witches stirred.

"As you all know, tidings were supposed to be reduced this year. But, unfortunately, it's worse than that."

Mutterings traveled through the circle.

"There will be no tidings."

Shocked protest erupted, but Morgaine squelched it quickly. "Silence! As you know, magic is a finite resource. It is regrettable, but there's only so much."

"But there's always been enough before," someone called out.

"Blame it on the Merriweathers," Morgaine said.

"Oh, that figures," Thea spouted.

Max, despite his efforts to not communicate with the Merriweathers, put a finger to his lips to hush Thea. They didn't need to draw Morgaine's ire.

"When the Blue Witch broke the Righteous Hex that kept the Merriweather witches from luring weak-minded men"—she looked at Max and raised an eyebrow—"to do their evil bidding, they took more than their fair share of magic. And now there's simply not enough."

"That's a lie," Amy said. "The Source is enough for all of us."

Morgaine turned on Amy. "You're a troublesome little bitch, aren't you?"

"That's what it says on my bumper sticker," Amy replied coolly.

But Max saw the fear in Amy's eyes, and no doubt Morgaine did, too.

"I should have let you follow them into the circle," she said, pointing a long, bony finger at Amy.

"Oh shit," Amy said. And then she began to levitate.

Morgaine held out her arm, directing Amy as she floated over the circle of fire holding the Merriweathers. Then she dropped her arm suddenly, and Amy fell into the circle, barely missing Andi before landing on her ass with a thud. The Merriweathers immediately helped her up.

"That circle is so small," Morgaine said. "If I'm forced to continue adding witches to it, someone is going to get crispy."

The veneer covering Morgaine's face faltered yet again, and this time it was more obvious. That little number had weakened her, and she was finding it more difficult to maintain her mask.

"How do we get our magic back from the Merriweathers?" someone asked.

"The Halifax family is here to rehex them," Morgaine said. "And then everything can go back to the way it was."

Armistead stepped forward. "That's exactly what we're here to do. Make everything just as it was before."

"Rehex them!" someone called out.

Morgaine turned to Max. "Care to do the honors?"

Max approached the ring of fire, looking Delia right in the eye. *Don't be scared.*

Sweat had broken out on her face. But Max could see she wasn't scared. She was pissed. And Max was glad, because it would make her more powerful. Even now he could feel it along the surface of his skin.

"I told you he was an asshole," Amy said.

Max turned away from Amy and the Merriweathers. "The hex requires a blood sacrifice. Any volunteers?"

Gasps erupted, along with some nervous giggles.

Morgaine stepped closer, and the flames of the fire made it look as if her bones were moving beneath her skin. "Choose one," she said.

CHAPTER THIRTY-EIGHT

Even though her skin was covered with a layer of sweat, Delia was ice-cold.

"Well," Amy whispered. "I was right. He's not bewitched."

Delia racked her brain, trying to come up with a way to protect her family, but how was she supposed to stand up to someone as powerful as the high priestess? Or, for that matter, people as powerful as the Halifaxes?

"Maybe you could try to bewitch him now, dear," Aunt Thea said.

Max was walking around the perimeter of the clearing, and every witch he passed seemed to suddenly find the need to examine their cuticles or tie their shoes.

"It looks like he's choosing someone for the blood sacrifice," Andi said. "So, he's kind of busy at the moment."

"Max isn't going to harm anyone," Grandma Maddie said. "Have some faith, for crying out loud."

Delia was trying, but it was hard. And what good was magic if she didn't know how to use it in a situation such as this? But then again, who could have predicted that she'd ever *be* in a situation such as this?

Max. That's who.

During one of their training sessions, he'd taught her how to create a field of protection. *In case anyone ever tries to rehex you*, he'd said. She hadn't been very good at it, and Max had become irritated over her inability to concentrate. Why would he work so hard to teach her such a thing if he was planning to rehex her himself?

Simple answer: he wouldn't.

Max continued walking, pausing briefly here or there, until he arrived back at their fiery cage, where he lifted the hood of his deep purple robe. His hair rose dramatically from static electricity before settling into its usual state, right down to the rakish lock hanging over his left eye.

"Hello, dear," Maddie said calmly.

The corner of his mouth curled ever so slightly, and with his right eye, he gave Maddie a slow wink. Then he turned around.

"Well?" Morgaine said. "If you don't choose someone for the blood sacrifice, I will."

She reached into the crowd and randomly yanked out Misty Herrera, dragging her to the center of the clearing. People cried out, and several had to hold back Misty's mom as Misty cried and struggled to break away.

"You," Morgaine said, looking at Luc. "The other brother, whatever your name is."

Luc stepped forward. "How may I be of service, Priestess?"

It was an unseasonably warm night (if you could say such a thing of a Texas night), and Morgaine's makeup had started to run. "Restrain this creature," she said, shoving Misty into Luc.

Luc caught Misty and wrapped his arms around her as she wriggled to break free. He whispered something in her ear, and she responded by stomping on his foot.

Luc groaned and cursed but managed to hold on.

Morgaine pulled a huge ivory-handled knife from the folds of her robe and held it out to Max.

Max took the knife, and Misty's eyes widened. But instead of bringing it to her throat, Max bent and began dragging it through the dirt.

"Man, that's going to dull the blade," Amy said. "Definitely won't make things any easier on Misty."

"Amy, hush," Delia said, and they all watched intently as Max made a huge straight line in the dirt. Then he stopped, turned, and began dragging the knife in another direction, Thea said, "He's drawing a pentagram." And she was right.

When Max was done, Armistead stepped forward with a container of Morton iodized salt.

Delia had seen enough movies to know what he was going to do with it, and sure enough, he started making a circle of protection around the pentagram.

"Ahh, yes. The old salt trick," Amy said.

When Armistead had completed the circle, he turned to Morgaine. "Priestess, would you be so kind as to step into the center of the pentagram?"

It was obvious that Morgaine was suspicious and didn't want to cooperate.

"We are about to perform very powerful magic," Armistead said. "The kind that uses power to seek power. And considering that a hex of this nature hasn't been performed in well over a hundred years, well, let's just say we're not relying on muscle memory." He smiled earnestly. "For your protection, Priestess, it would be a good idea to step into the pentagram."

Morgaine straightened, glanced at Max, who gave her a nod,

and then unceremoniously stepped over the salt and walked to the center of the pentagram.

Almost immediately, the body language and demeanor of the Halifaxes shifted. Glances were exchanged, and Luc let go of Misty with an apologetic smile. "Sorry about that."

The high priestess went on high alert. "What are you doing?"

Instead of answering the question, Max, Luc, and their parents scurried quickly to four of the five corners of the pentagram.

"Misty, hop on," Luc said, nodding at the fifth corner. And with only the slightest bit of hesitation, she did.

Morgaine began to literally growl as the Halifax family raised their voices:

To the ground
Your feet will meld
In this earthly realm
You're held

Armistead grabbed a handful of dirt and tossed it into the air. "Earth!" he said.

"Sky!" shouted Dorcas, raising her arms to the heavens.

"Fire!" Luc said, and the flames of the bonfire jumped.

It was Misty's turn next, and she began bouncing on her toes, as if she were participating in a trivia quiz. "Oh God, Oh God, Oh God…wait…water!" she shouted, clapping her hands.

Someone handed her a water bottle, and she quickly dribbled a bit on the ground.

Finally, Max, who stood at the top point of the star, formed prayer hands, brought them to his forehead, and uttered the final earthly element. "Spirit!"

A huge gust of wind rushed in, stirring up dirt, tangling hair, and whipping at the hems of everyone's robes. Morgaine unleashed a scream of pure rage as her upper body writhed and twisted. Her feet, however, remained firmly in place.

"Okay, so that's impressive," Amy said.

After a really long minute, the wind died down, leaving everyone in various states of disarray. But nobody looked as utterly disheveled as Morgaine. Slowly, her writhing morphed into a gentle swaying back and forth, and as she lowered her head, her hair hung limp in a style uncomfortably reminiscent of the vengeful ghost in *The Ring*. She smiled demonically at Max, and Delia didn't care for it one bit.

In the middle of all this, Constance timidly stepped into the clearing holding a bedraggled bouquet of flowers. "We've never had a high priestess at Hallowtide before," she said, setting the flowers on the ground in front of the pentagram. "I'm not sure we've provided a proper welcome."

"Good grief," Amy said.

Max cleared his throat. "Ah, but she is not a high priestess."

Morgaine, who hadn't taken her eyes off Max, raised a single eyebrow.

Constance, for her part, quietly bent over and retrieved the flowers.

"That wasn't salt you stepped over," Max said to Morgaine. "It was crushed demon stone."

A brief moment of silence was followed by a collective gasp, but Delia and the rest of her family remained clueless. "Witches can't step over demon stones," Amy whispered. "Only demons can do that."

Morgaine smiled, and the hairs on the back of Delia's neck stood at attention.

The biggest hurdle—getting Morgaine trapped inside the pentagram—was done. Max looked at Luc and wiped the sweat off his brow.

Their father stood in front of the bonfire. It was time to reveal the truth about Morgaine. The truth their mother had discovered when tracing the Gerards' lineage.

And it was a bombshell. Because there *was* no Gerard lineage. Not since the 1600s anyway.

"I'm sure you've all heard the story of the long-lost Philistina Gerard," Armistead said.

"It's his lecture voice," Luc whispered with an eye roll.

Luc was right. Max recognized the tone and cadence his father used when giving history lectures at Shadowlark Academy.

And yes, everyone knew the story of Philistina Gerard, who was rumored to be the lone survivor of a mass execution of witches in 1647. She'd been only thirteen at the time, and the method of her escape, and where she'd hidden, depended on who you were talking to. Because the details didn't matter. Her survival is what mattered. And her name became synonymous with hope.

"Sometimes," Armistead continued, "stories are just that. Stories. And unfortunately, the young woman who showed up, claiming to be Philistina ten years after her supposed escape, was not even a witch. She was a demon."

Morgaine started laughing. "Who is going to believe this fool?" she screeched.

The answer to that was pretty much everyone. Because Morgaine was definitely running out of stolen witch magic. She was looking more and more like a demon with every passing minute.

She gazed longingly at the willow tree, whose deep roots were fed by the ley lines. That's why she'd said there would be no tidings this year. Morgaine was planning on taking it all for herself.

"As you can imagine," Armistead continued. "The demon known as Philistina had a problem. She didn't have enough power to continue passing herself off as a witch for very long. She needed magic. *Witch magic.* And so she chose a group of Cor witches—the ancestors of the Merriweathers—and stole it from them."

Morgaine took a deep breath. "Don't leave out the best part," she said. "Where your ancestor fully cooperated by hexing the Merriweathers."

"Yes," Armistead said. "Quite regrettably, Wilmot Halifax hexed the Merriweathers, and their magic has been feeding the so-called Gerard family of demons ever since, allowing them to essentially live as witches, even to the point of ruling over Shadowlark and the witching world."

At some point during all the excitement, the ring of fire surrounding the Merriweathers had fizzled out. Max went straight to Delia's side.

"Is that true, Max? It was a Halifax who hexed us?"

Max nodded. "I'm afraid so. And I'm sorry. I was going to tell you."

Morgaine snorted. "And you came to this pathetic hovel of a town to follow in Wilmot's footsteps, didn't you, Maximus?"

Delia frowned. "What does she mean by that?"

Morgaine's shrill laughter filled the air. "Oh, you silly blue witch. Did you think he was here for the scenery?"

"I would never have rehexed the Merriweathers."

"You would have," Morgaine said. "But more importantly, you still will."

"I most certainly will not. And I don't even know why you'd want me to. Your jig is up, demon. You'll never rule Shadowlark again. In fact, you'll never even *see* it again. Your life of luxury in a magic city where everyone does your bidding is over."

"Unfortunately, I believe you. And it's all the more reason for me to get my witchy magic back. After all, I'm going to need it. I hear life's tough out there for a demon, Max."

Max was starting to get nervous. You never knew what a demon had up their sleeve. Nevertheless, he meant what he said.

The Merriweathers were huddled behind him, except for Delia, who was by his side. There was no way in hell—literally—that he was going to let them be rehexed.

"I hate to have to point this out, Morgaine. But you're trapped in a pentagram at the moment. I don't really think you're in a position to make me do anything."

His father stepped forward and put a hand on his arm. "Maximus," he said softly. "Never antagonize a demon."

"Too late," Morgaine said. "He just did."

"Oh dear," Maddie said behind him.

"I'm tired of playing," Morgaine said. "I know your father brought that dreadful hex book with him—"

"To burn it," Armistead said.

"Well, first, we're going to give it one last hurrah."

Armistead immediately turned to toss the book in the bonfire, and Morgaine twisted her head—way farther than anyone should be able to twist their head—and the fire instantly swelled, coming within inches of Armistead's face.

"Armistead!" Dorcas cried.

"I might be glued to the spot, but I am a demon," Morgaine

said. "I can still control a few elements. If that book burns, so does Armistead Halifax."

Armistead backed away from the bonfire, holding the book tightly against his chest.

"And let's see. In addition to the book, we still need our blood sacrifice," Morgaine said, moving her finger back and forth. "Which little witch will flinch..."

Delia's family rushed to stand in front of the cowering women. She moved to join them, but Max held on to her hand. "Stay with me."

"But, Max—"

Without taking his eyes off Morgaine, Max said, "Luc..."

"On it," Luc said, rushing to stand directly in front of the Merriweathers, who were brandishing their newly acquired wands with shaking hands.

"You don't understand the danger you're in, Morgaine," Luc said. "They have no idea how to use those things."

Despite the seriousness of the situation, Max had to stifle a laugh. But it caught in his throat when his parents joined Luc as well, one on either side, wands at the ready. And unlike the Merriweathers, they knew how to use them.

"This is touching, isn't it?" Morgaine said. "If this were a movie, it would be an inspiring moment. But it's not, and as they say here in Texas, y'all are in a heap of trouble."

Delia's hand trembled in his, and he gave it a good squeeze.

We're okay.

"Red rover, red rover," Morgaine called, "let the troublesome little bitch come over!"

"Oh God," Delia said. "That's Amy."

"No way," Amy shouted. "As we like to say here in Texas, come and take it."

Morgaine rolled her eyes—way farther than anyone should be able to roll their eyes—and then Amy was whisked up by an incredibly accurate gust of wind, and dumped inelegantly at the edge of the pentagram.

"So, we've got our hex book," Morgaine said. "We've got our sacrifice. And now all we need is for Max to, you know, do the damn thing."

"Never."

Morgaine clucked her tongue. "Never say never, Maximus."

Little sparks of light began popping on the ground at their feet, like firecrackers. "Come over here and open that book for your son, Armistead. Or those get way bigger." As if to prove Morgaine's point, one exploded right next to Dorcas, and the hem of her robe caught fire. She quickly put it out with her wand, but Armistead got the message, and he carried the book to Max.

"Open it to the original hex, please."

He did. And then he held it in front of Max.

"I take it you've still got that knife," Morgaine said. "The blood sacrifice is the first step, I believe."

"Um, Max?" Amy said. "I take back all the terrible things I said about you."

"Stop it, Amy," he said. "I have no intention of cooperating with that demon."

Morgaine smiled, showing jagged and pointy teeth that hadn't been there before. "Luckily, I prepared for this very possibility by bringing along a little friend. We're going to have to do this the old-fashioned way. All the way back to Wilmot's day."

The woods in this part of the park were fairly deep around the clearing, and Morgaine squinted, peering into the darkness. "Ah. There he is."

Max looked but couldn't see anyone.

"Come, imp," Morgaine said.

Had he heard her correctly? Did she say *imp*?

A dark shadowy figure floated out of the woods and into the clearing. It was almost formless, although Max thought he could somewhat make out a head and maybe some limbs. It looked more like an apparition than what Max imagined an imp to be. He'd never seen one in its natural form.

"Max," whispered Delia. "You don't think it's Nikki, do you?"

"Nikki never leaves the manor," Max said. "Unless he's a cat. And what would he even be doing here?" But there was something about the imp's movement that was incredibly familiar.

"Imps serve demons above all others," Armistead said. "Even above the witches they might be bonded to. They have no choice about it."

The figure paused when it got to Max. And up close, it was obvious that it wasn't just a dark shadow. It was more like a network of impossibly small, vibrating strings, almost iridescent at its center. And hidden in the midst of it all, just barely peeking out, were two green eyes. "Hello, Max."

Max's knees damn near gave out. The voice was staticky, as if it were being filtered through some kind of electrical device. But dear Goddess, it was Nikki's.

"Nikki," Delia gasped. She reached for him, then stopped.

"You can touch me," Nikki said. "In fact, I wish you would."

Delia tentatively reached her hand into the substance that was Nikki, and it reacted almost like fluid with small, pulsating waves.

The green eyes closed, and Max heard what he thought was a sigh.

"Don't make it weird," Luc said, and Nikki laughed. Or at least Max thought he did.

"I am so sorry you've been dragged into this," Delia whispered. "Can you ever forgive me?"

"I fear it will be you who needs to forgive me before the night is through," Nikki said.

Morgaine snapped her fingers. "Imp, come."

Nikki floated to Morgaine—he had no choice—and hovered in front of her. Max watched their interaction closely, noting that Morgaine didn't actually say anything. But they were definitely communicating.

Nikki suddenly became agitated. Or at least that was how it looked to Max. His form darkened and he vibrated, producing a high-pitched hum.

Max started to step into the pentagram, but his father stopped him. "No, son. Demon stones."

Son? His father had never called him *son* before.

Nikki floated back to Max and said, "I'm really sorry for what's about to happen."

"I don't like the sound of that, Nikki. What's—"

"Pardon me for interrupting," Morgaine said. "But isn't it funny how we're so much like our ancestors?"

No. Max wasn't like his ancestor. His ancestor had hexed the Merriweathers.

"I mean, look at me and Philistina. Just looking for the good life through a little witchy magic. And, Max, you're so much like Wilmot in your refusal to give it to me."

Max looked at his father, and they both breathed a sigh of relief.

We do not come from horrible people.

"And, Delia, you're so much like your ancestor Lucinda. Seeing what's inside people's hearts and then trying your best to give it to them. Spreading peace and love and standing by your Logos man—mens omnia cor be damned."

Max could suddenly imagine Wilmot and Lucinda so clearly. And he could *feel* their suffering at the hands of the demon Philistina. Suffering that had continued throughout the centuries.

"I don't know what you're planning, Morgaine, but none of us are cooperating. Not me. And not anyone in my family. And that includes Nikki."

Nikki's eyes glowed, and his head—or the thing that might be his head—leaned in to Max's until their foreheads (kind of) touched. "Don't you dare kiss me," Max said, trying to lighten the mood.

The green eyes grew even brighter, and Nikki laughed again. "Family," he said. "Thank you for calling me that."

"It's what you are."

Morgaine was growing impatient. "*Now*, imp. Let's get this over with. It's possession time."

Max's head snapped up, and he looked at Morgaine. "I'm sorry. You said what now?"

"Prepare to be boarded, Max," Morgaine said. "We're going to get that hex performed one way or the other."

"Possession? Are you freaking kidding me?" Delia said.

"That's how it happened back in the good old days," Morgaine said. "Wilmot wouldn't cooperate, and an imp stepped in. Literally. And to be clear, it was actually this imp's daddy who hexed your family. While inside Wilmot. Which I don't think was as much fun as it sounds."

"Oh, hell no," Max said, shaking his head at Nikki.

"Hell no," Nikki echoed.

"What did you say, imp?"

"Hell no," he said again.

"You're denying me?" Morgaine actually sounded stunned.

"Denied," Nikki repeated simply. And Max couldn't believe it, but he saw Nikki smile. He didn't know *how* he saw it, because there was no mouth to speak of. But it was definitely a smile, albeit an indescribable one.

"That was once, imp," Morgaine said. "Two more strikes and you're out."

"What does that mean?" Max asked. "Two more strikes?"

"It's a baseball term," Luc said. "But I don't think that's how she's using it."

Nikki just kept staring at Max, his back to Morgaine, as if having his eyes on Max was the only thing keeping him from floating away.

"Imp," Morgaine said, a little more loudly this time. "Daemonum possessionem!"

"Hell no," Nikki said, clear as day, and for the second time.

"Yeah, buddy," Luc said. "Show her who's boss."

"Luc," Dorcas said. "Be quiet. An imp can only deny a demon three times before…"

"Before what?" Max asked.

"This is your third and final chance to do my bidding, imp," Morgaine said, her voice low and gravelly and downright demonic.

"What happens if you deny her a third time, Nikki?" Max asked, not wanting to hear the answer.

"I am so grateful for all of you," Nikki said. "And right now I'm thinking of line dancing. And the taste of beer. And the smell of the antique shop. And that frozen macaroni and cheese that

Hartwell used to make in the microwave. And how being around all of you made me feel almost human."

A kernel of panic sprouted in Max's gut. "Nobody likes a sappy imp. So, stop it. Also, tell me what to do. Right now. I mean, holy hell, Nikki. What do I do?"

"What I think you should do is live your life the way Hartwell and Wilmot did. With your heart, Max."

"Imp!" Morgaine shouted. "Do my bidding, or be gone."

"Don't deny her, Nikki. We'll figure something out—"

Delia stepped in front of them. "Take my magic! That's what you want. And I'm offering it to you. Leave everyone else out of it."

All the Merriweather women echoed the sentiment in a cacophony of tears and begging, and Morgaine smiled, eating it up. "It's not that easy. I can't just *take* it. I am a demon, not a witch. The magic has to be diverted to me. And the hex does that. It's how Wilmot designed it. I only wish he hadn't put that key in there, the one that would allow a blue witch to break it. He was a sneaky, patient bastard."

Max could see everything that was about to happen right there in Nikki's eyes. And there wasn't a damn thing he could do.

"Daemonum possessionem!" Morgaine shouted.

"Nikki, this will be the third time," Max warned.

"I'll be free," Nikki said. And then, very softly, without taking his eyes off of Max, he whispered, "Hell no."

Before Max could react, either with words or actions, Nikki's form exploded into a sparkling iridescent cloud. And then, as they all watched, horrified, it fell to the ground as ashes.

Delia gasped and dropped to her knees, and Max wanted to do the same. But somehow, he remained standing, glaring at Morgaine as her wails of fury vibrated his very bones.

They'd been so foolish. How had they believed that simply exposing Morgaine as a demon would be enough? She wasn't going to stop until she got what she wanted.

Max looked at his father. "Dad," he said. "What should we do?"

He'd never called his father that before.

"Yes, Armistead," his mother said. "What *are* we going to do? It's not like we can leave a demon trapped in a pentagram in the middle of a city park. She'll burn the whole town down in her fury."

Armistead seemed to realize he was still clutching the book. He glanced at it and then back at Max. "We're going to do what we should have done in the first place. We're going to banish a demon."

"Do we know how to do that?" Luc asked with sweat beading his face.

"There's a demon banishment spell in this book," Armistead said. "But it will take Big Magic. And it will take all of us."

"I was born to do Big Magic," Amy said fiercely.

"Yes, you were," Armistead said. And then he turned to the witches hovering at the edge of the bonfire. "You were all born to do Big Magic," he shouted. "Now hurry! Circle around the willow tree."

"Come on," Max said, pulling Delia up. "We've got to go."

Something shiny caught his eye. "Are those yours?" he asked, pointing at a handful of small pebbles scattered about Nikki's ashes.

"Yes," Delia said, patting her pockets. "But they're just cheap fairy stones from the store. Leave them."

Chapter Thirty-Nine

Delia and Max hurried to the willow tree to join the others, leaving Morgaine behind in the pentagram, where she was becoming more agitated by the second. And the more agitated she became, the scarier she got.

"Hurry. Grab hands and form a circle," Armistead said.

Everyone excitedly did as they were told, with Delia and Max completing the circle.

Holding hands with Max was always exciting, but now, while magic was literally in the air, holding his hand felt downright electric. He felt it, too, and when he looked at her, in addition to the deep grief and shock of losing Nikki, she saw a bit of surprise.

"What is it?"

"Your magic is pulling at mine," he said. "Can you feel it?"

Not only could she feel Max's magic, but she could literally feel the ley lines running beneath her feet and rushing up the trunk of the willow tree.

With a wail of demonic laughter, a strong wind kicked up, and the willow tree's low-hanging branches, usually so lovely and docile, began furiously whipping in the air.

"Don't worry," Max said. "We've got this."

"We'll be doing an incantation," Armistead shouted over the wind. "And when we begin the chant, I'll need everyone to focus on bringing your magic to the surface of your skin, and actually out through your body. Can you do that?"

"No," Amy said, as a bolt of lightning struck very near, filling the air with ozone. "Most of us are out of magic."

Almost all the witches agreed, shouting *Same for me!* and *I've had no magic since April!* and *That's why we came!*

Armistead looked flustered for a moment, but then he recovered. "We're all going to do the best we can with what little we've got," he said. "Now, let us begin: daemonum vectigal!"

That was a mouthful. The women struggled with it, and it was more of a trainwreck than when Delia's grandma and aunts tried to sing "Happy Birthday" with any semblance of unity.

"Stop, stop," Armistead said. "Just say *Demon be gone! Demon be gone!*"

Everyone started chanting the new incantation with much more success. After a few rounds, they were totally in unison. Their voices rose in a monotone rhythm, and it almost felt as if they were one living, breathing organism.

Demon be gone! Demon be gone!

Another lightning bolt struck, and a couple of the women screamed.

"Don't stop," Armistead shouted.

As they chanted, Armistead took the book and began pacing around the pentagram. Delia could barely make out his voice against the din, chanting incantations in Latin, while Morgaine laughed and followed him with her eyes until her head eventually turned all the way around.

Delia felt her own magic rise. She could *see* the ley lines in her mind's eye. Max raised his voice, and Luc joined in even louder, and their hair rose, as if they were touching one of those balls of electricity you'd find in a museum.

Morgaine began howling, louder than the wind.

"It's working," Amy said. "Delia! I can feel it. I'm not supposed to have magic, but I feel it!"

A thin ring of light formed along the circle, and the tree itself began to glow. And then, Delia's hand, clasped tightly by Max, grew warm. Very warm. Max looked at her with wide eyes, and then a bright blue orb shot out from where their hands were joined. It flew to the willow tree, where it disappeared into the circle of light, and the circle pulsated and grew brighter. "We're stronger together," Max shouted in her ear. "Mind and heart as one!"

A red orb shot seemingly out of nowhere, and Amy yelled, "That was me!"

"Line of Corpus," Max said. "Red is magic of the body."

Just as the orb disappeared into the circle of light, two golden ones rose into the air.

"Animus!" Luc said. "Magic of the soul."

That was mind, heart, body, and soul. All of their magic. Together.

They chanted loudly as the air above them filled with orbs, and the ground beneath their feet vibrated with power. *Their power.*

Max squeezed her hand until it hurt. And she squeezed back. Because the current running through their bodies was so strong, it threatened to tear them apart.

Grandma Maddie's wild hair rose and danced in the wind. Her eyes were squeezed shut, and she clung to Fiona's hand on one side and Aurora's on the other. And Delia could clearly see the power that her grandmother had always had.

I come from a powerful line of witches, and our magic has always been the strength of our love.

A silver line formed at their feet, traveling from one witch to the next until it touched every single one. And then it burst forth like a geyser, shooting over their heads to land in the center of the pentagram, where it exploded in a prism-like blast of color.

Complete and total silence descended as they gawked at each other in utter shock. Only when their hair had floated back to their shoulders did they turn their attention to the pentagram.

"She's gone," Dorcas said. "The demon has vanished!"

All that remained of Morgaine was seeping into the ground as a puddle of black, gurgling liquid. "Back to the hellish depths," Max said. "Good riddance."

Cheers erupted and everyone hugged and laughed and cried. Delia looked at Max and felt a bit drunk from the rush of power. And others must have felt it, too, because someone started singing "Auld Lang Syne," as if the clock had just struck midnight on New Year's Eve.

Constance Fleming limped forward. Her hair was in knots and it seemed she'd lost one of her shoes. "Ladies," she said, smiling slightly while attempting to pat her hair into place. "I believe we've received our tidings."

CHAPTER FORTY

The stars were out. The party lights were on. And the music was playing. It felt almost like one of Hartwell's parties, except Hartwell and Nikki were gone. Would they ever feel normal again?

Delia leaned her head back against Max's arm and let the pounding jets of the hot tub work their magic.

"How's your back?" Amy asked.

"It's been better, and it's been worse. Banishing a demon is hard work."

"Yeah, but that was two weeks ago. You actually hurt your back chasing Splash with a broom after he pooped on your angora sweater."

"Like I said, banishing a demon is hard work."

"Speak of the devil—" Max said, pointing across the yard. "He's got a shoe in his mouth. And it's mine."

"Amy, you really gave me the gift that keeps on giving with that dog."

"Aw, he's just a puppy doing puppy things. A total innocent."

Grandma Maddie and the auntie brigade came out of the house, bringing tons of food and raucous laughter. "Is there room in that thing for me?" Grandma Maddie asked. "I wore my bikini under my clothes."

"There's plenty of room," Delia said. "Hop on in."

Max tried disguising a chuckle with a fake cough as Grandma Maddie slipped her dress off.

"My God, Maddie," Aurora said, sitting in a nearby chair and wrapping herself in a blanket. "Your legs are so white, they glow."

Delia snorted. Aurora wasn't wrong.

Maddie eased in with a sigh and leaned her head back.

"I don't know how y'all sit in those things," Fiona said. "It's like hanging out in other people's dirty bath water."

"Mm, thanks for that analogy, Mom."

"You realize when you swim in the river, you're in a fish's toilet," Thea said, sitting by the side of the hot tub and putting her feet in.

Max quirked his mouth, and the chiminea roared to life, adding a warm orange glow to the scene.

"Ooh, that's lovely," Fiona said, warming her hands. "I brought some marshmallows. Where's Luc?"

"He's inside making queso," Max said, and then he got very quiet, because, like Delia, he was probably remembering who had shown Luc how to make it.

Nikki.

Oh, how Delia's heart hurt. It was almost as bad as when she'd lost Hartwell.

"Max," Fiona said. "You said you had something to tell me. Is it good news? Or bad?"

Max smiled secretively, and Delia wondered what was up. "It depends on how you look at it," he said. "And can we wait until my parents come out? They're leaving for Shadowlark tomorrow. The investigation is just getting started, and they'll be testifying before the new Concilium."

"Are they in trouble?" Fiona asked.

Max shook his head. "Not at all. They're advocating for change."

"That's a relief," Maddie said.

Amy raised an eyebrow. "Who could have possibly known that the Body of Witchcraft needed all of its parts to function properly?"

Max gave Amy a side-eye, but Delia could see the hint of a smile on his lips. "Well, it turns out we Logos witches aren't as smart as we thought we were."

"I've been saying that all along," Amy quipped. "And for the record, I suspect that the so-called body includes other magical beings, as well."

Max nodded. "After reading his journal, I'd say Hartwell would agree with you."

Change was coming. Of that, Delia was certain. And it was exciting!

Luc came out with the queso and a bag of chips. His parents followed with a book and a bottle. "We brought spirits!" Dorcas said. "For a toast."

Armistead set the book on the table—the infamous *Clavis Hexicus*—and started pouring the tequila into colorful, plastic shot glasses.

"Max, everybody's here if you want to spill your big secret," Delia said. "I'm dying to know, so tell us."

"Well," Max said, accepting a shot glass from Luc. "I've decided against holding an open house."

"Max!" Delia said. "You're kidding, right? After all the work we've put in?"

She was freaking crushed! The house was gorgeous. Perfect, even. She'd been looking forward to showing it off.

"I don't think it's proper to hold an open house for a home that's not for sale," he said. "And sorry, Fiona. That might be the bad part for you."

"Did you say...?"

"I'm not selling the house," Max said. "I've been all over the world. And I've never wanted to live anywhere as badly as I want to live right here in Willow Root, Texas. I hope you can all stand having me as a neighbor."

Delia threw her arms around his neck. This was wonderful! "I'm so happy. You have no idea. Oh, Max."

He gave her a quick kiss, and his hazel eyes deepened in a way that promised there would be more later. "I was hoping you'd say that. Because you're the main reason I want to be here. And no, I'm not bewitched, so don't you dare suggest it."

Armistead had taught them all about Cor magic from another book Hartwell had left in the library, and the way Delia used hers was to discover the true desire of a person's heart. And sure, someone might think you could use that as a weapon, but as a Cor witch, she simply wasn't capable of it. Her magic *couldn't* be used that way. It came from a place of love, and love didn't hurt other people. But knowing the true desire of a person's heart did come in handy for figuring out what color they wanted to paint their bedroom.

Grandma Maddie held her shot glass up. "To our new neighbor!"

"Salud!" Maddie shouted, even though she didn't speak Spanish.

"L'chaim!" Andi said, even though she wasn't Jewish.

"Bottoms up," Thea said, and then, before anyone could add anything else, they all drank.

"Oh dear," Grandma Maddie sputtered. "That's the good stuff. Now, let's have another and make a toast to Nikki."

Delia glanced up at the manor while the glasses were being refilled. And she noticed Hartwell's bedroom light was on. She didn't think it had been on before. "Did someone turn that light on?" she asked, pointing.

Everyone looked, but nobody claimed to have done it.

"To Nikki," Luc said. "The best imp I ever knew."

Nikki was so much more than that. But how did you express a toast for someone who had sacrificed himself to save a woman's life, a family's magic, and one undeserving man's honor? What did you actually *say* about someone like that?

Max raised his glass. "To my friend."

Everyone drank quietly this time, and then Max turned away, pretending to mess with a setting on the hot tub, when he saw someone come out of the house.

He frowned and began counting heads, because he could swear everyone was here.

Eight, nine, ten, eleven...All here.

"Who is that?" Luc asked. "And why is he wearing a Speedo?"

Max got out of the hot tub with a sense of unease. Who just walked into someone else's home? In a Speedo?

"I swear that looks like Nikki," Luc said.

And Max was thinking the exact same thing.

Delia made a huge splash trying to get out of the tub, and it took both Luc and Max to extricate Maddie, and when they turned around—

"Don't get out on my account."

There was a moment of total silence while everyone tried to wrap their minds around what they were seeing. Or rather *who* they were seeing.

"Oh my God," Delia screeched. "Nikki!"

She was on him in a flash, and thankfully, Nikki caught her, hugging her tightly and laughing. "Was this a grand enough entrance?" he asked.

"Nikki," Max said. "How are you out here?"

"Are you asking how I'm out here on two legs instead of four? Or are you asking how I'm out here, in general, because you assumed I was dead?"

"Both!" Delia said, still clinging to the imp.

Max peered closely at Nikki, and wariness crept in. This person didn't look *exactly* like Nikki. His green eyes weren't as bright. His hair wasn't as black. His skin wasn't as obnoxiously perfect. In fact, it looked like he had a pimple, and holy hell, was that a five-o'clock shadow?

"Are those man whiskers rubbing on my face?" Delia asked, noticing the same thing.

"Yes. And they're not as fun as cat whiskers."

Max took a step closer. "You're human."

Nikki smiled. "Thanks for noticing, you monster."

Max just stood there, gawking like an idiot, until he was finally able to say, "I don't care what you are. I'm just glad you're back."

A few minutes later, after everything had calmed down and everyone had been hugged and more drinks had been had, the questions began. "So, do imps just, like, not die?" Amy asked. "Because you went *poof.*"

"Technically, imps are immortal. But that doesn't mean you can't kill them. It just means that if you don't, they can live a really, really long time. But there's also something else that can happen. Sometimes an imp can simply cease. And we stay that way unless something or someone decides we shouldn't."

"And you...did this thing?" Fiona asked. "You ceased?"

"Oh, I definitely ceased. But, apparently, someone placed fairy stones among my ashes and then wept on them. That was too much for fairies to ignore during a quarter moon."

"That was me!" Delia cried. "Fairy stones fell out of my pocket after you…ceased."

"Then I suppose I should thank you," Nikki said, with what Max still thought was a rather impish grin.

"But why are you human?" Max asked.

"Oh, that's simple," Nikki said. "The fairies granted me a wish as well."

"You'd rather be human than immortal?"

Nikki shrugged. "Being immortal isn't all it's cracked up to be."

"I imagine that's true," Luc said. "Especially if you're bonded to service against your will and even if people wanted to set you free, they couldn't."

"Yeah, about that," Nikki said rather sheepishly. "I kind of waited too long to tell you, and then it became awkward."

"Tell us what?" Max asked.

"Hartwell set me free as soon as he found the book of keys."

"What?" everybody said, practically at the same time.

Nikki blushed. "It's true."

Max didn't understand. "Then why did you stay? Why continue running around as a cat? Or being trapped in the house, acting like you couldn't deny a direct order?"

"After Hartwell freed me, I went home. And at risk of sounding like a sad country song, I discovered they'd mowed down my forest and put in a parking lot. My home was gone, and I never found my family."

"Oh, Nikki," Dorcas said. "That's terrible."

"So, I came back. And Hartwell took care of me and I took care of him, and he became my family. And then, when he died, you all became my family. Just like he'd said you would."

"Wait a minute," Max said. "We asked you if Hartwell had looked in the book for the key to free you."

"You didn't ask me if he'd found it," Nikki said.

Max was stunned. "Why didn't you tell us?"

"What if you'd known, when we first met, that you could just send me away? What would you have done?"

A huge knot formed in Max's throat, making it hard to swallow. And suddenly it became very still and quiet. Max reached out to touch Nikki's shoulder, but Nikki pulled him in for a hug instead.

After a moment, Armistead clapped his hands once, shifting the mood and effectively changing the topic. "I brought this book out because tonight we're going to figure out how this young woman broke that hex."

"Finally," Delia said, crossing her arms over her chest with a shiver. "Although I'm getting back in the hot tub to do it."

Max was getting chilly, too. "If anyone can solve this mystery, it's my dad," he said, getting in the tub.

"Yes," Luc said. "Dad is very good at that."

It was still a little awkward, but they were getting used to being less formal with their parents.

"Page thirty-two!" Maddie said. "Let's do it."

Armistead opened the book and read in silence. He made a couple of faces, and finally, he raised his eyes and said, "This is gruesome. And the spirit element renders it almost impossible. Add to that the fact that it includes a potion that you have to consume... Well, it's all rather intentional, isn't it? How would one break this accidentally?"

"We made soup," Maddie said.

The twins nodded.

"But we didn't put the baby in it," Thea assured Armistead.

"You do realize," Nikki said, "that Delia used fairy magic to break the hex? And fairy magic always includes humor or a joke of some kind. I mean, look at me," he said, laughing. "I'm sitting here in Speedos."

"What might that look like?" Armistead said. "If she used fairy magic?"

Nikki smiled. "Let me try and come up with an example. Let's say a spell called for a specific spice. Fairy magic might mean playing a Spice Girls song instead."

"Hm," Armistead said. "This is fascinating. So, the first thing this spell calls for is the boiling of an innocent."

"That's right," Thea said. "The boiling of an innocent, an agitated spirit, and the blood of the witch's true love."

"Let's think back to the night of your birthday, Delia," Luc said.

"We line danced," Nikki said. "It was a fun time."

Delia nodded. "And we ended up right here in this very hot tub."

"And that's how Splash got his name," Amy said. "He fell into the hot tub while the jets were blasting—"

"And spilled all our drinks," Delia added.

"Wait a minute," Max said. "Amy, what did you say about Splash earlier?"

"That he fell into the hot tub."

"No," Delia said. "You said he was an innocent."

Amy laughed. "But we didn't freaking boil him, Delia!"

Max stared down into the hot tub, thinking how it looked very much like a witch's cauldron of boiling water. "Hold on, here. I think Delia might be right. And when the *innocent* fell into the *boiling water*, he..."

"Spilled our drinks made with tequila!" Delia said.

"Agitated spirits!" Amy shouted. "Huzzah!"

Armistead went back to the book. "This is quite fun. What was next? Oh, here it is. The blood of the witch's true love."

"Max," Delia said softly. "Your bandage came off. Remember?"

"Yes," he said, leaning in until they were practically nose to nose. "And a single drop of blood landed in the water, just before midnight."

Armistead closed the book. "I think we just solved our mystery."

"But how did the fairies know?" Delia asked.

Max took her hands in his. "Try thinking like a proper Cor witch. What does your heart tell you?"

Delia didn't answer with words, but he felt her magic seeking his heart's desire. And he saw it in her eyes when she found it. "Oh, Max."

He kissed her deeply in front of their families, both born and found (and even *reborn*). And he knew with every fiber of his body, his heart, his mind, and his soul, that he was this witch's true love. And she was his heart's desire.

ACKNOWLEDGMENTS

Since I'm not one to suffer in silence, and since writing causes me great suffering, I'm always surprised there are so many people still speaking to me by the time I finally finish a book. This is where I thank those people.

The hardworking professionals at Forever couldn't quit me even if they wanted to, because it's their literal job to see me across the finish line. But there are definitely *easier* jobs, and what they do is a calling. I am especially grateful to my editor, Junessa Viloria, who always knows just what to say when I'm stuck or frantic or frantically stuck. Her insight and guidance are invaluable, but it's her temperament that I treasure most. Because let's face it, someone has to remain calm and cool while I write, and God knows it's not going to be me.

Thank you to Sabrina Flemming for her stellar first-draft notes (she has the perfect name for a witchy book), and to copy editor Penina Lopez, who finds all the needles in the haystack, and to production editor Anjuli Johnson, who ties it all up with a bow. Thank you to Caitlin Sacks for creating the cover of my dreams. And of course, I can't forget the superheroes in marketing and publicity, particularly Estelle Hallick (whose love of books and Muppets is contagious) and her partners in superhero-ing, Carolina Martin and Dana Cuadrado.

Thank you to my agent, Paige Wheeler, for always having my back, and to my writing coach, Jessica Snyder, for making me feel like an athlete in the world's loneliest and most sedentary sport.

Finally, thank you to the people who stuck by me because of codependency or their love of trainwrecks. This includes Amy Bearce, who listened to me agonize over every word—even the ones I deleted and retyped and deleted again—and Sam Tschida, who refuses to put up with my bullshit.

Thank you to my local writing buddies Sasha Summers, Jolene Navarro, and Janene Smith. I don't see them often enough, but when I do, they lift my spirits (and solve my plot problems).

And of course, thank you to my family for always loving and supporting and believing in me (seriously, they're worse than the Merriweathers), even when I can't think about anything other than "the book."

But the biggest and most lavish of thanks goes to you, my readers, for going on this grand adventure with me. I always hoped I could love my characters enough to make them real (can you guess what my favorite childhood book was?). But it turns out that what makes them real is you. Thank you for turning the pages.

About the Author

Carly Bloom began her writing career as a family humor columnist and blogger, a pursuit she abandoned when her children grew old enough to literally die from embarrassment. To save their delicate lives, Carly turned to penning steamy contemporary romance. The kind with bare chests on the covers.

Carly and her husband raise their mortified brood of offspring on a cattle ranch in South Texas.

You can learn more at:
CarlyBloomBooks.com
X @CarlyBloomBooks
Facebook.com/AuthorCarlyBloom
Instagram @CarlyBloomBooks
Threads @CarlyBloomBooks